THE THIRTEENTH APOSTLE

THE THIRTEENTH APOSTLE

Gloria Gonzalez

St. Martin's Press
New York

 For information, address St. Martin's Press, 175 Fifth Avenue, New York, N.Y. 10010

Design by Basha Zapatka

Library of Congress Cataloging-in-Publication Data

Gonzalez, Gloria.
The thirteenth apostle / Gloria Gonzalez.
p. cm.
"A Thomas Dunne book."
ISBN 0-312-08909-0
I. Title.
PS3557.04744T48 1993
813'.54—dc20 92-41829
CIP

First Edition: May 1993

10 9 8 7 6 5 4 3 2 1

For Thomas McDevitt, one
of the all-time great
New York newspapermen

CHAPTER ONE

The body slid over the iron railing of the seventeenth-story terrace and momentarily seemed to glide before the legs churned the air in a bizarre nocturnal jig.

The eyes, bulging in terror, threatened to pop from the skull.

Only the spindly brown hairs attached to the scalp relaxed, allowing the wind to fashion a casual coiffure.

A black size ten double E loafer landed on the fender of a taxi stopped at the light. The other shoe barely missed a jogger, who nonchalantly dodged the missile.

The body struck the burgundy canopy of the Park View Towers and thumped to the sidewalk.

The building's doorman, seated behind a circular desk in the lobby, was immersed in the *Daily News* sports section. He did not hear the body fall.

Nor did he notice the well-dressed Asian man who crossed the lobby and disappeared quickly through the revolving doors.

At that same moment, fourteen blocks south on Fifth Avenue, Cardinal Thomas Ryan McHugh sat in his living quarters adjacent to St. Patrick's Cathedral, wearing a New York Mets T-shirt and a New York Yankees cap as press photographers clicked away.

In Boise, Idaho, a grandmother made herself a cup of coffee from a new jar and settled down to watch television.

In Key West, Florida, a sailor polished the wood trim of a boat while his dog napped on deck.

A mile away, in the airport coffee shop, a stewardess argued with her married lover, who accused her of cheating on him.

On Duvall Street, Lt. Gabe Danford broke up a fight between a female impersonator and a transvestite.

At headquarters, the Key West police chief was in his office typing a letter to the Social Security Administration, alerting it to his impending retirement.

Across town, an elderly man sat on his porch weaving a fishing net from blue plastic twine.

Farther up the coast in a Miami nightclub, a Cuban man danced with his mother to the lively rhythms of Bobby Capo.

In Cleveland, a newspaper photographer cruised the city looking for a weather shot for page 3.

In a nearby Ohio suburb, a young mother sat in a neighbor's living room with a group of friends watching a Tupperware demonstration.

In Las Vegas, a woman playing a video poker machine drew a royal flush and collected 4,000 quarters.

Within months—seven of them would be dead.

CHAPTER TWO

Geraldine pressed her fingers against the red felt surface of the blackjack table. The grainy, liquor-stained texture absorbed the perspiration of her hands, perspiration caused by staring at thirteens and twelves.

She was down $600. Even the dealer was starting to look uncomfortable as he scooped up her chips after each hand.

She slid another green chip into the circle, wondering where her life had gone wrong. There's nothing like a relentless losing streak to cause one to examine philosophical beginnings. And suicidal endings.

Behind her, in the dark alcove cordoned off by thick red ropes, a country-western trio lamented that sex without love was like biscuits without gravy.

A grandmotherly type at the table got blackjack. Her third in twenty minutes. Geraldine pretended to be happy for her as she was dealt her usual thirteen, which quickly turned into twenty-three.

"We could set a record here tonight," the redhead sighed.

"You're just having a bad streak," said the dealer in the striped shirt with the black garters pinching his arms.

"Yeah," Geraldine nodded, "It started around 1950."

"Didn't you hit a video jackpot the other night?"

"That was two days and three thousand dollars ago," she moaned.

Picking up her few chips and the tall glass of grapefruit juice, she wandered over to the roulette table and lost fifty dollars in two spins.

Geraldine glanced about the casino, and guessed the time to be around 2:00 A.M. She owned four watches, all bought on previous trips to Vegas, but they sat crammed in the back of a drawer in her New York apartment.

The casino was practically empty, except for a small group around the craps table and a few weary gamblers sitting in the dark lounge listening to the western band.

Most of the blackjack tables were unoccupied, manned by bored dealers who stood at semiattention behind the wooden racks of chips. Three stragglers sat in the paper-strewn keno parlor watching the numbers light up on the board.

She strolled past the bank of video poker machines and out onto the sidewalk. The sky was dark above the pulsating neon explosion. She tried to remember the last time she'd eaten and vaguely pictured room service dishes next to the bed when she got up this afternoon. Or was it the day before?

It made no difference. It was either too early or too late to eat. She reached into her purse and uncapped a bottle of vitamin C. She popped three into her mouth—her only concession to good health. That and grapefruit juice—all she drank whenever she gambled. Alcohol was for amateurs.

She couldn't go back to the room broke. Not to lie in bed worrying about it. She headed down the block and darted into another casino where a brown-uniformed guard was half dragging a man out by his belt buckle.

"That bitch took the money right outta my pants when I was sleeping. She ain't got no right!" the drunk protested. "That's my money she's losing!"

"You don't disturb the customers. You come back in here you're going to jail."

Geraldine sidestepped the pirouetting drunk and entered the ladies' room near the all-night snack bar.

A cocktail waitress wearing a black miniskirt sat barefoot on the edge of the sink having a cigarette. Her red spike heels lay discarded on the tiled floor.

"How's it going, Ger?"

"Usual disaster," the redhead replied, leaning over the sink to soap the bad luck off her hands.

The girl nodded, "I ain't made enough to pay the sitter."

A cigarette ash fell on her satin skirt and she didn't bother to wipe it away. Underneath the purple eye shadow and black liner and orange cheeks was probably a twenty-year-old face. A weary twenty-year-old. And growing wearier. She had come to Vegas from Phoenix hoping to make it as a showgirl. She became a waitress after the headliner, a comic, got her pregnant and went back to his wife in L.A.

Geraldine glanced at herself in the mirror. The eyes were puffy; some traces of makeup remained. The red hair, which had been neatly upswept, now hung down in isolated copper strands. Her neck looked thinner. Her cheekbones appeared to be sharper. When the hell did she eat last?

Her mouth tasted like the shreds of tobacco lining the bottom of her purse. The white dress was wrinkled and one sleeve kept sliding off, exposing a bony shoulder.

"How long you in town for?" the kid asked.

"I don't start seeing some cards soon, I'm out of here tonight," Geraldine answered.

"Last time I looked, the progressive poker by the coffee shop was over sixteen hundred dollars," the girl yawned.

"Oh?"

"I played on my lunch break. Couldn't even get three of a kind. But maybe you'll be lucky."

"Thanks. I'll give it a shot." Geraldine took two five-dollar chips from her jacket and placed them on the sink next to the girl's cigarettes.

The young mother smiled. "I'll bring you a grapefruit juice."

Geraldine headed for the cluster of slot machines and took a seat near a woman who was furiously pumping quarters into two machines. Geraldine dug into her purse and came up with a handful of change.

The overhead neon sign advertised the current payoff at $1,683. She silently told St. Jude that if he let her win the jackpot she'd donate ten percent to his shrine and go straight home with the rest of it.

An hour later she bought fifty dollars' worth of quarters from the change girl and upped St. Jude's share to twenty percent.

Forty-five minutes and sixty dollars later bells sounded, sirens blasted, lights flashed. The change girl squealed with glee and rushed to congratulate a tiny wrinkled birdlike black man who smiled through two gold teeth.

"I just got off the plane! I only put in five quarters!" he told the crowd that had begun to gather.

Geraldine scooped up the few quarters in the metal tray and walked out of the casino.

She stood on the sidewalk staring at the sunrise that was uniquely Las Vegas. The orange sky, slashed with pink and purple ribbons, was a vibrant backdrop to the mountains that embraced the valley. Mother Nature's artist dueled with the neon canyon—and won. It was Geraldine's favorite part of the day. That brief time before the carnival lights bowed to the desert sun.

The January air, brushing against her open-toed sandals, was chilly. The temperature sign above Binion's flashed 57°, but it felt colder.

She walked slowly toward the taxi stand, trying to decide whether to draw another cash advance on her MasterCard. There was no point even trying the Visa. The machine had flashed Declined.

Which, roughly translated, meant she was over her $8,000 limit and if she didn't win soon—and big—there'd be hell to pay when the bill came in.

Geraldine paused at the corner and waited for the blinking figures to allow her to cross.

Women in fancy dresses shared the sidewalk with panhandlers, cowboys, teenagers, housewives, senior citizens, and middle-aged tourists in snakeskin boots.

She looked out-of-townish herself in the white linen dress and white sandals.

It was her Audrey Hepburn look, to her way of thinking, but everyone else said she resembled Susan Hayward.

Geraldine had once found herself at a Howard Johnson's lunch counter in South Carolina sitting next to a truck driver. She blurted out, "Tell me, why do you guys whistle at me when I'm rushing out to get a paper in the morning with my hair in curlers?"

"That's easy," the man smiled. "It's the curlers."

"I don't get it."

He explained that curlers were a sexy turn-on. "That's what my wife wears to bed. So if I see a pretty thing on the street with her hair rolled up it gets the juices going."

She persisted. "What about when you see a woman wearing a dress and heels?"

The driver laughed. "Then I think funeral."

She wrote an article about the conversation and sold it to *Redbook*. She used the money to buy a motorcycle, which was later demolished by a truck while parked in front of the courthouse. She was in court to pay a summons for failure to wear a helmet while operating a motorcycle.

Geraldine cast an eye toward the Four Queens and debated investing her last hundred. She told herself that no luck, good or bad, lasts forever. She was way overdue to get out of her slump. Any minute now it could change.

And if she hit it real big she could take a six-month leave from the newspaper and finally write the novel that would make her rich and allow her to move to Nevada. It wasn't just the casinos that drew her to the desert. She'd come to love the snow-capped mountains surrounding the city, the orange sunsets that left you breathless, the tumbleweed that blew in your path, the spaciousness of the midnight sky.

She had started the book ten years ago somewhere over Colorado on a flight home. She'd written two chapters but lost them in the confusion of meeting Castro after the plane was hijacked. She sold the article to *New York Magazine*—"Close Encounter of the Hijack Kind"—and spent the money on a twenty-seven-inch Panasonic TV that exploded one night, torching the apartment.

Geraldine crossed the street to Binion's Horseshoe and hesitated. Guilt wailed its siren song. She knew the message light was blinking in the hotel room with calls from Hal.

She wasn't up to another round of "Let's get married," "Why do you gamble so much?", "Are you fooling around?", and the currently popular, "When are you going to grow up?"

Her responses would be "Maybe soon," "It's all I know," "Don't start!", and "Next week."

She loved Hal. She even liked him. Mostly she admired him for being a writer who actually wrote.

She had sat, clutching his arm and a fistful of lucky charms, in the Dorothy Chandler Pavilion when he was nominated for an Oscar for best original screenplay.

He lost out to *Annie Hall.*

They left the ceremony, he in a tux, she in a Halston jumper, and flew home to get drunk in a Third Avenue saloon.

However mighty his literary talents, his true gift was drinking. It was like watching a legend in action. To see Hal pull up a stool at a bar was akin to watching Babe Ruth walk up to the plate. Spectators knew they were in for a hell of a show.

Yet she rarely saw him drunk. (One might argue she never saw him sober.) But he could go months without a drink when he was writing.

Between projects, the man drank, and did it better than anyone she had ever known—including a former city editor of the *New York Post.* (That feisty, sexy Australian could go through three shifts of bartenders and still be on his feet, days later, anchored to the same bar stool telling Rupert Murdoch stories.)

She sold a piece about Hal to *The New Yorker* (what it's like to be nominated for an Oscar and lose) and bought a mink jacket, which he tossed out the window of a San Juan hotel after accusing her of flirting with the wine steward.

How could she not love him?

Maybe she would marry him one day if he didn't get tired of asking.

Just because her three previous marriages ended ugly, was that any reason to be scared? (Probably.)

She decided to give the Horseshoe a shot. If she lost she'd go to the hotel, get some sleep, and take the next flight to Newark.

She hurried toward the casino, wedging herself through the bodies clogging the sidewalk. The sun was up now and the downtown area shook the sleep from its neon eyes.

Someone grazed her arm but she didn't react. The sidewalk was jammed with senior citizens disembarking from a bus.

Two sexy girls in cowboy hats and boots rushed toward the tour bus to hand out flyers for free souvenirs.

Delivery trucks merged with the early morning traffic. Weary gamblers shuffled by carrying plastic buckets jammed with coins. A woman in a long beaded evening gown walked arm in arm with a man carrying a six-foot pink panther, compliments of Circus Circus.

It took Geraldine a couple of seconds to realize that someone had her arm in a tight grip.

"Just do what I tell you."

Geraldine tried to yank herself free from the man, who strode quickly at her side, bracing his body next to hers. He increased the hold. "Don't," he warned.

He steered her easily through the crush of people, his arm encircling her waist. She tried to twist herself free but he merely pulled her closer. "Let me go!" she said.

He ignored her and continued marching swiftly, pulling her off her feet, half carrying, half dragging her across the pavement.

She tried to get a look at his face but her chin was crushed against his shoulder, making it impossible. She held her purse tightly at her chest but he didn't appear to be after the money.

Geraldine allowed her body to go limp, hoping to trip his gait, but he quickly pulled her closer, taking up the slack, and darted across the street. She looked around for a waiting car, expecting to be pushed inside.

"Look," she said hoarsely. "Take the money. And the jewelry. There's also a plane ticket."

He looked about nervously, and after a slight hesitation led her briskly toward the Golden Goose casino.

Geraldine offered no further resistance, fearing he'd swoop her away to unfriendly territory. GG was perfect. She knew two bartenders, a pit boss, three dealers, and most of the change girls.

The Golden Goose was without a doubt the sleaziest, trashiest downtown casino, but one of her favorites. She'd taken Hal there once, only to have him flee in revulsion.

It was a popular hangout for the city's derelicts, homeless, and panhandlers who regularly congregated in the keno parlor, smack at the entrance of the dingy casino.

The popularity was due in part to its proximity to St. Vincent's soup kitchen, which dispensed hot meals at breakfast and dinner.

The casino reeked of bad whiskey, body odor, and long ago cigarettes. The stained carpet underfoot had caught too many beer bottles. Ripped coin wrappers and plastic drinking cups littered the wells between the slot machines. A drunk was asleep braced against a stool.

"We just had a super jackpot winner on the quarter machine. The lucky winner, from Tampa, Florida, hit for twelve hundred and fifty dollars," a female voice boomed through the PA system.

"Don't do anything crazy," the stranger told Geraldine as he led her to the L-shaped bar buried against the far wall, guiding her quickly through the maze of slot machines, his hand clenched on her bare elbow. Once at the bar, he slid out a stool for her to sit on, but he remained standing.

Geraldine sat down quickly, pressing the purse against her lap. She told herself she was safe. He wouldn't make a move in such a public place. She glanced at the "witnesses" sitting at the bar—a middle-aged woman in a nurse's uniform and an old Mexican wearing a frayed cowboy hat and a sleeveless tank top. She glanced at the bartender—a woman for crissakes—whom she didn't recognize.

Sunlight penetrated the musty cavern but the bar remained cloaked in darkness.

"Don't do anything till you hear me out, Geraldine."

Fear roped her heart.

"How do you know my name?" The words came out in shaky spurts.

The barmaid walked over to take their order and Geraldine quickly lit a cigarette, noting with amazement that her hands were not trembling.

"Dewars," he said, glancing at Geraldine. "A Coke," she mumbled.

She exhaled the smoke in his direction, her first opportunity to examine him closely. Average height, slim, brownish gray hair long over the ears, darkly tanned, green-flecked eyes, overall a pleasant face, yet stern. Not a mouth that laughed easily.

"Forty-seven," he said.

She jumped at the sudden voice.

"Just thought I'd help you out."

Geraldine noted the gold chain around his neck holding a chunky, thick anchor.

"How do you know my name?" she asked.

"That was easy," he said, throwing a twenty on the bar. "The hard part was finding Susan Hayward." He stood facing her with his elbow leaning on the bar. A blue checkered shirt peeked out from under the satiny beige jacket.

"What else do you know about me?"

She was trying to place the accent and failing. It wasn't quite Southern, nor Texas-western. Certainly not Boston or New York. Nor ethnic.

"You work for a New York paper. You come to Vegas a lot and you play poker all over the country, wherever there's a game. You also lose more than you win."

He sat on the stool next to her. She noted the cowboy boots and the jeans with the ironed crease running sharply down the leg.

He eyed the players at the nearby craps table and scanned the immediate area.

"Look, friend," she said, "if you're in some kind of trouble, maybe I can help you." After I have you arrested, she told herself.

A woman playing a nearby slot machine screamed as an avalanche of silver dollars clattered into her bucket.

"We need to go somewhere we can talk," he said. "Your room at the Sands should be safe."

He knew where she was staying! Geraldine gripped the edge of the bar and entwined her foot through the rungs of the stool. If he tried to move her she'd be rooted securely.

"Geraldine, you can trust me."

She glanced around, hoping to spot a familiar face. The change girls were crowded around the jackpot winner.

"I'm sorry if I scared you. Just wasn't sure. They might've followed me. Besides, Hal said you were a yeller," he smiled.

Geraldine threw her head back and laughed. "I knew it! I knew it! Where is he! Where's the son of a bitch! Jesus Christ—did you have to scare me half to death!" She ran her fingers through her hair.

"Is he here?" she laughed.

"He's dead."

The man motioned for the bartender to bring another round.

"What?"

"I'm sorry."

Geraldine stared at his face. She searched the eyes for a clue. She stared at the mouth, hoping for a smile. Her hand shot out and gripped his jacket.

"What are you talking about!" Somewhere in her throat a scream was ready to explode.

He looked down and fiddled with the cardboard coaster under the drink. "His sister is staying at his apartment. Call her," he said, not meeting her eyes. "Tell her you heard the news from Owen."

Geraldine grabbed the change on the bar and fled. She was more annoyed than anything. For starters, Hal didn't have a sister. This was another of his stupid pranks, like the night he snuck into her bedroom dressed in an ape suit. She was sleeping and felt something grab her leg. She woke to find a giant gorilla beating its chest at the foot of her bed. Owen, she decided, was a wannabe screenwriter, looking to get lucky—with Hal's help—and had concocted the "kidnap" to score points with his mentor.

Geraldine raced to the pay phone in the corridor next to the parking lot. "You'll be dead all right when I get you!" She pushed a quarter into the slot and punched O for the operator.

Owen was at the cigarette machine, yanking on the lever, when she returned to the bar. She sat down and avoided his eyes.

"Was Ida there?"

Geraldine nodded. "I woke her. I didn't even know he *had* a sister."

"What did she say?"

First a single tear and then a parade dripped on her bare arm.

"That it was an accident. He was drinking and tripped over the flower box on the terrace and . . . fell."

The stranger lit a cigarette and handed it to her.

"It was no accident. He was murdered."

CHAPTER THREE

Geraldine paced the hotel room barefoot, holding the telephone and dragging the cord behind her. The white dress hung like a rumpled sheet on her body.

Owen's beige jacket was draped across the back of the chair. He stood staring out the eighteenth-story window. The sun was climbing slowly over the mountains. White patches of snow dusted the tops. Below, on Las Vegas Boulevard, a young couple in bridal finery emerged from a wedding chapel. Owen looked at his watch. It was a few minutes past 9:00 A.M. Back home he'd be baiting hooks. People here were getting married and walking out of casinos holding beer bottles. It struck him as unnatural.

A voice answered: "City desk."

"Mike? It's Gerry."

There was a slight pause before he asked, "Did you hear?"

"Yes. I'm flying home."

The man coughed. "We ran it on page two. AP called for a picture. The mayor gave us a quote and we have a call in to the governor."

She wanted to stop him. She didn't want official news. She didn't want this story confirmed. But she had to know. "Did anyone check with the medical examiner?"

"Called him myself. Hal had enough alcohol in him to—"

"You ever know him when he didn't?" she yelled.

"Take it easy, Ger. I didn't mean anything."

"I know," she said softly. "It's just . . . it hasn't sunk in yet. Mike, I don't know when I'll be back to work."

"Take as much time as you need."

She started to hang up and instead blurted, "He knew we loved him, didn't he?"

The man replied quietly. "Sure. He knew."

Geraldine licked at the tears on the corner of her mouth. "I'll call you tonight." She hung up smiling. Mike had loved him too.

After all, he did fire Hal twice. Once for sleeping through a six-alarm fire across from his apartment, and once for screwing the publisher's secretary in the conference room a half hour before deadline.

She sat on the edge of the bed and stared down at the floral carpeting. Her eyes hurt from lack of sleep. Her body felt crusty, like the sooted windowsills in her West Side apartment. Her scalp itched along the hairline and she couldn't remember when she'd washed her hair. She found it hard to remember anything.

Except Hal's face.

"You okay?" Owen asked.

She squinted at the sun coming in through the window. He noticed and slid the heavy drapes closed.

Geraldine lay back on the bed and rested her head against the padded floral headboard. "God, he was so special."

It was the first time she had ever referred to Hal in the past tense. It made her angry instead of sad. "I want to know everything."

Owen pulled the chair closer to the bed and sat down. "The hell of it is that when you get right down to it, there isn't that much to tell."

"I'll take whatever you have," she said, closing her eyes. They burned with fatigue.

The man rose saying: "You go in and take a shower and I'll order us some breakfast. Then we'll talk."

"I can't eat," she protested as he led her to the bathroom and turned on the shower. He spread the bathmat on the floor and slipped a thick towel from its metal holder. "Take your time," he said, closing the door behind him.

Geraldine sat on the toilet lid and cried. Her arm crashed into the cluster of makeup on the mirrored counter. She cried for the good times they'd had and for the great times they'd never have.

He was gone. For good this time. No more ape suits. No brawls. No late night slurred phone calls. No laughs. No sex.

She reached for the roll of toilet paper and blew her nose, angry that at this horrible moment in her life she could be thinking of something as inconsequential as sex. She decided she was truly an evil person and walked into the shower to cleanse her guilt.

Only when the water hit did she realize she was still wearing the dress, bra, and panties.

Owen had breakfast waiting when she finally emerged, wrapped in a bathrobe. The food was laid out on the circular table near the window.

"Okay, talk," she said, attacking the pancakes and coffee.

He said it had started a little less than a year ago in Key West.

"That's where you live?" she asked.

He nodded. "When I retired from the Coast Guard six years ago I cut all ties to everything and everyone. Instead of going home to Seattle, I went to the Keys. Got divorced, gave her the house, cars . . . kids."

She wondered how many but didn't ask.

"I bought a boat to take tourists out fishing. Between that and my military pension, I make a decent living."

A sailor. Who would have thought? She had him pegged as a rancher or a construction worker.

"That's how I met Hal. He chartered my boat. He was on the island working on a TV movie. About nine months ago."

Geraldine remembered.

A producer had hired Hal to do a remake of *Moby-Dick* and sent him to Key West to gain inspiration.

They'd sat in the lounge, at Newark Airport, laughing at the absurdity of the assignment.

Hal was in rare form. "The little twerp never even read the novel. Never saw the Gregory Peck movie. But he knows we can improve on it. The little shit wants to take this classic, this jewel, and turn it into a TV movie—you ready for this?—with Bruce Willis. Jesus! I heard that, my price jumped twenty thousand!"

So she sent him off to Florida to write his movie and she caught the shuttle to Washington for a poker game with some reporters from the *Post.*

Owen continued: "We spent two nights at sea drinking, shooting the breeze. We headed back 'cause we ran out of booze. First time that ever happened to me," he said, with a tinge of embarrassment.

Geraldine found herself strangely relaxed. Maybe it was the food, the first in many days. Or the fact that her hair was clean and she was redolent of rose talcum.

"After Hal went back to New York he sent me one of his books, which I read and liked. He called me a couple of times. Got the feeling he was looking for an excuse to come back."

Geraldine reached for the coffee pot and noticed a new pack of cigarettes. He thought of everything.

"A month later I'm having the oil changed and sitting in the garage reading a magazine. And there's his face. Hal. Looking right up at me. He wrote a story about the people that got poisoned by Tylenol."

Geraldine recalled the article. *Esquire* ran it in three installments.

"It was like part two so I called him and told him I'd like to read the rest of it. He sent it. It was waiting in the post office about a week later. I even showed it to my buddy, Earl. The ol' man got a kick out of it. Said he wanted to meet Hal next time he came down. Wanted to show him what real fishin' was." Owen smiled. It was a quick, unguarded moment.

"Couple of months later I'm having a beer with Wagon Master—that's Earl's CB handle. And he tells me about these two Japanese guys he took out on a night run. Guys were big spenders. Didn't blink when he asked for twice what he usually gets. At first they wanted to rent the boat without him but the ol' man wouldn't go for it. So Earl carried them out to the middle of the ocean. At midnight. They even had their own maps."

"Is that unusual?" Geraldine asked.

"Very," Owen said. "Most tourists can't tell a pond from a lake."

Geraldine wasn't sure herself what the difference was. Size? Depth?

"And these were no fishermen. Wore business suits. Spoke to each other in Japanese, but Earl says their English was perfect. Better than mine. They met up with another boat. A private yacht. They went aboard and stayed about an hour. Earl thinks he saw a man with a rifle but he wasn't sure. The man was standing off to the side, near the stern. They climbed back on his boat and Earl dropped them off on the pier."

Geraldine walked over to the dresser and started throwing clothes in the open suitcase. She went into the bathroom and scooped up her cosmetics, leaving the door open.

"Earl figured these guys were up to no good. Running guns, maybe coke. But he didn't see anything. Except, the next day he's cleaning the deck, and he finds a piece of paper with Townehouse written on it."

Owen lit a cigarette and leaned against the bathroom door, watching Geraldine apply her makeup.

"Earl forgot about it till he came across the story in the newspaper a few weeks later."

Geraldine plugged the hair blower into the socket beneath the wide mirror. "What story?"

"The woman in Idaho who was poisoned by Townehouse coffee. And the doctor in Texas."

Geraldine vaguely remembered something about it. It wasn't a coffee brand sold in New York, so the papers there gave it very little space. She fluffed her hair with the brush.

"I thought about that story Hal did on Tylenol, so I called him. Told him about the Japanese guys and the midnight cruise. He didn't seem to take it too seriously. Fact is, when I hung up, I felt kind of stupid having called. I didn't hear from him again till five days ago, when I got this telegram."

He removed a folded piece of paper from his shirt and handed it to her.

Geraldine read it quickly. "Went to Cleveland. You landed a big one. Arrive Wednesday. Flight 88. Stock the booze. Hal."

"Why Cleveland?" she asked.

"That's where they make the coffee."

Geraldine turned off the hair blower and set it on the counter. She turned to Owen. "When did you call him?"

"Three weeks ago yesterday."

That would have made it early January. She and Hal had spent New Year's together in New York and practically every day after . . . and he never mentioned a word. Two days before she left for Vegas, on January 16, he left a message on her machine that he was flying to L.A. for a meeting with his agent. By the time she returned the call, he'd left.

"Why did he lie about going to Cleveland?" she wondered.

"Maybe he wanted to check it out first."

Geraldine wasn't convinced. "Or maybe, being the competitive, neurotic writer he was, he was afraid I'd steal the story."

"Would you have?"

"In a minute!"

Owen met both flights from Kennedy and when Hal didn't show up, "I called his apartment and a woman answered. Said she was his sister. She told me what happened. I didn't know what to do, who to go to. Seemed to me like he found out something in Cleveland and they killed him. But it was nothing I could take to the police. Then you came to mind. He talked about you a lot those two days out in the water. I called your paper. They said you were in Vegas. I called every hotel, tracked you here to the Sands, and then I couldn't think of a message to leave you that would make sense. So I came out looking for Susan Hayward."

Geraldine said, "Hold on," and closed the bathroom door while she hurriedly dressed. The guy seemed normal enough but—that bizarre story implicating the Japanese in poisoning the coffee! Maybe all those years at sea did funny things to a person. Maybe veterans' hospitals were jammed with patients, ex-seamen, who told strange tales.

To insist there was a link between the Tylenol murders, the poisoned coffee, the glass found in baby food jars, and tainted soup cans in Nebraska was simply idiotic! The guy was a loony.

Copycat crimes happened all the time. "Son of Sam" had spawned an axe murderer who took instructions from his parakeet.

What probably happened is that Hal had gone to Cleveland, found nothing, and was merely going to Key West where he'd discovered an eager drinking partner. The telegram "You landed a big one" could mean anything. He might have stumbled on a totally different story idea in Cleveland, one he hoped to sell as a movie.

Her immediate problem was getting rid of the guy. As soon as she got back to New York she'd run a check on him. Anyone that wacko was bound to have left a paper trail of lunacy.

She applied some lipstick, pinned her damp hair behind her ears and swallowed a handful of Vitamin C. She left the bathroom and quickly gathered the rest of her belongings into the open suitcase on the bed.

"Don't believe me, do you?" He was sitting by the table, stacking the dishes neatly on the food service tray.

"I have enough to deal with," she said, checking her purse for the airline ticket. She added: "He could have fallen off the terrace in a drunken stupor."

The sailor slid the drapes apart and gazed at the mountains, which reminded him of Seattle. He'd never realized till now that he missed it. Some of it. The kids, mostly.

"You knew him a lot better than I did, but I drank with him for two days. When I docked at the pier he jumped off the boat and drove me to town. Ask me, I don't think he knew how to get drunk."

"Yeah, well," Geraldine said, glancing about the room. "I gotta go."

"There's something else," he said, not turning from the window.

She could hardly wait for this one. Aliens from Mars had taken over the White House and tampered with the vice-president's mind.

"What?" she said, not bothering to hide her annoyance.

"They also tried to kill me."

Geraldine stopped zipping the suitcase. "What?"

"Day after I got his telegram."

She looked at his face, trying to spot some tinge of weakness . . . some clue . . . some sign that he wasn't to be trusted. She found none. "What do you mean?"

"I was heading home after the bar closed. Before you get near the pier you have to drive under an old railroad overpass. It's a shortcut. Hardly any lights. Very little traffic. Most people don't use it 'cause the road is all tore up, but my car's old and can't hardly get any more dents."

"That night a rock comes crashing through the window at me. I'm here to tell about it 'cause I was reaching over to the radio and my head was bent. My car's in the shop right now with a hole the size of a watermelon."

Geraldine shrugged. "Maybe some kid?"

He shook his head. "I went back in the daytime. There was a bunch of cigarette butts. Person was up there a long time waiting. There were two holes in the ground alongside the overpass. Same kind of holes a ladder makes. I know 'cause I checked."

Geraldine asked: "What are you saying?"

"I'm saying that they found out about the telegram and figured I knew something."

"Are you saying the two are connected? The coffee and—"

Owen saw the flash of fear in her eyes. "Yeah. Puts us in a hell of a spot, doesn't it?"

Geraldine looked at him without flinching. "Us?"

"He was your friend. They're bound to know that. With you being a writer they probably figure he told you things."

Hal murdered? Over a story?

Impossible. But he was dead. Mike said so. Even the mayor. And Ida, the sister she never knew he had.

She started crying and didn't protest when Owen came to her side and cradled her shoulders. She continued crying as they rode in the cab to the airport.

And what, Geraldine wondered, becomes of all the memories? They don't tell you about that when someone dies. He goes off and you're left there with a stack of mental videos that no one wants to see.

What do you do? Carry the invisible baggage all your life until you die? And if you do meet in the hereafter do you fling it in his face? "Here! You carry it! My arm is broken."

What's the point of having memories if you're going to get stuck with storage fees?

Owen carried her bag to the boarding gate and waited till she disappeared into the covered passageway.

CHAPTER FOUR

After the funeral, Ida invited the mourners to Hal's apartment. There was a generous lunch for Geraldine, Mike, and the assortment of reporters, authors, hookers, bartenders, waitresses, sports figures, bookies, and politicians who had come to the service.

The mayor's office delivered three fruit baskets and six dozen pastries. Reilly's Pub supplied the liquor, and the neighborhood Chinese restaurant donated platters of egg rolls, spare ribs, and chicken wings. A famous Hollywood glamour queen sent two cases of Mexican beer.

Snow was falling lightly, powdering the gray city, as Geraldine stood alone on the terrace. The wind whipped at her coat and stung her legs. Behind her, the glass doors separated her from the people clogging the living room.

It was barely two in the afternoon but lights shone from all the apartment windows along the block. The shrouded sky between the buildings was swollen with icy currents. Below her on the sidewalk a man tried to walk a dog that sprang to catch the snowflakes.

She looked at the six square wooden boxes that lined the terrace. She had helped the carpenter arrange them in position. He cemented them to the terrace floor along the three-sided railing. A florist arrived later to fill them with soil and various greenery known to survive the city's winter as well as its brutal August humidity.

All that remained now were sickly, stubby roots clogged with dead leaves under a crust of soot-coated ice.

One box was out of line. It was pushed aside, standing near the folded furniture leaning against the east wall. It was that box that Ida said Hal must have tripped over in the dark.

Geraldine bent down and brushed the snow away with her gloved hand. She could see the thick round impressions of the glue, each about the size of a coffee cup, on the floor. One of the circles had a thin sliver of wood firmly embedded in it.

Geraldine lined up the circles of the flower box and tried to trip over it. Twice the terrace railing caught her just across the chest, making it impossible to scale it.

Even considering Hal's added height, she knew the four-foot barrier would have protected his body. She glanced quickly behind, checking to see if she'd drawn anyone's attention.

The mourners were lined around the food table with paper plates in hand. An unknowing visitor would have thought he'd wandered into a party.

Only Mike, she noted, appeared to be melancholy, sitting alone off to the side, nursing a club soda.

Geraldine looked down at the box and positioned her feet against the wooden edge. Then she raised her head, stared at a window across the street, and moved forward.

She fell and recovered quickly before her knees hit the cement floor. No one in the living room appeared to notice her stumble.

If Hal had walked out into the terrace on the dark January night, wearing just a cotton long-sleeved shirt and trousers, wouldn't the blast of cold air have revived his senses, even if he were drunk?

And what would have caused him to go out on the terrace to begin with? He hated winter. One of the reasons he became a screenwriter, he boasted, was to hang out in California.

A gust of wind swooped up and blew a metal magazine rack against her ankles. The thin legs of the plastic folded chairs trembled under the ropes securing them to the railing.

She wondered why the rack wasn't tied to the furniture. She leaned down and saw a section of the rope dangling free. She tried inserting the magazine rack and it slipped in easily on the second attempt.

Did Hal remove it? For what? There was one in the living room next to the couch. Why would he yank another one from the bundled furniture?

Or did someone remove it to use as a weapon? Did Hal hear a noise from the dark terrace and go out to investigate? Was he struck by surprise and his body thrown over the railing?

She examined the magazine rack and noted that one of the legs was damaged. Her hands were starting to numb, even with the protection of gloves. It was difficult to maneuver her fingers.

She turned quickly to the sound of tapping at the glass window. Ida smiled and pantomimed being cold. Geraldine replaced the rack and entered the living room.

She took off her coat and sat on the couch next to Mike.

The chubby man with the thick glasses and protruding belly reminded her of the Pillsbury dough boy, but without the smile.

"I should have married him," she said.

Mike didn't even glance her way as he answered, "For what? So he could die of gunshot wounds in some motel? You did the man a favor."

"I don't go to motels," she bristled.

"No, but he did, and eventually you would have caught him and shot him."

Geraldine laughed.

She knew about the women. Secretaries, computer programmers, movie stars, dental hygienists. She tolerated it as he did her gambling. It evened out. Somewhat.

"When are you coming back to work?" Mike asked.

"I need time."

"I need a reporter. How's two weeks?"

Geraldine groaned, "I can't even defrost my refrigerator in two weeks."

"A month. Tops. Otherwise, I'll have to let you go."

Geraldine smiled and waved at a baseball player, a shortstop with the Detroit Tigers, who often took her and Hal to dinner when he came to town.

"So fire me," she told Mike.

"If I have to. It's up to you. Talk is the paper's being sold," he said.

"That story's been going around for ten years."

"This time they're serious," he told her. "I can cover for you only so long."

"Mike, I just buried the best part of my life. I have to learn how to breathe again."

He patted her arm. "Thirty days, Ger."

Geraldine remained after everyone left. She helped an author fill doggie bags that would carry him at least a week. She also gave him cab fare and two bottles of rye.

There was a whole gaggle of writers that Geraldine dubbed the "Hal Landry Irregulars"—reporters, drinking buddies, college English students, poets who saw him as their guru.

He read their manuscripts, introduced them to agents, paid for their meals—but mostly he helped them face the blank page.

"Writing is not, as everyone says, a lonely profession," Hal believed. "It's a fucking lonely nightmare, especially when you're not earning enough to get drunk."

Who would cater to their silent dreams now?

It was nearing seven-thirty when Geraldine and Ida tied up the last of the garbage bags. While Ida napped on the couch, Geraldine sat at Hal's desk in the bedroom, rummaging through his notebooks and papers.

A file labeled Owen Ryder, Chief Petty Officer, Ret. drew her attention. It contained some notes, receipts for plane tickets to Key West, directions to the East Pier, and a picture of Hal and Owen sitting aboard the boat, *Nathan*. There was a second picture of Hal holding a beer near his lap while a hairy tan dog drank from the bottle. She wondered who had held the camera. Maybe the fishing trip hadn't been as unadventurous as the sailor recounted. She stared at the picture and tried to identify a white piece of clothing drying on the deck. A woman's bathing suit?

She lit a cigarette and dug through the papers, her hand grazing against a thick matchbook stamped Cleveland Ramada Inn. She opened it and found Hal's handwriting; he had scribbled "Marlene" next to a phone number.

"You're lucky you're dead," she muttered, " 'cause I'd kill you if you walked in now."

She stuck the matchbook in the folder and carried it to the bed. She reached over the bookcase and flicked on the overhead reading light.

The pillow still smelled of his cologne.

She stretched out and began reading. By the personal style of the writing, she knew that Hal had spoken into his tape recorder and later typed the notes.

It used to drive her nuts. They'd be sitting in a restaurant and he'd suddenly drop his chin and speak into his shirt pocket: "Give the mailman a limp. We can justify it by saying he had polio as a kid. Give the meek librarian a pit bull instead of a cat. Let's avoid the obvious."

She once asked him if he ever secretly taped their conversations.

"Ger, my movies are PG. With your language we'd never get a distributor."

The cologne was too distracting. Too recent. She flipped the pillow aside and sat up, reading leaning against the plaster wall.

> *His CB nickname is Fresh Paint. Have no idea what it means. Has a great boat,* Nathan. *Named it after some gal he was crazy about. Her father was an admiral with a bent sense of humor. Owen served twenty years in the military. Originally from Seattle, son of a lumberjack, he quit school and joined the navy, later transferring to the Coast Guard. He's got a dog that's an alcoholic, an ex-wife who dumped him for a refrigerator salesman at Sears, and three kids.*

Not that it mattered, but she liked the idea Owen was a father.

> *We gave up the fishing trip when we ran out of ice and rum but luckily they had plenty on land. Went to a bar down by the pier. There was a woman, Lily, who was hanging all over him. They took off and left me sitting there with a blind man, Joe, who talked my ear off about how he used to play baseball with Al Lopez up in Tampa when they were kids.*
>
> *A couple of weeks later the sailor calls me one night with some half-assed story about the Japanese poisoning the coffee supply.*
>
> *I pretended to be interested, not to hurt his feelings. Then I figured what the hell. I called my ol' buddy from AP, Roy Hingle, who's now with the Cleveland paper. According to him it was a quality control screw-up at the coffee plant and they cried "tampering" to avert lawsuits. I may go to Cleveland anyway just to see him.*

She examined the rest of the folder and found a hotel bill from the Cleveland Ramada Inn for five nights. He had registered on January 17 and checked out on January 22 . . . the day he died.

There were two MasterCard receipts for restaurant meals and a Visa slip from a florist for two dozen yellow roses.

Marlene had evidently made an impression. Geraldine felt the tears swarming and fought them off.

There was a car rental receipt from Avis and a cash advance voucher from American Express in the amount of $3,000.

Geraldine was puzzled. It was very unlike Hal to do that. Once when they were in Atlantic City she'd run out of money and tried to get him to use his credit card at the cashier's cage. He flatly refused, giving her a lecture on the inflated interest rates charged for such transactions. She didn't talk to him for days.

Why did he need $3,000 cash in Cleveland? She turned the paper over and saw where he had written "Joe A." Who was "Joe" and why did Hal give him money?

The last object in the folder made her heart lurch. It was a green laminated card that read Visitor's Pass. Townehouse Associated Food Industries.

She turned off the light and left the room, concealing the folder between the pages of an old *Newsweek.*

She hesitated a moment before closing the door, glancing at the bed that had provided the setting for many passionate encounters, some even including sex.

CHAPTER FIVE

Cardinal Thomas Ryan McHugh munched on a bacon cheeseburger and cold french fries in the rear of the black limousine. A chocolate milkshake stood within reach on the small lap desk beneath the reading lamp.

Outside the window, traffic crawled slowly along the New Jersey Turnpike. The snow had tapered off but the orange Caution: Roads Slippery sign still blinked from the overpass.

The inside of the window was fogged with cigar smoke. He swiped at the moisture with the hem of his black sleeve.

It was only nine o'clock at night but he was tired. He detested many of the ceremonial functions that he was forced to attend, like the one earlier tonight in Toms River for Catholic Charities. He looked forward to a hot bath, some blueberry brandy, and a good movie on the VCR. He hoped the housekeeper had remembered to light the fireplace in the bedroom.

The highway was peppered with red taillights and thundering gray trucks that whizzed past in a blur. He loathed New York winters, and thought fondly of his home in Louisville.

The reading lamp reflected on the car window as he skimmed through copies of the *New York Post, Daily News, Wall Street Journal,* and *New York Times.*

He liked the *Post* for the cartoons and sports section and the *News* for the restaurant and movie reviews. The *Times* was boring and the *Journal* almost unreadable, but he considered reading them a personal act of contrition.

His bifocaled eyes fell on a brief story on the *Times* obit page. He called out to his aide, Father Michael Murphy, who was seated up front with the driver.

"Who's this Hal Landry?"

The young priest woke with a start as the driver elbowed him.

"Excuse me?" he looked around quickly.

"Hal Landry. The *Times* has a story. The mayor attended the funeral. Who was he?" the cardinal snapped.

The priest tried to get his mind to function. He was surprised to see they were still on the turnpike.

He answered quickly. "He was a writer, movies mostly."

The cardinal frowned. "What does that have to do with the mayor? He write a movie that nut was crazy about?"

The priest wanted to shout, "If you read the damn story you'd know as much as I do!" but instead he spoke softly, as one would address a child. "He used to be a reporter and covered city hall for many years."

"Before my time," the rotund man said, smiling.

"Yes, Your Eminence," his aide replied. *Every damn thing was before your time! How long are you going to get away with that stupid, lame excuse?*

"That explains why I wasn't asked to speak at the funeral," the cardinal observed.

"No doubt," Father Murphy agreed, catching the driver's half smirk in the light from the dashboard panel.

"Should we send a letter of condolence, anyway?"

"It would be quite charitable," Father Murphy answered.

"Take care of it," the cardinal instructed, turning to his horoscope.

CHAPTER SIX

In the Willow Heights section of Cleveland, the young mother deposited her teenaged daughter at the movie theater in the shopping mall.

Marlene sat in the white Toyota and waited as the girl caught up to her friends in front of the ticket booth.

Her headlights framed the circle of young girls in their lookalike jeans, bulky down coats, and woolen leg warmers. From the back, it was impossible to pick out her own child.

Had it been that way when she was growing up? Probably. Instead of leg warmers it was ankle socks and black and white saddle shoes.

Marlene waved and drove off. She steered through the maze of cement barriers and stopped at a curbside mailbox to insert the letter. She heard it clunk to the bottom of the steel compartment. She rolled up the car window quickly, not wanting the heat to escape.

It was done. She'd written it. She'd mailed it. Somehow, it made her feel a little better. And somewhat foolish.

And . . . a bit romantic.

She'd only known him a week and had no idea who would open the card she'd addressed "To the family of Hal Landry."

She pulled away from the mailbox and drove out of the parking lot. She headed for the highway ramp and checked the rearview mirror.

The lights behind her were blinding. She glanced in the side mirror and could see the wide, long body of a gray van. She hated when they got behind her. The height of the wheels made the headlights shine right in the car.

But it seemed everyone in Cleveland had one. Even her husband, Gary, was starting to make sounds about buying one.

She paused at the Yield sign at the lip of the highway and waited for a break in the traffic. The van inched closer. She gunned the car onto the highway and relaxed, knowing she'd be home in ten minutes.

The car radio played "Strangers in the Night." She'd heard it thousands of times, but tonight she found herself listening to the words.

Was it only two weeks ago?

She had been sitting at the lunch counter of the diner across the street from the coffee plant. When the budget allowed, she ate there rather than at the company cafeteria.

On that rainy afternoon Marlene was drinking a cup of tea when Hal sat down on the stool next to her.

"Don't you work at Townehouse?" he asked.

She didn't recognize the face but the smile was pleasant.

"Division engineering," she told him.

The conversation progressed easily. She commented on his New York accent and he praised the cleanliness of her city.

It wasn't her city. She was from South Carolina and even though she only went back for funerals, she still considered it home.

Hal confessed to being from Alabama—and swore her to secrecy. "Even my agent doesn't know."

They shared their mutual longing for drive-in movies and drug stores with soda fountains. Porch swings. County fairs. Inflated black inner tubes in the water. A backyard tree house.

Somehow, she wasn't surprised to see him waiting for her by the gate at quitting time. Hal invited her to dinner, which she reluctantly declined. "Have to get groceries."

He offered to go along and push the shopping cart.

It was funny, shopping with a total stranger, buying extra-strength scented roll-on deodorant for her husband, who, in eighteen years of marriage, had never been inside a supermarket.

They met for lunch the next day, and Marlene learned he was a writer, doing research for a movie that was set in a coffee plant, much like the one she worked in.

No, the movie had nothing to do with the recent poisonings, he assured her. It was about a woman who inherits the business. Streisand was interested in directing it.

He gave her a copy of one of his novels and signed it: "To my new friend, Marlene." She admitted he was the first writer she'd ever met.

Surprisingly, he was interested in her story. Not that there was much to it. She got married right out of Thomas Jefferson High School to Gary, who sat across from her in biology. He now worked for the phone company. They had two girls, and when the youngest started school she went to work at Townehouse as a packer on the assembly line. She was later promoted to secretary and now worked for two engineers.

The next day, yellow roses were delivered to her desk with a note from Hal inviting her to dinner.

Marlene called home and told her daughter she had to work overtime.

She and Hal had a quiet dinner in the restaurant of the Ramada Inn, where he was staying, and later sat in the cocktail lounge where she drank her first mimosa—champagne with orange juice. He told her that Tom Selleck thrived on them.

They sat near the piano and Marlene requested "Moon River." She didn't pull away when Hal leaned over and held her hand.

In the morning there was a pass at the gate with his name, and she personally took him on a tour of the plant.

She went to his hotel room that night and left shortly after 1:00 A.M. She called in sick the next day and spent the afternoon with him at the zoo.

She didn't see or hear from him the next two days. He said he was scouting locations in the area.

When they did meet, he seemed preoccupied. She wondered if the writing project wasn't going well, but didn't feel it was her place to ask.

They drove to a seafood restaurant on the outskirts of town, and Hal apologized for his moodiness, explaining that he'd seen in the paper that a Japanese man had drowned. Joe Akido.

Why, yes! Everyone at the plant was talking about it! He'd worked at Townehouse sixteen years.

But how, Marlene asked, had he known Joe?

He hadn't. He happened to be on the waterfront when the cops fished out the body. "What kind of guy was he?"

Marlene pondered. "Quiet. Kept to himself. I met his wife and kids at one of the Christmas parties and they seemed nice. I think she had a lot of money. Or her family. Joe drove a Porsche and they lived over in Green Valley, the ritzy part of town."

It didn't occur to Marlene to ask what Hal was doing down by the waterfront.

The next afternoon she drove Hal to the airport and he gave her his address in case she ever decided to visit New York.

She watched him get on the plane carrying her gift, a teddy bear wearing a Cleveland Indians uniform.

She cried all the way home.

What totally shocked her was not that she had willingly shared his bed—though he was the only man she'd ever slept with besides her husband. What truly disturbed Marlene was her lack of *guilt!*

An almost stranger had seen her naked, stroked her body. Where was the shame, the remorse, the disgust, the hell and damnation the nuns had sworn would result from such behavior?

Certainly not in room 412 of the Ramada Inn. She could no longer drive by the building without smiling.

The smile faded that cold January morning. She was at her desk reading the newspaper while munching on a cheese danish. She had laid the newspaper flat on the desk to cut out the supermarket coupons when a brief paragraph caught her attention under the headline "Hollywood Writer Dies."

Normally Marlene would have skipped the story and turned to "Dear Abby." She had little interest in books, or movies, for that matter.

But all that had changed since meeting Hal.

So she read the AP story that told of his Academy Award nomination, his years as an award-winning journalist. She ran into the bathroom where she threw up her breakfast. She went home early that day and stayed in bed.

The song on the car radio ended and Marlene slowed for the approaching exit. Behind, the highway was deserted but for two headlights that made her wince.

She reached up to the rearview mirror and flipped the latch for night driving. The offending headlights were now two muted orbs in a black velvet backdrop.

She clicked on the right turn signal and eased the car to the far lane, braking slightly for the familiar sharp incline.

She glanced in the mirror and noticed, with relief, that the headlights were gone.

She came around the wide turn and caught a glimpse of some movement in the outside mirror. She strained for a better look. Something was approaching quickly. But it had no lights.

CHAPTER SEVEN

Owen piloted the boat against the choppy waters as he headed for a reef in the Gulf of Mexico. The sun had only been up an hour. The air was still crisp with the night's breath.

His destination was Gator Cove, a small island popular with scuba divers, shell collectors, and photographers. Every local artist had sketched the half-mile of sandy beaches and coral reef.

The speckled coral shells had names like *Tonna Perdix, Natica Canrena* and *Cyprae Exanthema.* He knew this only because many of his neighbors had christened their crafts after the local shells.

The cove, with its palm trees and colorful birds, was a regular stop on the sightseeing excursions. He always avoided the main docking area and took his passengers to a remote slice of the reef.

The sailor was looking forward to the outing. It'd been weeks since Luther, the terrier now asleep at his feet, had romped freely. He used to let him run on the marina, but a new group of live-ins complained.

Owen never had a dog as a kid. His mother, who was asthmatic, had a natural dislike of animals.

Then, last spring, he was sitting on deck, anchored to the pier, when the brown mutt, wadded with gum and tar, hopped aboard and drank thirstily from his gin and tonic. He finished it, and a can of beer, before settling down for a nap.

He came back the next night and helped Owen devour a pizza. He also gulped down a vodka and orange juice before dashing off to chase a Doberman.

One day he never left. Owen adjusted to his new roommate. It just meant buying extra booze. He named him Luther after a hairy cook aboard the USS *Hudson.*

Owen steered the craft and thought of Geraldine. He hadn't heard from her since Vegas and wondered if he would.

It was a dumb move. He should've kept his suspicions to himself. He wondered if he'd been motivated by Hal's sudden death, or had he used it as an excuse to meet the woman he'd found so intriguing from Hal's description.

Probably a little of both.

Owen glanced to the deck and found it difficult to look away from Gigi.

His passengers had arrived shortly before daybreak as planned. He was unprepared for the gorgeous creature that climbed aboard.

Her companion, a chunky, dark man with bad skin, introduced himself as Gino. Three cameras dangled from his neck. A leather case hung from his shoulder.

She said her name was Gigi and held out a slim, tanned hand while the other gripped the rim of the white Panama hat that threatened to blow away. He couldn't see the eyes behind the blue-tinted glasses, but the smile was dazzling. Movie star quality. As was the body in the strapless peach jumpsuit.

He made it a practice not to get chummy with his passengers, other than to extend the normal hospitality of a well-stocked bar, fishing gear, and fresh bait.

On one of his first trips a client accused him of coming on to his wife. The enraged woman pushed her husband overboard and Owen had to jump in to save him. It cost him a wristwatch given to him by shipmates in the North Atlantic. In the struggle to rescue the husband, the man had thrashed his arms in panic. The watch was yanked free.

The wind picked up strength and he quickly adjusted his course to trap it in the sails. The boat maneuvered easily over the whitecaps churned by a passing motor launch.

The sudden choppiness failed to disturb Gino, who slept soundly on the lounging chair.

Gigi sunned herself on deck wearing only a silver metallic bikini bottom. Her long blonde hair hung in thick ropes over the caramel-colored breasts. The lean, angular body glistened with suntan oil.

Owen squinted against the sun at ten o'clock in the sky. It was going to be a hot one today, he knew, as he watched the woman's body—a willing offering to the sun god.

She was on her back, her pelvic bones protruding sharply against the thin slice of material cutting high across her thighs.

She caught his gaze and flashed a smile beneath the sunglasses.

The CB radio momentarily distracted him.

"Fresh Paint, how's it going?"

Owen recognized the wheezing voice of Wagon Master.

"Not bad, Earl. What'cha up to?"

"Have to go to the feed store. The chickens ain't eating and Molly's convinced they sold us a bad batch. How was Vegas?"

"Okay. Didn't hang out that long."

"You meet up with that gal?"

"Yeah. She went home for the funeral."

"You truckin'?" the old man asked.

"Heading out to the cove."

"Carrying any freight?"

"Two."

"If you're not doing nothing tonight, stop on over for dinner. Molly says we don't see you no more. How's seven-thirty sound?"

"Good."

"You can bring Lily."

Owen turned his back to Gigi and barked into the mouthpiece, "Why the hell would I want to do that?"

"I don't know. Ran into her the other day. She wants to know where you've been hiding. Sure is a pretty lady," the old man said. "If I was forty years younger—"

"You'd be in jail."

He laughed. "See you tonight."

Gigi sauntered into the cabin, a white towel rolled across the back of her neck. One blonde braid covered a nipple, the other rested against the end of the towel.

"Got a drink?"

Owen gestured behind him to the bar.

She stumbled and grabbed on to his arm for support. He caught the aroma of almonds and cocoa butter. She took her time releasing her grip.

He heard her open the refrigerator and remove the ice cube tray. Her high heels clacked on the wooden floor as she crossed the cabin to tune the radio. She changed the easy listening station to country music. She fumbled with the bottles on the bar and swayed across the floor, holding on to the walls for support.

She carried a drink and sat on the wooden captain's chair a few inches away from Owen.

"What do you do for fun?" she asked.

"Sleep."

"Alone?"

"Usually."

"Not much fun in that."

He didn't respond. It was all he could do to keep his eyes from the naked breasts.

"You're not a born-again Christian or gay are you?" she smiled.

Owen busied himself with the charts. "I'd take it easy with that rum today. That sun's gonna be hot."

"I got a talent for it," she said, raising the glass. "Everybody has a talent . . . for something. What's yours?"

"Staying alive," he said, glancing at Gino.

She shrugged. "I just work for him." She leaned over and put her drink on the wooden floor. She rose slowly. "I bet you have many hidden talents." She slid her hand across the front of his white, cutoff jeans. "I bet you're loaded . . . with talent," Gigi cooed, undoing his zipper.

Owen gripped the wheel as she dropped to her knees and swallowed him.

A large chunk of driftwood slammed against the side of the boat, causing Gino to stir in his chair. He looked about quickly and yelled over the waves, "Where's the girl?"

Owen yelled back, "She went down to eat."

CHAPTER EIGHT

It was past midnight as Geraldine lay in bed watching an Edward G. Robinson movie. Fourteen stories below, a truck rumbled noisily as it sprayed the street with salt.

Not that she could have slept. She was exhausted emotionally, physically, mentally, but unable to sleep. She'd tried calling Owen but got no answer. Not that she was starting to believe his crazy story—she just felt like hearing his voice. And maybe, if she steered the conversation smoothly, he'd invite her to Key West to go sailing.

She might have told him about the Townehouse pass if he'd answered. She might have mentioned the $3,000 withdrawal. And maybe not. After all, what did it prove? Nothing. Only that Hal went to Cleveland, met some dame, and sent her flowers. Probably a stewardess. Or cocktail waitress. Hal professed a fondness for working women. Intellectuals, professionals, business types, left him cold. Or so he claimed.

"I'm a writer. That makes me a professional," she'd argued.

"You're a gambler. That makes you a degenerate, which in turn, makes you incredibly desirable. To a point."

She stared at the collection of clowns gazing down from the shelved walls. The leader of the pack, an authentic Howdy Doody, sat proudly on the dresser, grinning with wooden gums.

Hal hated the room. "It's against all human decency to make love on Sesame Street," he protested.

The walls were a soft lime that ended at the deep forest green carpet. She had seen the decor in a Sears catalogue and copied it. Next to the bed, within arm's reach, was a brown knee-high refrigerator permanently stocked with Diet Pepsi and Malomars. On nights when Hal slept over, she threw in bottles of Mexican beer and a slab of fresh Gouda cheese. And when the budget allowed, smoked shrimp and cocktail sauce.

It was her own corner of the world. She did most of her writing in bed with a portable Smith Corona propped on a suitcase. The telephone sat huddled in the bookcase/headboard along with pens, notebooks, dictionaries, and reference books. Telephone directories for most major cities across the country sat in a pile next to the bed, serving as a night stand.

The living room was the library, housing a vast collection of books, albums, and now unusable Beta movies.

She would never forgive the Japanese for retiring the Beta format when her film library numbered over a thousand titles. It was their revenge for Nagasaki, she was convinced.

The kitchen served as the storage area. Friends were entertained at restaurants. Like most serious gamblers, she wasn't a social person. It took time away from the cards.

Sometimes it bothered her. The thought of growing old alone. But she rationalized by saying to herself that she'd probably die young and not have to worry about it.

Edward G. Robinson lay mortally wounded when the phone rang.

"Sorry I couldn't get back to you earlier. I was out on a story," Roy told her. "So—how you been?"

"Fine," she said, reaching for a cigarette.

"Terrible about Hal," he blurted.

"That's why I called," Geraldine said, flicking the lighter. "Did you see him when he was in Cleveland?"

"Sure did! Son of bitch looked great. We only had an hour. I had to go to the aquarium and take pictures of a fucking whale."

"Was he okay?"

"Oh, yeah. A she. Had a baby. Big deal."

Geraldine said: "I meant Hal. Was he his usual self?"

"Yeah. Why?"

"Nothing. Just last time I saw him I thought he seemed to be under some kind of stress."

There was a slight pause from the other end. "What are you saying, Ger? He jumped off the fucking terrace?"

"No! He just seemed a little depressed."

Roy laughed, "Hell! With all that Hollywood money? Shit! I

should've gone to L.A. years ago when he called me. I wouldn't be taking pictures of fucking whales. A person gets tired."

"I know."

"You still at the paper?" he asked.

"More or less."

"Mike still running tits and ass on three?"

"And page six."

Roy's tone changed. "I have to admit. Sometimes I miss it. You must, too."

"I'm still here," she yelled.

"That's not what Hal said. He said you spend more time in Vegas. When are you going to learn you can't beat 'em?"

She groaned. "I'm not trying to beat 'em, Roy. I just want to get even."

"Never happen. Not in a million years. I got a brother-in-law who goes to G.A. meetings, leaves, and plays fifty dollars on the lottery. It's a sickness. Listen to what I'm saying."

She didn't need a lecture in the middle of the night from a guy who got his job by marrying the editor's daughter.

"Hal say anything that stuck in your mind?"

"Not really. Talked about the idiots in Hollywood. Man, I couldn't believe the *Moby-Dick* story. Oh, yeah! And the floater."

Geraldine gripped the phone. "What?"

"A floater. They pulled him out of the river and I took the picture. Usual crime scene crap. No Pulitzer. But Hal seemed to know the guy. Had me dig out my whole roll and bring it to the hotel."

She turned on the bedside lamp and grabbed a pen out of the Mets mug behind her head.

"Did he . . . ah . . . take the pictures with him?"

"You know better than that. I could've got my ass in a sling just for taking them out of the building. Anyway, the guy was a nobody. A goddamn factory worker."

Her heart quickened. "Townehouse?"

"Yeah. You knew him, too?"

"No." Her throat tightened.

"Listen, Ger, I still got two rolls to develop before deadline."

"Sure, Roy."

"If you ever get out here, give a call."

"I will."

"And tell Mike," he laughed, "all the photographers here drive company cars—with telephones."

"He'll be thrilled," she said.

"See ya."

She rested the phone on her stomach and stared at the wavy static lines tumbling across the TV screen. She dialed Owen and let it ring eight times before giving up. He was either sailing or sitting in a bar. He'd cautioned her that the phone only worked when the boat was docked.

It annoyed her that it was after midnight and he was out somewhere carousing.

It aggravated her that she'd been trying to call him for days.

It truly bothered her that he hadn't called, if only to ask about the funeral. Hal was a friend, right? You'd think he'd show some interest. Common decency said that when a mutual friend died, you stayed in touch!

Wherever he was, she hoped he was miserable.

Geraldine had no way of knowing that her wish was being granted that very moment.

Owen was in the vet's office, staring down at the lifeless form of Luther.

CHAPTER NINE

Marco Luiz DelCampo was not happy. The two men seated in his living room were not happy. Outside his Biscayne mansion, the ocean waves whipped at the sea wall. It told him that God was not happy.

"We have a problem here," the slim, immaculately groomed man stated. His dark hair curled tightly against the scalp, framing amber eyes that seemed to be in a perpetual squint. The angular nose could have been a surgeon's prized accomplishment. The tawny cocoa skin was smooth and unlined. It was the face of a man who looked in the mirror often and liked what he saw. "How do we solve it?" he asked in a clipped Spanish accent.

Marco settled into the leather chair, careful to maintain the crease in the gray slacks. Chunky gold rings adorned the thin, almost feminine fingers.

The two Japanese men averted their eyes, each fearful of speaking first.

When the silence grew uncomfortable, Yan-San Tokumura spoke, "We know the writer had a meeting with Joe Akido and he spent much time with the woman secretary. Also the photographer."

He added, somewhat smugly, that the woman was no longer a problem.

Marco strolled to the wall near the fireplace and straightened a Dali that was slightly askew. He was careful not to touch the microchip at the base of the frame that was linked to the security system.

"What else?" he asked, his back turned.

The men exchanged nervous glances.

"We know that he sent a telegram to the boatman in Key West who went to Las Vegas soon after. Probably to meet the writer's girlfriend."

Marco reached over the fireplace and adjusted an errant peach-colored rose that drooped in the crystal vase. The gardener failed to cut the stems properly and would be reprimanded.

"The fault is mine," Yan-San continued. "I allowed sentiment to blind me. You had misgivings about Akido and I dissuaded you."

The other, David Ko, found his voice. "I share the blame." He did not mention his failed attempt at the overpass against the sailor. He still wore a bandage under his trousers where his leg had scraped against the jagged wall as he hurried down the ladder.

"Do you know what writers do?" Marco asked.

The men looked at each other and quickly turned their attention back to Marco.

"A baseball player plays ball, a baker bakes, a cook cooks, . . . and a writer writes."

Marco walked to the glass wall and gazed down at the ocean invading his property with a relentless fury. His yacht bobbled like a child's toy in the distance.

"Where are his notes? By your count, he had meetings with three people. Where are they?"

Yan-San replied, "The nature of the . . . assignment was such that it only allowed for a hurried search. I had to act quickly. The search was . . . incomplete."

Marco continued staring at the raging ocean spitting giant mouthfuls of foam. "Perhaps a second visit—"

Yan-San assured him he would see to it at once.

"Good. We'll talk when you have something to say." His tone signaled their dismissal.

The men hurried from the room, pausing at the outer door for the electronic buzz to allow their exit. Marco accommodated them by pushing a button near his chair.

On the other side of the door, an armed guard sprang to the sound and led them along the corridor, where another sentry escorted them downstairs.

Past the glass-domed atrium and the music room, the guard led them to the main entrance. He watched as they silently climbed into the car parked in the circular driveway.

Another guard, positioned on a balcony above Marco's terrace, waited until the car swept around the massive fountain, and signaled the gatekeeper.

When the vehicle cleared the grounds and disappeared into the thicket of tropical foliage, the gatekeeper announced its departure into a walkie-talkie.

Marco strolled onto the terrace and felt the salt air swirl beneath the immense striped canopy that shielded the balcony. Raindrops fell like a shimmering curtain from the edges of the canvas.

Marco understood God's anger and assured Him that all would soon be well in His kingdom. He asked to be forgiven and prayed for the strength to do His bidding.

Marco implored Him to look into his, Marco's heart and see the pain that he carried for having failed. A searing pain that only victory would heal.

His tears were in earnest.

Within moments the raging wind calmed to a lingering breeze. Seagulls squawked overhead, heralding the passing of the storm.

Marco took it to mean he was forgiven.

This time.

CHAPTER TEN

Ida sat on the living room floor surrounded by cartons. She'd been at the task for three days and was beginning to see the proverbial light at the end of the proverbial tunnel.

She took the autographed baseball and wrapped it carefully in tissue paper. She placed it in the box labeled Sports, which contained clippings, photos, letters, the entire sports section of the *Daily News* when Willie Mays retired, a cocktail napkin signed by Dwight Gooden, all-star game programs, and a moldy brown clump of earth with a note attached: "Infield, Shea Stadium, the day Mets clinched the '69 pennant."

The more she packed, the more she found to pack.

It had been painful at first, poring through the personal belongings of her brother. But resolve, and a desire to return home, had set in.

She attacked the job with her usual efficiency. The Salvation Army was coming to pick up the furniture, appliances, and dishes. The New York City library was sending a truck for the books.

Geraldine wanted only the framed photo of herself and Hal sitting on a pair of donkeys in Cuernavaca.

Hal's files, personal papers, notebooks, and manuscripts were going to the Literature Department of Alabama University, in accordance with his will.

Ida was keeping only the clothing. Her husband, Harry, was about the same size, and he needed a new wardrobe. Even a used one. The last time he'd bought a suit was when they got married.

She told the Puerto Rican doorman he could have the liquor and three cartons of cigarettes she found in the bedroom closet. He seemed more eager to have the shoebox filled with "parsley," which she also gave him.

She packed Hal's clothing in suitcases and set them aside to take home.

The phone rang and she got up slowly to answer it. She'd been sitting on the floor for hours and the knees didn't appreciate sudden movement.

Whoever it was hung up just as she lifted the receiver. The second time that day.

CHAPTER ELEVEN

That same afternoon, Owen walked briskly across the high school campus and got into the dented pickup truck waiting in the No Standing zone.

The old man woke at the sound of the door opening.

"Done?"

"Yeah."

Wagon Master turned on the ignition. The truck lurched forward, causing the bucket of crabs in the open back to splash its saltwater.

The cheerleading team was drilling on the athletic field as they rolled out of the parking lot.

"What did he say?" the old man asked.

Owen leaned his elbow out the window and stared at the splattered insects coating the windshield.

"Said I was lucky I stuck to beer."

Earl reached for the cigar on the dashboard and stuck the soggy end in his mouth. He didn't bother lighting it.

"What was it?"

Owen removed sunglasses from his shirt pocket and wiped them on his sleeve.

"The vodka."

Earl's head shot around. "Is he sure? For crissakes, he's only a damn teacher."

"He's sure."

"It don't seem possible."

"Shit, Earl, he's got more goddamn equipment in that lab than the Russians have. It was arsenic! Plain and simple."

The old man shook his head slowly. "Poor ol' Luther. I figured the drinking would do him in eventually, but not that way."

A police car cruised past and the officer behind the wheel tooted hello. The sailor recognized Gabe and waved back.

"So what are you going to do?"

"How the shit do I know," Owen lashed out.

Earl didn't appreciate being yelled at, but let it ride. He'd never seen his friend this out of control. Not even when his ex-wife said she was sending the kids for a week and didn't.

The sun baked the interior of the truck as they drove in the midday traffic. The road was clogged with new cars, all bearing rental stickers. A sure sign the Yankee invasion had begun.

"You gonna report it to the police?"

"Hell, no! I'd be out of business in a week. It'd be all over town—except they'd have it that two tourists died on my boat."

Earl didn't dispute it. Billy lost his coffee shop when the cashier came down with an infection. People were convinced it was AIDS and stayed away.

"The teacher, will he keep his mouth shut?"

Owen shrugged. "I gave him fifty bucks."

"You have any idea who did it?"

"Yeah," Owen said, recalling the scent of almonds and cocoa butter.

"You gonna tell me?"

"No."

The old man chomped on the cigar and spit the butt out the window. He rested his skeletal arms lightly on the steering wheel, feigning uninterest, but the tight lines deepened around the mouth.

"Maybe you better stay away from the boat for awhile. Come by us. Just till things settle down."

"Can't do that," Owen replied sharply.

They drove along Truman Avenue and got caught behind the sightseeing Conch train that spirited tourists to the Hemingway house and other attractions.

"Must be snowing up north," the old man groaned. "Pretty soon you won't be able to move around town."

Owen wasn't listening. He was angry at himself. At Hal. At Geraldine. Even the old man, who had started the whole thing with his stupid theory about Japs poisoning the coffee. Luther would have been alive if he'd never taken Hal fishing. Hal getting killed was one thing. He almost asked for it when he decided to play reporter. All Luther wanted was a drink—and Owen had obliged.

"If you don't want to stay with us, I got that other place on Columbus Avenue. Got no tenants at the moment. Whole house sitting there empty."

Owen shook his head. "Just drop me off home."

"That's not smart."

The sailor yelled, "Forget it. Okay?"

Earl twisted the wheel hard and gunned the cranky engine past the Conch train, missing an oncoming car by inches.

"Fine," he snarled. "Just do me one goddamned favor. Sign *Nathan* over to me!"

Owen turned sideways and peered at the old man from behind the sunglasses. "Why?"

"When they wheel your body off the boat I'd hate the surrogate judge to auction her to those goddamn Yankees over in the condos."

Owen didn't conceal his disgust. "You have two damn boats. What the hell do you need another one for?"

"So I can sell it to them goddamn Yankees over in the condos!"

Owen laughed. He couldn't help it.

The truck rattled down the road and Owen felt the tightness ease in his throat. Drops of rain peppered the windshield in spite of the hot sun scorching his arm through the open window.

Coming from Seattle, where it always rained, but never when the sun was out, it had taken him time to get used to the Florida climate. That, and the accents. The Southern drawl was further compounded by the way they abbreviated words and spun them together in a sing-song fashion. He spent his first year asking: "What?"

There was also the loneliness to contend with. Then he met the old man at the bait store. Tall, over six feet, weighing maybe 145, Earl looked tubercular. He walked bent forward, as if blown by a perpetual gust of wind, the spine rippling through the shirt.

His knobby, curled toes protruded from sandals too small to contain them. His skin was burnt brown, like the edges of an overbaked pie. The face was birdlike, with a sharp, pointed nose beneath two small, watery blue dots that passed for eyes. His most spectacular feature was the long mane of dark hair that blew about his ears, reminding Owen of the Indian on the buffalo nickel.

For his part, Earl, a fisherman like his father before him, felt a kinship with the retired sailor.

And so that the younger man wouldn't get too cocky, he tagged Owen Fresh Paint, to remind him that no matter how long he lived on the island, he'd always be a newcomer.

CHAPTER TWELVE

Geraldine and Ida sat in a small Italian restaurant on Second Avenue. The dining area, ten tables at most, was cordoned off from the gray pizza oven by mock wood railings shaped like thin bread sticks.

The atmosphere was gloomy, the decorations tired, and the ambience had ambled off years ago. But the pasta primavera was the best in town, and the veal scaloppine a close second.

"I'm glad you called," the white-haired woman said, sitting properly straight, a blue sweater hugging her shoulders.

"How've you been?" Geraldine asked.

"Okay," Ida answered. "I'm holding up."

Geraldine poured a glass of wine from the decanter on the table and handed it to her companion, who shook her head briskly.

"I hardly ever drink."

"Taste it. It's very light."

The woman looked about the small room, almost as if expecting to see someone she knew, and sipped. She smiled. It *is* nice."

Geraldine ate silently. Ida barely touched her food but drank three glasses of wine. Geraldine ordered a bottle for her to take home to Alabama.

They left the restaurant and walked the six short blocks to Hal's building.

The night air was brisk. The snow was gone, but some clumps remained along the curbs, now stained with black soot and dog droppings.

Geraldine walked Ida to the entrance and watched as the doorman let her into the lobby.

She hailed a cab and went home. Her phone was ringing as she unlocked the door. She raced to it, dropping her purse and keys on the floor, hoping to hear Owen's voice.

It was Ida.

Sobbing: "I was robbed!"

CHAPTER THIRTEEN

Now that God had forgiven his transgression, Marco was renewed with a fiery desire to prove himself worthy.

The only burdens that remained now were the sailor and the woman.

Burdens, he was certain, that God would help him remove swiftly.

God would not allow them to abort the mission that had begun forty-four years ago when Marco was born in Tres Cruces, a tiny village eighty kilometers from Havana.

Legend had it that a wealthy landowner came home from the fields one night to discover his wife in the passionate embrace of a local merchant. Enraged, he executed the couple along with his housekeeper, who had witnessed the disloyalty, and tied their bodies to three wooden crosses on the dirt road outside his farm.

It was said that the village was cursed, and vegetation failed to flourish. Animals died and the people withered and moved away. Flowers refused to bloom and birds to sing. The one brook that fed the hills dried to a parched crater.

Miraculously, on the day the husband died, it began to rain and continued for twenty-eight days. The thirsty soil absorbed each precious drop and produced a mighty crop. Soon the people returned.

Marco grew up hearing of God's benediction.

He came into the world on his mother's bed in a tin-roofed shack without electricity or plumbing. Baths were taken in the backyard, in a huge metal tub, with water supplied by a hose hooked to a neighboring well.

His mother gave birth to six children and saw three die before they reached the age of two.

She attributed it to God's will, not poverty or lack of medical care or malnutrition.

Her husband died an old man at the age of thirty-eight. He collapsed in the sugar cane fields a few feet from twelve-year-old Marco, who worked alongside him, hacking away at the stubborn vegetation.

The boy ran crying the five miles home to break the news to his mother. She was sitting on the porch rocking the baby and fanning the heat from her face. The baby that she didn't want to get too attached to in case God also required her in Heaven.

"Papa esta muerto," the youngster wailed.

She handed Marco the infant while she went into the house and lifted the wooden floor plank under the kitchen table. She reached below the termite-ridden boards and retrieved the milk bottle containing her life savings.

Nine pesos and change.

She dug deep into the narrow neck of the bottle and removed a nickel. She gave it to her son and told him to borrow the neighbor's bicycle and ride into town to call his uncle at the bakery. He would know what to do about the funeral.

She attributed her husband's death to God's will and not exhaustion, exploitation, oppression, ignorance, or misfortune.

At the graveside, the elderly, toothless priest echoed her sentiments.

"God's will be done. Amen."

For the young widow, there was a strange comfort in hearing the familiar words for the fourth time.

Three months later when the six dollar rent came due and the kitchen jar yielded not quite four, the family moved to the grandmother's house.

Marco occupied the screened porch, which deterred spiders but not the relentless sun nor the army of flying insects. He'd lie awake at night on the floor mat cushioned of sugar sacks, vowing to avenge his father's death.

The priest was wrong. God's will did not claim his father. American greed, American industry murdered his father.

Many had died before . . . many would die after. He knew this because his father had warned him.

At night, after work, sitting in the back of the open truck, shirtless, his grimy legs hanging over the side, his father would preach: "Each day our people die so Americans can put sugar in their coffee.

"And before the undertaker can remove the corpse another body is given a machete to continue the death chain that binds us in ignorance and servitude.

"Break the chain, little Marco. Don't let it grip you or your sons.

"Rip it free with your strong hands and strangle those who will try to stop you."

Other times, sitting under the tree behind the house, his father would rant against the Catholic Church and its indifference to the people's suffering.

"Where is the church when our people are dying in the fields? Where is the spiritual compassion for these innocent souls whose only crime is they were born poor?"

It fed his rage to see the local priest driving an American Ford when he called on the villagers. A housekeeper who worked in the rectory told of the huge amounts of food wasted each night. Food that could have fed her family, but which she was not permitted to take home to her children.

He never blamed God for the crimes of the church. He was absolute in his belief that God shared his anger.

"Marco, a man can open a business and have the noblest intention of providing for his customers and his workers. He can be truly an honorable and generous man, but then, one day, he dies. The business falls to other people. They have only one intention . . . to make more money."

Sometimes the conversation would take place in the cafe where the men gathered nightly to play dominoes and drink dark, sweet coffee, laced with hot milk.

"The church today is not the church that God envisioned. It is not the church His son, Jesus, died for.

"Do not blame God for the ignorance and greed of the priests and pope who claim to represent Him. They will burn in the same fire of damnation with the thieves and child molesters.

"God is good and merciful. If He takes our children, as He did your brothers and sisters, it's to sit them beside His throne in everlasting happiness. They sing with the angels."

Marco didn't question why God needed those three little voices.

At age fifteen, he was sent to Miami to live with an aunt who enrolled him in school. She led him to the front door of the building and handed him a paper bag containing a sandwich, a pear, and hunk of sweet bread.

He entered the building and darted out the back door—smack into a card game in the schoolyard. That was to be his closest brush with formal education.

He sold his lunch for a quarter and parlayed it into twelve dollars. His father had taught him much, not the least of which was how to play poker.

With his dark good looks, easy smile, polite manners, and humble demeanor, the young man quickly came to the attention of Enrique, a small-time hood.

Initially the assignments were minor. Marco would get a job as a grocery delivery boy and case the houses in the better sections of the city.

He soon graduated to stealing government checks out of mailboxes. He was later promoted to numbers running, and eventually to whiskey distilling in Enrique's warehouse.

On the side, he made money entertaining lonely northern women who migrated to the beach hotels in the winter to escape equally icy husbands. He provided the needed warmth, for a price.

At age twenty-three, Marco sent for his mother and sisters. He settled them into a comfortable house in Fort Lauderdale. It was the first time mama had seen a television, or an indoor bathroom with a tiled tub and a toilet you flushed instead of emptying the slop jars in the woods each morning.

There were two telephones and a refrigerator that did not require a daily supply of ice. In fact, it was so clever, it made its own ice.

America was truly a magic land. In time, mama discovered supermarkets, movies, pizza, beauty parlors, and bingo.

Marco also arranged for his mother to learn English. A tutor was hired and lessons were given daily at the kitchen table. Within six months she could read some of the sales circulars printed in the newspapers.

Within a year, she could travel the city on public transportation and read the street signs. In the sixth year, she was calling numbers at bingo whenever the priest had to officiate at a wedding. In her eighth year in Miami, she became an American citizen and knew all the state capitals.

Marco also excelled. By age twenty-nine he owned an oceanfront home, a restaurant, a jewelry store in Tampa, and a half-interest in a stud farm in Ocala.

He also had six Delta and Eastern Airlines stewardesses and seven cargo handlers on his payroll who brought in the drugs he distributed from Miami to Jersey City.

To his family and friends he was simply the owner of a Cuban restaurant and the proprietor of the Marco Travel Agency on Collins Avenue in Miami Beach.

He could be found there most days, closeted in his office, while two pretty bilingual clerks booked cruises and special tours.

It was a happy, orderly life, insured by his vast fortune and a loyal circle of bodyguards.

When mama visited the palatial home, the sentries knew to conceal the weaponry. Their presence was easily explained. "You know papa never trusted banks. I keep a lot of money in the house."

When his sisters married, Marco felt he had served his father well. Now it was time to avenge his death.

But then he met Kate.

Tall, thin, as American as peanut butter, with hair the same color. She was thirteen years his senior and a former dancer with the American Ballet Company, who had retired after a serious auto accident damaged the nerves in her leg. She came to Miami for the therapeutic weather and opened a dance studio for children.

She walked into the travel agency one April afternoon to book a cruise to Alaska. Something about the woman caused Marco to rush to her side.

He ushered her into his private office. His hands shook as he asked her name. His knees trembled when he learned she would be gone two weeks.

Marco impulsively invited her to lunch, which led to dinner the following evening. They picnicked the next afternoon, followed by a moonlight swim in his pool.

When Kate sailed to Alaska, he booked the adjoining cabin.

They were married by the ship's captain beneath a canopy of stars, with a glacial ice cap as their witness.

When Marco brought Kate home to meet his family, mama's only comment was, "Why her?"

With his arm around Kate's waist, he replied in Spanish, "I don't know." He was only certain of one thing. He couldn't live without her.

The next morning mama paid an emergency call on Senora Cruz, the local gypsy, whom one only consulted in the gravest matters of life, death, or revenge.

"The American woman is nice," mama told the gypsy. "A little old, a little skinny—but nice. Still, she is not for my son. She can only bring him unhappiness. I need to know if she has drugged my Marco or has he inherited the genes of my grandmother, who used to dance naked on the porch."

The gypsy woman, with orange hair and tits the size of basketballs, fondled the empty pack of Wrigley's spearmint gum that Kate had discarded in mama's wastebasket. She closed her eyes and chanted an old Xavier Cugat melody.

When she returned from the beyond, or wherever Cugat fans go, she told the weeping mother, "I don't know."

It was to become a familiar lament among family observers.

That Marco was genuinely happy was obvious to all. He gave up smoking and took vitamins. He stopped going to the racetrack and discovered ballet.

He quit playing dominoes and took piano lessons with Kate as his beaming maestro. He traded rice and beans for wheat germ and broccoli.

Three years into the marriage he became a registered voter and earned his high school equivalency diploma.

Six years later he became a member of the Chamber of Commerce and within eighteen months was elected president.

One night as she was driving home from a recital at her school, Kate's Pinto was rear-ended by a taxi and exploded into flames, killing her instantly.

She was buried two days short of their eleventh wedding anniversary.

The grieving husband was devastated.

His screams could be heard throughout the mansion.

Mama hired a doctor and an ambulance crew to remain nearby during the cemetery service.

It required two aldermen, a chunky police sergeant, and a hefty jai alai player to stop Marco from throwing himself into her grave.

Medical specialists from New York's Columbia Presbyterian Hospital and Baltimore's Johns Hopkins were flown to Miami to diagnose Marco.

He had not uttered a word in months and would eat only peanut butter and wheat germ on rye toast.

He refused to leave the house. He closeted himself in the bedroom, staring at their wedding picture.

He sat for hours looking at the scrapbook. There was Kate with the governor cutting a ribbon to the new hospital wing. Kate, in her floppy hat, designing costumes for her ballerinas. Kate on a bicycle. Kate washing the dog with a hose. Kate hosting mama's birthday party.

After extensive tests, the medical opinion amounted to: "I don't know."

Fearing for her son's life, mama again consulted Senora Cruz, who was now a brunette and the owner of a video store.

The gypsy visited Marco's home accompanied by her hyper chihuahua, and spoke to Marco privately in the bedroom.

She emerged two hours later, emotionally drained, and told his anxious mother: "I don't know."

Months later, at the tearful pleading of mama, who said that God came to her in a dream and asked to speak to Marco, the wounded husband reluctantly ventured from his home and accompanied her to church.

He sat dazed and bewildered in the strange surroundings. As his mother gripped his hand, Marco heard Father McDevitt sermonize on the evils of big business.

"God was not a businessman. Jesus was not a businessman. Only Lucifer. When he traded the apple for Eve's soul."

Then—as if a candle had been lit in the darkest recess of a dungeon—Marco turned to his mother and said the words she would never forget to her dying day: "You're hurting my hand."

Mother and son left the church crying tears of joy.

The next evening he invited his entire family to join him for dinner at his restaurant. Eight limos were dispatched to collect the sisters, nieces, nephews, aunts, uncles, and assorted in-laws.

The family marveled in disbelief as Marco dazzled them with his charm and hospitality, not to mention his ability to consume Cuba libres.

Relatives who had been saying their rosaries since he married Kate watched in astonishment as he swept his mother across the dance floor to the frenzy of the Latin beat.

The five-man Afro-Cuban band played as if the gods themselves could hear the celebration!

He was his old self again—maybe better, for this one didn't yell at the waiter for spilling a pitcher of sangria.

The intoxicated revelers, delighted to have Marco back after an absence of twelve years, wondered what had brought on the dramatic change.

The unanimous opinion was: "I don't know."

The next day he asked Gigi, the blonde barmaid, to dinner. Within a week he bought her a condo, which he helped decorate.

He knew now why God had called Kate to His side. It was right there in the morning paper. The Pintos had been recalled for a tendency to explode on contact.

Big business had claimed its last victim.

Marco had let his father down. He'd been distracted by his love for Kate, so God had removed her to firm his resolve, to insure that the promise would be kept.

Marco vowed to do what the Great Depression and many Democratic presidents had failed to do.

Aided by the Almighty's will, he would single-handedly destroy big business.

To slay such a mighty dragon would require a financial war chest. Drug money was good, but a mere pittance when compared with TV residuals.

So he became a TV producer with offices in Burbank.

His company, Kaystar, quickly acquired a reputation for bold moves and innovative programming. He was credited with bringing back westerns to the home screen.

In six years, via three successful sitcoms, a game show, a late-night talk show, a mini-series, and a sweetheart syndication deal, he accumulated wealth to rival the national treasury of a small republic.

Unlike his drug trade, which still prospered, he didn't have to bribe cops and judges—just an occasional TV critic. They could be had with wine and book certificates. Not to mention Hollywood junkets and lunches at the Polo Lounge.

He closed the offices in Burbank, knowing the residuals would lubricate his empire for generations, thanks in part to the theft of writers' royalties and credits.

He returned to his Biscayne villa and sat in front of the television to begin his crusade for God.

He watched every commercial. He read the *Wall Street Journal.* He clipped coupons from the Sunday papers. The more America consumed, the more he became consumed.

And through it all he was unswervingly convinced that Kate approved.

He could picture her now, flicking a hand through her strawberry-blonde hair, whispering in that breathless little girl's voice:

"I know."

CHAPTER FOURTEEN

Geraldine got to Hal's apartment just as the police were leaving.

Ida was sitting on the couch staring at the wreckage about her ankles. Books, papers, manuscripts, files littered the living room. Cartons, ripped open, were tossed about like scattered toys.

Geraldine crossed quickly to the bedroom and found a similar scene. Except for the fact that the walls were standing, one might have mistaken the damage for a Kansas tornado.

The mattress was flung off the bed. Every dresser drawer had been dumped on the floor. The three metal filing cabinets stood open and empty. Even the drapes had been yanked from the rods.

"Unbelievable," Geraldine groaned. She took a moment to compose herself before joining Ida. "What did the cops say?" she asked, tiptoeing around the mess.

"Nothing. I have to make a list of what's missing and take it to them tomorrow. They were only here five minutes. It's not like in the movies, is it?"

Geraldine threw off her coat and bent down to retrieve a baseball enclosed in a small plastic capsule.

Ida sat huddled at the end of the couch hugging a pillow. Two of the seat cushions lay across the room against the terrace doors.

"They didn't look for fingerprints or anything. They didn't take any pictures. They just said make a list."

Ida pointed to the torn boxes. "All that work for nothing."

Geraldine looked around for a place to sit, but every inch of the room was buried under books, clothing, record albums, and other debris. She shoved an armful of clothes off the piano bench and sat.

"Why would anyone do this?" Ida moaned.

"Probably some junkie," Geraldine lied. She knew it wasn't a robbery. Hal's camera and binoculars still hung from the bookcase. The stereo system was intact. Also the TV and VCR. She reached down and examined a carton marked "University of Alabama." It was ripped cleanly with a knife.

"Any idea what's missing?" Geraldine asked.

The woman shook her head. "Nothing, as far as I can tell. He had some watches and rings in a box on the dresser. I was going to pack that last to see if you wanted any of it. It's still there. Right where I left it."

Three cartons filled with glassware and dishes remained mostly undisturbed.

"I haven't even called Harry," Ida said, her voice close to breaking. "He didn't want me to come to New York to begin with."

Geraldine walked over to the door and inspected the locks. There was no obvious sign of tampering.

"How did he get in?"

Ida shrugged. "Who knows? The cops said these crooks have gadgets—"

Geraldine checked the kitchen. Boxes of frozen food had been torn open and thrown on the floor. Milk and juice cartons had been emptied into the sink. The orange and white liquids collected into a thick pool around the dishes. Even the laundry powder had been emptied on the counter.

She leaned against the sink, fighting the wave of nausea that crept up her throat. Her hands felt cold and clammy against the porcelain surface.

This was no junkie. This was Hal's killer, back to get what he'd missed the first time.

Geraldine reached over and turned on the faucet. She cupped her hand under the water and swiped her neck with the cold. She kept her head straight, afraid to look down for fear of getting dizzy. When she felt sufficiently able she returned to the living room and told Ida: "You can't stay here. You're coming home with me."

Ida didn't protest. She gathered a few clothes and followed Geraldine out of the apartment.

Down in the lobby, while the older woman waited by the entrance, Geraldine took the doorman aside and asked if he'd seen any strangers in the building.

She waited while he retrieved the guest book. One single name, which could be Chinese or Japanese, caught her attention.

"Oh, yeah. He was delivering for the Chinese restaurant."

"Did you ring the apartment where he was going?"

"Probably. I don't remember, exactly. Listen," said the man in the burgundy coat with the copper buttons, "if I called up every time a pizza or deli man came, I'd be on the phone all night. I got other stuff to do."

Geraldine started to press him further, but the newspaper on the counter stole her attention.

Roy Hingle's face smiled under the headline: "Newsman Slain."

CHAPTER FIFTEEN

Owen sat at the counter of Ruby's Cafe with Lt. Gabe Danford, who was on his lunch break.

"I'm trying to find a girl," Owen told him.

"Who isn't?" the lieutenant laughed, as he ogled the young waitress. A former Triple A ballplayer, Gabe still looked able to hit one a mile. Big, with round hairy arms, thick chest, hard stump of a neck, the sight of him in uniform was enough to disarm any criminal.

The family-owned restaurant across the street from the courthouse was a popular hangout for cops, politicians, and lawyers. Today being Saturday, and the courthouse closed, business was slow. Only a few of the green booths were occupied. The overhead fans whirled with a buzzing hum. Cardboard hand-lettered signs listing the menu covered most of the dingy walls.

Owen stabbed at the apple pie in front of him. "I'm talking about a specific person. I only have a first name and I'm not even sure if it's real."

The officer scooped up a forkful of grits. "Occupation?"

"Said she was a model."

The man laughed, "They all do."

The sailor wasn't in the mood for his jaded observations. "You're supposed to be a cop. Help me out here!"

Gabe brushed toast crumbs from his sky blue shirt. The gold cloth shield with the Key West insignia hugged the massive shoulder. A slight scar that caught the corner of his mouth was the only distraction in an otherwise average face.

"Is this important or you just want to get laid?"

Owen tapped out a cigarette from his shirt pocket. "What the hell difference does it make! How do I track her down?"

Gabe shrugged. "Start with the modeling agencies. She local?"

"Don't think so," the sailor said. He sure as hell would have remembered her.

"Try Miami, Orlando, maybe Tampa. Make some calls. What does she look like?"

"Blonde, twenty-eight or twenty-nine, greenish eyes, around five-three, a hundred and ten pounds, tanned."

Gabe joked, "If you find her, give her my number."

"Shit!" Owen called for the check and threw money on the counter.

The cop's hand flew out and grabbed Owen's sleeve. "All right. Jesus! Sit down."

Owen straddled the stool.

"She have an accent? Any identifying marks? Unusual features? A limp? Freckles? Beauty mark?"

Owen shook his head.

"She drive?"

"Came in a cab," he answered.

"Smoke?"

The sailor looked up at the fan, feeling his temperature escalating. "Who gives a shit?"

"Hey, take it easy!" the lieutenant warned. "I nabbed a guy once on account of his cigarettes. Smoked something called English Ovals. Even the cigar store in town didn't carry 'em, but the gift shop at the hotel did. And they remembered the creep."

The waitress dropped the check next to Owen's plate and scooped the money off the counter. Owen waited till she walked away.

"She came aboard with a photographer, we sailed a couple of hours, and they left. I didn't notice any limp or any freckles! I'm not even sure about the color of the eyes. She had tinted sunglasses but she looked like the type that would have green eyes—if that makes sense."

Gabe had never seen his buddy so worked up. The nicotine-tipped fingers shredded a napkin into slivers.

"How'd they pay you?"

"Cash."

Gabe dunked the toast in the coffee. "You got a problem."

The sailor got up quickly. "Thanks. I'll call you when I don't."

He had started to walk off when Gabe yelled, "Hey, I heard about the dog. But I didn't kill him! So lay off."

Owen returned the angry tone: "No. But she did."

The cop gaped at him. "The blonde? Why the hell would she do that?"

Owen took a seat and stared at the glass dairy case containing red and green Jell-O in stemmed dishes. A can of whipped cream lay on its side nearby.

"Because she thought I had the drinking problem."

Gabe drew in a breath. "You mean . . . she poisoned the dog, instead of you?"

"You got it."

The cop hunched the big arms around his plate as if protecting the food. He looked at his friend and wondered if maybe he'd been out in the sun too long. He looked normal enough. Clean. Combed. Same polished boots and bell-bottom dungarees. Face was tired, the eyes a little sunken, but nothing alarming.

Gabe knew Luther well from their fishing trips. He even had a picture of the dog in his locker. Drinking from a beer can.

"You report it?"

"No. And you're not going to either."

The cop could imagine the chief's reaction if he went in with such a story. The entire police force was secretly saving five bucks a week, per man, in anticipation of the bastard's retirement. They were going to blow it on a party as soon as he walked out the door.

Gabe wiped his mouth and reached for a stick of chewing gum in his pocket.

"You saying this blonde tried to kill you—and got Luther instead?"

Owen looked away. "Something like that."

"Why? What did you do to her?"

"I never even met her," Owen said. He was sorry now he'd called Gabe. It was stupid. And dangerous.

"You're saying some dame you never saw before shows up on your boat and tries to kill you?"

"Forget it. I'll handle it," Owen mumbled.

The cop lifted his cap and smoothed down the hair under the tight brim. "What is it you're not telling me?"

Owen got up. "I'll catch you later."

"Catch me now," Gabe told him.

Owen kept walking, even though the cop called his name twice.

CHAPTER SIXTEEN

It took Geraldine and Ida three days to repack the cartons and send them to their various destinations. No police report was filed; nothing was missing.

On the morning of February 7, an unseasonably warm day, Geraldine took Ida in a cab to Kennedy Airport.

"If you ever find yourself in Alabama, we're fifteen miles out of Selma due east, past the Little League field and two blocks up from the Sunoco station," the woman said as they sat in the waiting area near the boarding gate.

"Maybe you'll come back for a visit and bring Harry?" Geraldine smiled.

"Maybe." Ida reached into her purse and removed a wadded-up piece of tissue. She handed it over to Geraldine. "I want you to have this."

Geraldine unraveled the clump and found a thick gold ring with an amber stone. It was Hal's college ring from NYU.

Geraldine said, "Thank you." Seeing people off at airports always made her sad. There was a finality to the ritual that disturbed her. Sometimes she felt sad because she wasn't the one going on the trip. Today, even though she'd only known the woman a few days, the sadness was genuine.

"Oh, I almost forgot," Ida said quickly, reaching into the small shopping bag next to her leg. She dug down and removed a stack of mail held together with a thick rubber band.

"I'm not good at this," Ida said handing over the small bundle. "Could you take care of it? You probably know most of the people anyway."

"What is it?" Geraldine asked.

"Condolence cards. They've been arriving all week."

Geraldine started to say something comforting just as an overhead voice announced the boarding.

"Well," Ida said, gathering up her parcels. The area was suddenly clogged with people jockeying for position.

"Call me when you get home," Geraldine instructed.

The woman's eyes suddenly moistened and Geraldine pretended not to notice. She hugged her quickly. "Have a good trip."

Geraldine watched her disappear through the gate entrance.

Later that night, Geraldine lay in bed unable to sleep, unable to concentrate on the movie on the tube, unable to read the book that lay a few inches away next to the empty pizza carton.

A gentle rain peppered the window behind her head. She could hear it striking the fire escape.

She was feeling anxious, somewhat depressed, and definitely hyper. And it had nothing to do with Hal's death. Nor the fact that she'd been unable to reach Owen. Or Mike's call to remind her that if she didn't report to work by the end of the month, not to bother.

The depression and anxiety had to do with the fact she hadn't gambled since returning from Vegas.

There'd been calls from Detroit and Bucks County, Pennsylvania, about poker games, and two Atlantic City casinos had sent invitations to upcoming blackjack tournaments.

She had the fever—and it would soon pop the thermometer. Only another addict could understand.

Hal never did. On her last birthday he sent her a framed poster from Gamblers' Anonymous, with the phone number circled. She figured he stole it from a subway platform.

She needed to touch cards. To stare at their beautiful markings. To agonize and celebrate with each fall. To smell the crispness of their texture.

She needed to play!

She tried to explain it once in terms Hal could understand.

"Picture it's a warm, summer evening and you're sitting in a box seat between home and first base. A cool breeze is blowing from Flushing Bay. You're with friends, drinking a foamy beer, eating a hot dog, and Tom Seaver's on the mound, pitching like his car is double-parked. It's the ninth inning and the Mets are ahead six runs. One out and they win the pennant."

Playing poker was like that—only better.

But Hal never bought it. "It costs me seven bucks for a seat at Shea. Costs you a thousand. Mets lose, I get over it on the way home. You lose, I hear about it for months. Where's the fun? It's an obsession."

He was right, of course. There were some hands, played years ago, that still elicited remorse.

But there were also those sweet moments plastered across her soul. Like the time at the Gold Coast Casino where she raked in $22,000 on a pair of nines. Or in the backroom of the VFW hall on Staten Island when she drew the fourth king.

Right now she'd settle for a low-stake kitchen game, a glass of grapefruit juice, and the stunning oblivion that made the game so intoxicating. Reality never intruded on the hand being played.

Geraldine reached across the bed, pulled her purse strap up from the floor, and removed the stack of letters. She slipped off the rubber band.

She recognized some of the names on the return addresses: Hal's Hollywood agent, his accountant, the chiropractor on West 83rd Street, his typist, barber, an editor at *Playboy,* a playwright, and an assortment of drinking buddies.

She also recognized the name Lysette, the hatcheck girl at Sardi's. Geraldine was surprised to learn she lived in Queens. The planet Pluto would have been her guess.

There were also cards from the Writer's Guild, the Director's Guild, Disney, Orion, TriStar, and HBO.

One postmark drew her attention. Cleveland. She tore the envelope open and read: "With my deepest sympathy, Marlene."

The receipt for the roses instantly flooded her thoughts. An overwhelming sadness attacked. She knew that this was the last woman to sleep with Hal.

She felt empty. And used. And bitter. Angry. Stupid. Wasted. Hurt. Lonely. Afraid. Afraid she would hate him forever—and terrified she wouldn't.

She lit a cigarette and called the airport. And then, because she was feeling sorry for herself, she tried Owen. There was no answer.

CHAPTER SEVENTEEN

Just before 9:00 A.M., David Ko stood by the newspaper rack thumbing through an issue of *Consumer Reports* while keeping an eye on Geraldine, who bought cigarettes at the gift shop counter in Newark Airport.

He was angry. He had tickets to the Knicks game that night and instead he was about to board a flight to Cleveland.

He could ice her right there and be done with the whole thing, but no, Marco only wanted her followed. And there was no reasoning with the man.

Geraldine took the change and carried her small overnight bag to the boarding lounge for her flight. Ko put the magazine back on the rack and followed the beige woolen coat that ended above the knee-high leather boots.

He took a seat on a small plastic chair a row behind her, next to a family with four unruly kids. Ko knew that the safest way to blend into a crowd was to invade a disorderly group. People tended to ignore such mayhem, whereas a man or woman sitting alone often drew a glance.

With his camera dangling across his pressed suit, Ko looked like a prosperous Japanese tourist. Probably here to buy real estate.

He watched as Geraldine strolled to the large windows overlooking the tarmac. Her hair was tucked under a beige cap. A brown plaid woolen scarf hugged her neck and dangled freely.

She looked like a suburban mother awaiting her husband's return from the corporate wars, rather than the pain in the ass that had screwed up Ko's plan to return to Barcelona where his family awaited in the newly purchased villa with its marble courtyard and goldfish pond.

She was his last assignment. Once she was removed he owed Marco no further allegiance. He could begin the life so carefully planned eight years ago when he placed the first bottle of Tylenol on the supermarket shelf.

But the maniac wanted her spared—for now.

Ko had no illusions about the man. He was deranged. If nothing else, his scheme to kill the pope proved his insanity. Only Yan-San's repeated protests averted the act.

Why risk all that they had accomplished with such a bold move that was doomed to failure, Yan-San had pleaded. He showed Marco pictures he'd taken at the basilica and impressed on him the hazard of such a deed.

Marco had relented, and for the moment at least, the pope was safe.

Ko watched the beige coat and the gloved hand holding a leather briefcase. It would be so easy. It would take less than five seconds.

He could walk directly behind her in the crush of travelers passing through the boarding gate. The knife could suddenly appear in his hand, and one flashing quick plunge into the beige wool, perfectly aimed, would cause her to stumble. As the crowd rushed forward to assist her, he could stand aside, let them pass, and easily walk away in the confusion.

Ko had suggested the exact scenario fifteen minutes earlier to Marco, who immediately dismissed it.

The Japanese man was concerned that Marco was saving her for March 27, which would delay his Barcelona departure even further.

Marco, for reasons of his own, was obsessed with that date. The first Tylenol poisonings had occurred on March 27. The team was assembled for the first time on March 27 in Miami, with recruits arriving from all over the country under the painstaking selection of Yan-San. The pope's death had been planned for March 27, two years ago, before logic prevailed.

Ko watched Geraldine as she gazed at the airplanes taxiing past the glass wall.

It would be so easy. So effortless. So clean.

It'd been almost two years since he moved his family to Spain. He'd not been there to see his daughter take her first steps. Soon she would be talking, and strangers would hear her first words.

He felt in his pocket for the comforting handle of the steel blade that would spring open at his touch. It was childishly easy to get it past airport security. He merely concealed it in the thick leather strap of his camera and handed it to the guard before passing through the metal detectors. The move hadn't failed in five years of crisscrossing the country.

Ko watched a young mother sitting a row away, feeding her infant. He recalled the aroma of warm milk and longed for his daughter. The more he thought of his daughter, the more he hated the redheaded American. She was all that stood between him and his family.

He didn't regret the years in Marco's service, for he'd been handsomely paid.

But enough was enough.

It would be so easy to kill the woman now and disappear through the crowd. He could be at Kennedy Airport and bound for Spain within hours.

Naturally, he would call Marco and tell him. After he was safely out of the country. Once in Spain he would be untraceable. He had led Yan-San to believe that his family was in Switzerland.

Besides, loyalty was merely a word of infinite definitions, depending on who chose to define it.

Was it loyal of Marco to have Joe Akido killed?

It was no secret that Akido was displeased with his share of the money. He felt, to his mind, since he was the only one of the team to be involved with both the Tylenol and the coffee plant sabotage, he deserved a larger reward. He had mentioned as much to Marco at the midnight meeting aboard his yacht when they sailed from Key West.

He had presented a persuasive, nonargumentive case, keeping in mind all the while whom he was addressing—a deranged maniac.

The exchange had embarrassed Marco and he soon after ordered that Akido be watched at all times.

If David Ko killed the woman now instead of waiting for specific orders—everyone knew she was doomed—where was the disloyalty? Either way she'd be very dead.

Across from him, the baby's head dropped into the soft cradle of her mother's elbow, and fell asleep. The mother's silent joy was so obvious as she nestled the baby that he had to look away.

His fingertips probed the knife as the boarding announcement sounded. He rose slowly and reached for the thin garment bag. He grabbed up his camera case and moved swiftly toward Geraldine, who was now approaching the roped entryway.

His hand quickened about the knife. Only three people separated them.

Marco would just have to understand.

After all, he'd taken all the risks and given up years of his life. It was cruel to expect him to wait another month when she had to be eliminated eventually.

Better now.

As one hand held out the boarding pass to the young steward, the other twisted slowly in the coat pocket and worked the knife to a vertical position. The wooden ridges of the handle felt comfortably familiar.

The steward pulled the airline ticket from its folder and allowed him to pass. Ko sidestepped a dawdling couple and hurried through the covered passageway.

It was too perfect.

The beige coat was an arm's length away, and any second now she would have to slow for the crush of passengers stalled at the nose of the plane.

A circle of bodies stood patiently waiting to board. She would have to stop. Behind him, an army of passengers approached quickly.

Perfect. In a moment he would be totally concealed.

Ko edged closer toward the beige coat. He was near enough to see the copper strands of hair peeking out from under the cap. She brought her hand to her ear and he caught a glimpse of a ring with an amber stone.

Behind him, the family with the unruly kids halted inches from his back. The kids dashed ahead gleefully, to the annoyance of the other standees. He worked his way through the pressed bodies and slid out the knife. He felt for the small silver nub and depressed it. The blade jumped free like a snake's tongue.

His eyes only saw beige wool. A thin seam of brown threads ran down the back of the coat, accentuating the spine. He could smell the mustiness of the wool. Soon it would mix with the odor of hot, syrupy blood.

Geraldine stood unmoving, half leaning against the side wall.

Ko was suddenly pushed forward, blade in hand; he stumbled and went down on his knees. The knife fell from his hand. He quickly recovered it.

Behind him, the mother apologized profusely for her son's clumsiness.

CHAPTER EIGHTEEN

Cardinal Thomas Ryan McHugh woke at 8:30, as was customary, and lay in the four-poster bed sorting mentally through the day's agenda. There was a wedding scheduled for seven, the niece of an aide to the Queens borough president, and the African ambassador was due for lunch, but other than that, the day belonged mostly to himself.

The cardinal nudged the fat, graying terrier sprawled at the foot of the bed atop the paisley comforter.

"Pepper," he poked the dog with his toe. The dog didn't move. Besides being grossly overweight and blind in one eye, the fourteen-year-old animal was slightly deaf. And obstinate.

"Move," the cardinal poked harder.

The dog raised its head, shook off sleep, and wobbled on its short legs to its master's side. The man stroked the animal's neck and offered his cheek for a good-morning lick. Pepper obliged happily.

The cardinal climbed out from beneath the bulky covers and felt the thick warmth of the Persian rug beneath his feet.

He reached over and picked up the dog—not an easy task considering its weight—and placed it on the floor. It'd been a long time since Pepper could jump on and off the high double mattress on the raised platform.

Pepper waddled to the large mahogany doors and waited while the cardinal opened them. The dog scampered downstairs to the kitchen where the housekeeper, upon seeing him, would put on the coffee and call the janitor to walk him.

The cardinal crossed the bedroom to the tall, stately windows draped in heavy gold satin and pulled them aside to glance out on Fiftieth Street. A cop on horseback sat drinking a container of coffee, holding it with gloved hands. The wind whipped at the litter along the street and sent a newspaper to rest against the horse's brown leg.

The cardinal put his chubby fingers to the window pane and felt the coldness of the day. A steady stream of people darted along the street, rushing to work. The #27 crosstown bus pulled away from the curb at Saks Fifth Avenue.

He unlatched the window and pushed the frame outward a few inches, feeling the icy February air on his fingertips. Yes, it was definitely a good day to stay indoors.

He walked to the adjoining bathroom, turned on the gold faucet, and let water run in the sink. He flicked on the one light switch that illuminated the sink area. The purple ceiling light, which was always on, remained trained on the wicker baskets of plants lining the eight-foot vanity counter.

He reached automatically for the pills on the glass shelf and filled the crystal tumbler with water. He downed one thyroid pill and a blood thinner.

He opened the door to his dressing room, and due to his unusually light schedule and the fact he intended to stay indoors, he chose brown slacks and a white V-necked sweater.

He took the hairbrush on the dressing table and whacked at the white mane that threatened to conceal his ears. He looked in the mirror and wasn't pleased. The face was growing a third chin. The eyelids drooped with fat, threatening soon to cover the milky blue eyes.

He'd tried the Bloomingdale's, Pritikin's, RAF, Canadian, Scarsdale, and grapefruit diets. Through it all, he gained nineteen pounds.

His only consolation was that the mayor, who'd suggested them, gained forty.

The cardinal finished dressing and walked down the rosewood staircase, pausing to bless himself before the life-sized oil painting of Pope John the twelfth.

He continued down the long foyer, past the portraits of Cardinal Spellman, President Kennedy, Fiorello LaGuardia, Mayor Koch, and Eleanor Roosevelt.

The orange and purple stained glass windows at the far end of the corridor cast a garish glow on the face of young Kennedy.

It always disturbed the cardinal. He had asked the janitor to remove the portrait to his bedchamber but the housekeeper vetoed the idea. Since the residence hadn't been painted in twelve years, the portrait couldn't be moved till one of a similar size was found to replace it.

Mrs. Chadderton was not easily overruled. She'd been a fixture at the rectory long before the cardinal's tenure. Her mother had served under Spellman.

The cardinal entered the kitchen and took a seat at the butcher block table beneath the hanging forest of copper pots.

It was his favorite room in the mansion. He liked sitting near the open brick stove.

His aide, Father Michael Murphy, entered with copies of the *Times, Post, Daily News,* and *Newsday.* Certain stories, like the nuns arrested in Baltimore at an antiabortion rally, were circled boldly in red.

"Good morning," Mrs. Chadderton said, carrying a plate of fresh apple muffins to the table. "What are we feeling like today?" she asked.

The cardinal didn't hesitate. "Spanish omelet."

She needn't have bothered to ask. It was the third time this week.

"Good morning, Your Eminence," the young priest said, taking his place at the table where his usual tea and cinnamon bun awaited. "Sleep well?"

"Very well. Winter agrees with me."

Pepper waddled into the kitchen and took his place near the cardinal's feet. The cardinal broke off a piece of buttered toast and fed it to the dog.

Phones rang in the distance, to be silenced by the office staff who worked unseen in separate quarters.

Father Murphy slid the newspapers across the table.

The cardinal saw his face on the front page of the *Times* over a headline: "Gay Protesters Stage Rally on Steps of St. Patrick's Cathedral. Leaders Angrily Demand AIDS Hospice." He pushed the paper aside.

"I'm tired. I'm restless. I need to get away."

Mrs. Chadderton, at the stove, smiled to herself and prayed for a long vacation.

Father Murphy took off his glasses and tucked them in the pocket of his black shirt. "Where would you like to go?"

"Anywhere. Anywhere where they don't have faggots and protest marches. I need tranquility. Peace of mind. Fun!"

"I see."

"Do you?" The older man rested his thick arms on the lace placemat and leaned forward. The gold crucifix on the rope chain touched the table. "I don't think you appreciate the pressure I've been under lately. If it's not the queers, it's the abortionists, or the homeless. I can't take much more."

Mrs. Chadderton, whose niece was evicted when her building went condo, was tempted to sprinkle the black pepper generously—but didn't.

The priest noted the slight, accusatory manner. "Have I done something to displease you, Your Eminence?"

The man waved his chunky hands. "Did I say that? Don't get dramatic! I just need a change of pace."

"It's understandable," the young man smiled. "I'll get your appointment book." He got up quickly and left the room.

He managed to conceal the smile he felt.

"They say Tahiti is beautiful," the housekeeper said as she chopped a tomato.

"I was there four years ago. Too hot. Food is ghastly."

Father Murphy returned with the thick leather ledger and spread it open on the table. The glint from the copper bottoms of the pans overhead reflected off his glasses.

"Your schedule is very tight. Extremely. Until—" he turned the pages quickly. "Easter Sunday. You have a few weeks then. There are some minor commitments but nothing crucial. We shouldn't have any problems rescheduling."

"Fine. Easter Sunday it is. When is it?"

The priest closed the ledger. "A little over six weeks away."

"Perfect. Where shall we go?" the cardinal asked, swiping at the dog that whined at his feet.

The small priest with the tiny, delicate features and balding head coughed softly.

"Your Eminence, my vacation starts the day after Easter. I purposely selected that time, with your knowledge and approval, because of your light schedule."

The cardinal slathered the toast with raspberry jelly. "So I'll go alone. I've done it before. But where should I go?"

"The world is yours," the priest responded.

The cardinal leaned back and shook his leg quickly to release Pepper's hold. The dog yelped and ran over to attack the other leg.

"Do you have anything to feed this dog?" he snapped. "He won't let me eat!"

The woman threw a chunk of sausage on a paper plate and yelled at the dog, "Here!" She told the cardinal, "When he's too fat to climb the stairs, don't expect me to carry him."

The cardinal refrained from mentioning that Pepper had climbed his last step six months ago.

The dog munched hungrily with his few remaining teeth, and the cardinal turned to the priest. "That show we watched the other night on PBS. Where was that spectacular country inn? The one where you needed reservations two years in advance. Sweden?"

Father Murphy answered, "France. One of the small provinces known for its vineyards."

The cardinal groaned. "I hate the French. They're impossibly rude. And no humor whatsoever. Still—" he thought of the picturesque inn with the white tables and windows overlooking a glade with a running brook. For a four-star meal he could put up with a few ignorant Frenchmen. "Arrange it," he said.

Mrs. Chadderton took the news happily. He'd probably fly over and sail back, which, with any luck, would keep him away a few weeks. Now, if she could only get him to take the damn dog. Or send it to his sister in Louisville.

"I'll start on it immediately," Murphy replied.

"Clear it through the usual channels," said the cardinal, not concealing his distaste for church politics.

The priest gathered the ledger and stood up.

"You might convey my regards to the French ministry and have them alert the European press to my arrival. Nothing formal. Maybe just a brief press conference at the airport. Nothing extraordinary. Maybe a one-on-one interview with their Ted Koppel. You might wire a personal note to the religion editor of the Paris *Herald.*"

"I'll get right on it."

Mrs. Chadderton tossed the sausages in the skillet and looked at the calendar clipped with a magnet to the side of the refrigerator.

She leaned across the stove and flipped the page over. Easter fell on March 27. She hoped the days would speed quickly.

CHAPTER NINETEEN

The flight was uneventful. Geraldine even managed to snooze.

She hurried through the Cleveland airport and walked directly to the Avis counter, where she picked up the keys to a Toyota. She suffered a slight anxious moment when the clerk ran the MasterCard through the electronic gizmo but it cleared, to her amazement.

Geraldine headed to a bank of pay phones and dialed the number on Hal's matchbook. She didn't know exactly what she'd say to Marlene, but she'd think of something.

"Townehouse," a breezy female voice answered.

Geraldine was startled. "What?"

"You've reached Townehouse Coffee. Whom would you like to speak to?"

Geraldine tried to sort and evaluate the unexpected news. Marlene, with the roses, worked at the plant. She leaned her head against the metal phone box and enjoyed the coolness on her forehead.

"Are you there?" the woman asked.

"Can I speak to Marlene?"

The voice on the other end hesitated a moment. "Are you a friend?"

"Yes," Geraldine lied.

"Well, I'm sorry to report that Marlene . . . passed away last week."

Geraldine found it hard to speak. Her chest hammered. A tremble shot through her body. Dead?

Was that why she hadn't heard from Owen? Was he lying dead somewhere too? She glanced about the terminal. Each strolling pedestrian was a threat. Was she being watched this moment? She eyed two redcaps who stood leaning against a tall luggage rack. She turned swiftly to glance behind and found a strange man, weary and disheveled, staring at her. If he was waiting to use the phone, the next one was unoccupied. Why was he standing there?

"Hello?"

Geraldine spoke into the phone. "Sorry . . . you . . . I . . . didn't know." She recovered and said quickly, "I lost her home number. Could you give it to me? I'd like to pay my respects."

"Certainly. Hold on."

Geraldine took off her coat and crushed it into the small opening between the wall and the phone. Her arms were saturated with sweat. Her fingertips felt numb as she rummaged in her purse for a pen.

The voice returned and gave her the number, which Geraldine quickly scribbled on the car rental folder.

She hung up and dialed before losing her nerve. She caught her reflection in the silver sheen of the phone box and wondered if those wrinkles around the mouth had been there yesterday.

A man answered.

"Hi. My name is Geraldine. I was a friend of Marlene's. I heard what happened and I'm only going to be in Cleveland a few hours—" She knew she was talking too fast but she couldn't stop herself. "I was wondering if I could stop by the house and speak to you for a few minutes."

"Why?" he asked, the voice barely audible.

"I really can't explain on the phone. I'll only stay a few minutes."

There was a long silence and then: "Okay."

A half hour later, the man who opened the door and led her inside the modest house was wearing a telephone company jumpsuit with "Gary" sewn on the shirt pocket.

He was in his mid-thirties, stocky, with a muscular body honed by the outdoors. The hair was sun-bleached, the eyes a chocolate brown.

"I just made a pot of tea."

"I'd love some," she said, following him to the kitchen. She quickly took off her coat and draped it across her arm.

Geraldine glanced at the living room. It was crammed with family photographs, all of blonde kids. Sports trophies filled a glass case over the TV set. The furniture was old but clean. A laundry basket piled with clothes lay waiting.

The husband led her to the wide kitchen. It was a cheerful room with a collection of bright ceramic roosters circling the cabinets.

"People always make fun of my drinking tea, seeing as how Marlene worked at the coffee plant."

Geraldine sat at the table and offered a weak smile.

"Is that how you knew her?"

Before she could answer he stuck out his hand. "I'm Gary."

She nodded, "Geraldine."

"Where did you say you were from?"

"New York."

A child's coloring book and crayons lay on the table next to a half empty cereal bowl.

She tried to avoid the pain in his eyes.

"How did you know my wife?"

Gary walked from the stove carrying two mugs.

Geraldine took time to blow the hot liquid, hoping for inspiration.

"Actually, I never met her."

The man's face hardened.

"A friend of mine did," she said quickly. "And he said if I ever came to Cleveland to be sure to look her up. He was a writer. His name was Hal Landry. Maybe she mentioned him."

Gary shook his head. "How long ago was it?"

"A couple of weeks ago."

Geraldine tried to keep her voice light. She reached into her purse for a cigarette. "Mind if I smoke?"

He shook his head. Gary gazed at the circles in the tea as he stirred the liquid. "What do you mean his name . . . 'was'?"

Geraldine tensed. She puffed on the cigarette and slowly reached for the cup. She purposely kept her eyes averted. She didn't want him to see something that might set off any alarms. "Heart attack."

Gary nodded.

Geraldine asked, "And . . . Marlene—?"

"Car accident. Hit and run."

Geraldine's knees trembled under the table. She placed her hand on her lap and held the cup with the other. I should never have come here, she berated herself. This is insane. I'll never pull it off.

"Was she . . . alone?"

"She had just dropped off our daughter at the movie. Van came out of nowhere, hit her. Kid on a motorcycle saw it but didn't get the plate. Happened too fast."

It didn't surprise her that Marlene had kept her meeting with Hal a secret. Which posed a new problem. She needed desperately to come up with a story that wouldn't strain the husband's credibility nor add to his grief.

She removed her hat, smoothed out her hair, and hoped the extra seconds would inspire her with brillance.

"What did your friend want with my wife?" He fixed his eyes squarely on Geraldine's face.

"Well . . . Hal was writing a book." It even sounded dumb to her.

The husband interrupted: "Was your friend from New York, too?"

"Yes."

A door opened upstairs, emitting loud rock music.

"Look, lady, I don't know you. You don't know me. But I don't think you came all the way from New York to have a cup of tea." He gripped the spoon and used it as a pointer. "What's this all about?"

Geraldine returned the stare, hoping her eyes conveyed sincerity. She couldn't weaken now.

"Love," she blurted.

"Beg your pardon?" his voice displayed more than a tinge of sarcasm.

"Hal was working on a book when he died. About love."

Gary wasn't impressed. "That so?"

Geraldine smiled, "Good old-fashioned, romantic, boring, married love."

Gary fiddled with the napkin holder on the table. She noted the thick wedding ring and fought the nervous flutters rippling her chest.

"He ran ads in newspapers all over the country asking married couples to share their thoughts on the subject. And your wife wrote to him. He came out to interview her."

What could almost pass for a smile crossed his face. "Would be like her to do something like that. She was always reading 'Dear Abby.'

And the movie star gossip. You should see her Elvis Presley stuff. Had to build four shelves."

Geraldine breathed easier. "To be honest, Gary, I was hoping maybe Hal had mentioned me to Marlene. You see, she was one of the last people to see him alive."

The man turned away and looked over at the sink, perhaps picturing his wife as he'd often seen her bent over the dishes. "Does it get easier?"

"People tell me it does," Geraldine said softly.

She felt dirty and wretched and evil. There was no way she would ever forgive herself for this intrusion, this charade, this ugly masquerade. It was ghoulish. Here she was sitting in the bright yellow kitchen with the wall plaque of General Schwartzkopf's face smiling from across the room, lying to a husband who would never know his wife had been murdered.

"I hope so," he mumbled.

"If it's any consolation," she said softly, "Hal said that if every married couple in America was as happy as the two of you, divorce lawyers would be extinct."

The husband got up and walked to the refrigerator which was decorated with a lot of colorful magnets. Many of them had to do with the Cleveland Indians or the Browns. He removed a container of milk, sniffed it, and carried it to the table.

"How come she never mentioned any of this to me?"

"She probably wanted to surprise you. Hal was using real names in the book."

Geraldine stayed an hour, looking at the family album, the daughter's cheerleading trophies, and Marlene's Elvis collection.

She learned that the inside gossip at Townehouse blamed the poisoned coffee on employee negligence. Powerful insecticides were kept on the premises for rodent control. Someone accidentally confused the powder with the cleansers used to disinfect the cooling bins. It'd happened before, about eleven years ago, but they caught it immediately.

"I'm glad you stopped by," he said, walking her to the car. "I guess the book died with him."

Geraldine nodded. She glanced at the bicycle lying on the brown lawn and the basketball hoop over the garage door.

"But at least you know she really loved you."

Gary held the car door open. "She still does."

Geraldine drove directly to the circular, modernistic office atop a grassy hillock that was the publishing plant for Cleveland's morning newspaper.

She parked in a visitor's slot and walked across the airy, tree-lined walkway to the main entrance. The beauty and cleanliness were somewhat unsettling. She thought of the *New York Post,* where reporters stamped their feet walking to their cars in order to alert the rats that scuttled underfoot, inches from the East River. However, the view of the crisscrossing Brooklyn and Manhattan bridges made it tolerable.

Geraldine spoke to the receptionist in the lobby and a copy boy was summoned to take her to the sports department.

The editor, a rotund former minor league pitcher, welcomed her warmly. As often happened, they discovered they had mutual friends on various papers.

The man was equally mystified by Roy's death and eager to talk about it. She learned that he'd been shot while sitting in his car at a traffic light. The paper had posted a $10,000 reward but no witnesses had come forward.

Roy Hingle was not only his best photographer but also his son-in-law; the man was quick to speak well of him.

"He wasn't a drinker. Didn't fool with drugs. Didn't gamble. Didn't owe anybody any money. Was a good father and husband. It just doesn't make sense. You always read these stories where someone says it was a 'senseless murder.' Never paid it any mind before."

Geraldine wanted to ask if she could look at some of the pictures Roy had taken the week he died but decided against it. She'd gotten off easy with Gary. No sense pushing her luck.

She thanked the man for his time and sent her condolences to his daughter. They shook hands and Geraldine left.

Instead of leaving the building, she crossed to the city room and sought out the copy boy. She found him at a corner desk near the AP wire machines.

"Can you get me an issue of the paper for every day going back two weeks?" She put a twenty-dollar bill on the desk.

"Sure can!"

"I'll be outside," she said and hurried away. He found her twenty minutes later in the reception area and gave her the bundle.

Geraldine checked into the Ramada Inn printed on Hal's matchbook.

It disturbed her to think that he'd stood at the same desk signing the registration card. That he'd used the same elevator. That he might have exchanged a joke with the bellman who now carried her bag. That he might have . . . brought Marlene to the room.

She waited as the bellman unlocked the door and flicked on the lights. Maybe he remembered Hal. But she was afraid of the answer.

Geraldine forced the thoughts away and took a quick shower. It was growing dark outside as she slipped into a pair of slacks and blouse. She eyed the stack of newspapers on the bed and decided to tackle them later.

Food was a priority. But first she dialed her answering machine in New York. There was a call from Ida saying she'd gotten home safely and Owen—to her instant relief—said he'd been trying to reach her for a week "and this is the only time I'm talking to this damn thing!"

She smiled at his voice and had a sudden, strong urge to see him. Maybe she wouldn't wait for an invitation. Maybe she'd surprise him. The thought amused her.

There was a message from a Dallas businessman offering to send his plane to fetch her for Saturday's poker game.

Geraldine was tempted. Very.

There were two hang-ups and a call from Mike saying the clock was running.

Geraldine dialed Owen's number and let it ring eight times. She covered her disappointment by ordering two cheeseburgers and a Bloody Mary from room service.

After dinner, when she could no longer postpone it, she gathered up the newspapers and began examining each photo for a Roy Hingle credit.

She came across the pregnant whale and smiled. The third paper yielded results on page 11.

It showed a drowning victim, identified as Joe Akido, thirty-four, being pulled out of the water.

"Police theorize that the Townehouse maintenance supervisor fell into the water. His car was parked nearby and no suicide note was found."

Joe A.

The blue credit card receipt leapt to mind.

Why did Hal give him $3,000?

Who else knew about it—and killed them both?

And why Roy?

Marlene?

She walked to the window and glanced out.

Outside the ninth-story window, Cleveland slept. Three lanes of traffic rolled beneath the hotel. She hadn't noticed it in the daytime, but now, far in the distance, a bright red neon sign flashed Townehouse Coffee. Curls of white smoke puffed from the factory's towers.

A yellow, illuminated bell tower with green dots outlining the face of a clock told her it was twenty past ten. The temperature blinked 48°.

She took off her clothes and slipped into a nightgown. She removed the furry slippers from the suitcase and put them on her feet. She flicked the television to a John Wayne war movie and soon fell asleep. She woke with a start when an announcer yelled at her to buy a car.

She looked around the room quickly. The room was lit and a half-smoked cigarette lay on the ashtray atop the bed. The phone was resting on the bedspread where she'd placed it before dozing off. She propped herself up on her elbow and tried to see the bell tower, but the clock was obscured by the rain outside the window. Only the red Townehouse letters were visible through the haze.

She reached to the foot of the bed and grabbed the phone.

He picked up on the fourth ring.

"Owen?"

"Yeah?"

"Where the hell have you been? I've been trying to get you for two weeks. I thought we were in this together. You get me the hell involved in this mess and then you take off and go fishing! People are being murdered left and right and you—"

He groaned. "Who is this?"

"Geraldine, goddammit!"

"It's the middle of the night. What the hell time is it?"

"I don't know," she said, looking around. "They never have clocks in hotels."

She liked the husky not quite awake voice and wondered if he slept in the nude. She instantly hated herself for wondering.

"Where are you?" he asked.

"Cleveland. Sound familiar?"

"You nuts?"

She heard the telephone fall and what sounded like bodies crashing into furniture.

"Owen!" she screamed.

Something toppled to the floor. A refrigerator? Bookcase? A body?

"OWEN!"

She heard a grunt, followed by a moan, and then nothing.

Geraldine hung up and dialed the operator. Her hands trembling, she could barely write the numbers as the woman put her through to Key West information. She dialed the police department, punching the bed with each ring.

"Officer Powanda. Can I help you?"

"Is this Key West?"

"Was the last time I looked."

"My friend is being murdered! You have to send someone now! Right away!"

The officer laughed. "Ethel, honey, don't fool around. I'm getting off in an hour."

"Asshole! He could be dead! Do you hear me?"

The man instantly adopted an official tone. "Name and address?"

"Owen. I don't remember his last name. He lives on the marina. Will you hurry!"

"What marina, lady? We have three. Four if you count—"

"Nathan! That's it. He lives on his boat, *Nathan.*"

"I still need to know the marina."

"Shit. Send the cops to all of them! If he dies—" She hung up, dialed the boat, and got a busy signal.

Officer Powanda left the switchboard and entered the lieutenant's office, pausing to tap on the glass door in case he was reading *Playboy* again.

"Some foul-mouthed bimbo just hung up on me. You should've heard the names she called me. Real sicko. Said her friend was being murdered on his boat. Didn't have his address, naturally. Didn't even know his last name. Must be a full moon tonight. Said his boat was called *Nathan*."

Gabe threw the magazine on the floor and jumped up from behind the desk.

"That's Owen! Call Dave and Frank. Have them meet me on the East Pier. Send the ambulance. You get the woman's name?" he yelled.

"No, sir," the patrolman responded.

Danford pushed him out of the way and ran out the door strapping on his holster. "Better call the chief."

"At this hour? He won't like it."

"Fucking do it!"

Gabe was out of the building and in the car with the siren screaming before Powanda could bring himself to dial the chief's home number.

Geraldine paced the room, stopping to light a cigarette that was already lit.

She dialed the boat for the tenth time and connected with the same busy signal. She put on a pair of slacks over the nightgown, grabbed her purse, and raced from the room.

She took the elevator to the lobby and entered the cocktail lounge, taking a seat at the end of the bar.

She squinted in the darkness, feeling for the top of the stool. The only light was a pink gel aimed at the cash register.

It took a moment to make out the form of the bartender at the far end of the horseshoe-shaped counter. It was the white towel in the waistband that drew her attention. He walked toward her, smiling.

"What can I get this lovely lady tonight?" he asked.

"Scotch. Double. Water on the side. And five dollars in quarters."

He backed off. The lady was definitely not in the mood for small talk. "I don't think I have that much change."

"Just get it," she told him.

He walked off mumbling as Geraldine looked about the large room. A young couple sat on high-backed wicker chairs next to a large fish tank built into the wall. Small couches and round tables surrounded a tiny dance floor. A fireplace with gas logs was tucked into a corner.

She didn't notice the Asian man who slipped quietly away.

"What in God's hell happened here!" the lieutenant growled. He shone the flashlight in the cabin and trained it on the busted chair and broken bottles.

"Nothing," Owen said. He was sitting on the floor holding a towel to his face. His arm was caked with blood. A chunk of skin hung loose from his shoulder. A thick knobby welt ballooned above the eyebrows.

The blue lights of the police car invaded the small windows.

"Looks like a goddamned armored division rolled through here. You okay?"

"I'm fine," Owen said just before he passed out.

Geraldine splashed some water in her drink and promised the Virgin Mother that if Owen lived she'd never touch another deck of cards for the rest of her life.

"I know I've made that same promise before but this time I really mean it. Please, let him live."

She could only recall having felt such gripping, suffocating terror once in her life. When she awoke from surgery and saw the doctor. It was that horrible moment before he said, "Benign."

The bartender returned with a paper cup filled with quarters. "My tips," he explained.

She scooped up the cup and raced to the phone in the lobby. A cleaning woman in a blue uniform swiped at the white sand in the ashtray by the elevator. A man sat half-dozing, surrounded by pieces of luggage.

She dropped some coins into the phone and dialed. An operator's mechanical voice told her to drop more.

"Officer Powanda."

"Did you send someone to the boat?"

"We have two cars there right now. You the one who called before?"

"Is he all right?"

"Don't know. They're not back yet. Can I have your name?"

"Let me speak to your superior," Geraldine insisted.

"I'm the only one here," he said sharply. "Give me your number and I'll have the lieutenant—"

She hung up and called the boat. The phone was still off the hook.

Geraldine returned to the bar and sipped the drink slowly, forcing herself into an artificial calmness. The sailor was tough. Hal had said it himself. All those years at sea had conditioned him physically. He was probably strong enough to deflect a bullet, she convinced herself.

And even if he was wounded, she reasoned, the cops knew emergency procedures. They could keep him alive till the ambulance arrived.

Maybe he wasn't even hit. That's why the phone was off the hook. He knocked it over when he chased the attacker.

Please, God, let him be alive.

Geraldine bowed her head and noted to her horror that she was wearing the furry slippers. She began laughing and didn't stop even when the bartender rushed over.

"You okay, lady?"

She laughed till the tears flowed. The young couple stopped talking and stared.

"Maybe you should get some sleep," the bartender leaned over and whispered.

"Yeah," she nodded. "Maybe I should."

She put some money on the bar, picked up her glass, and said goodnight.

"Lady, you can't take the drink with you."

Geraldine stopped, turned, and in a voice that trained actors paid top money to acquire, yelled, "Try . . . and . . . stop . . . me."

She marched to the elevator stomping her furry pink feet.

She opened the door to her room and fumbled in the darkness for the light switch. She ran her hand against the wall, sliding it up and down, left to right, feeling about for some type of plastic bump.

She threw the door open wider, allowing the hallway light to penetrate.

She continued searching and finally found it on the right hand wall instead of the left.

Geraldine froze. She didn't know where the light switch was because:

1. The bellman had turned it on.
2. She'd never turned it off.
Someone had been in the room.

Geraldine didn't stop to see if anything was missing. She grabbed the suitcase, scooped up the clothes in the bathroom, and fled the hotel still wearing the nightgown under her slacks. A cab took her straight to the airport. She paused long enough to tell the Avis girl where they could find the car.

The following morning, David Ko was sitting in the hotel coffee shop looking out the window when an Avis mechanic got into the Toyota and drove it away.

CHAPTER TWENTY

Police Chief Ford Baker was by nature a lazy person. His mother often said that if laziness were an Olympic event, he'd win the gold and silver medals, and tie for the bronze.

As a kid, he'd paid friends to do his homework and deliver the newspapers.

In the army, he wrangled an assignment with *Stars and Stripes* and spent his tour of duty following the division baseball team throughout Europe.

After leaving the service he returned home to Florida and joined the police force when his grandfather, the mayor, assured him a desk job.

He never married, some say, because Leona never found any of the women he dated suitable for her son. He kept company for a few years with the woman who ran the bait shop, but when she moved west he didn't follow.

The chief's life centered around fishing and hunting. And his Tennessee cabin.

He began dreaming of retirement after two years on the force. Since age twelve, when he read *Huck Finn,* he knew exactly what he wanted to do with the rest of his life. He wanted to spend it in a log cabin in the woods, sitting on the porch watching the deer. He wanted to get up in the morning and dunk his toes in a backyard creek.

Four times a year, Ford and his mother would get in the car and drive north to the remote retreat. They didn't rough it. The cabin was equipped with color TV in the den and bedrooms, a jacuzzi, and a satellite dish that brought in the Dodger games from California. He built a hothouse a few yards from the brook, where his mother grew roses and herbs. She also had a vegetable garden and he indulged himself with a trailer-sized tool shed. They counted the days till his retirement, when they could live year 'round in their mountain paradise.

When the phone rang, at 2:38 A.M. that morning, Chief Ford Baker was one month and six days from liberation.

He was also sound asleep and hours away from a fishing trip to Turtle Key.

Lieutenant Gabe Danford walked into the chief's office and placed the typewritten report carefully in front of the man.

"What's the story?" the chief asked.

"Not sure yet."

"You fucking better have one for getting me over here!"

Danford nodded. "Doctors say it'll be sometime tomorrow before I can talk to the victim. He sustained multiple stab wounds. Fourteen stitches in the arm, lost a lot of blood. Got a knot on the side of his face the size of a grapefruit. Some broken ribs. Two fractured fingers."

The chief leaned forward in the chair. The hazel eyes, still puffy with sleep, glared with hostility.

"Who did it?"

"Don't know. We searched the dock, parking lot. Talked to a woman out walking her dog. She didn't see anything. We searched the area garbage cans. No sign of any weapon. Even checked the dumpsters at a restaurant nearby."

The chief looked at him with disgust.

"Someone sure as hell heard something because they called. We get that woman's name?"

The lieutenant was tired and emotionally spent. The blood got to him. He could still smell it. "No, sir. We know she was calling long distance from a pay phone. Powanda heard the money drop."

He felt like his legs would cave in under him any moment but he didn't dare sit. Not in the chief's office.

Ford reached for the report and took his time reading, knowing the deliberate silence would aggravate the lieutenant.

"Coke deal?"

"No, sir," Danford said quickly. Maybe too quickly.

"That right?"

"I've known Owen a long time, chief. Straight as they come. We go fishing, have a couple of beers now and then. Believe me, he's clean."

"Womanizer?"

The lieutenant took a moment before answering. "No more than any other single guy in town."

"Gambler?"

"Not really. He had a few bucks on the Super Bowl. Other than that—"

"Drinker?"

"Yeah. But I never saw him drunk."

The chief flung the papers across the room and jumped up from the chair.

"What the fuck we talking about here? Goddamn saint? I don't give a shit if he's the fucking pope! Somebody was out to kill him and I want to know why."

"Yes, sir."

It was bad enough to wake him on the eve of a fishing trip, but to stand there and give him this bullshit about some fucking do-gooder—!

What really pissed him off was the fact he didn't recognize the victim's name. It meant he was one of those northern yuppies new to the city, here to destroy it with more car fumes and their goddamn petitions. It seemed whenever two of 'em got together they drew up a petition against something.

"I want the name of the woman who called. If Saint Owen doesn't give it to you, make a copy of the recording and play it around town and see if anybody knows her."

The lieutenant's hands suddenly grew clammy. Sweat beads erupted at the back of his neck.

"Sir . . . we can't do that. Officer Powanda didn't have the machine turned on."

He could feel the chief's silent fury and knew the old man's blood pressure was touching Mt. Everest. Any minute now the purple veins would balloon in the twisted nose that had been busted by an irate female impersonator he'd arrested. The chief, who stood over six feet, with arms the size of ham hocks, leaned across the desk, his face flushed red. Even though awakened from a sound sleep, he'd arrived in a white starched shirt and pressed slacks. He'd also taken a moment to splash on cologne and clip on the antique watch fob that hung from the gun belt. The silver-peppered hair was wet-combed straight back.

"Why not?"

Gabe shrugged.

"That damn Ethel been calling here for him? That bitch calls one more time I'm having her locked up and you can tell him that!"

"Yes, sir." Lieutenant Danford wondered if he'd done the right thing by not mentioning Luther's poisoning in the report. If the old man found out he was withholding information . . .

The chief swiped his stubby fingers through his hair. "I want this friend of yours run through the computer. He shows so much as a parking ticket, I want to know about it. Got that? You check his car?"

"No, sir."

"He has one, doesn't he? Or does he flit around on goddamn wings?"

The lieutenant was beginning to feel like the accused. He regretted mentioning he knew Owen. "He has a red Chrysler."

"Check it!"

The lieutenant hesitated, glancing down at the desk. "It's kinda late to call the judge and get a warrant. Don't you think?"

The chief came around from behind the desk and confronted the officer. "Who the fuck said anything about a warrant? You hear me mention warrant?"

The lieutenant mumbled, "No."

"You go down to the fucking car—this minute—bust the fucking window if you have to, bust the fucking lock on the trunk, and if the son of a bitch comes in with a complaint you amend the report to say the perpetrator must have damaged the vehicle before or after the commission of the crime. I have to teach you goddamn *basic* police work at three o'clock in the morning?"

"No, sir. I'll take care of it."

"You have someone posted at the hospital?"

The young officer swiped at the sweat trailing down his neck. "I didn't think it was necessary."

"And that's why you're a fucking lieutenant and you'll never be chief as long as I live—and even after I'm dead—if I have anything to say about it. Get a man over there. Now!"

Gabe started for the door, only to be stopped by the chief's command.

"One more thing," the chief said, striding over to the coffeemaker sitting on the window sill. Gabe was glad he'd thought to start it brewing.

"That jerk Powanda, I want him off the desk. Assign him to the beach. Couple of months dealing with lost kids and beach balls on the highway, he'll get the message."

Gabe hid his pleasure behind the stony expression.

"Also—spread the word to the men that anytime they spot Ethel's car anywhere in town she is to get a ticket. I don't give a shit what for. Parking. Taillights. Dice hanging from the mirror. I better come across her name a whole lot."

"I'll drive by her house on my way home," Gabe told him. "She lives on my block and she always parks up on the grass."

The chief smiled. "And we have a city ordinance against that, don't we, lieutenant?"

"Yes, sir."

"And while you're there," the chief said, pouring a cup of coffee, "see if her garbage cans are covered. We also have an ordinance about that, don't we?" He spiked the coffee with four sugars and stirred it with a fountain pen.

"Certainly do. And weeds."

The old man nodded and waved him out of the office. He went to the window and peered through the venetian blinds at the illuminated flagpole across the lawn. Six police cars sat idle in the lot. The sprinkler splattered drops of water on the grass in a rhythmic pattern. The night was clear and moonless, harbinger of a cool, crisp morning, perfect for fishing.

He thought of the fat mullet that swam freely, no longer in danger of his hook. He crossed to the desk and sat dejectedly thinking of the stacks of cartons packed in the garage. The house was sold and the new owners were due to move in the first of March, less than a month away.

No goddamned weekend sailor—more than likely a dope runner—was going to stand between him and retirement.

He'd shoot the son of a bitch first.

CHAPTER TWENTY-ONE

Owen woke up in a fog—literally. It took him a few moments to realize it was smoke, from a cigarette clasped in Geraldine's fingers.

"It's about time, fella," she smiled. She was sitting on a chair with her stockinged feet propped up on the bed.

He grinned. The pain on the side of his face brought him back to reality. His mouth tasted as if it was glued together with soggy bread crumbs. He ran his tongue over his lips, but it just scraped the blistered skin. He tried to move but the effort was tiring.

Geraldine walked over to the nightstand and filled a plastic tumbler with water. She held it for him as he drank, slowly at first and then thirstily. "Easy," she laughed. "It only looks like vodka."

Owen moved in the bed, inching his way higher on the pillow. "How long have you been here?" he asked.

She glanced at the ashtray on the floor. "Oh, about a pack and a half."

"How long have I been here?"

"Three days."

She sat next to him on the bed, careful not to jar the hand that was tubed to a bottle dangling over the bed.

"You have company," she whispered. "They've had a cop outside your door since you got here. I told him I'm an old girlfriend from San Diego. They think I made the call the night you were attacked. I denied it."

Owen glanced at her, his eyes focusing on the tight beige slacks and brown sweater. The red hair was caught away from her face, exposing huge gold hoop earrings. The makeup was a little dramatic, even for the gay crowd on the island, but on her it looked . . . nice. He'd forgotten how pretty she was. "I'm glad you're here."

She smoothed the sheet over his legs, bare beneath the cotton gown. "Anything hurt?"

He moved cautiously, raising a leg, then an arm. He tried lifting his head from the pillow but the pain shot up the back of his neck.

"If it's attached to me, it hurts."

She reached over, propping his pillows. She hooked her arm around his chest, grabbed on to the metal railings at the headboard, and hoisted him into a semi-sitting position.

"Who did it?"

Owen looked away. "The same people who killed Luther."

"Who's Luther?" she asked, sitting on the edge of the bed.

"My dog. That's what I was trying to tell you on the phone. You realize you saved my life?"

"How?"

"You woke me. Bastard was already in the room. Another couple of seconds—"

"How many were there?"

"Not sure. Maybe two but it could've only been one. What did you find out in Cleveland?"

She told him about Marlene and Ida's burglary and Roy and Joe Akido. She told him about finding the American Express voucher for $3,000 and that someone had entered her hotel room.

He didn't say anything for a long time. She lit a cigarette and handed it to him. "What the hell have we gotten ourselves into?" he asked.

"There's more," she said. "Someone broke into my apartment."

She saw a flash of anger cross his face. The lines tightened around his mouth.

"When the hospital said you were going to be all right, I flew home. The place was destroyed. Nothing was taken. Whatever they were looking for, they didn't find it."

He looked at her with the sun dancing in the long copper strands and was struck by the childlike softness of the woman.

"Gerry," it was the first time he recalled using her name. It felt comfortable. "We have to end it. We have no business in this. Too many people have died."

"You can quit if you want. But I'm not." She pulled her hand away.

Owen rolled over on his side to face her. "Hal would tell you the same thing."

She laughed. "I never listened to him when he was alive. I'm not going to start now."

"You find this funny?" he asked.

She didn't appreciate the condescending tone. "Four people are dead! And a dog. Besides the ones who took Tylenol or drank coffee or had soup for lunch. How the hell can we just walk away from it?"

Geraldine told him about Hal's funeral and how she went through his papers and found Marlene's name with the phone number.

"Hal found out something from her. Maybe she introduced him to Joe Akido and whatever Joe told Hal, it was worth three thousand dollars. I don't know where Roy Hingle fits in except he took the picture of the body."

"Do you know if Hal saw Roy?"

"Yeah. Roy told me they got together for an hour or so. Why?"

The sailor raised himself on his elbow. He glanced toward the partially opened door and saw the brown uniformed leg of the cop sitting sentry.

"Hal was being followed. Everyone he spoke to is dead. He sent me the telegram from Cleveland. They knew about it and figured I knew something."

Geraldine asked, "And my apartment . . . the hotel room?"

"His notes. They want his notes. Whatever Akido told him, or the woman."

"But there are none," she protested.

Behind her, in the corridor, the cop coughed, causing her to flinch.

"All he had was a manila envelope. That's how I knew your boat's name. Some receipts. Marlene's number. Nothing else."

"Where is it?" he asked.

"Right here," she said, digging it out of her purse and handing it to him.

"I'm keeping it," Owen said. He leaned over the side of the bed and stuffed it under the mattress. "You can't go back to your apartment," he said calmly.

She avoided his eyes.

The overhead paging system announced that visiting hours were over in the maternity ward. Grandparents were reminded to stop by the reception desk for their complimentary fruit basket.

"Gerry, I'm just a sailor. I know boats, ocean currents, and something about fishing. You're a writer and you know a little about gambling."

"Very little," she pointed out.

"It doesn't make us detectives," he said.

She glanced at the face that sported the beginnings of a beard. The hospital gown could almost pass for Coast Guard white.

"Why did you get divorced?"

His smile froze. "What the hell does that have to do with anything?"

"It doesn't. Just curious."

"How'd you find out?"

She pointed to the mattress. "Hal's file."

He started to say something just as a nurse entered carrying a medicine tray.

Geraldine caught a glimpse of the cop reading a paperback just before the woman closed the door.

Geraldine rose quickly, knowing she'd be shooed from the room. She welcomed the dismissal. She'd taken a cab from the airport, and the New York clothes, especially the panty hose under the slacks, didn't wear well in the ninety-two-degree Florida humidity. A shower would be delicious.

She reached for her suitcase near the door and didn't see Owen spring from the bed. She looked up to see him grab the aluminum pole attached to the plasma bag, and fling it, like a sword, at the nurse.

In the same instant, Geraldine saw the gun with the long thin muzzle peeking out from under the tray.

The woman fired. The bullet plopped soundlessly into the pillow that still bore the imprint of Owen's head.

He yelled at Geraldine to get down and lunged for the white form.

His fingers grabbed air as the nurse dove through the closed window.

CHAPTER TWENTY-TWO

Chief Ford Baker arrived into a scene only the Marx Brothers could have orchestrated.

The hospital room was squeezed to the limit by an army of bodies scurrying about taking pictures, drawing diagrams, and dusting for prints. A detective questioned two doctors while three nurses awaited their turn.

The chief bellowed, "Everybody out!"

There was a stampede for the door as he yelled, "Except you!" He pointed to Geraldine. The last person barely cleared the door before he slammed it.

The chief stood over the bed where Owen lay with his leg secured to a bulky ice pack.

He had sprained his ankle jumping at the nurse.

"Talk." The chief ordered. He removed his cap and held it against his side.

"Got a cigarette?" Owen asked.

"No, but I got a jail cell with your name on it and it won't pose no problem finding one for your ladyfriend."

Owen sat up slowly. "And I've got a lawyer who'll have you on charges faster than you can say 'pension.' In case no one told you, I'm the victim. Not the criminal."

Geraldine did not like the way the conversation was going. In all her years as a reporter she had learned one granite truth: Don't argue with cops. The pen might be mightier, but they owned the bullets.

The chief barked, "We can talk here or in the ambulance on the way to my office. But make no mistake, we *are* going to talk."

"My dog was poisoned. Somebody tried to kill me the other night, which is why I'm here. You have a cop posted outside my door—and the stupid son of a bitch lets a man dressed like a nurse come in here carrying a gun!"

The chief bit right through the cigar. He threw the stub out the broken window, which still bore a swatch of white linen caught on a jagged piece of glass.

"You wanna know how I see it?" Baker asked. "I say you've been dealing coke with some unfriendly people. I say you did them out of some money and they mean to collect your ass."

Geraldine remained rigid in the chair, her hands demurely crossed on her lap.

"Search my boat."

"We did. It's clean but that don't mean diddly piss to me. You're into something and I want to know what it is. And as for you," he turned to Geraldine, "empty your purse. Right now!"

"She's not involved in this," Owen shouted.

"It's okay," Geraldine said. She unzipped it and dumped the contents on the bed.

They watched silently as the chief took his bifocals from his pocket and examined each scrap of paper.

"Newspaper reporter?"

"You can call my city editor and verify it."

"Oh, I intend to. Have no doubt about that. New York? Should've fucking guessed!"

He rummaged through the clutter of address books, lipsticks, eye shadow, cigarette lighter, and held up a plastic, pink case shaped like a flat sea shell.

"What the hell is this?" he asked.

Geraldine mumbled, "Birth control pills." She stared at the ceiling, not actually seeing but feeling Owen's amusement. She was glad she'd left the Mace cylinder at home.

He rummaged through her wallet and stepped back when a clay chip tumbled from one of the plastic compartments. Geraldine gaped as a twenty-five-dollar green chip from the Lady Luck Casino hit the bed.

Damn, had she known it was there, she could've played another hand.

The chief turned the chip in his hand and squinted at the markings. He tossed it aside.

"Everytime we have a commotion in queer town, the instigator is down here from New York. You got any normal people up there?"

Geraldine bristled. "Some. The rest are in the police academy."

"Well, I got a story for you, Miss Geraldine," he said pocketing her driver's license. "I can get a warrant for your arrest as a material witness and have you locked up. We got a recording of your voice the other night and a patrolman who doesn't cotton to being called an asshole, even if he is one."

The chief sorted through the rest of the stuff and held onto the Newspaper Guild ID, press card, and Social Security card.

"You can pick these up at my office tomorrow."

"Cut the horseshit!" Owen told him. "You got a murderer lying out on the sidewalk. Why don't you find out who he is? How'd he get the uniform? Gun? Who is he?"

"Suppose you tell me."

Geraldine walked across the room and glanced out the window. A circle of cops stood by the body covered with a green hospital blanket.

Farther across the lawn, a family carrying pink balloons and flowers laughed as they walked toward a station wagon. The irony of life and death did not escape her.

"What if," she said, "he wasn't alone? What if his partner is at the airport this minute waiting to board a plane? An Asian passenger might stand out."

The chief turned slowly. "I thought you never got a look at him. That's what my man said. How'd you know he was a Chink?"

"Someone mentioned it," she answered.

"That so?" the chief smiled. It was not an expression designed to win one's affection. He reached across Owen and grabbed the phone, thumping it on his lap as he sat on the bed. He dialed and shouted into the receiver.

"Get someone over to the airport and bring in any Japs hanging around. I don't give a shit what excuse you use. Make up whatever you like. I gotta teach you goddamn police work on my day off!"

Owen leaned over quickly to protect his ankle in case the man "accidentally" dropped the phone.

The weight of his body, shifting to the far end of the bed, momentarily exposed the brown envelope tucked under the mattress. Geraldine spotted it and froze.

She edged her way toward the bed and quickly yanked the sheet down, draping it over the side of the mattress.

"You tell the mayor I'll call him when I'm done. Could be two weeks from now!" The chief slammed down the phone and marched to the door. He threw it open and yelled at the detective to enter.

"Find out what time visiting hours are over. Get all the plate numbers in the lot and check them out with personnel. If you got a car unaccounted for, I want to know about it. Also see if any uniforms are missing. Who's searching the building?"

"I got two men on the roof and one in the basement. They'll meet on the third floor."

"I want the people who were on duty on this floor, and all the elevator operators, in the cafeteria in ten minutes. Also," the chief told him, "collect all the visitors' passes. I want to know if one's missing."

He waited till the man left and turned to Owen. "I spoke to your wife in Seattle last night."

The sailor jerked his head around. "What the hell for?"

The chief tucked his thumbs in his belt. "Maybe you were hot shit out on the aircraft carrier, but as far as I'm concerned you're just another drifter looking to score some easy money, and, fella, you picked the wrong town. Your dog was poisoned? You report it?"

"No," Owen said, quietly.

"Why not?"

The sailor averted his eyes. "What's the point? He's dead."

"By the way," the chief said, putting on his cap, "the perpetrator did some job on your car. Detroit wouldn't even recognize it. Tore it up somethin' awful."

He turned to Geraldine, "Don't try leaving town. I'd hate to have to send someone up to that great city to get you. Never know, he might come back a faggot." He walked out.

"A real charmer," Geraldine observed.

Owen inched his body across the bed, closer to where she sat. He whispered, an eye cocked to the cop sitting outside.

"How'd you know he was Asian?"

"Just a guess."

He reached out for her arm and pulled her closer. The sweater felt soft under his touch. He could smell the musky floral perfume.

"It's over. Right now. Let the cops handle it."

Geraldine laughed, "Who, Wyatt Earp?"

"He has resources. The FBI, labs, computers. We've got nothing." Owen said.

"We have resources, too."

"Yeah? Like what?"

"A boat. A press card. It just requires a little money. You have any?"

"Some," he said. "Not a whole lot."

She smiled, "May not take a whole lot."

Something about the smile made him uneasy. "What are you getting at?"

"You know I play poker."

He groaned. "Hal mentioned it."

Geraldine leaned over the bed, the top of her body lying across his arm. "Every town has a game. I know, 'cause I've played in most of them. Usually a cab driver or a bartender can point one out."

Owen regarded her with suspicion. "You hustling me?"

"Maybe. You decide when you get to know me better."

"Ger, nothing personal, but since I've known you I've been stabbed, had my boat torn up, my dog poisoned, my car trashed. And Wyatt is looking to throw me in jail."

"Hear me out," she said. "You stake me and we nab these guys. We'll hand 'em over to the cops and I'll write the book. We split the money and you can sail to Tahiti, be a wealthy beachcomber. And," she said somberly, "I get to finish what Hal started."

Owen reached over to adjust the ice pack against his foot. "We could get killed. You," he emphasized, "could get killed."

"You think Wyatt Earp can prevent it? Strange as it sounds, I'm your best shot at staying alive."

Owen dropped his head to the pillow and stared at the ceiling. "No. I don't like it," he told her flatly.

She leaned closer, bringing her face within inches of his. "Then you shouldn't have made the call to Hal."

CHAPTER TWENTY-THREE

Marco waited by the pay phone outside the 7-Eleven on Topper Road in North Miami. When it failed to ring at 3:00 P.M. he knew something was wrong. He went to his car and sat another twenty minutes with the windows rolled down. When he finally gave up and drove away, he was certain that Kuni Hamada was dead.

Of the six, Kuni was his favorite. Not as clever as Yan-San, or as aggressive as Ko, and not nearly as ambitious as Akido. But he was, Marco recalled sadly, the most enthusiastic.

An enthusiasm born, no doubt, from being raised in an American internment camp in Arizona following the bombing of Pearl Harbor.

He was the oldest member of the team, but his eagerness had prompted Marco to relax his restrictions. Marco thought of Hamada's wife and sons in Philadelphia, and though he'd never met them, he shared their grief.

As he drove along the rainswept highway, he remembered when Kuni was stricken by a rare disease. Marco paid the medical costs and faithfully monitored his progress.

His only comfort, as he drove south on I-95, was that somehow, some way, his friend would be avenged. He knew without question that Kuni Hamada now reigned at God's side. A bright new star would flicker in the universe in his honor.

Marco steered the gray Lincoln off the highway ramp, staying discreetly behind a school bus. The air conditioner hummed softly as mellow Spanish music filtered from the rear speakers. Outside the window, pink and lime green stucco roofs raced past his vision. It reminded him of his homeland.

He blessed himself and asked his father to welcome Kuni to his embrace. "He is a valiant soldier in our struggle. Tell him he will rejoice in our victory. Soon, papa."

Marco headed for the beach to await David Ko's phone call on the public phone near the refreshment stand.

He would no longer restrain him.

CHAPTER TWENTY-FOUR

"Goddamnedest story I ever heard," Earl told Geraldine as they sat in his pickup truck on the beach.

The sun was setting, slashing the sky with bold purple strokes. The ocean, which an hour earlier had glistened neon blue, was now a drab gray blanket ruffled by foamy whitecaps. The salt air wafted through the open window. In the distance, a platoon of sea gulls glided overhead.

"You bring the money?" she asked. She tossed a cigarette out the window and watched two gulls zero in.

"Yeah." The old man leaned across her lap and punched the glove compartment twice before it fell open. He removed a brown bank envelope and handed it to her.

"Thanks. You find out about the game?"

Earl leaned against the door and let his arm dangle out the window in the night breeze. Four teenagers in a dune buggy with oversized tires caromed past, spitting sand on the hood of the truck.

He spoke softly. Geraldine had to lean forward in the seat to hear him.

"I've known Owen just about since he moved here. He's a very agreeable person. Don't mind telling you, I kinda look on that fella like a son." The thin sunken cheeks deflated further as he took a drag on a cigarette. The skeletal frame in the red-checkered shirt and black trousers relaxed against the door. "If anyone hurt him, I'd tend to take it personal."

Geraldine caught the warning. "Earl, I'd never hurt him. Not intentionally, anyway."

He remained silent for awhile and then said simply, "That's fair."

She had the urge to reach over and pat his arm, but didn't.

"There's a game, once a week, down at Mae's boarding house. Don't know which night. Been years since I played."

Geraldine lifted her hair and caught the cool breeze on her neck. It was hard to believe that she'd started the day slushing through snow. "Could you put in a word for me?"

"I suppose."

"It has to be soon," she urged him.

"This whole thing's my fault," he said. "Your friend dead and that woman leaving those young 'uns . . . I should've thrown that damn paper away and said nothing." He stared at the ocean and made a sound that alarmed her. Then she saw he was laughing.

"We used to bring Luther out here and let him run. Son of bitch could damn near catch the gulls! Fast! He'd jump up in the air and twist around so pretty, almost like he was floating. Amazin'."

Geraldine slipped off her shoes and rested her feet on the suitcase under the dashboard. She was worn out. And hungry. And in desperate need of a bath and shampoo. But for the first time in a long while, she felt wonderfully at ease. Even the noxious smell of dead fish coming from the tub in the back of the truck was no longer offensive. The sky was totally dark to the left. Yet the other half still gripped the last rays of sunlight.

"I got a house. Nothing fancy, but clean. Bought it here when we got married. I go by there once a week and keep it up. Propane tank should be full. Ain't rented it out since last summer. Got a phone. And TV. You're welcome to stay there."

"If it's got a bathtub, I'll take it," she smiled.

Distant lights twinkled across a causeway bridge. Two strollers in bathing suits squatted on the shore to collect sea shells.

"Earl, I want you to know that today was only the second time I've seen Owen. I went to Vegas to play cards and get away from everything. Hal, my job, my life. I don't know if this will make any sense to you but . . . I'm glad you didn't throw the paper away."

The old man glanced at her. There was no smile, no reassuring change in the emaciated features, but a silent warmth radiated from the stoic face.

"Gotta get you a CB handle," he said. "How does Poker Chips sound?"

Geraldine laughed. "It says it all."

CHAPTER TWENTY-FIVE

Horse hockey!" Leona Baker flung her slipper across the living room.

The police chief sat on the couch stroking Ginger, the calico cat, as Fred slept curled next to the rocking chair.

"I got everything packed. I changed the address at the post office. They'll be sending our mail to Fox Creek, Tennessee."

Her son said, "Don't worry. We're going."

"Why don't you just throw their asses in jail!"

The thin, sparrowlike woman smoothed the cotton house-dress against her spindly legs. The wrinkled, liver-spotted hands sported three large rings.

"It's not that easy. He's retired military. And she's some hotshot newspaper reporter from New York. I so much as look at her cross-eyed, she'll have some Jew lawyer on my neck."

"Horseshit! You ain't just anybody. You're the police chief. That still counts for something, don't it?"

He grunted, "Goddamn mayor was calling all day. Tells me there's an election this year. Like I give a good goddamn."

The old woman's head shot around quickly. "He threaten you?"

The chief winced as Ginger sprang up on his lap to stretch. Her claws dug into his bare knees below the Bermuda shorts. He chased the cat off.

"He said, without actually saying it, that I can forget about retiring till we close this case. Said it didn't look good for nurses to be jumping out of hospital windows. Told the dumb son of a bitch it wasn't a nurse, it was a Jap dressed like a nurse, and he says, 'Same thing.' He's your cousin, you talk to him." Ginger amused herself with the tassles on Ford's loafers.

"He's from the idiot side of the family," Leona said. "Never cared for any one of 'em but I'll go out to the house after supper and slam him on the side of the head if you want. He's not ruining our plans!"

The chief grinned. "Wouldn't look too good in the paper, the chief's mother getting arrested for beating up on the mayor."

Leona thundered, "But it'd feel good."

Ford stretched out on the couch and smiled. His mother never disappointed him. The years, all eighty-three, had not diminished her fiery spirit. And as he was known to say, the oak hadn't fallen too far from the tree.

"You know a commercial fisherman in town named Owen?"

Mom leaned forward with that familiar glint in her squinty eyes. She resembled a hunting dog who lived for the chase. Her short brown hair, which she touched up to hide the gray, was caught in a rubber band atop her head.

"Owen who?"

"Last name is Ryder. Keeps a boat on the East Pier."

She glanced down at the heavy braided rug beneath her feet. "Owen? That what you said?"

He nodded. He could almost see her sorting through the cobweb of names and faces. Whenever the historical society or the town librarian was stumped for a name or long-forgotten incident or news event, they called Leona. She didn't need to consult any book. Just her personal memories.

"He go by any other name?"

"Not that I know of."

The woman screwed up her face and wiggled her cheeks rapidly from left to right. "Owen. Owen."

The chief reached over and patted her arm. "Ma, it's okay. Can't expect you to know everybody. Besides, he's new."

The old woman sprang forward in the chair. "Big? Good-looking? Lot of hair, falls down on top of his eyes. Has a red car?"

The chief grinned.

She continued, "Thin. But not skinny. Wears cowboy boots."

"You are unbelievable!" he beamed proudly.

Leona sat back in the rocking chair and sighed contentedly.

"Took me time 'cause I ain't seen him but once. But I remember him. Nice man. Polite. Friendly. What he do?"

"How'd you meet him?" the chief asked.

"At the beauty parlor. Few years ago. I was getting my hair done and so was Lily. You know Lily. She has the souvenir shop."

Ford nodded. He didn't mention that for years he'd had his eye on the woman, who, for his money, was the prettiest one he'd ever seen. He'd shared a picnic table with her once at the firemen's annual supper and she seemed to want to see him again, but he never could get up the courage to find out.

"He's her boyfriend. Or was then. He came to the beauty parlor to pick her up and gave me a ride home. Very nice. Brought me right to the door," Leona said. "Very friendly. What did he do?"

"He's the one that Jap tried to shoot before he went out the window."

Leona pursed her lips. "I don't believe it."

"He's involved in something. And I mean to find out."

The old woman fiddled with her hair, snapping and unsnapping the rubber band. It was a gesture she did absent-mindedly when reading or watching television. Or like now when deep in thought.

"Why don't you go down to Lily's tomorrow and buy some . . . postcards?"

CHAPTER TWENTY-SIX

Marco Luiz DelCampo was furious. The coffee plant was back in operation. Tylenol sales were soaring. Mothers had resumed buying baby food. The soup company was racking up sales.

He'd destroyed nothing!

On the contrary, the food industry was basking in favorable and profitable gains due to its attention to innovative packaging. Even Dannon Yogurt quietly unveiled a new tamperproof container.

Were the truth known, Marco could probably garner the Nobel Prize for forcing industry to safeguard its products. Even Ralph Nader, in his unending struggle, never accomplished such sweeping revisions.

He regretted now not killing the pope, as he'd planned. But he'd allowed himself to be dissuaded by Yan-San and the others, who feared for their lives in carrying out the mission. There was no use explaining that God was guiding his every move and dispensing His protective love and therefore no harm would come to them.

Kuni had sacrificed his own life because he believed in the nobility of the mission. God allowed him to die so the others would champion the cause.

Yet, they didn't believe.

And that's where he differed from his soldiers. Marco did not fear death. He welcomed it. It was his passport to Kate. He knew without question that God would not summon him till his earthly promise to his father was fulfilled.

Marco walked out to the terrace where his housekeeper had breakfast waiting under the canopied tent. Copies of the New York newspapers, delivered to the gate each morning, lay next to his plate on the round, glass-topped table.

He poured a cup of the thick, dark Cuban coffee and reached for the *Daily News.* Another mob rub-out in Brooklyn. Twelve dead in a Queens tenement fire. A police captain in Manhattan was indicted for selling confiscated drugs. Cardinal Thomas Ryan McHugh, wearing a pilot's cap, was shown on a picket line outside the striking TWA terminal.

Marco turned to the horoscope column and found his sign, Capricorn. It read: "Recent business reversals will bear fruit under Pluto's transit in the days ahead. What is now unclear, will soon crystallize."

He smiled.

CHAPTER TWENTY-SEVEN

Geraldine woke the next morning to the sound of the phone ringing. She sat up and looked around. It took more than a moment to place the surroundings. The room looked like a page in a 1930 Sears catalogue.

Lace doilies adorned the dark, heavy vanity bureau with its three-sided mirror cradled in wood. A floor lamp with a glass globe stood alongside the bed. An oval braided rug lay atop the gray linoleum floor. Venetian blinds covered the two high windows behind frilly, criss-crossed sheer pink curtains.

Then she remembered it was "the shack" in Little Cuba.

She followed the ring to the parlor and found the black phone on a small circular table near the window.

She was only wearing panties and a T-shirt so she grabbed the phone quickly and edged away from the window.

"Hello?"

"I get you up?"

"It's okay," she said, recognizing the Wagon Master. "I had to get up early, anyway."

"It's two-thirty in the afternoon," Earl told her. " 'Round here, you get up after seven you're either sick or dead," he added, somewhat disapprovingly.

"Well, I might be. I won't know for sure till I have some coffee," she answered.

She stood in the shadows of the brooding, musty room and glanced out the window at the porch with the wooden veranda that covered the length of the house.

"I stopped by Mae's. They play tomorrow night at eight. I told her you were my niece. She'll introduce you to the regulars. I'll see a few of 'em today and mention you."

"Great."

"Don't forget to go see the chief. He's not one to mess with," he warned.

"No problem," she assured Earl.

The living room, with its tabletop black and white Emerson TV and the crocheted afghan flung over the couch, reminded her of summers at her grandmother's house in Toms River, New Jersey. She could almost smell the floral talcum powder that came in a lavender colored tin.

Earl told her: "I'm gonna go see how the Fresh Paint is drying. You need anything?"

"No, I'm fine."

"You need somethin', you call me. Told Molly you're a friend of his. That's all she knows."

A chicken with a spray of red feathers scooted across the porch and stopped to peck at the floorboards.

"You have chickens?"

"Used to. Why?"

"There's one on the porch," Geraldine gasped.

"Probably belongs to the people across the street. Gotta go," he said. "Call the chief."

"I will."

She hung up and peeked out the window at the chicken, which was thumping flat-footed across the porch. This was the closest she'd ever been to one, and she had no desire to get closer. Geraldine searched for the kitchen and put a pot of water on the stove. The small, square green formica table matched the wallpaper with tiny green windmills. Despite its age, the house was well tended. And immaculate.

She looked out the kitchen window at the jungle of banana trees and bushes that separated the property from the house next door. A thin purple lizard darted about the rusted skeleton of a child's bike. A woman's voice peppered the air with Spanish. The sky was overcast, threatening rain. A breeze ruffled the curtains over the sink. She made a cup of instant coffee and carried it into the parlor. She settled next to the phone on a needlepoint hassock and dialed the police.

"The chief in?" she asked.

"Who's calling?"

"Geraldine. He'll know."

Ford Baker came on the line a minute later.

"Reporting in, as ordered," she said with just a tinge of civility.

"Good."

Was it her imagination or had Wyatt Earp mellowed? The "good" sounded almost pleasant, like the forerunner of a cheery "morning."

"Spoke to that fella, your boss, up in New York. Not that I understood half of what the hell he said."

Geraldine laughed: "He's Australian."

"That what it was? He seems decent enough. Wanted to know what you're doing in the middle of an attempted homicide. Told him I'd like an answer to that, too."

Geraldine didn't like the way his tone changed. "Can I come over and pick up my stuff?"

"Your boss said he expects you to cooperate with this office."

"And I would," she said quickly, "if I knew anything."

"Bullshit."

So much for mellowness.

"You pick up your ID, anytime, at the desk. What hotel you staying at?"

"Holiday Inn," she lied. She didn't even know if they had one in town.

"I'll be in touch," he said and hung up.

Geraldine showered and threw on a pair of white dungarees and a red/purple Hawaiian shirt with pink flowers. She brushed her hair away from her face and pinned it behind her ears. She applied some light makeup and marveled that with all she'd been through, she still looked halfway decent. No new wrinkles had popped up to offend. The few gray strands, she told herself, gave her needed character.

She strolled out to the porch and sat on the wooden steps, resting against one of the circular pillars that supported the weatherbeaten veranda. Thirty years ago the house must have been a gem. A waist-high wrought-iron fence with fancy lattice work enclosed a tiny front yard. Large, hexagonal red clay stones marked the narrow walkway. The metal porch swing hanging from chain ropes, she knew without testing it, would squeak.

A rain-heavy breeze swept around her bare feet as a cockroach the size of Rhode Island scampered across the yard and darted under the fence.

She quickly tucked her legs beneath her.

The houses along the street, pink, chocolate brown, or sky blue, were relics of better days. Torn screen doors, broken cement steps, lopsided, unhinged gates, peeling paint. . . . But the abundance of greenery, palm trees, flowers, colorful bushes, concealed many of the blemishes.

A dark woman around forty, wearing shorts and a Tampa Bucs orange T-shirt, stepped out on the porch next door, cradling an infant.

"Chi-Chi! Get back here," she yelled in Geraldine's direction. She whipped off her sandal and banged it against the side of the house. The chicken flew off the porch and disappeared through a hole in the fence.

"Sorry," the woman said. She turned to the racket behind her and let off a barrage of Spanish. A teenage girl appeared, scooped up the infant, and stormed back into the house.

The woman slid a rocking chair to the far end of the porch. "You just move in?" she asked in a musical accent.

"Last night," Geraldine smiled.

"I'm Cecelia," she said.

"Geraldine."

"You got kids?"

"No. No husband," Geraldine said.

"You're lucky," the woman answered.

"Change his diaper!" the woman yelled through the screened window. To Geraldine she shrugged, "They think love is making babies. Then they don't want to do the work." She sighed and swatted at a fly. Her blonde hair was upswept à la Betty Grable, a jarring contrast against the dark skin. Though overweight, with flabby arms peeking from under the orange shirt, the body was shapely. Huge breasts drooped almost to her waist.

"You from New York?"

"Yes," Geraldine said.

"The guy who rented last year was from Queens." The woman leaned over to whisper loudly across the narrow alley. "He was a pato!"

Geraldine mentally jiggled her high school Spanish. "A duck?"

The woman laughed, putting a hand over her mouth. Her slim fingers sported long, polished nails. "No. He didn't like women. Just men. You know?"

Geraldine knew. "Oh. Yeah."

Cecelia leaned over the side of the porch. "You want to go shopping? I have to go to Sears. We can eat at McDonald's."

Geraldine replied quickly, "Sure!" She needed a ride to police headquarters and Cecelia looked like the type that wouldn't ask questions.

Ten minutes later, Cecelia was sitting in a dented, mustard-colored Pontiac in front of the house when Geraldine emerged. Furry pink dice with black spots hung from the mirror along with a large medallion of the Virgin Mary. A miniature statue of St. Lazarus stood magnetized to the dashboard.

Cecelia had changed into a cotton dress and white heeled slippers. Large silver hoop earrings dangled inches from her shoulders.

Geraldine got in the front seat, squeezing around Marlboro cigarette packs, baby bottles, and empty soda cans.

Cecelia, who smelled of recent perfume, apologized for the condition of the car, saying she was waiting for her disability case to be settled in order to buy a new one.

"Not new, just newer," she said, driving off. "I'm gonna have it all ready for when my boyfriend gets out of jail." She volunteered, "He broke into a restaurant. All he took was cigarettes." Then she added, "Stupido," and laughed.

Geraldine recognized the hospital as they drove past. She glanced at the red brick building and suddenly found herself longing to see Owen.

"You know what happened there yesterday?" Cecelia asked. "A nurse got into a fight with her boyfriend, a married doctor, and jumped out the window." She grinned, "My cousin is a janitor there."

The woman drove along the back streets, explaining her license plates were overdue and she didn't have the money to get new ones.

"I'm a beautician," she said proudly, "but I hurt my back and now I can't do shampoos."

Bouncy Cuban-African music played on the car radio as the announcer pitched for Goya beans.

"You got a boyfriend?" Cecelia asked.

"Used to," Geraldine answered, staring up at the gathering clouds. Tiny drops slid down the windshield.

"You're better off," the woman said. "All they bring is trouble."

Coming out of McDonald's, the blonde grandmother spotted a former boyfriend and yelled to him in Spanish. They hugged and laughed as Geraldine flagged down a taxi.

CHAPTER TWENTY-EIGHT

Lieutenant Gabe Danford was at Ray's Car Wash at 4:33 P.M. when his beeper went off. The patrol car, chained to the ground rail, was in the wax cycle as he stood chatting with the owner. He used his phone to call headquarters.

"Danford here," he told the desk officer.

"Hold on for the chief."

Gabe groaned. He was technically off duty but he knew better than to return the car unwashed. Whatever the chief wanted, it could only spell disaster.

His wife, Maryanne, was home preparing a barbecue to celebrate his fifteenth anniversary on the force. They were supposed to be on a five-day trip to Disney World but the chief abruptly canceled all vacations. The family cookout, complete with a hired clown for the kids, was a last-minute substitute.

"Where are you?" the chief asked.

"The car wash."

"That dame from New York just left here in a cab. Star Taxi. Get over there and find out where he took her."

Gabe knew he was courting serious trouble but plunged ahead anyway.

"Sir, I was due off forty-five minutes ago."

"That a fact?"

He plunged deeper. "Maryanne is having a party for my fifteen years. Everyone'll be there in an hour."

"Well, I'd sure hate to have you disappoint all those people. I mean, what with murderers and dog killers and faggot Japs running around loose! Why don't you run on home and make it a retirement party instead?"

Gabe swallowed hard. "I'll check the cab." He didn't wait for the black teenager to hand-dry the car. He got in, blasting the sirens to annoy and terrify fellow motorists, and sped to the taxi stand, where he waited impatiently while the dispatcher called the driver back to the office.

The Spanish driver with a gold front tooth said he took the woman to the General Car Rental outside the airport. He didn't mention that she had asked about poker games and he had given her the number of his cousin, who ran one in the back of the grocery store.

An hour later the lieutenant returned to headquarters and told the chief: "He picked her up by McDonald's and brought her here. Then they went to General where she rented a blue Thunderbird, license 497 SBB. Paid with a Visa card issued by a New York bank. Said she was staying at the Holiday Inn. I went over there. Spoke to the manager. She's not registered."

The chief sat back in the chair with his feet on the desk. A brown, mushy cigar burned in the ash tray. "She talk to the driver?"

"Weather. Seafood restaurants. Usual tourist crap."

The chief took the cop's notes and threw them atop a pile of computer printouts.

"How long she rent the car for?"

"A week."

The chief removed his legs from the desk, bent down to the bottom drawer, and gave it a hard kick. It came unstuck.

"You have a party to go to, don't you?" the man said.

"If it's all right." The young officer dared not smile.

"You might need this." He handed Gabe two bottles of Chivas Regal that he removed from the drawer. "Tell Maryanne I'm sorry about the vacation. I'll make it up to her."

The lieutenant held the bottles close to his chest like two prized trophies. "Thank you." He hurried to the door and paused to say, "Sir, maybe you'd like to stop by after work. And bring your mom."

Chief Ford Baker grunted, not bothering to look up from the paperwork.

Lieutenant Danford took it to mean, "Get out!" and fled.

The chief got up and locked the door. He went to the refrigerator and took out a beer bottle, twisting the cap open. He checked the air conditioner and turned it up a notch. Let the new chief worry about the electric bill. He'd be gone when it came in.

He went back to his desk and reached for the file marked "Ryder, Owen." He spread it open on the desk. The phone button blinked and the voice on the intercom alerted, "It's the mayor."

"I'm not here."

He skimmed through the papers that included military records, bank statements, motor vehicle printouts, property taxes, the marina lease, car payments. There was also a typed transcript of the chief's conversation with the wife in Seattle, medical testimony taken from the doctors, photographs of the exterior and interior of the boat, and something that now caught his attention.

He didn't know how he missed it the first time. The title for *Nathan* was cosigned by Earl Smithers.

He'd known the ol' geezer all his life. He wasn't the type to take out a loan for a stranger . . . and a Yankee, at that.

The chief locked the file in the top drawer of the desk and finished his beer. He walked to the coat rack and took down his gun holster.

It was still early. He could drive by Earl's on his way home.

The white button blinked again.

"Officer Daniels calling."

The chief picked up the phone. "Yeah?"

"I went by Shirley's like you said, but he's busy with two funerals and his man told me he'd have the report sometime tomorrow. I told him you wanted it right away, but he said that's the best he can do."

"That so? I'll handle it," the chief said, and hung up. He pushed the intercom and told the officer on duty, "I'm heading home. I'll check in later."

The chief put on his jacket and left by the side door that led directly to the parking lot. He got in his '79 Cadillac and headed toward Sweet Water Creek where the old man lived.

It was almost dark when he turned into the dirt road running alongside the creek. The Yankee developers hadn't discovered this area yet—or maybe they were discouraged by the mosquitoes and the perennial floods.

Huge, gnarled tree trunks, bent with age and a century of hurricane winds, bowed over the road, dripping with stringy Spanish moss that slapped against the windshield.

He guided the car around the deep puddles in the road. He drove past two weathered shacks and stopped at the end of the cul-de-sac in front of Earl's house.

The porch light was lit but the rest of the house was dark. Earl's white pickup truck was gone and Molly's station wagon was nowhere to be seen. His headlights caught the cemetery of crab traps strewn about the yard like square tombstones. A large mound of fishing net lay alongside the porch steps.

Ford didn't bother to get out of the car. He thought of leaving a note but decided instead to confront the old man without warning.

Ford backed the Cadillac into the yard, turned the wheel sharply, and drove off.

He couldn't imagine what connection Earl had to Owen. Sure, they were both sailors and hired out their boats, but so did dozens of others in Key West. Besides, Earl was known to be very tight with a nickel.

Why would he take out a loan for a Yankee that wasn't blood kin?

Since he was close to the waterfront, the chief decided to swing past the souvenir shop.

He turned east on Front Street, past Old Mallory Square with its Fish Museum and tourists shops. He found the store, brightly lit, with the beach towels hanging on a high clothesline over the door's entrance. The chief parked at a meter, not bothering to feed it, and crossed the narrow street quickly. For a winter weeknight, the sidewalk was crowded with strolling tourists. Two taxis sat idly in front of Manny's Seafood Restaurant with the pink neon crab blinking on the roof.

The chief went into the store, his entrance announced by a bell chime tacked to the screen door. A few customers lingered about the racks of bathing suits.

Lily spotted him from behind the counter and smiled. The chief nodded and headed for the wire rack that held hundreds of postcards. He took his time selecting his purchase, all the while glancing about the tiny store.

He waited till the customers left and took his postcards to the cash register.

Lily, a tall, handsome woman with dark hair braided around

her head entertwined in a colorful scarf, seemed genuinely happy to see him.

"Hi, Ford. How's Leona?"

"Good," he said, reaching in his pocket for a fresh cigar and wondering if it was all right to light it. Lily slid an ashtray toward him on the glass-topped counter.

"I didn't see her at the firemen's picnic. I meant to call and find out what happened."

Ford lit his cigar and dropped the match in the ashtray shaped like an alligator. "She's been busy packing."

Lily smiled. The white, even teeth shone against the tanned, angular face. "That's right, you're leaving. Bet you're excited."

He decided to come right out with it. The element of surprise usually worked. "Terrible thing, that business with Owen."

Lily sighed. "Awful! I called him this morning. He said he might get out tomorrow. He was very lucky."

"Good thing you weren't on the boat that night," the chief said.

"You're telling me! I almost did go by, but I heard he'd gone to Las Vegas. Didn't know he was back."

The chief felt a sudden tinge of excitement. He remembered the casino chip that had fallen out of the reporter's wallet. From Vegas.

Now that he thought of it, she seemed surprised to see it. Like she didn't know it was there. Couldn't have been in her purse too long. That meant they were in Vegas together.

Ford Baker decided to take his own gamble. He placed the postcards on the glass counter and mentioned casually, "That's right! She said they'd been in Vegas recently."

"Who?" Lily asked.

"The woman reporter. The one from New York. She was visiting Owen in the hospital when the Jap took a shot at him."

"Oh," Lily said, gathering up the postcards. The beautiful, theatrical face seemed to slump. Her hands quickly gathered up the postcards. "Will that be all?"

"Yeah."

She rang up the sale and seemed anxious for him to leave.

"Well, you take care," he said, gathering up his change.

He left, secretly pleased. Maybe the Jap missed his shot, but there was no telling what a jealous woman could accomplish.

CHAPTER TWENTY-NINE

In celebration of the feast day of his mother's saint, Santa Josefina, Marco arrived at her house in Fort Lauderdale with gifts, flowers, a fresh-killed chicken from the butcher, and the New York newspapers, which she read for the cartoons.

"You give me too much," mama protested, making her son comfortable in the cozy, screened back porch that looked out on the L-shaped swimming pool.

He welcomed these visits, which allowed him, for a few hours, to bask in warm tranquility.

Mama hugged her son and hurried back to the kitchen to keep a watchful eye on the *ropa veja* she was cooking. Beside the stove in a deep caramelized pan a creamy flan was cooling.

He had tried, without success, to have his chef duplicate her skills, but even though the ingredients were identical, and mama herself had coached him, the results were disappointing.

His shoes off, his feet hoisted comfortably on the leather footstool, Marco settled back in the recliner to watch television.

Mama came in, removed her apron, and sat in the rocking chair browsing through the newspapers.

"You work too hard," she told him. "For a man who owns a restaurant, you are too skinny. You need a wife."

He sipped the dark, Cuban coffee that his mother served in small porcelain cups the size of thimbles. "*You* never married after papa."

The old woman shrugged. "How could I? In my heart, we are still married."

He glanced at the baseball game on television that the satellite dish beamed from San Juan. It saddened him to think how much his father would have enjoyed sitting at home—with his coffee and hot chunk of buttered bread—watching a game.

The old man had been a pitcher in the Cuban league, but marriage and the parade of children forced him to seek work in the sugar fields. He retired from baseball with a 192-36 record, which, as far back as anyone could remember, still stood.

Marco found himself staring at his wedding picture, taken aboard ship. Mama had it displayed on a corner table, crowded with framed photos of relatives.

He knew that his mother had never fully accepted Kate, but it was understandable. To a Cuban mother, a daughter-in-law was a rival. Had he married Princess Grace of Monaco, mama would have remained similarly aloof.

To her credit, Kate accepted the situation. She felt that in time, when it became apparent she was there to stay, mama would relent. But she died before the thaw.

Marco gazed at the picture and remembered how the white flower in Kate's hair had scratched his cheek as he held her close. The ship's photographer had caught a sliver of the moon in the background; in the photograph it appeared like a halo above her head. He found it very appropriate.

He turned his attention back to the television, surprised to find that the game had ended and in its place was an evangelist in a dark robe with a gold collar.

"These three—greed, anger, and malice—are the three fires of the world!" the man was saying.

"Greed breeds greed. Injustice breeds injustice. Who among us will put out these fires? Who among us will lead God's mighty army and strike a blow for justice?"

"I will," Marco swore silently.

"Who among us will restore our dignity?"

"I will," Marco vowed.

"Who will carry the torch of justice and humanity?"

"I will," Marco promised.

"I say to you, hear God's tender voice. Let Him show you the path to righteousness. Let His song fill your heart and rejoice in the beauty and truth that is Jesus!

"Let Him lead you into His kingdom of glory where love and justice and truth prevail!

"Open your heart and allow Him to enter. Reach out and take His hand. For as God watched over the child David, so will He be at your side in your battle."

Mama stirred in the chair, her white hair tucked neatly in two long braids that now rested on her shoulder. Her mouth was open and the dentures made her appear to be smiling.

Marco looked at the picture of his father on the wall and told him he would not fail. He would see to it. No longer would he rely on others to fulfill his promise.

The time had come for him to act. The blow would be mighty and Godlike in its force.

Marco glanced at the newspaper that had slipped off his mother's lap to the floor.

A picture of Cardinal Thomas Ryan McHugh, wearing a chef's hat, caught his attention.

"Even God's disciples shall not be spared!" the evangelist warned.

Marco stared at the screen. He looked back at the newspaper photo.

"For as God sacrificed His only begotten son, so shall His mighty leaders relinquish their earthly throne."

Marco reached for the newspaper and held it with trembling hands.

"Only then will the message be heard—in all the nations of the universe," the minister vowed.

"It's in your hands," the minister said as a group of teenagers, dressed all in white, mounted the stage singing.

Marco read the brief article below the picture. The cardinal, in preparation for his upcoming trip to France, had visited the French embassy. The story noted that McHugh would depart immediately following Easter mass on March 27.

The newspaper fell from Marco's hands as if an unseen force had yanked it away.

March 27. His father's birthday. Marco's wedding day. The date of Kate's death.

There was no mistaking the message. God had spoken to him. A child could see it! This was no hidden message.

The cardinal had to be sacrificed. And Marco had been chosen to do the deed.

He walked into the kitchen and glanced at the calendar hanging next to the refrigerator. He lifted the page to March and saw a bold red pencil mark around March 27. Mama's shaky scrawl read: *"Cumpleano,* 70." Her husband's birthday.

Marco's skull pounded with excitement. He could hear only the angelic choir singing from the television two rooms away.

It was fitting that his father's seventieth birthday would be remembered throughout history.

His exhilaration subsided when he realized he had only a matter of weeks to carry out his destiny.

CHAPTER THIRTY

Yan-San Tokumura walked with a purposeful but leisurely stride across the airport parking lot in Key West, carrying a small bag. A camera dangled from his neck.

He eyed the vehicles with cardboard sun shields, the newest fad to enthrall the American motorist. It enabled him to steal a car easier in broad daylight. He no longer needed to crouch low on the front seat.

Yan-San felt lighter than air. His spirit was as buoyant as the afternoon breeze that swept his face. The palm trees in the distance seemed to bow in a silent welcome.

In a matter of days he would be free to resume the life he had dreamed of, fueled by Marco's generosity. Unlike the other members of the team, his wealth would not enrich a foreign government. He would spend the rest of his days in his beloved Kyoto, surrounded by family.

Three hours earlier, in an empty church pew outside Miami, Marco had wished him well on this, his final assignment, saying that perhaps one day they'd meet again.

The team had performed with the highest excellence, Marco said, and credited its success to Yan-San, who had recruited them from all parts of the United States.

The praise was nice but the money that accompanied it, now tucked safely inside the briefcase, was much more comforting as he walked briskly along the parked vehicles in the bright sunlight.

He tried four cars in the long-term lot before finding one with that day's parking ticket in the glove compartment. He checked his watch. It was a few minutes past noon. The car had been clocked in two hours ago, and with any luck its owner was high in the friendly skies, not to return for a few days.

A copy of *Forbes* magazine lay on the front seat. The cover story featured the ten richest men in the world, seven of whom were Japanese.

Yan-San took that as an omen that all would go well. Within seconds, he had the engine purring.

He drove up to the booth and paid the parking fee. He swung out to the exit ramp and headed for the local streets. He was overdressed for the Florida sun so he slipped off the jacket when he stopped at the first light.

An open package of Dorito corn chips lay on the dashboard, tempting him. It could be hours before he ate, he rationalized as he poked his fingers into the cellophane bag.

Leona Baker glanced out the window of the city bus that was taking her to the eye doctor. She looked at the man eating the salty chips and turned away quickly, with stern disapproval. She loved the damn things and her cardiologist strictly forbade them.

Yan-San veered from the main road and sought less-traveled residential streets. He pulled into a small open-air laundromat. A woman in a bathing suit with two small children was busy tossing wet clothes into the dryer. A thin black man, probably the janitor, sat dozing by one of the machines.

At the rear, a wooden fence concealed the building from neighboring homes. Yan-San drove around to the back and parked at an angle to the large metal garbage dumpster. He waited a moment, listening for any sound of approaching visitors, and quickly opened the suitcase. He removed two blue and yellow New Jersey license plates and a screwdriver. He got out of the car quickly and replaced the Florida tag, tossing it deep in the trash bin. He was proud of himself for bringing an extra set of screws. New Jersey required two plates while Florida only issued one. It was that attention to detail that was his trademark.

He drove toward Truman Avenue, searching for the intersection of Cypress, where Kuni had kept an apartment prior to his suicide plunge.

Yan-San did not mourn his death. The man failed twice to kill the sailor. He had no choice but to die.

Although Marco was a bona fide madman, Yan-San knew he was capable of inspired wisdom. For example, his naive belief that all

Japanese men looked alike. As it turned out, it was a perception shared by many Americans as well.

Eight years earlier, Marco had told him: "I want you to find eleven Japanese men, thirty to thirty-four years old, of the same height, weight, and skin tone. We will assemble an invisible army." The only required trait was the willingness to kill on command.

Yan-San had come to Marco's attention during an aborted drug buy in Camden, New Jersey, that left two dead. Yan-San whisked the Cuban safely from the scene, making an instant decision to side with Marco rather than with his partners.

It led, a year later, to Yan-San sitting on Marco's yacht off the coast of Iberia, listening silently as he outlined his plan to poison the American public.

Yan-San wondered at the time if Hitler's generals had listened as dispassionately when they first heard of the ovens.

It took Yan-San a mere seven months to carry out the order. Two men were recruited in Philadelphia, one in Tampa, one in Boise, Idaho, another in Puma, Texas, one each in San Jose, Jersey City, the Bronx, Atlanta, Reno, and Cleveland.

To each were sent identical dark blue business suits and a matching wardrobe, down to the socks and shoes. A hairstylist was dispatched to each man's home to unify the cut and hair color.

One was excused early in the planning stage when he suffered a torn knee ligament, resulting in a noticeable limp. Another was removed after he was arrested for drunken driving and his fingerprints recorded. A third was excused when it was discovered that he had a male lover. Homosexuality was an aberration to Marco.

When the "soldiers" gathered for their first meeting aboard Marco's private Falcon Jet, even Yan-San marveled at the results. He felt surrounded by mirrors.

Precise instructions were given regarding American slang and modes of behavior. It would not do to antagonize strangers. Americans tended to remember rudeness.

Before arriving in any city, the soldier often knew more about its history than did its natives.

Yan-San found the small house on Cypress easily enough, even though none of the details—the avocado tree on the front lawn, the striped metal window awnings, the wood-carved mailbox at the curb—had been written down.

Yan-San drove by the house slowly, paying particular attention to the older man, no doubt the owner, who pushed a loud lawn mower across the front yard.

The pink-shingled two-story house sat far back from the street. The side entrance to the ground-floor apartment, along the driveway, was clearly visible, as was the doormat where Yan-San knew an extra set of keys was taped to the underside.

He drove around the block checking for any restricted parking zones. He searched the backyards for dogs and fences. He quickly mapped an escape route, should one be required.

A school bus lumbered down the tree-shaded street and Yan-San automatically recorded the time. He glanced at the mailboxes along the street and noted that they appeared empty. He would have to learn the delivery time.

He was confident he'd be in Kyoto within days.

CHAPTER THIRTY-ONE

Owen waited till the nurse collected the lunch tray and picked up his cigarettes and lighter. He strolled out of the room, nodding at Officer Powanda, who sat doing a crossword puzzle.

"I'm gonna walk down to the TV room," Owen said, yanking at the string belt on the pajama bottoms.

The officer glanced at him uninterestedly and went back to the penciled squares.

It was just minutes past two in the afternoon. The elevators discharged clumps of visitors.

Owen strolled to the end of the corridor, and as expected, the patient lounge, with the box TV and folding chairs, was empty.

He closed the door halfway and lifted the glass ashtray from its bulky round pedestal. He dug his hand into the circular canister. His fingers closed on the plastic bag and quickly removed it.

He stuffed the bag inside his waistband and let the pajama shirt dangle over the bulge.

He walked from the room and glanced down the corridor at Powanda, who was now chatting with a nurse. Neither looked his way.

Owen darted beneath the Exit sign to the staircase and came out on the second floor. He hurried to the men's room, entered the first stall, and took the clothes out of the paper bag.

He changed quickly and discarded the bag and pajamas in the wastecan. He hurried from the room, down a flight of stairs, and out the main entrance, where Earl's pickup truck was waiting.

The old man gunned the engine and whipped the truck to the stairs just as Owen's feet touched the pavement. The sailor had barely jumped in before the truck was coughing down the driveway and into the stream of traffic.

"Everything go okay?" Earl asked, keeping an eye cocked to the side view mirror.

"Piece of cake," Owen smiled.

Once out on the highway, he felt safe enough to ask, "How's Geraldine?"

"Good," Earl said. "I got her fixed up for the game tonight."

"My car ready?"

The old man nodded, "Picked it up this morning. Bumper had to put a new lock on the trunk. Cops really did a job on it."

Owen rolled up his shirt sleeve and welcomed the sun on his arm. He yanked off the bandage and let it fall out the window. The raw, puckered skin under the zigzag stitching stung in the hot breeze.

"Got something for you," Earl said, sliding an envelope across the seat.

Owen tore it open and found a room key on a plastic holder stamped: Bay Villa Motel. Room 211.

"Friend owed me a favor," Earl explained. "Drove up there yesterday. You got the room for a week."

Owen looked at the skeletal form in the green khaki shirt and patched pants. Did he imagine it or did Earl look older? The face appeared even more sunken.

"Your place isn't safe. Not sure mine is either," the old man said. "I went to your bank." He gestured toward the glove compartment.

The sailor didn't bother to count it. He stuffed the money in his shirt pocket. "Thanks." He reached behind the seat to a tub of ice filled with just-caught fish and beer cans. He palmed a beer and snapped it open. "After today, you're retired from this," he told Earl.

"Shit!" the old man grumbled. "You ain't got no business in it yourself. You had any sense you'd dump it in Ford's lap. Let him deal with the fucking Japs. You and that gal are just advertising for trouble." The old man sucked on his pipe, making loud hollow sounds.

He'd never spoken so directly to Owen before. He felt uncomfortable doing it, but he knew he'd feel worse if he was killed. "You in love with her or something?"

"You've been out in the sun too long," the sailor laughed. "I'd sooner tangle with a crocodile."

The old man didn't say anything, but found himself silently annoyed when Owen began humming to the radio. What he could find to sing about with cops and murderers chasing him was beyond Earl's comprehension.

CHAPTER THIRTY-TWO

"What the hell do you mean, gone?" the chief yelled into the phone.

"I . . . I . . . was in the bathroom. Came back and he was gone. Doc said he'd released him this morning. Said you knew about it. Bastard snuck out wearing pajamas."

"Put that son of a bitch doctor on the phone. Right now," the chief ordered.

"Yes, sir." Officer Powanda threw the receiver on the empty hospital bed and ran down the corridor, frantically poking his head in all the rooms. He found the doctor and dragged him away from a patient.

"His medical condition warranted release," the doctor told Ford Baker. "Hospital beds are scarce."

"So are cops!" the chief thundered. "I can't be assigning cars to cruise around the whole town lookin' for him. You were supposed to notify me."

"I have a hospital filled with sick people. I don't have time to play cops and robbers," the doctor said sharply.

"Put the officer back on!"

The doctor handed the phone to Powanda and marched out of the room.

"I'm here, chief."

"Weren't you told not to leave your post until someone relieved you?"

"I was only gone two seconds! He had on pajamas. Told me he was gonna go watch TV in the patient lounge."

"I'm writing you up!" the chief roared. "It's going in your fucking file. It's gonna be there the rest of your fucking, miserable life. You understand that?"

"Yes, sir." The officer cupped the phone tightly to his ear, fearful that the nurses across the hall could hear the raving maniac.

"I have another job for you. You fuck this one up—turn in the badge! Got that?"

"Yes, sir!" Powanda stood at attention, not sure the old bastard couldn't see through the phone.

"Find out that doctor's name. Call it in—immediately—with the license plate number of his car. Can you handle that?"

"Yes, sir."

The chief hung up and flung his coffee cup across the room. The Styrofoam cup slid off the wall and dribbled brown liquid across the PBA clothing allowance notice. He stormed out of his office and marched to the sergeant's desk.

"Powanda is going to call in a motor vehicle plate. Belongs to a doctor in town. His wife just reported it stolen. Send it out over the radio. Every shift. Tell the men to exercise caution. We're dealing with a junkie here who goes around impersonating doctors. Probably stole his wallet and ID, too. No matter what story he gives, detain the bastard. Tell him on orders of the mayor."

The chief walked back to his office grinning. God, sometimes the job was so much fun he could hardly contain himself. Not only would he nail the prick but he'd get the mayor also. Once the doctor was hauled in, the mayor could kiss off his fancy campaign contributions.

No one held a grudge worse than a doctor, unless it was a greedy lawyer, and it wouldn't take much doing, over at the country club where the morons hung out, for one to spread the word that the mayor was an idiot.

Hell, Ford had been preaching that gospel for years.

CHAPTER THIRTY-THREE

Mae's boarding house, it was rumored, was haunted by a naked ghost.

The original owner of the sprawling gothic structure was a sea captain who had it built in 1887 for his bride. He hung himself in the attic, it was whispered, because she gave birth to a negro child. The wife was never seen again, fueling gossip that her body lay buried in the yard.

The gingerbread house with its fancy lacy wood trim sat vacant for years, till a Yankee railroad baron purchased it for his family. The current owner, Mae, grew up in the house where her grandmother worked as a maid.

If there was a ghost, locals said, it knew better than to mess with Mae.

It was dark, almost a quarter to eight, as Geraldine drove to the poker game. She was tired. And anxious. Owen had called earlier to say he was okay. That's it. He wouldn't even tell her where he was staying, brushing off her concern with, "I'll be in touch."

She returned his coolness with, "Fine," and hung up. She replayed the conversation in her mind as she searched for street signs in the quiet residential area.

She found the house on a secluded dead end. The large structure, with its circular wooden porch and overhanging chiseled carvings, was impressive even in the darkness. A solitary street lamp illuminated as high as the front steps. Two amber lights at either side of the front door revealed most of the porch, till it curved out of sight.

Geraldine parked and gave her hair a quick check in the mirror. She was wearing a beige linen skirt and vest over a pink blouse that she'd bought at Cecelia's insistence at Sears. Her hair was caught tightly in a bun and she'd kept the makeup to a minimum.

She was nervous as she hurried up the stairs, careful to stay in the shadows. She was always apprehensive at any poker game, but the stakes here were more than just money.

Geraldine stood by the screen door, not knowing if she should enter unannounced. An elderly couple sat at a checkerboard in the living room. A Perry Como record played from one of the open upper windows.

She rapped softly on the edge of the door and heard one of the checker players yell, "Mae!"

"It's open," a woman called.

Geraldine entered and was greeted by a robust black woman swathed in an African print robe and pink sneakers. Her hair was twisted in thin braids that hugged the scalp. Geraldine liked her on sight. "Mae?"

"You must be Geraldine!" The woman hugged her with flabby arms. "They're waiting on you, honey."

Geraldine followed her past the parlor and the dining room where a young woman cleared off the dishes. The table seated twelve, and judging from the amount of china and glassware, all of the chairs had been occupied.

"I never knew Earl had a niece," Mae said. "But then, he don't talk much, does he?"

"No," Geraldine smiled. "Not a whole lot."

A television sat, on but unwatched, in the den where a silvery cat slept on a wicker table. Another cat stretched out near the banister at the foot of the stairway.

"Earl tell ya how we operate?" Mae asked. She paused to dust a picture frame with the hem of her robe. The aroma of floral incense swirled about the house. "We cut a dollar out of every pot and five from the last hand. That entitles you to food and drink. Most of my people are in bed by midnight so we ask you keep it quiet at that hour."

She led her to a room behind the staircase and slid open a heavy mahogany door that revealed a group of men sitting around a table.

"This here's Geraldine," she told them, "and don't none of you get smart with her." To Geraldine she whispered, "They're pussy-cats," and dashed off to answer a ringing phone.

"Hi," a tall, thin man in his fifties, wearing white slacks and a blue golf shirt, extended his hand. "I'm Patrick Shirley but everyone just calls me Shirl. Glad to know you."

The other men at the poker table stood up and introduced themselves.

There was Bumper, a tow truck operator; Rudy, a retired mailman; Herman, a bartender; and Phil, an auto parts salesman.

Her nervousness vanished.

"Thanks for letting me sit in," Geraldine said, taking the one open spot at the table. They had diplomatically seated her away from Bumper's cigar. The roly-poly man was aptly named, and his infectious grin was heartening. She felt very at ease, for just a moment forgetting why she was there.

"A drink?" Phil asked.

He gestured toward a long table at the opposite end of the room covered by a white linen cloth and supporting an array of booze that would have impressed even Hal Landry.

Funny, the way that man always popped to mind. She wondered if it would always be that way.

"A beer would be nice."

The men smiled and the atmosphere immediately relaxed.

The table was laden with platters of sandwiches, salads, cake, pies, fried chicken wings, fruit, and a bucket of barbecued spare ribs.

"This must be that famous southern hospitality," Geraldine observed.

"Mae believes in doing it up right," Phil agreed.

Herman quickly helped himself to a sandwich and didn't bother to reach for a plate. "If you're around Thanksgiving, Mae puts out a whole turkey with stuffin' and yams. Christmas she does a pork."

"Food's food," Rudy said. "Let's play."

Six decks of unopened cards sat in a pile in the middle of the table.

"I'm ready," Geraldine said, taking some money from her purse and laying it on the table.

"Then let the madness begin," Shirley said as he closed the sliding door.

An hour later, Geraldine was down over a hundred and had yet to see better than two pair.

But she did have a handle on her partners. Bumper was a wild man who bet on anything; Phil was conservative and never called a bet unless he was loaded up; Shirley never raised, Rudy tended to bluff, and Herman was quick to fold. But if he didn't, he had it.

Two hours into the game, wondering how she'd ever pay Owen back, she took in a pot with a heart flush and won the next four hands.

She started to unwind. Her relaxation index rose in direct proportion to the chips stacked next to her cigarettes. She casually inquired, "Have any of you seen an oriental man in town the past couple of days? A tourist."

"Alive?" Shirley said, producing the laughter he anticipated.

"I gather that's exactly what she meant," Bumper said, opening for five.

"Shirl's the local funeral director," Herman explained. "After a while you get used to his jokes. They're all . . . deadly."

"One I saw was very dead," Shirley said, squeezing his cards slowly with his thumb. "Went through a window at the hospital."

Geraldine's knees shook under the table. She tried to focus her eyes on the cards in her hand but her mind raced wildly. "I read about it. Was he from around here?"

"Philadelphia," Shirley answered. "Jesus, Phil, you deal nothing but garbage." He threw his cards in the center of the table.

"Tough," his opponent laughed. "See your five," he told Bumper, "and raise you five."

"You better have 'em 'cause I ain't running," Bumper said.

Geraldine had to ask what the bet was and matched it even though she couldn't remember what she held.

"Did the family claim the body?" she asked.

"Cops don't know who he is. We're not even sure he's from Philadelphia. But he was wearing a medical alert bracelet from a hospital there."

"I'll take two," Bumper told Phil. He nervously relit the cigar. The pot was turning out to be the biggest of the night and all he needed was a little help.

"Hope that's not the guy you're looking for," said Rudy.

"No," she answered quickly. "I was shopping at the mall yesterday and some guy rear-ended me. Busted a taillight, dented the gas tank.

And took off! I don't want to report it to the insurance company. I'd like to find him, have him pay for it."

"How you know he's a tourist?" the fireman asked. He held up two fingers for two cards.

Geraldine pretended to study her cards intently while attempting to come up with a plausible answer. It seemed to her that everyone was waiting—and staring.

"When I jumped out of my car and ran over to his, I saw a lot of maps on the dashboard. Then he took off," she said matter-of-factly. "I'll open for ten."

Everyone but Phil dropped out.

"Full house," he announced.

She checked her cards quickly and found herself staring at two threes, a four, a six and a jack. "Take it," she told him.

She leaned across the table and buried her cards deep in the discard pile. If anyone saw them they'd know instantly she didn't belong in that hand.

"I'll keep an eye out for him," Bumper told her. "I'm on the road all day long. Besides, I know most of the Chinese families in town, not that we have that many."

Geraldine scribbled Earl's number on a napkin. "Call me at my uncle's."

"We get a lot of orientals coming into the restaurant," Herman said. The men laughed. "If you want Geraldine's number, why don't you come right out and ask for it?" Rudy said.

Herman scowled and picked up his new cards. They must have been as ugly as the last ones, going by his expression.

Bumper examined his cards and announced, "The price of poker just went up."

"That bracelet. Was the guy sick?" she asked.

"He was sick all right," Phil cut in. "Heard he was dressed like a woman. One of the cops told me. They didn't put that in the paper."

"Who the hell cares? Deal! I'm down seventy bucks," Rudy grumbled.

"That's not all," Shirley smiled. "He dyed his hair."

Geraldine coughed on the cigarette smoke.

The funeral director shrugged. "His hair was black to begin with. No gray that I could see, but it was definitely dyed."

"Doesn't make sense," she thought aloud.
"We talking or playing cards here?" Phil said. "I open for three."
Bumper had to remind her, "It's up to you."
Her mind was on the Philadelphia corpse.

CHAPTER THIRTY-FOUR

Shortly past 1:00 A.M., when Mae knocked on the door to ask if they needed anything before she went to bed, Owen drove his car slowly, with the headlights off, to the parking area alongside the pier.

He cut the motor and allowed the car to ease silently into a slot by the administration building.

The single-story brick structure served as a post office/clearing house/storage space for waterside residents. Two elderly sisters manned the office during the day and a security guard patroled the area at night. More often than not he sat at the desk watching television, which is where he was tonight as Owen crept out of the car silently.

The night was quiet but for the rhythmic lapping of the water striking the jetties. He heard an anguished infantile wail, but he quickly realized it was a cat's mating cry. Still, it unnerved him.

He crept around the building and mounted the rear steps of the wide red oak deck. He crossed quickly to the far side, darting about the picnic tables and vending machines.

He could see the security guard asleep with his feet on the desk, next to a Burger King bag.

Owen grabbed the side of the flag pole at the edge of the porch and climbed to the top railing of the three-slatted fence that surrounded the deck. The pole was slippery with mist and he lost his footing. He grabbed the rail as he tumbled forward and threw his ankle around the pole, stopping his fall, his head inches from the stairs.

He looked beyond the thick shrubbery at the foot of the pier and spotted the police car hidden in the mangrove bushes. A cop sat alone in the front seat smoking a cigarette. Owen was close enough to see the red tip burning like a tiny beacon.

He got down quietly and hurried along the side of the building.

A rat jumped out of a garbage can and ran across his feet. Owen slammed himself against wall, his elbow striking the window pane with what sounded like a roar to him. He held his breath waiting to hear the cop burst from his vehicle, but the only sound was his own heavy breathing.

He waited two full minutes. He thought he'd heard the security guard stir but couldn't be sure. When he felt it was safe, he darted into a cluster of trees, close enough to the water to hear a fish splash.

He quickly undressed and bundled his clothes into a ball, which he stuffed into the crevice between the thick roots of a tree. Concealed by the bushes, crouching low to the ground, he made his way toward the dock and silently slipped into the water.

He swam under the dock and around the bobbing boats. The salt water stung the stitches on his arm as he made his way toward *Nathan.* She was four slips down on the pier and he had to swim wide around the monstrous houseboat kept by his neighbors. The thing was an eyesore in daylight and now a treacherous obstacle in the slimy, oil-slick water.

A dead sea gull floated in his path and he made no move to circle it. He merely pushed it aside.

Just as he got a clear view of *Nathan*'s hull, his neighbor, Frank, came out on deck, and dumped a bucket of water over the side of the houseboat. Owen ducked quickly to avoid the splash.

The man retreated and Owen swam on, his hands slipping as he reached for the ornamental railing just above the water on *Nathan*'s hull. He inched his way around the boat and sprang forward, latching onto the side of the pier. He hoisted himself over the dock and stepped quietly onto the deck.

He couldn't see the police car, but neither did he see anyone running toward the slip.

Owen entered the cabin and threw off his wet shorts, he hobbled about naked, and cold, till he found a towel and some clothes.

The blue lights of a Coast Guard cutter dotted the horizon, but it was too distant to pose any danger.

He felt his way in the darkness. The only light was from a pole lamp trained on the water. He hurried to the head, where he crouched down near the toilet and removed a floorboard. It ripped away with a noise that sounded like a gunshot.

He dug his hands in the deep recess. His fingers closed around a plastic bag and yanked it from its mooring. He reached in and removed the gun.

CHAPTER THIRTY-FIVE

Yan-San Tokumura crouched quietly in his car across the street from the marina.

He, too, had spotted the police car earlier in the evening while pretending to take pictures of the sunset from the dock.

A routine call to the hospital told him that the patient had been released.

Similar calls to hotels and motels had failed to turn up the woman. It was of little concern. If he found him, he'd find her.

As Marco had wisely observed, "A cook cooks, a writer writes."

He could have added, "A sailor sails."

Yan-San did.

His patience was rewarded when shortly after 1:00 A.M. he spotted the red Chrysler, headlights off, pull into the dock.

It was almost too easy, he thought, smiling.

Now it was only a matter of time before he led him to the woman.

CHAPTER THIRTY-SIX

It was five-thirty the following day when Owen parked behind Leon's Tavern. There were only four cars in the lot, but he had to jockey for space in the cramped quarters.

A slice of an alley separated the dilapidated bar from the poultry store next door. The stench of live chickens was enough to make one flee—even into Leon's.

He didn't like the place, or the owner, but it was well hidden and besides, Gabe had picked it.

A cruising police car would not spot his vehicle from the main road. Tourists were not lured inside by its rundown facade or the single blue sign on the grimy window advertising Beer on ap.

Despite having spent the night in his car, Owen was feeling good. He'd showered at Earl's and called the redhead, who happily reported winning three bills.

They agreed to meet at nine behind the bleachers at the high school baseball field.

Owen entered through Leon's rear doorway, ducking his head below the dingy fishnets trailing from the ceiling. The phony nautical motif, with rusted anchors and bloated starfish, was another reason he avoided the bar.

That, and the smell of stale cat piss.

Leon's was a throwback to waterfront saloons, the kind Jack London wrote about and that everyone else thought was glamorous. He'd seen enough of them in his years at sea. They reminded him of being broke and lonely.

Owen took a seat at the far end of the bar and said hello to blind Joe, sitting near the entrance, his Seeing Eye dog asleep at the foot of the stool. He ordered a bottle of beer for sanitary reasons. Leon didn't know from clean glasses.

Behind him, the jukebox played Kenny Rogers's "Lady." Two fishermen that he recognized from the bait store stood off to the side tossing darts. A wall fan shuffled the hot, pungent air, positioned not to sweep the dollars off the bar.

Leon, a surly Armenian with black tufts of hair sprouting from all parts of his body, sat behind the bar inspecting a mound of pennies with a magnifying glass. He'd been doing it ever since anyone could remember, and the joke was that by now he'd forgotten what he was looking for and only did it so he wouldn't have to talk to customers. Which was fine with most. They only came there because his shots were the cheapest in town.

An hour later, and at least ten hearings of "Lady," Gabe still hadn't showed.

The blind man tapped his way to the jukebox, stepping on his dog's tail in the process. The dog didn't seem to mind. Probably happened forty times a day.

Owen looked at the clock in the shape of a diving suit over the bar and saw it was almost seven. Soon he'd have to meet Geraldine. The prospect brightened his mood.

Finally the door opened and Gabe slid onto the stool next to him.

"What the hell took you so long?" he asked the cop. Gabe was wearing a Dolphins shirt and dungarees over sneakers. His baseball cap read Gilmore's Paints, the name of his Little League team.

"Car broke down. Got it towed to the police garage. Then I had to wait for a ride. Told Maryanne I'd be home early. Two beers and I gotta go."

Owen was pissed. "Can't you call her?"

"Hey, I ain't seen the kids all week! Thanks to you, the chief has me running around like a maniac. Only reason he gave me the night off is that with all my overtime, I'm makin' more this week than he is."

Owen told Leon to bring them a beer.

"How you feeling?" the cop asked.

"Good. What do you have for me?"

The young cop glanced about the room and lowered his voice, "If the chief ever found out—"

"Hell with him! Bastard trashed my car. He's got cops hiding by my boat. What the fuck did I ever do to him?"

Gabe hunched closer. "If he even knew I was here talking to you . . . he wants your ass."

The lieutenant felt guilty talking about the chief, almost expecting him to pop through the door and haul him out. Gabe didn't even know why he'd agreed to meet Owen. Maybe because he felt bad about personally trashing his car.

"What have you got for me?" Owen persisted.

The cop made wet circles on the bar with the beer bottle. "We're talking about my job here."

The conversation was momentarily halted by the scraping sound of the back door opening. It was a natural reaction, since only regulars used the rear entrance.

Owen spotted Lily before she saw him. She took a seat next to Joe and reached down to pat the dog. She acknowledged the sailor with a slight smile.

She must have seen Owen's car when he drove in. Her store was across from the alley.

Surprisingly, he was glad to see her. She looked great. The dark eyes in the tawny skin were set off by the white halter blouse. He'd known many Greek women while stationed in Athens, but few had that hungry, feline demeanor that he found irresistible.

Owen told Leon to put her drink on his tab and she pretended not to hear.

"I don't have much," Gabe told him.

"I'll take whatever you have."

The cop turned his back to the others. "Look, I don't want to hit this too hard, but if the chief ever found out, I'm through."

"You made your point. Twice."

Gabe nodded. "Guy drove to the hospital in a stolen car. Swiped it from in front of a bank. Belonged to one of the tellers."

The two dart players finished their game and left, stopping to whisper something to the blind man.

"She reported it stolen two days before he jumped out your window. I personally checked the car with the owner, and the only thing we found was a local map he could've picked up anywhere and a book of matches from a restaurant in Miami. Owner said she hasn't been to Miami in ten years."

"Maybe her husband—?" Owen asked.

Gabe shook his head. He remained standing with his elbow leaning on the bar. "She's a widow. No one drives the car except her."

"Anything circled on the map?"

"Nothing."

"What restaurant?"

The cop reached into his pocket and removed a small notebook. "El Rincon del Cuba on Palmetto Street." He tore off the spiral sheet and placed it on the bar.

Owen tucked it away in his shirt pocket. "What else?"

"Guy had absolutely no ID. We found his clothes behind the pipes in the boiler room. We figure he changed there into the nurse's uniform. We lifted a couple of prints and ran 'em off to the FBI but that takes awhile."

Owen seriously doubted that anything would come of it. Whoever they were, they'd made few mistakes from Cleveland to New York. There was no reason to expect they'd suddenly get careless.

"Any idea who the guy was?"

"Negative. We checked every hotel and motel. An oriental guy would tend to stand out."

"What about the body? The medical examiner turn up anything?"

The lieutenant shrugged. "He's out of town so the body went over to Shirley's. He's slower than shit. We haven't even seen his report yet. But from what he said on the phone, don't look for any surprises."

Owen stared at his drink. "That's just great."

"He did mention something," Gabe said. "The guy had some kind of disease. One of those alphabet Latin things with a hundred letters. He had to take medicine for it every day. It'll be in the report, if we ever get it."

For a sickly man the bastard put up a hell of fight on the boat, Owen told him.

"He have any bruises on him?" Owen was sure he'd gotten in a few blows.

"Like I said, we have to wait for the report."

Owen jumped when Joe misjudged the rim of the bar and his beer stein crashed to the floor. A sure sign he'd had enough to drink.

Gabe grinned, "A little nervous these days."

Owen caught Lily's smile and looked away, feeling foolish.

Gabe threw some money on the bar. "Gotta go."

"Thanks for coming."

"That's okay," Gabe smiled. "I'm doing it for Luther." He yelled down the bar at Leon to call him a cab.

"Forget it," Owen told the bartender. He reached for his car keys. "Take mine. I'll get a ride home with Lily."

"You sure?"

"Go ahead," Owen told him. "Keep it till you get yours fixed."

Gabe grabbed up the keys. "Catch you later." He hurried away.

Owen focused his attention on Lily, who was half-turned, facing the television set over the pool table. He tried to recall the last time they'd been together. A year? Two? Three? There'd been midnight cruises, weekends in St. Thomas, X-rated movies on the VCR, late night suppers on her terrace. Then she started talking marriage. Asking where he'd been. It ended with arguments. Angry letters. Threats. Telephone hang-ups at three in the morning, checking if he was home.

He watched as Lily picked up her drink, said something to Joe, and walked toward him. Her smile said she knew she looked good.

Owen slid his cigarettes and drink aside to make room for her.

She was smiling and tossing her dark hair about her bare shoulders when the explosion ripped the door off the hinges and flung it across the room, striking the jukebox.

Lily was blown off her feet and slammed against the pool table.

Joe toppled backward and fell on the dog.

Leon spun like a frenzied ballet dancer into the row of liquor bottles propped along the mirrored wall. The glass disintegrated into a shower of silvery pellets.

The beer drum exploded, sending a gusher of foam to the ceiling.

Owen was propelled across the room, crashing into the wall rack of cue sticks. He knew before he hit the ground that Gabe was dead.

CHAPTER THIRTY-SEVEN

Geraldine drove past the entrance of James Monroe High School and took the second road, marked by a large illuminated sign listing the baseball schedule.

She followed the white arrows implanted curbside on the grass to the parking lot. A vacant orange school bus sat alone. She looked around for Owen's car and realized she had no idea what he drove. It didn't matter, hers was the only car in the area.

She looked through the windshield to the skeletal outline of the bleachers, far in the middle of the field. If he was here, he was well hidden. She decided to wait in the car. He must've seen the headlights. She kept the engine running and half-listened to the country-western singer on the radio.

Geraldine adjusted the outside mirror, positioning it to give her a clear view of the road behind her. No headlights were visible.

The night was clear and quiet. Lightning bugs flashed about a few feet off the ground.

She rolled down the window, hoping to hear Owen's approach. He had to be here. Somewhere. Wasn't the military famous for punctuality? The digital clock above the radio read 9:04.

Then she remembered. He'd said the bleachers. He was probably hiding there somewhere. He'd probably left his car on the road and walked over.

Geraldine turned off the engine, grabbed her purse from the seat, and got out of the car. She marched directly to the ballfield. Her high heels immediately sank in the mushy ground.

All around her, unseen sprinklers shot thin streams of water at her ankles. She dashed around the "phhhttt" pulsating jets and made it behind home plate. The hem of her dress clung to the back of her knees, plastered by the water.

She half-stumbled up the first wooden platform, banging her knee in the process.

Geraldine climbed to the third row and walked carefully to the center, selecting a vantage point that included the parking lot and the main road.

Where the hell was he?

A slight breeze touched her bare legs. It felt nice. Back in New York, the people were shoveling out from under nine inches of snow. And as usual, there was no heat in her building. One of the messages on the answering machine when she called that morning was the super announcing there was no hot water due to boiler repairs.

Sitting here, looking out over the dark baseball field, with only the sound of the water sprinklers spritzing the air, she felt strangely at peace. Partly because Owen would soon be at her side. Also the quiet. And the soothing aroma of wet grass.

A palm tree nodded at the night like an overgrown feather duster. A host of stars dotted the cloudless sky. What harm could possibly intrude in such a serene setting? Even the chirping crickets, so alien to her normal environment, failed to arouse any anxiety.

Geraldine lit a cigarette and blew the smoke into the night. A single light over the centerfield fence shone on a rolled-up log of tarpaulin. The rest of the ballfield was bathed in darkness, only the white base lines dimly visible.

She leaned back and rested her elbows on the bleacher bench behind. A welcome breeze licked at her neck.

Two headlights turned from the main road and traveled up the path past the wooden signboard.

She tried not to get her hopes up. It could be someone lost, looking to make a U-turn.

The car was moving slowly. Geraldine stood up on the bleacher to get a better view. The headlights bounced over the speed bump. The car turned slowly toward the lot and stopped on the other side of the school bus, blocking her vision.

Geraldine quickly descended to the ground just as she heard the car door slam closed.

She walked toward the figure now moving rapidly in her direction.

"Hey!" she waved. "What took you so long?"

The form moved through the darkness at a fast pace. She tried to see his face, but he was still too far away.

"You're late, fella."

The dark figure was now within a few feet. Geraldine could almost see his face. She started to run forward and stopped. She gasped. "What are you doing here?"

The figure halted.

"There's been a bad accident," Earl said.

CHAPTER THIRTY-EIGHT

The next morning, a young black man in a beige suit and tan, pointed-toe alligator shoes sat waiting in Chief Baker's office.

Outside in the corridor, an army of reporters and two television crews shouted questions just as the chief stormed through the door yelling, "Get out of my way!" He slammed the door shut and confronted the man.

"You still here?" he asked LeRoy Thomas. "I told you you're wasting your time."

The chief went behind his desk. "I'm busy, LeRoy, what do you want?"

The young attorney, who had graduated summa cum laude from Rutgers University and had turned down a prestigious offer from a top Wall Street firm, sighed audibly.

Forget the fact that he was in *Who's Who,* a Jaycee man of the year for the State of Florida, or that he was due to argue before the United States Supreme Court in behalf of an AIDS victim . . .

Sitting across from Ford Baker, he could still recall the sheer terror of being seventeen that night by the railroad yards.

He and Yolanda Clark were going to town in the backseat when the chief, then a sergeant, shone the flashlight in the car.

It was difficult, LeRoy discovered, to intimidate a man who had nailed you ass-naked. But he tried.

"You can't hold him forever," he said.

"I can detain him seventy-two hours as a material witness and then charge him with manslaughter and bind him over without bail until the grand jury convenes."

"Horseshit," LeRoy said.

The chief shrugged. "So sue me, counselor. But that motherfucker don't walk."

"Look," LeRoy sighed, "I don't know the man. Met him for the first time half an hour ago. I'm here as a favor to Lily. I talked to the guy. He seems normal enough."

"He had a goddamn dog that was an alcoholic! You call that normal?"

"He could be Ted Bundy for all I know, but unless you're prepared to formally charge him with a crime, I have to, in all fairness, ask you to release him."

"Fuck off."

LeRoy inspected his manicured fingertips. "Is that your official response? Because if it is, I'd like to get a stenographer in here to record it."

"Don't give me bullshit lawyer talk, LeRoy!" the chief thundered. "I knew your mama when she was bagging groceries at Kash 'n Karry and your brothers were stealing doughnuts from the bakery. I used to carry your daddy home when they'd run him out of the pool hall. So just 'cause you went up north to school and got white women shacked all over town, don't give me your shit!"

The phone rang and the chief reached over, yanked the cord from its innards, and flung it off the desk.

"Gabe is dead and that son of a bitch sitting in the basement is gonna fucking rot in there till he talks."

LeRoy Thomas, sporting a six-hundred-dollar suit and two-hundred-and-fifty-dollar shoes, suddenly felt ass-naked again.

"He's as much a victim as Gabe."

"That so? Then how come he's alive and Gabe's over at Shirley's in a plastic bag! That is—pieces of him!"

LeRoy didn't have an answer, just a powerful urge to wring Lily's neck.

The chief tilted back in his chair and took a cigar from his pocket. He jammed it in his mouth, not bothering to light it.

"Do me a favor, LeRoy. Get the fuck out of here."

The young attorney leaned over and picked up his French leather briefcase.

"And if I see your face here again, I'll have you and your girlfriend up on fornication charges. It's still in the books, counselor, look it up."

LeRoy stood and headed for the door just as an officer dashed into the room, red-faced and huffing.

"He's gone, chief!"

"Who?"

"The prisoner."

CHAPTER THIRTY-NINE

Geraldine never slept. She sat up all night, waiting for the sun, anticipating Earl's call.

Her first instinct had been to rush to the emergency room, but the old man quickly forbade it, saying the place was crawling with cops and reporters. He had managed to see Owen for a few moments and assured her he was okay. Earl went directly to the ballfield from the hospital.

He brought a message from Owen that as soon as he got out they'd meet at Bay Villa, forty miles north.

Then just before midnight, while she was sitting alone on the porch trying to decide what to do next, Earl called with the news of Owen's arrest.

Geraldine had her head in the sink washing her hair when the phone rang the next time. She reached for the towel and sopped the suds off her face.

"Howdy."

She immediately recognized Wagon Master. The voice sounded strained. "Something wrong?" she asked.

"Remember that batch of fresh paint I told you was downtown last night?"

"What about it?"

"It peeled off."

Geraldine gripped the side of the sink.

"What?"

"Went AWOL."

She dabbed nervously at the wet strands of hair plastered to her cheeks. "Jesus!"

The old man coughed. "You know that place we talked about?"

Geraldine forced herself to remember. It was a hotel. No, a motel up the coast. Spanish. "Vaguely. It'll come back to me."

"They'll be needing some fresh paint. Tonight. After it gets dark," he told her.

"All right," she answered.

"You take care."

He hung up.

She stood for a moment staring at the phone. Outside, she could hear Cecelia hosing down the back porch. The chickens squawked angrily as the blonde woman laughed and splashed them with water.

Geraldine held the towel to her head and raced out to the backyard.

CHAPTER FORTY

Yan-San Tokumura loved America. He knew he would miss it when he left.

He especially loved Americans and their open friendliness. Occasionally you'd run into a repulsive oaf, but by and large they were a free-wheeling, simple-minded bunch.

Children, really. With a child's willingness to please.

Take for instance the two senior citizens he was sitting next to now on a bench outside the post office.

Wearing a white polo shirt and white linen slacks, Yan-San had stopped to ask directions and got caught up in conversation.

The two elderly men, obviously long-time friends, made room for him on the bench, eager to hear a new voice, especially one with such an unusual accent.

Yan-San inquired about the best fishing spots and they asked him the price of a meal in Tokyo.

"I heard you can spend six hundred dollars just for two people at a regular restaurant. And nothing fancy, at that."

The other couldn't believe it, pointing out that his first car only cost $200.

Which led the conversation to the car-bombing that was on the front page of the paper on Yan-San's lap.

"A person ain't safe in their own backyard anymore," the senior citizen opined.

Yan-San asked if they knew any of the people who'd been sitting in the bar when it happened.

"Hell, yeah!"

The oldtimers, eager to impress the tourist, tried to outdo each other in supplying details. One could hardly wait for the other to stop talking.

Yan-San learned that Joe, a blind man, was in the hospital with a broken hip. His sister was watching over the dog, who got cut with some glass but was basically okay. The bartender got hit the worst. Lost some teeth. His foot was broken where the beer keg crushed it. One eye was cut bad and they didn't know if he'd lose it or not.

His biggest worry was financial. He didn't carry any insurance.

Lily, they said, was damn lucky to be alive. She'd been sitting right by the door a few minutes before it happened. She had some bruises but nothing serious. Hell, she opened the store today, so she couldn't be too bad.

"Her boyfriend got the worst. It was his car that got blown to hell."

Yan-San immediately perked up. "Does she have a dress shop?"

Naw. Gifts. Souvenirs. Junk like that. Up the block from the bar, in fact. Right there on Front Street.

Yan-San told them he might've seen her. He went into a shop in that area to buy film. Big, blonde woman?

Lily? No. She's big, all right. Real tall. But black hair. Lots of it. Looks Indian, kinda.

Yan-San sat with the men until they left to have lunch at the VFW Hall. They invited him along but he declined politely.

Instead he walked to a corner phone booth and dug in his pocket for the yellow page he'd ripped out of a telephone directory that morning.

He scanned the heading Automobile Rental, and dropped a coin into the phone.

Using an excitable tone, but not loud enough to be overheard by pedestrians, he told the woman who answered he was stranded in the Palm Gate shopping mall and couldn't locate his wife or their rented car.

They became separated while in the store and if he could only find the car. . . . He couldn't remember the license number, or even the color. She rented the car under her name, Geraldine St. Claire.

Only two clerks, at different agencies, refused to give any information over the phone, citing company policy.

The sixth agency cheerfully informed him that his wife was driving a blue Thunderbird, tag number 497 SBB.

Yan-San was smiling as he got into his car and drove away.

It was no wonder that America was rapidly declining as a world power. Its people were undisciplined. Lazy. Unschooled. Unmotivated. Spoiled. Cowardly. Crude. Naive. They worshipped rock stars over statesmen. They had no sense of history. Nor respect for it.

They were a nation of children thrashing about in a luxurious playroom, not knowing which toy to reach for next.

Only an American could have conceived the fast-food industry. It summed up the nation's philosophy.

Yan-San was proud of that afternoon's accomplishment. He was so enraptured that he allowed his guard to slip for just a moment.

He never noticed the tow truck that followed him.

CHAPTER FORTY-ONE

It was an eerie night, with few clouds and just a slash of a moon. The air was cold and frisky as Owen piloted the *Lady Luck,* Earl's boat.

The sailor was tired. The tight bandage across his rib cage made steering an agonizing chore. His legs felt weak. His body was drenched in sweat. He'd been fighting off dizzy spells since he set sail an hour earlier. His feet were swollen in the moccasins. A thick vein at the ankle throbbed for attention.

But no matter how bad he felt, he was alive. And Gabe wasn't. He could never face Maryanne. It was cowardly. And he knew it.

Owen spotted the gaudy lights along the shore and swung the craft inland. He cut the engine and let the waves push him toward the beach of the Bay Villa resort.

Not that he had anything against purple, green, blue, and orange illuminated palm trees, but the Santa sleigh permanently riveted to the roof of the motel was a bit much.

Owen maneuvered the boat to the pier and secured it to the rusty spike. He gathered up his canvas bag and walked briskly across the beach past a young couple, covered by a blanket, who sat playing cards by the light of a kerosene lamp.

His feet scattered the sand, causing tiny fiddler crabs to burrow deeper in their holes.

Owen found himself panting for breath and rested against a palm tree till the dizziness passed.

Farther up the beach, a trio waded into the water, lanterns held high, in search of crabs.

Owen thought of the many nights he and Earl had scouted the same waters and wondered if life could ever be that simple again.

He crossed the beach, snaking through the maze of anemic trees, and headed toward the six-tiered concrete structure with the picture windows facing the ocean.

Only a few of the rooms had lights on. At this time of the year, the motel was nearly empty. He glanced at the few cars and hoped one of them belonged to Geraldine.

CHAPTER FORTY-TWO

Chief Ford Baker parked the police car in the no standing zone outside the convention center.

Three pretty girls in white dresses stood at the entrance of the dome-shaped building handing flowers to visitors. A male barbershop quartet in striped shirts, bow ties, and straw hats sang while one strummed a banjo.

The chief sat in the car a few minutes. His stomach felt queasy. Damn ulcer acting up again. It hadn't bothered him for years. Not since he bought the cabin and began planning his retirement. Now his dreams were quickly evaporating.

The mayor was threatening to revoke his pension, tomorrow's paper would run his picture under the headline "Prisoner Escapes," and his men, who made no secret of their dislike, were laughing behind his back.

Even Ethel, who accumulated eight summonses in three days, had hired a lawyer to sue him.

His head throbbed as he opened the car door and got out.

The chief refused a carnation as he briskly entered the huge exhibit hall. A wide banner welcomed the Associated Funeral Directors of North America.

The stadium-sized cavity was sectioned off into a maze of booths where salesmen hawked their wares, from coffins to limousines.

Models in bikinis paraded about serving appetizers. The public address system entertained with Elvis Presley's "Jailhouse Rock."

The chief made his way through the crunch of conventioneers, pausing at a booth that featured a salesman wearing a gorilla suit. The man was selling video equipment which he swore "even a monkey can operate."

The chief bypassed the ape and found a uniformed guide.

"Where can I find Patrick Shirley?"

The guard pointed toward the bar under a garish sign, dotted with drawings of cocktail glasses, that read Hospitality.

The chief spotted the mayor and police commissioner lingering by the food wagon and quickly retreated, losing himself in a crowd gathered by a shiny black limousine. A blonde model in a shimmering red dress explained the car's features in a breathless voice.

Behind the bar, two young women wearing slinky black gowns dispensed drinks as Patrick Shirley supervised.

"Great party, huh, chief?"

The funeral director, wearing a white linen suit, came from around the bar.

"Goddamn disgusting if you ask me," Ford told him.

"Hey! You only live once. And believe me, we know!" Shirley laughed.

"Whatever happened to dignity in death?" the lawman asked, refusing a margarita from the barmaid.

"That's for the paying public. We're here to spend a couple of bucks, see old friends, catch up on the latest technology." Shirley consulted a brochure. "You have to see Booth Forty-nine. The guy has a line of custom-made coffins. Say for instance you're a cop. Hell, you can be buried in a mahogany baby shaped like a badge. Or a gun even.

"Or say you're a baseball fan—we can bury you in a replica of first base."

Ford told him, "That's sick."

"Liberace's family bought one shaped like a piano."

The chief kept a close eye on the mayor, who was milling through the crowd shaking hands.

"I called you a couple of days ago," Ford said.

"I've been busy as hell. You don't put something like this together overnight."

Shirley glanced about the teeming stadium, obviously proud of his accomplishments. If nothing else, he was certainly assured of a prominent mention in the next issue of the National Funeral Directors' Association *Quarterly*.

"I called about the jumper," the chief said.

A middle-aged man attired in a brown leather suit hurried by. He slapped Patrick on the arm. "They're giving out trips to Hawaii. Booth Thirty-three." The man took off after one of the bikini gals.

Shirley whispered to the chief, "He owns a string of parlors from Houston to New Orleans. He could buy Hawaii for crissakes," he snarled.

"The jumper," the chief persisted. "Had on one of them medical bracelets."

"It's all in my report," Shirley said, smiling at a woman who asked him to autograph her program.

The chief waited till she left.

"Yeah, well put it in fucking English next time! What the hell is that disease?"

"Myasthenia gravis."

Patrick waved at an attractive woman and leaned over to tell the chief. "She's one of the few female directors in the business. Operates out of Los Angeles."

"You wanna have this conversation in my office?" the chief threatened.

Shirley sighed. "It's a disease that attacks the nervous system. People who have it can usually live a normal life if they take their medication every day. But if they don't, they wind up on a respirator."

"What about the hair dye? He do it himself? Was it a professional job or what?"

Shirley shrugged. "Hard to tell."

The ape man dashed to the bar and ordered a banana daiquiri. Shirley screamed with laughter.

The chief yanked Shirley by the sleeve, dragging him to a nearby corner. "Cut the shit," he warned.

"Jesus!" Shirley said, smoothing his white linen jacket. "Little touchy these days."

"Yeah, I'm touchy. I got my man lying in a black bag. And he's got a wife and three kids who want some answers!" Purple veins expanded on the chief's neck.

"I'm sorry about Gabe," the man said, staring down at his drink. "Terrible, terrible thing."

"What else about the Jap?"

Shirley looked up at the man's face. He saw something that disturbed him. "This have something to do with Gabe?"

"It ain't none of your fucking business. What do you know about him?"

"Nothing," Shirley said quickly. "But I can call the hospital in Philadelphia and see what I can get. They probably have some record on him, seeing as how they issued the bracelet."

"Do it!" the chief ordered. He spied the mayor moving toward him. There was no way to avoid a confrontation.

The mayor's face was contorted with anger. He was marching quickly toward the chief just as a county politician pulled him away and steered him toward a small group.

"I'll take care of it as soon as I get back to the office," Shirley promised.

"Make sure you do."

The chief walked away.

"Ford! Ford!"

He pretended not to hear the mayor as he walked out of the building.

CHAPTER FORTY-THREE

In a small cemetery west of Fort Lauderdale, Marco sat on a pink marble bench facing Kate's grave. The afternoon sun felt warm on his back. A slight breeze rippled the white roses in his hand.

Four stately pine trees shaded the area. It was a restful oasis, for both of them.

Marco had purchased the six adjoining lots, assuring him privacy on his visits.

The headstone was carved from pink marble imported from an Italian village outside of Palermo. The same marble was used to create a two-foot ledge bordering the gravesite. At each corner of the square ledge sat a sculptured cherub with angel wings of white marble, which now cast a tender shadow on the tomb. He leaned over and placed the roses in the porcelain vase cemented to the earth.

A few yards away a squirrel hopped about, stopping in a frozen stance by a tiny American flag that drooped at the foot of a neglected headstone.

Marco rose slowly and touched Kate's picture, which smiled at him from the headstone.

"Soon, my angel," he whispered.

He brought his fingers to his lips and then placed them on the gold letters of her name.

"Te amo," he said.

CHAPTER FORTY-FOUR

Owen left the motel room and walked down the back stairs to the beach. The fishermen were still wading near the shore and the only other person in sight was a jogger running along the water's edge.

Owen circled the motel and entered the bar from the highway, rather than risk going through the lobby.

A young barmaid wearing a skimpy pirate outfit was laughing with two customers sitting at the bar.

A middle-aged couple occupied a booth near the kitchen. The few tables were empty. His eyes scanned the booths against the far wall. He saw her immediately.

He could feel himself grinning as he crossed the tiny dance floor.

"Hi," Geraldine smiled. She rose and gave him a quick kiss on the lips, brushing his nose with the brim of her hat. The kiss was one of those Hollywood kind, made famous by talk show hosts. But the perfume was real.

Owen slid into the seat across from her. He noted the two empty glasses.

"Been here long?"

"An hour, maybe."

The chubby candle on the table illuminated her face. Her lips were parted in a half smile. The large eyes looked softer, younger. More alive. Her skin boasted a new tan. The hair was buried under a wide hat, with a scarf that dangled to her shoulder. He'd never seen her more beautiful. He wanted to say so, but didn't.

"You feeling okay?" she asked.

"I'm getting there," he said, reaching for her glass. He tasted the sweet liquor and quickly put it aside.

"I heard about your friend. I'm sorry."

Owen moved to the far end of the booth, leaning against the wall so he could keep a watch on the door. The barmaid glanced over and shouted, "Want a drink?"

He called for a Dewars.

Geraldine told him, "It's on me." She reached into her purse, took a handful of bills, and slid them across the table.

He gathered up the money, all except two fifties, which he pushed across the table next to her pack of cigarettes.

"A tip?" she asked.

"Why not? You worked for it," he said pleasantly.

"How the hell did you escape?" Geraldine asked.

"Just walked out."

"Just like that?"

He described the commotion of TV cameramen, newspaper reporters, and photographers.

"Cops had me in a cell in the basement. They opened it to let this lawyer come in to see me." He lit a cigarette and tossed the match near the ashtray.

"When he left to go see the chief, nobody bothered to lock up after him. Cops were too busy trying to get on television. So . . . I left."

Geraldine sighed, "Not too smart." She stared at the face she had come to trust. There was something about him that made her feel protected.

Though he looked nothing like him, Owen reminded her of her stepfather. Theirs had been a tangled relationship. War and peace. He taught her to play poker when she was eight and by age fourteen was taking her to games with his fellow longshoremen.

Her mother's disapproval was tempered by the steady income Geraldine provided through her winnings.

Most of the money went toward tuition at City College. She took journalism because next to poker it seemed the easiest way to make a living.

The barmaid brought the drink. Geraldine even liked the way he held the glass. His hair grazed a corner of the forehead. The nose was a little too large and the eyes a tad too small, but the overall effect was very agreeable. Extremely so.

"How'd you get a lawyer?" she suddenly asked.

"Lily sent him."

She wondered why the news depressed her.

"Lily?"

He looked away. "A friend. She was in the bar when it happened."

Geraldine instantly thought of Hal's file and his notes about the woman pawing the sailor. She was starting to feel somewhat annoyed. She couldn't help asking, "What was she doing there?"

He picked up the subtle tension and found himself secretly enjoying it.

"She runs a shop across the street. In fact, when I lent Gabe my car, I was counting on getting a ride home from her."

Geraldine didn't ask what else he was counting on getting.

"You think the guy rigged your car while you were in the bar?"

"Don't know. I was there a couple of hours."

She suddenly didn't hate Lily. He might not have lent the car if she hadn't been there.

"Was she hurt?"

Owen replied, "Earl says bruises mostly. How was the poker game?"

"Not bad," she smiled. "One of those magical nights gamblers pray for. When I needed a card, there it was."

He didn't doubt it—especially if she was wearing the backless/frontless outfit she had on tonight. The red dress crisscrossed in the front and dropped down in the back. Her thin arms were bare except for two chunky gold bracelets. Any player would have had trouble concentrating on the game. Not to mention the musky perfume that wafted his way each time she reached for the ashtray.

"But did you learn anything?"

"I learned that when Bumper opens for ten, you better fold," she chuckled.

Owen was not amused.

"Okay," she said, striking a somber pose. "I picked up some information on the guy who came after you in the hospital. Asian, approximately five-seven, a hundred and sixty pounds, around thirty-five years old, good physical condition, no missing teeth, two caps, lower jaw, gall bladder was removed eight years ago, type O negative blood, and . . . it appears he lived in Philadelphia. Any of this mean anything to you?"

The sailor shook his head and concentrated on his drink.

Geraldine shrugged and again consulted the notes, which she kept buried in the purse on her lap. "He suffered from a rare nervous disorder which isn't life-threatening, unless you don't take your medication. He also dyed his hair two shades darker, although there was no apparent need. His hair was thick and dark—no signs of gray or even random white hairs." She crossed her arms over the purse.

"Nice work," Owen said.

She leaned her elbows on the table and tilted her body forward. "Joe Akido is the key. Has to be. Hal gave him three thousand dollars. For what? What did he know that cost him his life? And why would he tell Hal? For the money? I don't think so. Drove a car worth more than I am. Revenge? I'm liking that a lot."

"You think he poisoned the coffee?"

"Hell, yeah. If not personally, he set it up. I'm telling you—Akido's the key."

"Maybe, maybe not. The jumper . . . do you know if he had any friends in Miami?"

She stared at him a long moment. "Miami?"

Owen told her about the matchbook found in the stolen car parked in the hospital lot. "He was in Miami. He's from Philadelphia. What was he doing in Florida?"

"How the hell do I know? Maybe he went to Sea World!"

She was expecting lavish praise—hearty applause, metaphorically speaking—and here he was skipping lightly over her prize catch and concentrating instead on his own fishing hook.

"These guys are careful," Owen pointed out. "They don't make mistakes. He jumped out of a window rather than get caught. He stole a car. He removed all clothing labels. Why did he hold on to the matchbook?"

"Because," she pointed out heatedly, "it wasn't important. He forgot he had it."

Owen hunched forward across the table. "Maybe somebody in the restaurant will remember him. He could've paid with a credit card. I say we go find out. Okay, it isn't much to go on—maybe he got the matches to pick his teeth. Do we even know if the bastard smoked? So we go to Miami. What's the big deal?"

"I say we go to the FBI," she answered firmly.

His head jerked up quickly. "What happened to the 'greatest story of the century'?"

"Let somebody else write it," Geraldine replied, looking away.

Owen covered her hand with his. "Are you that scared?"

Geraldine's eyes instantly clouded with tears. "For you, not me."

Something about her voice alarmed him. "Gerry, what's wrong?"

She looked up from under the hat, saw the genuine concern in his eyes, and burst into tears. Not soft little sobs or tiny gasps for air, but loud, body-shaking, face-streaking, nose-dripping tears.

The more she tried to stop, the more a new spasm would attack. She felt humiliated but couldn't stop.

Owen waited helplessly for the tears to subside. Her face was buried in her hands, all but concealed beneath the hat.

He walked over to the bar and grabbed up a couple of cocktail napkins. He carried them back to the booth and slipped them under the hat, like a schoolboy sliding a note under a door.

She offered a watered down smile. "It came to me the other day that with . . . Hal gone . . . you're about the only friend I've got." It sounded as awkward as she felt saying it. "If something happens to you . . . I may have to do something drastic, like get a dog or a parakeet."

She didn't fake a giggle for fear it would trigger more sobs, and she needed desperately to retain the tattered remnants of her dignity.

"Let's go to Miami," he said pressing her hand between his. "If it doesn't pan out, I'll go with you to the FBI."

She nodded quickly. "Okay." Her sorrow evaporated. "Okay!" she grinned.

He jerked his hand away quickly and stared across the room. She followed his gaze to the television set above the bar.

A Barbi-doll anchorwoman sat at a desk speaking into the camera. Behind her shoulder, Owen's face filled the screen.

One word, "Sought," was imprinted above his picture.

Geraldine looked at the screen and moaned, "Jesus."

CHAPTER FORTY-FIVE

I'm not gonna starve to death," the old man yelled into the kitchen phone. "I used to be in the marines, you know. They taught us how to eat snakes raw."

"Just don't bring 'em into my house," Molly yelled back.

They talked another few minutes, with Molly assuring him she'd be home as soon as her sister could fend for herself, maybe a week or ten days, and not to forget to pay the phone bill and water.

They hung up and he looked at the dirty dishes in the sink and wondered if she'd miss 'em if he threw them out.

In their thirty-eight years of marriage, they'd only been separated twice. Once when he took a highway construction job in Tallahassee, and when her mother died.

Now Molly was back in Winter Park with her relatives and he dreaded the idea of being alone for a week. Maybe more.

They'd argued all the way to the bus terminal. He couldn't understand why her brother-in-law, with all his money, couldn't pay a nurse to come look after his wife.

"They'll have you scrubbing floors and cooking," Earl vowed. "Probably ironing, too. And the cheap bastard won't even feed you."

They sat silently, like zombies, on the bench waiting for the bus to arrive. When the boarding was announced, she grabbed up the suitcases and stormed through the pneumatic door.

"You always hated my family," she accused him.

"There's a lot 'bout 'em that's hateful," he told her.

He took three wadded fifties and thrust them in her hand. He lingered a moment hoping for some sign of concern, but Molly had snapped, "They ain't too crazy 'bout you either."

Earl flicked off the kitchen light and crossed the parlor to the screened-in back porch.

The pink neon bulbs of the Flamingo A-1 Used Cars sign across the creek illuminated a wide patch of the land behind the house. The pink neon rippled in the black water. He could make out the silhouette of his rowboat, hoisted on cinder blocks, on the grass.

He could see the tops of the tomato plants in the trailer-sized garden where he grew zucchini, lettuce, bell peppers, and okra.

The room was chilly, so he threw on a flannel shirt. Like everything he owned, it smelled of fish. He put on a pair of heavy socks under the frayed slippers.

The room was crowded with fishing gear, crab traps, bait buckets, coffee tins filled with lead weights, kerosene cans, lanterns, a basket of cork circles, boxes of wicks, and hundreds of feet of netting.

It was his favorite room in the house. The only furniture was a floor-model radio, a rocking chair, hassock, and a refrigerator he used for storing bait.

Molly hated it. Called it the city dump.

He shuffled over to the far corner near the chair and saw that his eyeglasses and ashtray were still there from the previous night. Good. It saved hunting.

He pulled the hassock toward the light and sat down. He reached for the tarnished, harpoon-shaped needle and lifted a section of the net off the floor.

He put on his glasses and examined where he'd left off. Outside, his dog chased something into the creek and thrashed in the water.

"Blackie," he yelled. "Come out of there 'fore you catch pneumonia!"

The dog scooted up the bank, heading straight for the back door. He waited till the old man let him in before shaking the water off his body.

"Goddamn!" Earl yelled. "Get out of here!" The dog darted between his legs and ran to the kitchen. Earl heard him under the table, his nails scratching the linoleum, as he tried to curl the blanket under his wet legs.

Ever since he was a pup and Molly used to keep him warm on a blanket near the stove, the kitchen was Blackie's domain. They had long grown accustomed to his stench as they ate their meals.

Someday he'd get around to adding a dining room like Molly wanted.

Earl sat back down on the hassock, adjusted the lamp shade to give him the most light, and began working. The thin, spiderlike fingers wove the harpoon needle expertly through the tangle of small, square hoops.

A mound of blue netting lay in a heap at his side. A thick ball of clear blue plastic twine rested on his lap.

Earl reached into the coffee can and pulled out a steel weight shaped like a tiny pyramid. He attached it to the hem of the net, counting off the spaces from the last cork.

A car's headlights took his attention. He saw them before hearing the engine. It moved slowly through the grove.

The car stopped alongside the house. If Blackie heard it, he didn't give any indication.

The old man pushed the net aside and got up slowly. He walked over to the far wall and flicked on the light switch that illuminated the backyard. He could make out the figure of a large man climbing out of the car.

"Earl? It's Bumper."

"Come around back."

Earl greeted him at the door as the dog ran at top speed from the kitchen, barking at the screen door.

The old man ordered, "Get!"

Blackie barked twice, letting him know he was only doing his job, and disappeared into the kitchen.

"Come on in," he told Bumper.

The burly man stooped his head to enter. "You weren't sleeping, were you?"

"No. Just working on a net. For Sam over at the courthouse. Sit down. Want something to eat?"

"No, thanks," Bumper said. He made his way carefully through the maze and sat in the rocker. "Is Geraldine around?"

The old man returned to his weaving. "No." The question caught him by surprise and he covered it by pretending to hunt for his needle.

"Think she went to a movie. Didn't say exactly. Why?"

Bumper reached down and picked up a corner of the net. "Nice."

"Heard that was some poker game the other night," the old man said. He reached over and turned off the radio. "You make it out alive?"

"Barely," the mechanic laughed.

He was wearing a white shirt and clean trousers. He'd even taken time to comb his hair. Earl couldn't ever remember seeing Bumper in anything but grease-stained overalls.

"You know when she's coming back?"

"Nope. But I can have her call you if she don't get in late."

Bumper shook his head. "I have to be up at five to go to Homestead and pick up a wreck."

The old man tried to sound unconcerned. "Up to you."

Bumper stood. "Just tell her I saw a guy who might be the one she's looking for."

Earl's fingers held the needle in mid-air. He avoided looking at his visitor. "Who is that?"

"Chink who hit her car. Tourist. Had Jersey tags."

Earl kept his eyes on the blue plastic twine. He paused only to adjust the glasses on his nose. "You talk to him?"

"No. I followed him to a place out on Cypress." Bumper jammed his hand into his shirt pocket and brought out a scrap of paper. "Forty-eight. Two-family house. He went in the side apartment, by the driveway. I figured I'd pass it along for what it's worth."

Earl took the piece of paper. "I'll tell her."

Bumper bent over the old man's weaving. "How come you never told me about your niece before? Hiding her?"

The old man coughed. "Hell, she's one of them career women. I'm lucky to get a Christmas card."

Bumper sighed, "She sure can play cards."

"I'd never tangle with her," Earl answered. "Took my car payment last time she visited."

"She's a looker, too," Bumper said, staring out toward the creek. A rabbit skittered from the garden carrying something in his mouth. "She got a boyfriend?"

"Two or three. I lost track."

Bumper nodded. "Figured that." He crossed to the door and opened it. "Well, just tell her I came by. I'll keep looking in case that ain't the guy."

"Thanks. I'm sure she'll appreciate it."
Earl waited till Bumper got in the car and drove off. He hurried to the kitchen and read the phone number off the wall calendar. He dialed Owen's room and let it ring ten times before hanging up.

CHAPTER FORTY-SIX

Monday mornings were usually depressing for LeRoy Thomas, but this one promised to be the granddaddy of them all.

He sat in his office above the Rite-RX drugstore in the shopping mall and contemplated fueling his Piper Cub and taking off to the Fiji Islands or wherever one escaped to find whatever it is that was missing. That "whatever" didn't even have a name, but he knew he'd know as soon as he found it.

His secretary had called in sick with "female problems." His car's transmission was bucking again. The dentist wanted $3,000 for his daughter's braces. The IRS was pressuring him for $8,577, and when he got to the office he found an envelope under the door with the key to the apartment he'd leased for his girlfriend.

She hadn't bothered to include a note. No "Let's keep in touch." No "Sorry it's over." No "It was fun while it lasted." And, he noticed, she didn't return the jewelry. Maybe her new boyfriend wore it on stage.

The Australian rock singer with the stringy blond hair and dangling earrings. A rhinestone cowboy with tattoos.

They could fucking die together.

But the main source of his depression was that today was his fortieth birthday—a clear signal that his life was half over.

And what did he have to show for it? A couple of good suits, a house mortgaged to the hilt, and a plane that was also showing its age.

LeRoy glanced out the window and watched a chubby housewife push a grocery cart to her car. The sign on the Triplex Cinema advertised three movies, the titles all ending with numbers.

His life had not gone according to plan, and here it was almost over.

LeRoy opened his second pack of cigarettes for the day—it wasn't yet lunch time—and flipped the newspaper to the sports page. His attention flew to the weekend recap of the jai alai payoffs.

His throat constricted as he read the outcome of the fourth and ninth trifectas. His 718 combo—for the first time ever—came out in both games, paying a whopping $3,520 and $2,330.

He punched the desk.

He wanted to ring Lily's neck. By helping her out, for free no less, it had cost him a bundle.

He heard the outer door open and glanced up at the redhead who smiled. "Hi." She crossed through the reception area and took a seat across from his desk.

LeRoy rose quickly, extending his hand.

"Do we have an appointment?"

"Sort of," she smiled, taking his hand. "I'm Geraldine St. Claire."

"LeRoy Thomas," he answered.

The name and the face meant nothing to him but he hardly cared. He was mesmerized by the stunning woman who now rose from the chair and glanced in the adjoining room where a Xerox machine and paper shredder were housed. She inspected the bathroom briefly and returned to his office, glancing at the framed diploma and the black and white photos of vintage airplanes. One photograph showed the attorney in the open-air cockpit of a small bi-wing.

"You're a pilot?"

"You from the board of health?"

Geraldine shook her head, smiling. "You have a partner?"

"I solo."

He was intrigued by the striking woman behind the dark, round sunglasses.

He figured her for a divorce case, probably a dirty one, with lots of property to divide and a business or two to liquidate. Maybe a house up north and a fat portfolio of blue chips.

"Can I buy you lunch?" she asked. "I'm here on behalf of a friend."

"I'd love to but I'm very busy," he told her.

"Even busy lawyers have to eat."

She stood facing him across the desk. A blue scarf was braided through her hair. It matched the blouse that fit snugly into the white jeans.

He was sure of one thing. He'd never seen her before. He definitely would have remembered.

"Who exactly is your . . . 'friend'?" LeRoy asked.

Geraldine leaned over the desk, turned the newspaper to the front page, and placed her finger on Owen's picture.

They drove to a roadside restaurant twenty-five minutes north on U.S. 1. By the time the waitress brought the food, Geraldine had finished talking.

"It's a little early for April Fool's Day," the black attorney said, grinning.

Geraldine did not remove her stare.

"First this guy kills everybody with Tylenol and now he's after you and your boyfriend?"

Geraldine corrected him. "He's already killed my boyfriend. Now he's after Owen."

LeRoy smiled. "Sorry, it's hard keeping track of the bodies."

Geraldine bristled.

LeRoy leaned across the table. "Look, I don't want to get involved."

Geraldine shrugged. "You're already semi involved and we need someone with credentials. Someone who can gather information without setting off alarms."

LeRoy laughed, "Honey, I got alarms going off right now and they're telling me not to mess with this."

"Okay," she said. She gathered up her purse and pushed her chair away from the table.

"Hold on," he told her. "Look, I'd like to help you. Nothing personal, but your friend is a real hardass. And not too bright. Hell, I'd have had him out on bail. But he took off!"

Geraldine sat back in the chair and looked at the lean, athletic man with the dark oval eyes. A small scar at the corner of his lip gave him a perpetual smile. Thin white strands of hair curled about his ears.

"Besides, if any of your story is true, we're dealing with some very nasty people. A person could wind up dead. I also have an office to run. I can't be tied up with something like this. Who's gonna pay the bills? Who's gonna deal with the clients? And what if you don't catch 'em and you don't sell your book? One third of nothing is shit!

"Maybe you made this whole thing up to gain sympathy for your friend. Hell of a way to cop a plea, gal."

The voice was shrill, almost feminine. She wondered what impression he made on a jury. Probably a very positive one. A small smile crossed her face.

"You're going to go for it, aren't you?"

LeRoy laughed and stubbed out his cigarette.

"No way, José! I wouldn't touch it with the pope's blessing."

Geraldine observed, "You're coming in."

The lawyer averted his eyes. "Keep dreaming, lady. I don't know what you're smokin' but you better give it up."

Geraldine faced him squarely. "LeRoy, I've played poker since I was twelve. It put me through college. Stop playing games and tell me why you're going to help us."

The black man looked at her, his face not displaying any twinge of emotion. His strong cheek muscles did not flinch. His eyes did not waver. His hands remained flat on the table. His voice did not rise above a whisper. He stared down at the paper placemat with drawings of pink seashells. His fingers traced the scalloped edge.

"Because," he said, mostly to himself, "it's my birthday and maybe you're the present."

CHAPTER FORTY-SEVEN

Yan-San Tokumura sat in an open-air cinder block hut on the public beach.

Graffiti covered the structure, and hurricanes had torn the foundation, but it still afforded shelter from the rain now striking the sand.

The beach was deserted and only a single boat sailed the horizon under gray clouds.

He gazed at the angry foam caps and thought of an aborigine tale. The elders of a primitive tribe guarded a holy place hidden high in an Australian mountain cavern—a hazardous two-day climb.

The secret sanctuary was known for 40,000 years as Hawk Dreaming. It was a temple where troubled tribesmen came to gather strength and inspiration from the spirits of their ancestors. Often the seekers died on the journey, victims of animal predators or the elements.

But those that completed the journey, it was said, were amply rewarded in spirit and resolve.

Yan-San inhaled the salt air and allowed himself to indulge in Hawk Dreaming.

He had scoured every inch of Key West and had come up dry. Most likely, the sailor and the woman had fled, but he was reluctant to give up the hunt.

If the primitive tribesmen could endure hunger, scavengers, torrid heat, and a 19,000-foot climb where the prevailing winds, it was said, could rip the skin off a man's body, he could continue his search.

Besides, he reminded himself, they were Americans and subject to all the failings of the race. Discipline was not a national credo.

Soon they would emerge . . . and he need only wait.

CHAPTER FORTY-EIGHT

Chief Ford Baker and his mother rushed from the car, darted through the rain, and entered the house by the kitchen door. The garage was blocked with boxes and furniture to be picked up by the movers.

Leona shook the water from her dress and unpinned her black hat. "I'll go change and then make lunch."

The chief removed his suit jacket and placed it over a chair. He loosened the tie and went to the kitchen window, cranking it slightly from the top to let some fresh air into the room. The rain slashed fiercely against the jalousie panes, blurring the view of the backyard. He liked rain. As a kid, when his friends ran from the creek, fearful of thunder, he'd stay in the water, floating on his back, not wanting to miss any of it. It fascinated him, even now.

The funeral had been a messy business. It scared him to see how Maryanne had aged overnight. Maybe intense grief could do that. Or fear.

He'd run into her a week ago at the supermarket, chasing her kids down the aisle, and she bore no resemblance to that woman today sitting at the grave.

He listened to the water hitting the roof and wondered why it always rained on funerals. Was it, as the Latins believed, that the saints were weeping? He wondered about people who lived in desert areas. Did sudden sand storms attack mourners?

The chief took a beer from the refrigerator and carried it into the parlor. He sat on the couch, undid the tight laces on his black shoes, and slipped them off. He let his head fall against the needlepoint pillow and closed his eyes.

Images crowded. The long procession to the cemetery with six motorcycle escorts. Officers from as far as Tampa and Tallahassee had filled the church. The tiny coastal town of St. Joe had sent a contingent of seven.

He was proud of the way his men had conducted themselves during the service. Not one had broken down. Even the mayor, to his credit, was subdued. And when the hearse drove slowly past the police station, the officers on duty stood somberly in the rain to salute.

It had moved him.

Many of his men had come up to him individually at the graveside to offer condolences. Two of them he hadn't seen in months or spoken a word to in maybe a year. He would make it a point, in the future, to seek them out. Even Powanda and Ethel had expressed their sorrow, and he was touched.

He dozed off and woke to the sound of his mother calling, "It's ready."

Ford was still wearing the black trousers and white shirt as he walked barefoot into the kitchen. He sat at the table facing his mother, who now wore a cotton house dress, exposing the bony arms.

"Maryanne is going to be all right," she said off-handedly. "She's got spunk. And she'll do right by those kids. I plan to invite them up to the cabin for Christmas. The kids would enjoy the snow."

The chief nodded, "For sure."

The knot in his stomach tightened. The signal to tell her. As with any unpleasant duty, it was best done immediately.

"The mayor told me when we were leaving the church that he's canceled my retirement."

Leona held the fork mid-air. "What?"

"Just until this business is done with," Ford answered quickly.

"And what do I tell the people who bought the house? Do I ask 'em if it's okay if we sleep in the garage? Or maybe we can pitch a tent near the septic tank?"

Ford gave her his "don't make me crazy look" and said, "I'll handle it."

He didn't add that he was secretly happy. He had no intention of leaving till Gabe's killer was caught. Retired or not, he would have stayed near.

Leona sputtered, "I already went to the post office. In three weeks all our mail is going north."

"I know, I know."

The chief was suffocating in his long-sleeved shirt. He hadn't worn one in years. His arms were too bulky and felt constricted.

"Well—do you have any leads?"

"Nothing. Not a goddamn one! Got cops in thirteen states looking for that son of a bitch sailor. Hasn't showed a hair. I even stopped by Earl's house the other day. Found out he cosigned for the bastard when he bought his boat."

Leona stared him down. "You aren't thinking Earl's involved in this? No sir! Finer man, outside of your father, you'll never meet."

"I know Earl hasn't got anything to do with it but I still want to talk to him. Maybe he can put me on to something. Someone. Has to be real chummy with him to sign a bank note. You don't do that for just anybody."

Leona dug into the omelet and started to say something but caught herself. It was a habit that often annoyed her son but today incensed him.

"What? Tell me."

The woman looked up innocently, as if a stranger had approached her at a bus stop. "Huh?"

"What were you gonna say about Earl?"

"Nothing," she swiped the damp strands of hair from her neck. "Just thinking of the day he got married. Molly was the prettiest bride I ever saw."

He found it hard to believe. Every time he saw the woman she was wearing workman's overalls and a flannel shirt.

"I was there the day they got back from their honeymoon in Thomasville, Georgia. We had a little party for them at their house on Columbus Avenue. In fact, your father fixed the fruit punch—with that hooch he used to make in the garage. People were drunk for a week."

Ford asked, "They lived in Little Cuba?"

Leona laughed. "It used to be pretty back then. When Columbus Avenue was something to see. And their place was like a little doll house. It doesn't look like much, now. But I still see him there once in awhile cutting the grass. I go by there on my way to the doctor."

The chief was confused and said so. "But they live by the creek. Have for as long as I can remember."

"They moved there after Molly's mother died. But they never sold the other house. Earl rents it out. Has for years."

He asked, "Where on Columbus Avenue?"

"Right off Eighteenth Street. The second house from the corner, with the fence. And rose bushes. I'm pretty sure the address is twenty-five twelve. Why?"

"Nothing," he said, reaching across for the pot of tea. "Just curious."

CHAPTER FORTY-NINE

The snow was eight inches deep and still falling as Cardinal Thomas Ryan McHugh stood outside St. Patrick's Cathedral waiting for his limousine.

"Where is he?" he barked at Father Murphy. "We're going to be late. Forget about makeup! They'll just push me in front of the camera."

Father Murphy glanced up Fifth Avenue. The wide street, with snow banks shrouding the curbs, was deserted but for a police car, far in the distance, and a wheezing bus whose clacking wipers could be heard in the stillness of the early evening.

A tri-state storm alert was in effect and motorists had been warned to stay off the roads. Both the Lincoln and Holland tunnels were closed. The George Washington Bridge was reporting delays of three hours due to high winds and abandoned cars.

Thirteen homeless people had frozen to death in the previous twenty-four hours. Two tenements in the South Bronx burned to the ground, killing one fireman, as tenants turned on gas stoves to keep warm. All three metropolitan airports were closed and Amtrak service was suspended between New York and Washington, D.C.

"Something must have happened," the younger priest replied. He pulled the fur collar up to his ears and stuffed his hands deep in the pockets of the black coat. "Why don't you wait inside and stay warm?"

Above him, the spire of the cathedral stood like a golden arm reaching out to the universe.

The massive figure of the cardinal, encased in a black mohair coat and Russian sable hat, paced anxiously. "The show starts taping in forty minutes. You can be sure the mayor's in makeup."

Father Murphy looked down the block. The police car had only managed to travel inches. The street lights went from red to green without cars to respond to the silent commands.

"At last!" the cardinal shouted, pointing a finger at his driver, who came running around the corner, propelled by an icy blast of wind. He lumbered through the curtain of snow.

"Fucking car was stolen!" the driver yelled up to the figures on the steps.

The cardinal stepped forward. "What?" His foot slipped on a bumpy crust of ice under the snow and sent him tumbling backward down the stairs.

Father Murphy screamed his name and rushed to the cardinal, who was sprawled on his back, a huge black whale on a sea of white.

As he lay on the ground with fresh snow powdering his face, his last thoughts before passing out were of the mayor sitting under the studio lights.

CHAPTER FIFTY

The following evening, under a cloudless sky, Geraldine sat in the mustard-colored Pontiac by the Western Union office on Duvall Street in Key West waiting for Owen to appear. They had left Bay Villa early that morning—separately.

Shortly before nine, she saw him emerge from the shadows and tooted the horn twice.

Owen jumped in the back and stretched out on the seat. "Where'd you get the jalopy?"

She explained the trade with her neighbor, who was delighted to be driving a new car for the first time in her life. "I may have trouble getting it back," Geraldine laughed.

"Where we going?" he asked.

"LeRoy is putting you up in an apartment his girlfriend vacated recently," Geraldine said. "Very recently."

She drove slowly, glancing at the envelope on the dashboard where she'd scribbled the directions. The city streets were mostly deserted. The March chill kept the natives holed up.

A police car sidled by at the intersection and Geraldine turned the corner slowly in the opposite direction. It meant going out of her way, but there was no choice. Owen's picture was in the paper again, this time with a reward posted by the PBA.

She watched the police car in the rearview mirror and saw it make a U-turn directly behind her. Her heart thumped in her throat as the car approached quickly.

The red lights flashed, bouncing off the buildings on both sides of the street. She cried, "Oh, God."

Owen could see the lights from where he lay huddled in the darkness. "Don't panic," he told her as he eased himself slowly to the floor.

Geraldine trembled. Her hands gripped the steering wheel tightly. Her leg stiffened on the gas pedal. She suddenly remembered what Cecelia said about the expired plates. How could she have been so stupid!

The car approached swiftly. She could see the outline of the figure wearing the cop's uniform in the rearview mirror.

Maybe she could jump out of the car and stop him before he got near.

Maybe she could run for it.

Maybe she could pretend to be sick and distract him long enough for Owen to escape.

Maybe she could . . .

The police car sped past her and raced ahead, out of sight.

Ten minutes later she pulled up to the garden apartment complex and LeRoy ushered them into the empty living room.

"Excuse the mess," he joked, gesturing to the three folding chairs that consisted of all the furniture in the room. A rolled-up sleeping bag lay in the corner.

The lawyer was wearing a green velour sweater over tan slacks. Four thick strands of gold chains hung across his neck.

The window shades were pulled down. Square dust marks in the shape of picture frames dotted the blank walls. The lady had obviously taken everything.

LeRoy caught Geraldine's glance. "She left the ice cubes and a couple of glasses." He went into the kitchen and came back with three Mickey Mouse glasses and a bottle of wine.

"I bought some sandwiches, in case you're hungry," he said. He sat on the chair and leaned it back against the wall.

"Where do we go from here?" he asked.

Geraldine told him about Earl's message from Bumper. "Maybe we should go check out the apartment on Cypress."

"Too dangerous," LeRoy answered.

"I could go alone, later tonight," Owen suggested.

"No way!" the lawyer shouted. "You're staying put right here. Your face is all over the TV. All you need is to run into your pain-in-the-ass 'concerned citizen.' "

"We just can't do *nothing,*" Geraldine moaned. "He can't hide up here forever."

"I don't plan to," Owen said. "I'm going to Miami."

LeRoy looked at the redhead. "What's in Miami?"

She explained about the matchbook found in the jumper's car.

"You're chasing shadows," the lawyer told him. "But I'm not against your getting out of town. Sydney, Australia, would be better—but I can live with Miami."

"I have a friend on the Miami *Herald,*" Geraldine blurted out. "Actually, he's more like an ex-husband."

Owen looked at her and then just as quickly averted his eyes.

"Hey, if we decide to go to the FBI, he'd be a good person to set it up for us," Geraldine offered.

She glanced at Owen, sitting cross-legged on the floor, his hands behind him. The silver ID bracelet with the Coast Guard insignia hugged his wrist tightly. A relic of innocent times.

He spoke to the lawyer, "Can you do something for us?"

"What?" He sounded suspicious.

"Talk to someone in that Philly hospital. See what you can get on our jumper."

The lawyer swayed his head slightly. "Forget it. Medical records are a bitch. You need a court order. And when you're dealing out of state . . . it's not worth the hassle. You could spend months."

Geraldine brought him a fresh drink. "We're not talking official. You know how to schmooze. Unleash that deadly charm."

"Which one is that," he said sarcastically, looking about the empty apartment, "the one that makes women flee?"

They drank and made plans to meet at the private airstrip shortly after dawn. LeRoy described his plane and gave them directions, using back roads. It was agreed that he would fly them to Miami.

He made it appear he was going out of his way to do them this big favor, when in reality he had a ladyfriend there, and his ego required a little stroking about now.

Shortly after midnight, Geraldine hitched a ride with him to Little Cuba and left the Pontiac for Owen, saying, "Can I trust you to stay out of trouble for a few hours?"

"There's some towels and a couple of blankets in the linen closet," LeRoy told him, his hand on the door. "If she should call . . ."

Geraldine tugged at his arm and led him away.

"She's not going to call. It's over. Don't torment yourself."

LeRoy nodded, "Yeah."
They drove in silence to the house on Columbus Avenue.
"See you in a couple of hours," she told him.
His mind seemed to be elsewhere.

CHAPTER FIFTY-ONE

As they sat on the bare living room floor mapping their strategy, Yan-San walked away from the pier.

He'd made two passes by the boat, once during the rainstorm and again after dark. Both times, a police car sat in the vicinity, thwarting his efforts to get closer.

He reminded himself of Hawk Dreaming and summoned the will to be patient.

Shortly before ten, Yan-San decided to call it a night. He got into his car, the second one he had stolen in as many days, and headed for his apartment.

In a town the size of Key West, it was dangerous to keep a stolen car too long. Although the cars were taken from the airport, and even if the owner was traveling, there was a chance a relative would spot the vehicle.

Yan-San was stopped at a red light when something drew his attention to the car facing him at the other side of the intersection.

He leaned against the steering wheel and forced his eyes to focus on the license plate of the Thunderbird.

The light changed and he didn't move. The car behind him honked twice. The driver hung out the window and yelled at him to move.

Yan-San watched as the Thunderbird approached slowly and drove alongside him.

He turned his head and squinted at the retreating bumper. A smile erupted.

He made a quick U-turn and followed the blonde woman, certain she would lead him to the redhead.

CHAPTER FIFTY-TWO

LeRoy dropped Geraldine off on Columbus Avenue and instead of driving home swung by the funeral parlor.

The white lawn sign was illuminated and he could see lights in the upstairs residence.

He pulled into the circular driveway and noted that the visitor parking lot was empty. Evidently viewing hours were over.

Inside, Patrick Shirley was in the main parlor spritzing the floral arrangements with a mixture of water and club soda.

He glanced at the male corpse in the silk-lined casket and reached in to straighten a wrinkle in the suit's lapel.

It was those minor details that he prided himself in providing to his clientele. Like the water and club soda. He knew of no funeral home that maintained fresher flowers.

He once had a wake that ran eight days because the family elected to wait for one of their members to be freed on parole. The floral display withstood the judicial delay.

Patrick emptied the brass floor ashtray near the entrance and turned off the lamp over the visitors' book. Again, someone had pocketed the pen. He resisted putting them on a chain, but if the vandalism continued he would be forced to.

He glanced at the gray carpeting and determined that it didn't need vacuuming. He turned off the parlor lamps and left the soft amber spotlight shining on the casket. One never knew when a family member would be struck by an urge to pay a midnight call. He liked to be prepared.

Again . . . it was one of his touches.

Patrick walked to the main door and peered outside to make sure the lawn sign was properly illuminated. It was then that he saw LeRoy Thomas walking quickly up the path.

Shirley hoped nothing had happened to one of his daughters. Teenagers meant classmates, two full sets of relatives, teachers, cheerleading friends, football squads . . . always required the main viewing room.

Patrick unlocked the door.

"LeRoy."

"You busy?"

"Just tidying up," he said, extending the plastic water bottle with the long nozzle.

"There's something I need to talk to you about."

"Let's go in my office," Patrick said, leading him to a small, nicely furnished room.

LeRoy had never been in a funeral home after hours. The smell of flowers was suffocating. He wondered how many dead bodies were in repose.

Patrick sat in a high-backed leather chair and gestured his visitor to the tweed couch.

"What can I do for you?"

In these situations it was never wise to open a conversation with, "How's the family?"

"I'm working on a case. It concerns the man who jumped out the hospital window."

Patrick stared at his visitor. So much for the big parlor.

"What about him?"

"I want to know who he was."

"I have no idea," the thin man smiled. His face was remarkably unlined and youthful despite his sixty-odd years. LeRoy wondered if he was using some of his own embalming fluid cosmetically. The idea caused him to shudder.

"I only did the autopsy. It's all in my report, which I gave to the chief. He can tell you whatever you need."

LeRoy sighed. "Shirl, I can't go to him. I'm working on this quietly."

Patrick shrugged and spritzed the flowers on his desk. "I'm sorry. It's out of my hands."

LeRoy reminded him, "You owe me."

The funeral director averted his eyes. "LeRoy, we've been friends many years. I laid out your father. I was the first white director in the county to administer to negroes."

LeRoy's voice rose. "And you wouldn't have a license to operate if I hadn't saved your ass at the hearing."

When LeRoy was two years out of law school, Shirley had come to him with a delicate matter. His career, his life was in jeopardy. Authorities were threatening to revoke his credentials. A civil suit was the least of his problems, but he couldn't survive if he lost his license.

And all because he'd picked up the wrong body at the hospital, believing it to be an indigent, and sold it to a medical lab.

An honest mistake. An innocent misdeed. The licensing board, however, and the grieving family, felt otherwise.

"I pulled your nuts out of the fire. It's payback time. I need information."

Shirley nodded. "I'm not an ungrateful person."

"Good. Who was he?"

LeRoy waited as the man crossed the carpeted room to a wooden file cabinet. He flicked on an overhead lamp and ruffled through the files. He pulled one out and carried it back to the desk.

LeRoy took a notebook from his pocket and clicked his gold pen ready.

"There's not much. The man's name was Kuni Hamada. He was under the care of a Doctor Riad. Address was listed as 4344 Chauncey Avenue, but the hospital said that a letter sent to him at that address was returned by the post office. He'd obviously moved and left no forwarding address. No next of kin was listed. Occupation was furniture salesman and he carried no health insurance. He suffered from a serious respiratory affliction but was controlling it with medication. He dyed his hair and had chronic athlete's foot. Otherwise healthy." Shirley closed the folder.

"That's it?"

"You're lucky we got that."

"Got an address for the doctor?"

He shook his head. "But it shouldn't be hard to get. He's associated with the hospital. Riverside Memorial, Philadelphia."

LeRoy closed the notebook and stood. "Thanks."

"Anytime."

Shirley walked him to the front door and watched him leave. He debated calling the chief to mention the strange visit.

You never knew when you would need a powerful law enforcement officer on your side. Even one about to retire. He went back into his office and looked up the chief's home number in the Rolodex.

Shirley glanced at the clock on his desk. It was ten past eleven. He hesitated. It could wait till morning.

He turned off the lamp but lingered by the desk in the dark room. The chief could be a nasty son of a bitch if he felt he'd been crossed.

He flicked on the lamp and quickly punched the numbers into the phone. If Leona answered, sounding sleepy, he'd hang up.

Chief Ford Baker picked up on the second ring.

CHAPTER FIFTY-THREE

When LeRoy dropped her off in Little Cuba, Geraldine found a note from Cecelia jammed in the handle of the screen door.

"Went to bed. See you in the morning. Love the car!" The last words were underlined.

Geraldine walked into the kitchen, dug through the cupboards for something to eat, and settled for a can of tomato soup. She put it on the stove to heat and dialed her New York apartment.

No big surprises. The woman from the collection agency threatened to take her to court unless she received a check by registered mail immediately. The promotions director from the Golden Nugget reminded her of the poker tournament set for Easter week. Ida called to say hello. MasterCard wanted to know when they could expect payment. Hal's agent said they were having a memorial service in Hollywood on the tenth. Mike informed her she was officially off the payroll.

She went into the living room and turned on the small black and white television. She flicked through the channels and had few choices. A rerun of "Gilligan's Island" won out over a rerun of "Green Acres."

She was starting to undress a few minutes later when Leroy called to report on his meeting with Shirley. She scribbled down the information.

"Nice work."

"Get some sleep," he told her. "Meet you by the hangar."

Geraldine stuck the note in her purse and went back to the kitchen to stir the soup. The sides of the pot and the spoon were covered with an orange fuzz. Not exactly a gourmet delight. She turned off the stove and allowed the soup to cool.

Outside, the neighborhood was quiet. The porches were dark. She missed New York. Especially the greasy pizza at the corner stand where she played ten dollars a day on Lotto. She wondered if any of her numbers had come in.

She told herself that the whole nightmare could be over in a matter of days. If the restaurant lead didn't pan out, she'd convince Owen to go with her to the FBI. Let somebody else write the book. All she wanted was Owen's name cleared—and her old job at the paper.

She was feeling more optimistic than she had in days as she entered the bedroom and pulled the suitcase from under the bed.

She walked to the closet and reached for her clothes.

A hand flew out from between the wire hangers and gripped her wrist.

Geraldine screamed.

A dark figure sprang from between the garments and clamped his hand over her mouth.

She felt a thick ring pressed against her lip and tasted blood on her teeth.

The same hands pushed her backward, increasing the grip on her neck. Her eyes widened in terror.

The Japanese man smiled.

His face was inches away. She could smell the chewing gum on his breath. She fought to slip from his grasp as his eyes shone with amusement. He yanked a handful of hair and brought her face down to his shoulder. "Sayonara," he grinned.

Geraldine kicked up her knee and cracked it sharply against his testicles.

He planted his foot on her stomach and sent her flying into the dresser. The wooden knobs struck her in the kidney as she slumped to the floor.

The man raced to her side, grabbed her by the hair, and crashed his fist into her face. She felt the ring puncture her cheek.

Geraldine crumpled whimpering, her eyes on the dark shoes. She prayed for the next blow to come. The one that would end the pain searing through her skull.

She lay on the floor with her face pressed against the cold linoleum. She felt a wetness behind her ear. She wanted to dry it off but her hand wouldn't move. She felt the wetness reach her neck. She stared at a thick dust ball trapped under the metal wheel of the bed's box spring.

She waited for the merciful darkness to close in. Her thoughts were of Hal.

Geraldine heard a distant ringing sound. Telephone? Tea kettle? Alarm clock?

There was a thump. The floor under her face vibrated. She winced at the pain in her cheek. She felt her eyes closing.

From the living room came the theme song of "Gilligan's Island" and a voice saying, "It's okay. It's okay."

The blood trickled, hot and sticky, from the corner of her mouth. It tasted sweet.

"It's okay," the voice repeated.

She felt herself being lifted. She tried to get the eyes to focus but they fought to close.

She felt arms around her, carrying her away. Then the softness of the mattress under her body. She wanted to sleep but her head jumped and jerked even though she silently willed it to stop. If only she could sleep for a few minutes . . .

"Come on! Babe!"

She tried to focus her eyes. White milky swirls obscured her vision. She blinked to erase them.

"Drink this."

She was lifted to a half-sitting position and felt the hot liquid against her lips. She swung her arms wildly and turned her face away. The inside of her mouth was on fire. Then the warmth slid down her throat and curled inside her chest.

"One more."

She focused on the cup held to her mouth. Her eyes followed the hand and trailed it up . . .

"Owen?"

She tried to clutch him but the pain crippled her efforts.

"It's okay, babe. I'm here."

He sat on the bed and cradled her shoulders as he held her head to the cup.

"That's all I could find. Tomato soup."

She wondered why he had spilled the hot liquid on the back of her neck. Her ear burned.

Owen dabbed at her face with a wet cloth. "You're going to be okay. You hear me?"

She nodded.

"It's all over. You're safe. Do you understand?"

She looked down and screamed.

The Japanese man lay on the floor, his eyes open, gaping at the ceiling.

Owen pulled her close, holding her head against his chest as she struggled to get free.

"Geraldine, he can't hurt you. You understand? He can't hurt you."

She gave up the struggle.

"Don't pass out on me. Babe! Come on. Hold on!"

She nodded slowly and gently pushed herself away into a sitting position.

"I'm okay," she said, not looking down. She glanced at the sailor and buried her face in his chest. "Is he dead?"

"Yeah."

The body lay no more than a foot away on the floor next to the bed. She tried not to look but her eyes drifted . . . first to his jacket . . . the legs . . . the dark shoes.

"Why did you come here?" she asked Owen.

"Couldn't take the sleeping bag. Came over to use your couch."

"How . . . how . . . did he—?"

"I shot him," Owen said softly.

"Jesus."

"Can you move?" he asked her.

"I think so," she said. She looked away. "Is my face bad?"

"You've been prettier," he answered.

She felt behind her ear to the wet clump of hair and removed a bloodied hand. "Oh, God."

"Let me see." He tilted her head and carefully separated the tangled wad of hair. He dabbed at it with the wet cloth. "It's not too bad. Looks a lot worse than it is. You want to go to the hospital?"

"No."

She took the cloth from his hand and patted the area till the cloth came back white.

"I have to get rid of the body," he said. "Now."

"All right."

She pushed her hands firmly against the bed and steadied herself long enough to stand up. She gave her legs a moment to support the weight. Just to be sure, she leaned against the edge of the mattress. Her head was beginning to clear. The fuzziness was edging away.

"Did you check him for ID?"

"Nothing. Just a set of house keys. And car keys."

A sudden wave of nausea overcame her and she sat quickly. Her legs dangled over the side of the bed as she looked down on the body. Her stomach tightened at the pool of blood leaking from under the man.

She found herself staring at the dark suit and the high-polished shoes. The tie was nice. Not something she would have picked out. A little too conservative, but definitely expensive.

He looked strange lying on the linoleum floor, his arm partially flung under the bed. It was the eyes that bothered her the most. The way they stared at the ceiling.

"Where are we going to put him?"

"Out in the back porch, for now."

She watched Owen grab the man by the legs and drag him from the room, the dark suit jacket slopping the blood into a thick straight line, like a bright red highway divider. She gripped her throat and tried not to throw up.

Chief Ford Baker hung up from his talk with Shirley and walked into the living room, where his mother sat dozing on the couch. He took a jacket from the hall closet. He went into the kitchen, wrote a note for Leona, and left it on the table where she'd be sure to see it.

Shirley's call had disturbed him. LeRoy was obviously making inquiries in behalf of the sailor. It meant Owen had to be close by.

His first instinct was to drag the lawyer in for questioning, but he was reluctant to make such a move. He couldn't risk a race war. The city of Miami had exploded over an incident involving a black motorist and the arresting officer who claimed the driver was drunk and unruly. Like it or not, LeRoy would have to be handled delicately. It was the temper of the times.

However, he was the chief of police and still commanded some power, however eroding. He reached for the wall phone and dialed the control tower at the airport. He spoke to the agent in charge.

That done, he put on his jacket, strapped on his gun, and left the house.

He got in the car and headed toward Little Cuba, with its bodegas and voodoo flower shops. And *carnicerias* and cigar stores where you could still pick up a hand-rolled Hav-A-Tampa.

Even at night the area had a vitality that contrasted sharply with the yuppified flavor of the town.

Once Key West had been a haven for artists, beachcombers, adventurers, drifters, writers, bandits, con men, and just plain folk, down on their luck, in search of new beginnings.

It was a town that protected its own and kept secrets.

But that was before the real estate developers and Yankee dollars swooped down to erect their glass palaces. Soon it would look like Orlando with wall-to-wall tourist attractions. He was getting out at the right time.

The chief drove through the narrow streets. A pack of dogs swooped from a vacant lot to chase his car, but gave up when the leader stopped to scratch his ear.

In a front yard cluttered with rusted autos, two teenagers were dismantling a car engine, using the light of a table lamp hooked to a long extension cord. The chief smiled at their ingenuity.

He turned on Columbus Avenue and noted with surprise that Irene's Bakery was now José's Cafe, specializing in Cuban sandwiches and café con leche.

He drove slowly down the dark street and spotted the house. A single light burned inside. The homes alongside were dark and silent. Across the street, a white-haired woman in bathrobe and slippers sat on a porch swing feeding a baby.

The chief glanced at her and the woman looked away.

He slowed the car and proceeded to the corner, where he drove around the block. When he returned the woman with the baby was gone.

The chief slowed the car and parked in front of the Thunderbird with the car rental sticker on the bumper.

He was more saddened than angry. He hated to think of having to arrest Earl for shielding a fugitive, if not on the old man's account, for what it would do to Molly. He'd deal with that when the time came.

The chief got out of the car and reached under his jacket. He jiggled the gun handle loose in the leather holster. Not that he expected to use it, but it was comforting to know it was there.

Ford had only fired his weapon once in the line of duty. He had been a rookie, on the job six weeks, when he was sent to a robbery in progress at a grocery store.

He fired a warning shot at the fleeing bandit and struck the Coca-Cola sign above the drugstore. The incident had earned him the moniker The Coca-Cola Kid. The officers refrained from using it in his presence after he made sergeant.

He climbed the porch steps quietly and peered through the screen door. The house looked empty, but the blue tint of a TV screen illuminated a sliver of the living room.

The chief knocked on the wooden molding of the door and waited. Down the block, a woman marched onto her porch and flung a bucket of water in the air. A cat screeched and darted under the house.

He knocked again. A figure emerged. From the backlighting he could tell it was a woman, but the face was obscured by shadows.

The woman stood behind the screen door, her voice weak and breathy, as if she'd awakened from a deep sleep.

"Chief. What . . . what can I do for you?"

He recognized the New York accent. "Can I come in?" he asked.

She seemed to hesitate a moment. "Okay." She stepped back.

He noted the slacks and a blouse, so it didn't appear that he woke her. He pushed the door open and entered, his arm grazing the familiar bulge under his jacket.

She held her hand to her head and made no move to turn on a light. "Listen, I'm very tired. Can we . . . talk . . . in the morning?"

He had started to answer when Geraldine suddenly slumped. He lurched forward and caught her before she hit the floor. He half carried, half dragged her to the couch. He looked around for a light switch and rushed to the lamp across the room. He hurried back just as her eyes fluttered open.

The chief leaned over her and winced at the sight of the battered face.

"Who did this?"

"I'm okay," Geraldine moaned, struggling to sit up. She focused her eyes on his knees as she waited for the room to stop spinning. "Just . . . give me a second."

"You're going to the hospital," he said. "Where's the phone?"

"No," Geraldine groaned.

"The sailor did this?"

Geraldine mumbled a weak protest.

"How long ago did he leave?"

She swayed for a moment and he caught her just as she toppled backward against the couch. He saw the wide slash of blood coating her neck.

The chief propped her against the pillow and ran out to his car, where he called the paramedics. "Hurry!" he ordered.

Ford dashed back into the house and saw she hadn't moved. He took a handkerchief from his pocket and placed it gently behind her head.

"They're on their way," he assured her. "Just hang in there."

Geraldine didn't have the energy to protest. If only she could sleep for a little while.

The chief propped the couch pillows around her so she wouldn't tumble on the floor and ran outside to wait. He heard the ambulance screeching in the distance and dashed into the street to wave it down.

Two attendants jumped from the rear and ran up the porch steps after the chief. They didn't bother with the stretcher. They carried her out.

Ford jumped in the back of the ambulance and sat on a small stool near her unconscious form. The bright lights revealed the torn, blood-soaked blouse. The long red hair was matted with clumps of dried blood.

He grabbed the handrail as the ambulance sped off. He wedged himself closer. If she died en route, he wanted to hear her last words.

She walked out of the emergency room three hours later sporting a round bald spot behind her ear where the doctor had shaved her hair off to stitch her skull.

Chief Ford Baker was waiting, propped in a wheelchair, by the nurse's station.

"You up for some breakfast?"

She smiled. Strangely enough, she was glad to see him. "Sure."

They walked across the street to the all-night diner, and Geraldine went to the ladies room to assess the damage. The bruises on her face felt worse than they looked. The eyes were puffy, swollen into fatty slits. The gash across her nose would be uglier in the days ahead. The teeth, though loose, would tighten up on their own, the doctor assured her.

There was a deep slash running down her cheek where his ring had peeled the skin off cleanly. The lips were swollen and cut where she'd bit into them. She grabbed up a long sleeve of paper towels and draped it along the front of her blouse to conceal the blood stains.

She had definitely seen better days.

Coffee, orange juice, a platter of French toast, and bacon awaited her when she slid into the booth across from the chief.

They ate silently. A few customers stared at them curiously, but looked away quickly when the chief glared back.

She ate with gusto despite the soreness in her mouth. The chief asked her what she smoked and walked over to the counter, coming back with a pack of cigarettes.

They were on their second cup of coffee when he broke the silence.

"Doctor said you're a lucky lady."

She laughed. "He hasn't seen me play poker."

The chief leaned back in the booth and took a cigar from his shirt pocket. The clock over the pastry case read ten to four. In another hour or so the sun would be up.

"You see a lot of sorry things in my line of work," he said, "but I never had the stomach for men who abuse kids or women."

Geraldine nervously shredded the paper napkin beneath the coffee cup.

"You don't even have to swear out a complaint. Just tell me where he is."

Geraldine sighed. "It wasn't Owen."

"Bullshit."

"I'm telling you the truth."

"I've got cops all over the state of Florida looking for him. It's only a matter of time. Days. Maybe hours."

"He didn't do it."

The chief lit the cigar and flung the match away. "He won't hurt you again. I'll fix it so you won't even have to testify."

Geraldine raised a fingertip to her swollen lip. It felt hard. "I went to a bar. Met this guy . . . we had a couple of drinks . . . and I brought him home."

The chief spun his body around in the seat, peering out the window. "Bullshit!" A truck lumbered past, glowing like a Christmas tree, outlined in amber lights. "What you take me for, gal? Some stranger had done that to you, you'd be on the phone with the governor! TV people! You'd be in my office carryin' on like a banshee."

She quickly killed the smile.

"I'm trying to help you here. Just tell me where he is," the chief said softly.

"Can't," she shook her head. "You'll hurt him."

"Might. Ask me, he needs hurtin'."

Geraldine sipped the coffee, using the teaspoon to insert the liquid into her mouth.

"Isn't it remotely possible . . . just pretend for a second . . . that you're wrong about Owen?"

The chief nodded, "If he's innocent, let him tell me. I'll listen."

"And then you'll arrest him."

She suddenly felt weary. The combination of the painkillers and the food were having its effect.

"I have to get some sleep or I'll pass out right here," she told him.

He could see from the lines pulling at the corners of her mouth that she wasn't faking. He paid the bill and used the phone next to the cash register to call for a police car.

They drove in silence back to the house.

"I'll be in touch. You can count on it," he told her.

They got out of the vehicle and Geraldine followed him to his car.

"Thank you . . . for everything."

The chief pulled away, squealing the tires.

She waited till the red taillights disappeared and then entered the house.

"You here?" she whispered in the darkness.

"Yeah."

She jumped at the closeness of the voice. Owen was sitting on the couch. She groped her way across the room.

"You okay?" he asked.

"Yes," she said, dropping next to him on the couch.

The house smelled of pine oil and disinfectant. She could detect it on his clothes.

"Where is he?" she asked.

"All taken care of."

She followed the red glow of his cigarette.

"How—"

"He's gone," Owen said emotionlessly.

"Where?"

He tapped out the cigarette. "For a ride."

Geraldine was taken aback. "You dumped him?"

"Sort of," he replied.

"What do you mean?" she said sharply. This was no time for charades.

"He's in the trunk of the chief's car."

CHAPTER FIFTY-FOUR

On their way out of town, Owen insisted they check out the house on Cypress Street. Geraldine waited in the car as Owen crossed the road and headed quickly for the white clapboard house. The sun was rising and soon the street would awaken. He didn't have much time.

A bakery truck lumbered by. Owen plastered himself against the side of the house, keeping an eye on the dog who slept on the neighboring porch. The truck scooted from view and Owen hurried along the macadam driveway. Upstairs, above his head, he heard a toilet flush.

Owen dug the keys out of his pocket and opened the door on the first try. He closed it quietly and snapped on the flashlight, beaming it on the small entranceway.

The tiny apartment was compact. A bedroom, kitchen/living room, and bath. It was also immaculate. And dark. All the window shades were drawn. He swept the main room with the beam, careful not to scan the picture window. The orderliness struck him as odd. Not a magazine, ashtray, or piece of clothing announced that someone actually lived there.

He crossed the few feet to the kitchen and opened the refrigerator door to give him more light. Two bottles of mineral water, one opened, stood on the otherwise empty metal racks.

A drinking glass was propped upside down on the plastic dishrack alongside the sink. The garbage pail was empty.

Owen went into the bedroom. The closet yielded a single dark suit. Below it was a small suitcase.

A car cruised by slowly and Geraldine tensed. She scrunched lower on the seat and peered over the dashboard as the car continued on.

She glanced nervously at the house and saw a window shade rise on the second floor. A man in a white undershirt walked past the window.

Another car turned onto Cypress Street. It moved slowly, leaving a smoky green exhaust trail.

She nervously lit a cigarette and stared down the driveway where Owen had disappeared. Her eyes scanned the immediate area and saw the dog. She silently willed it not to wake. She reached up to the steering wheel and clutched the keys jutting from the ignition. She would give him another few minutes.

What was taking him so long? She moved up on the seat, keeping her body angled in the shadows. She jumped at the sound of a door closing and saw Owen rushing toward her. She reached over to push the door open.

He got in the car grinning. "Bingo!"

She slid quickly to the passenger's side as he started the engine and tossed something on the seat between them.

She picked up the circular object. It was a small, amber plastic container, the kind issued by pharmacists. She read the typed label bearing a Philadelphia address.

CHAPTER FIFTY-FIVE

"He's dead," David Ko told Marco over the phone.

Yan-San the clever one. The most ambitious. The meticulous artist. The leader.

"Are you positive?"

"He was supposed to call me at midnight."

All he asked was, "The sailor?"

David Ko didn't hesitate. "Appears so."

"What do you recommend?" Marco asked, as if politely consulting a waiter.

"He told me about a lawyer who visited the sailor in jail and helped him escape. I will start there."

Marco said "Fine" and hung up.

First Akido, then Kuni, now Yan-San.

Marco walked away from the public pay phone next to the Taco Bell in the shopping mall. He took the escalator to the parking level and got into his car.

Yesterday's edition of the New York *Daily News* lay on the front seat, open to a picture of Cardinal Thomas Ryan McHugh in his hospital bed.

The story said that the sidewalk injury would not keep the cardinal from officiating at Easter Mass, in three weeks, nor would it postpone his goodwill visit to France.

The photo showed the cardinal surrounded by floral displays and smiling at a nurse who autographed his leg cast.

The nurse was bent over the bed, partially concealing the open door, which was visible in the right-hand corner of the picture. At first it had escaped Marco's attention and then he had been mystically drawn to the small lettering that grew prominent under closer inspection with a magnifying glass.

It was then that he saw the grainy black and white 27. The number of the room.

He took it as a another sign from God. A direct message to him that the time had come.

Less than ten miles away from the Miami mall, under threatening clouds and a slate gray sky, Geraldine and Owen stepped out of the twin-engine plane and hurried across the windswept runway, trailing behind LeRoy.

They waited out of view as the lawyer entered the smallest of the six hangars and reappeared minutes later.

"I'll be at this number the next three days," he said, handing Owen a slip of paper. "A girl will answer," he said smugly. As they headed for the taxi stand, LeRoy told them, waving for a cab, "Try to keep out of trouble."

Owen flagged down a second cab and had the driver take them to the Howard Johnson's motel on Collins Avenue.

They arrived ten minutes later and silently appraised the eight-story structure on the beach. Owen nodded and Geraldine paid the driver.

"I'll be right back," she told the sailor.

He sauntered around the building, his face partially hidden by the wide-brimmed cowboy hat and dark glasses. He glanced across the parking lot and noted the rear exit.

Geraldine emerged minutes later. "We're all set." She led him quickly through the small lobby and up the rear stairway to their second-story room. She was taken aback by the one double bed but if Owen noticed he didn't let on.

They took turns showering and while she busied herself at the mirror applying makeup, the sailor called Earl.

"Anything in the paper today?" he asked.

"Nothing," the old man told him.

Owen tensed. "He had to find the body by now."

"Happened to me, I sure wouldn't be announcing it," Earl pointed out.

She brushed her hair slowly, stealing glances at him as he sat on the edge of the bed.

His hair was still damp from the shower and she could smell his talcum powder across the room. The white T-shirt gripped his chest tightly. The thick gold chain with the anchor rested on the stretched neckline.

A bath towel was wrapped across his midsection, ending just slightly above the knees. The legs were tanned and hairy. Thick purple veins, like clumps of grapes, knotted the knees, caused, no doubt, by years of walking the steel floors of a ship.

Still . . . it was a nice body.

Owen gave Earl the phone number and hung up.

CHAPTER FIFTY-SIX

It was one in the afternoon when Chief Ford Baker parked in his reserved spot at police headquarters and entered the building through the main entrance.

He usually liked to sneak up on his men unannounced, which is why he had two doors in his private office, enabling him to enter unseen by the front desk. It tended to instill discipline. Often the men didn't know he was in the building till he bellowed orders.

Accustomed to his ploy, the cops always checked the parking space. When it was empty, word would spread quickly, greatly relaxing the atmosphere. Each squad selected one of its officers to keep tabs. It wouldn't do to have the chief pop in on a gin game in the locker room, or a confiscated XXX-rated movie.

But Ford had also been a patrolman, so he sometimes took a cab and got out a block from headquarters, entering by the rear door.

Or he'd hitch a ride with a neighbor. Once, for a week, he rented a different car every day and parked it in the visitor's lot.

Today he was too angry and preoccupied for such charades. He marched straight to his office and slammed the door shut. Pink phone memos flew around with the blast of air. He picked up some of them and glanced at the others. Didn't matter. Most were from the mayor.

Hours later he was on the phone with the emergency room doctor who had treated Geraldine when Patrolman Powanda stopped in to see if he wanted dinner.

The officer, looking to get Saturday night off, volunteered to drive over to the coffee shop by the courthouse, knowing the chief had a passion for their crab cakes.

As expected, Ford took him up on the offer and threw a ten on the desk.

"It's on me," the officer said, heading for the door. "By the way," the cop added, "you better get those fish out of your trunk. Smells real ripe." He walked out, leaving Ford Baker staring.

The chief waited a few moments, grabbed his car keys, and dashed to the parking lot.

Two cops were leaning against a police car, enjoying a joke. The punchline went unfinished as they scurried away at the sight of the man.

The chief rushed to his car and inserted the key. Before he could twist it, the trunk lid slowly rose open.

Yan-San's gaping eyes greeted him.

Geraldine drove silently as Owen consulted the street map on his lap. He'd been painfully quiet since she'd called the Miami *Herald* and spoken to her ex-husband, Buzzy James, whose car she was now driving.

The two exes chatted like old pals, catching up on the highlights of the past fourteen years. She was happy to hear he was the assistant sports editor and the father of twins.

If he was curious or suspicious or alarmed as to why she needed a car immediately ("Could I come down to the paper and pick it up right now?") he didn't inquire. After all, with Geraldine, the unexpected was the norm.

Owen's only comment was, "What kind of a name is Buzzy?" He didn't really want an answer and kept his attention on the street map.

"Turn here," he said, pointing to an unfinished furniture store. "Two blocks, make a left. Should be right on the corner."

The neighborhood was definitely Cuban, with its bodegas and sidewalk clothing racks. A vegetable stand with wooden baskets of mangoes and avacadoes displayed a large tin tub filled with tall, gnarled stalks of yucca. Children cavorted on the sidewalk while bored-looking women sat on the row of porches.

Geraldine steered around a maze of wrecked cars belonging to an auto body shop. Two Spanish men sat at a sidewalk table playing dominoes. A beer bottle clothed in a paper bag sat near one man's foot.

It reminded her of New York, where the old men sat in Washington Square playing chess. She found herself missing the city. She hadn't had a good slice of pizza in weeks. Nor a decent cheeseburger.

A block away, Gigi, in tight pink Spandex pants and a pink scarf tied about her blonde hair, left the restaurant and hurried to her sports car parked at the hydrant.

She threw the leather pouch with the cash receipts on the front seat next to the shopping bags. She made a quick U-turn, spinning the tires on the wet surface, and drove away as Geraldine's car made the left.

"That's it," Owen said, peering at the red brick facade with the dwarf palm trees at the entrance.

"I could go in alone," she suggested. The restaurant had its own parking area strung with hanging lights. And more palm trees.

She eased the car next to a Lincoln Continental and a Corvette.

A youth in a white shirt, dark pants, and vest hurried over to open the car door.

The chief closed the trunk quickly and strode back into the building.

There was not one scintilla of doubt in his mind that the fucking sailor planted the body while he was in the hospital with the woman.

The son of a bitch was in the house all the time and he hadn't fucking checked it! Stupid! Stupid! He berated himself. The bastard was right there in the house with a fucking dead Jap and I'm playing fucking good Samaritan with his girlfriend.

The chief entered his office and locked the door behind him. It took him a few minutes to find the right key, it was so rarely used. He stood by the door panting. A pain shot up through his leg. His heart was pumping too fast to keep up with the collapsed veins.

HE WAS RIGHT THERE! IN THE NEXT FUCKING ROOM!

If it had happened to one of his men he would've brought him up on charges and kicked him off the force.

MAYBE SIX FEET AWAY! ALL I HAD TO DO WAS LOOK!

The chief gripped the edge of the water cooler, drawing comfort from the cold. He leaned over, pressed the small blue button, and cupped the water in his hands. He swiped it across his forehead.

His breathing was under control now and he made his way slowly to his desk. He could hear laughter from the hall and what sounded like a basketball bouncing on the tile floor. He figured it to mean a lost kid being entertained. Or one of his men goofing off. Either way, he didn't care. The phone rang and he ignored it. His heart rate calmed as he walked slowly to his desk and sat down. The cigar in the ashtray didn't tempt him.

HE KILLED THE BASTARD AND PUT THE FUCKING CORPSE IN MY CAR!

As he saw it, he had three options.

1. Report it.
2. Dump it where it would be found.
3. Bury it.

He stared at the amber buttons blinking on the phone. He glanced away and looked at the bulging employee folder on his desk.

HOW WAS HE SUPPOSED TO DEAL WITH FUCKING VACATIONS AND COMP TIME WHEN A DEAD JAP WAS THIS MINUTE STARING AT THE ROOF OF HIS TRUNK!

He grabbed up the cigar and didn't bother to relight it.

The first option, reporting the body, presented a problem. "Well, Ford, how'd that body get there?"

Even the chickenshit, imbecile mayor would have enough common sense to ask the question.

So long, pension. Hello, disciplinary charges.

So long, Tennessee. Hello, K-Mart security, $4.25 an hour.

So long, mama. The news would kill her.

There'd also be a ton of reports, probably involving the FBI, whose fingerprint files they'd have to use. And reports meant waiting for lab findings on hair particles, carpet fibers, stomach contents, clothing labels, fingernail scrapings, dust analysis.

WHILE I WAS RIGHT THERE GETTING HER AN AMBULANCE!

Ford could visualize the headlines: "Police Chief Takes Murder Victim for a Ride."

"Death Was His Copilot."

"Mayor Suspends Chief."

He would be held up to public ridicule, probably fired—and for what?

A FUCKING JAP WHO PROBABLY GOT WHAT HE DESERVED.

And if he didn't, hey, too bad. Pearl Harbor.

The second option was more desirable. He could wait till dark and dump the body where someone would be sure to find it.

But it also brought problems. For one, he'd get stuck with the investigation. And what if the FBI guys didn't fuck up the way they usually did, and traced the body to his trunk?

What if they were able to lift his thumb print from the victim's suit? He had stupidly placed his hands on the man's chest to see if he was breathing.

The phone rang and he grabbed it out of habit. His heart was pounding like a drill press. "Ford Baker."

"Chief, this is Cabral over at the airport."

It took him a few seconds to place the caller. "Oh, yeah." He had known him since he was the star slugger in high school. A pleasant kid, always polite and easy-going, he'd passed up a minor league career to go to college.

"How's your mom?" Cabral asked.

"Good. Real good," the chief answered. He held his hand to his chest, convinced Cabral could hear the hammering through the phone. "What can I do for you?"

"I just came on duty and saw that memo where you'd called. I went through the flight logs and I noticed that LeRoy flew out this morning. So, I figured you'd like to know."

"Where'd he go?"

"He filed a flight plan to Miami."

The chief grew excited. "Was he carrying any passengers?"

"He didn't specify. These guys never do, no matter how many times we tell 'em."

The chief thanked him. "You'll let me know when he gets back."

"Absolutely."

The chief hung up and became aware of the sweat caking his body. He turned instinctively to look at the air conditioner and heard its familiar buzz.

So LeRoy had flown the coop—taking them along and leaving him with a dead body.

The chief stared across the room at the Alaskan poster with the fisherman in a red-checkered cap holding a thrashing salmon over the foamy waters. The sun glinted off the silvery tail as droplets of water slid to the man's rubber boots. Behind him, a clump of trees stood stately against a rushing waterfall.

All things considered, the chief decided, life would be much simpler if the Jap just sayonaraed away.

CHAPTER FIFTY-SEVEN

David Ko lost little time. He was in Key West three hours after the call to Marco.

He took a motel room near the airport. He didn't go near the Cypress apartment, knowing it'd be futile. In the years since he joined the team, Yan-San had never once neglected to call as prearranged.

He remembered their last conversation. "When I find the lawyer, I'll find the sailor," Yan-San told him.

Ko didn't possess his friend's patience, nor his devotion to detail. Yan-San once admitted he was enslaved to the "minuteness of invisible truths." Ko had never forgotten the lyrical phrase. He had no idea what it meant exactly or even if it was a quotation from some piece of literature, but it fit his friend perfectly.

And because he wasn't similarly blessed, he picked up the phone in the room and dialed.

"Mr. Thomas's office," a young woman answered.

"Hello. A friend recommended that I see Mr. Thomas. Is it possible to get an appointment for this afternoon?"

"I'm sorry. He's out of town."

"When do you expect him back?"

The woman laughed. "Your guess is as good as mine. But I'll be hearing from him later. I could have him call you back."

Ko coughed, "It's vital that I speak to him. Did he say where he was going?"

"All I know is he's in Miami."

Ko persisted. "Do you know what airline? Maybe he—"

"He flies his own plane," she said impatiently. "Just leave your number and he'll call you."

Ko hung up feeling pleased with himself. Maybe he wasn't the gifted scholar his predecessor had been, but he could hold his own. He gathered his suitcase and left the room. He took a cab to the small airfield that jutted up against the main airport and approached a young mechanic fueling a plane.

"Hi," Ko smiled. "Maybe you can help me. I was supposed to go up to Miami with LeRoy Thomas this morning. Got up late. Now I have to meet him at the airport there and I forgot the name."

"Probably Curran Field. That's where most of 'em go," the teenager said. "Call and find out if he's tied down."

Ko hesitated and fumbled for his wallet. "I haven't mastered your American phones yet," he said sheepishly. He removed a ten dollar bill. "Could . . . could you call for me?"

The kid jumped in the company van. "Sure. Come on."

Ko rode with the teenager to a small one-man office adjacent to the hangar.

The kid grabbed up the desk phone, checked the number in the Rolodex, and dialed as he lit up a Marlboro alongside a huge No Smoking sign that covered most of the wall.

"Joey? Kevin in Key West. Good. Listen I'm trying to see if one of our guys tied down this morning."

With his free hand he flipped through a loose-leaf notebook bearing scribbled entries. He turned the pages till he found the one he wanted.

"Grand Jury X7670."

David Ko silently blessed his good fortune.

"Thanks. Talk to you soon." The kid hung up. "He's there. Curran Field."

Ko thanked him and left. He found a phone booth a block away and called Marco. "I'm coming back," he told him. "They're in Miami."

CHAPTER FIFTY-EIGHT

Geraldine and Owen drove from the restaurant in silence, both confined to their solitary fears. The foray had produced nothing but a tasty bowl of black bean soup and yellow rice with chicken. She was even too depressed to point out, "I told you so."

The prospect of going to the FBI, which had seemed like such a smart move a lifetime ago, now appeared downright foolish and dangerous.

For starters, Owen would be turned over to the Key West police. There was no doubt in her mind that others in the Japanese network were picking up the scent, ready to pounce. How long could she run with no money and no prospects of getting any?

Returning home was out of the question. If they were able to track her to Little Cuba, her New York apartment was certainly being watched. Besides, there wasn't any job to return to and more than likely not even an apartment, as she hadn't paid the rent for February or March.

Geraldine brushed her hair from her face and stole a glance at the sailor, who was driving with equal lethargy. His elbow protruded from the open window as one hand held the wheel.

"Got any ideas?" she asked, trying to sound perky.

He threw her a half-smile. "Do you know there's a string of islands in the South Pacific that don't even show on any map?"

Geraldine said, "Really?"

"We anchored there for maneuvers one winter, back in sixty-eight. A person could get lost easily."

She pictured a clump of sand out in the middle of the ocean battered by hurricanes and infested with crawling creatures. "What are you saying?"

"That a person could disappear . . . forever."

Tears jumped to her eyes. She was stunned by the sadness that suddenly washed across her soul.

"Are you serious?"

"We don't have too many options," he said with a calm resolve.

She stared out the car window. She pretended to be fascinated by the scenery that blurred behind the tears.

They arrived at the motel and took the back stairs to their room. Owen had the key in the lock when a dark figure materialized behind them: "Don't move!"

Geraldine spun around and was swinging her purse like a weapon when the man shouted, "Hey! It's me!"

"LeRoy!"

Owen pushed him in the room quickly, turning to make sure no one had witnessed the charade. He flung the keys on the dresser. "That was stupid."

"How'd you find us?" Geraldine asked, scurrying about turning on lamps.

"Earl." The lawyer noted the double bed as he took a seat next to the window.

Owen leaned against the dresser. His bulk seemed to overcrowd the furnishings in the cramped room.

"What are you doing here?" the sailor asked.

"Got anything to drink in this place?" LeRoy asked.

"No," Owen answered, too sharply, Geraldine felt.

LeRoy sighed. "You know your jumper? The one from Philly? He didn't have any health insurance."

Geraldine stole a glance at Owen. "So?"

LeRoy was enjoying the attention and meant to drag it out. "You'd think a hotshot New York reporter would've checked it out. I'm just a poor, country lawyer—"

"Cut the horseshit, LeRoy," Owen bristled. "You have something to say, say it!"

"Not very friendly, is he?" the lawyer asked Geraldine.

"The jumper," she persisted. "What about him?"

LeRoy unbuttoned his leather aviator jacket, revealing a brown silk shirt. "I made a couple of calls today. Those Philadelphians are really downright neighborly. May fly up there sometime."

Geraldine could feel the tension. "That's nice, LeRoy. What did you find out?"

"Well, the guy had a lot of medical problems and Shirley mentioned he had no health insurance. Got me to thinking."

He reached into his pocket and pulled out a yellow slip of paper torn off a legal pad. He handed it to Geraldine.

She unfolded it and read: "Marco's Travel Agency. Marco DelCampo." The name was familiar. Where had she heard it?

"That's the guy who paid his bills," LeRoy pointed to the paper. "Has a travel agency here on Collins Avenue, on the nine hundred block. Maybe the guy worked for him at one time."

Owen looked at Geraldine. "What do you think?"

"It's worth a shot."

To her mind, it sure as hell beat hiding out in a snake-infested island a million miles from a casino table.

Even if it didn't pan out, it kept the chase alive—and the slim hope they were getting somewhere.

Owen told LeRoy, "We'll follow it up. Thanks."

The lawyer stood quickly. "Gotta go."

Geraldine followed him to the door. "How long you going to be in town?"

"Depends on the lady. She flies for Delta. If they call her in, I'll leave in the morning." He grinned, "That part you keep out of the book. Ciao."

They waited till they saw him leave the hotel, and Owen told her, "Let's go."

Ten minutes later they were in the car driving north on Collins Avenue.

"What do we do when we get there?" she asked.

"I'll wait outside. You go in and get some travel brochures. Look the place over. Count the doors, windows. Figure out what's the easiest way to bust in tonight."

Geraldine was scared. "What if—"

"You're not out in five minutes, I'll run in."

She didn't like it. If this Marco was involved, he probably knew what she looked like.

"Maybe we should wait," she said nervously. "Do a little background check on him. I could have Buzzy ask around the *Herald.*"

Owen didn't respond.

He was staring at a figure half a block away, crossing the street to a small sports car parked at the curb.

He hunched closer to the windshield and slowed the car to a crawl.

Geraldine followed his gaze to the blonde in the pink knee-hi pants and white heels. Even from a distance she could tell that this was an exotic creature.

The slim woman, with a figure off the cover of *Sports Illustrated,* was now leaning to open the door of a green sports car. The gold link ropes of the shoulder purse glinted against the tanned body. The blonde hair curled out from under the pink scarf.

Geraldine found herself suddenly annoyed. Here she was about to risk her life and he was drooling over Miss November! But she also found she couldn't avert her gaze. The woman was incredibly beautiful.

Owen slowed the car to the curb, halting behind a mail truck in a restricted zone. They still had a clear view of the woman now getting into the car.

Geraldine poked him. "Can we get back to reality here?"

Owen watched as the woman settled behind the steering wheel and adjusted the sun visor. He waited till she pulled away and made a quick U-turn behind her.

"What are you doing?" Geraldine glanced back at the travel agency they were leaving behind. "You crazy? Hey—she's probably married!"

Owen replied, "Not Miss Gigi."

Geraldine stared at the green Jaguar ahead, slipping easily into the traffic.

"You know her?" she gasped.

Owen nodded. "We met once. When she killed Luther."

And at that instant, Geraldine remembered. She dug quickly into her purse and removed the small black packet of matches with the silver-embossed palm trees she'd taken earlier from the restaurant. On the back cover, under "Genuine Cuban Cuisine" was printed, "Marco DelCampo, proprietor."

Geraldine waited till the car stopped for a light and jumped out.

"What are you doing?" Owen shouted.

"Don't lose her! I'll meet you back in the room," she said. He didn't have time to protest—the green Jaguar made a left at the intersection and he slid in behind it.

Geraldine got back to the hotel room at around 10:30 that night and found it empty. She checked the bathroom and saw a white towel neatly hung across the shower bar. She knew he'd returned and gone out again. She located him in a bar three blocks from the motel, shortly after midnight.

He was talking to a woman in a tight sweater who promptly moved away when Geraldine threw her purse on the bar and sat next to Owen.

"Don't mean to cramp your style," she said, eyeing the brunette with the purple eyeshadow and clunky earrings. She looked like one of the television models for a dating service. The ones that slither and breathe heavily to the camera.

"I thought you took off," he said. The cowboy hat all but obscured his face. He had not turned to look at her.

From the cigarette butts in the ashtray and the peanut shells in the small lacquered basket, she figured he'd been there a few hours.

The bar was a pretentious yuppy hangout with neon sculptures of Monroe's lips and Bette's eyes on the stark wall. A neon telephone with its innards exposed sat prominently midway down the pink formica bar. Brass ceiling fans twirled overhead.

A slim young man with a dancer's body, wearing a yellow cardigan and white slacks, stood behind the bar filling drinks. A neon menu listed the entrées on the far wall next to a garish caricature of Laurel and Hardy.

She detested the place.

"Why didn't you leave me a note?" Geraldine asked, noticing he'd taken the time to put on a fresh shirt and jeans. He looked annoyingly attractive.

"You leave a note when you ran out of the car?"

The brunette, sitting three stools away, pretended not to hear the exchange.

Geraldine fumed. "I went straight to the *Herald* and spent the day researching back clips. I was with the women's editor for over an hour."

Why the hell was she explaining herself to a pervert who, the minute her back was turned, sought out Miss Dial-a-Porn? And,

Geraldine swore silently, if the bimbo looked at her one more time *her* innards would be visible on the bar.

"You see ol' Buzzy?" Owen asked.

"Yes. As a matter of fact."

He chuckled.

Men, she realized, were all neurotic. This conversation was depressingly similar to many with Hal. And here there wasn't even a relationship.

Her hand drummed nervously on the bar. She told herself, when this is all over, if the Japs don't get him, I will. But now was not the time.

"Our friend Marco is a very shadowy character. He's definitely dirty. Drugs. But he's never been arrested. Seems he has many friends in high places. The governor has cruised on his yacht, so have a couple of U.S. senators. Originally from Cuba, he used to be married to an American ballerina. She died a couple of years ago. They lived in a mansion out in Key Biscayne."

"More like a fortress," Owen said.

She was momentarily taken back.

"I saw it today," he explained. "What else?"

"Besides the restaurant and the travel agency, he has real estate and a horse farm in Ocala. He and his wife were very socially active—symphony, museum, that kind of stuff. He's the main benefactor on that arts complex going up downtown. Sees it as a memorial to his dead wife. Maybe he's our man, maybe not. He could be a regular businessman."

"Restaurant owners don't need armed guards," Owen said. "The gate around the house could hold back a military tank. The hedges have electrical sensors. There are cameras scanning the property. The place is guarded twenty-four hours a day by armed men. Behind the house, along the water, is another sentry post and three Dobermans in wire kennels."

Geraldine softened. "Guess I don't have to ask where you've been all day."

"I went back an hour ago," he said. "The night crew is on duty."

Geraldine placed her elbows flat on the bar, close to but purposely not touching his arm. "You followed Miss November?"

He nodded. "She went in the house and never came out."

"It doesn't make sense," she said. "Why would a guy with all that money want to poison the country?"

Owen shredded the cocktail napkin with his thumb. "It wasn't done for profit. None of it. If you read Hal's stories you'd know that. No one made a dime off it."

Geraldine said, "If he is a coke dealer it would explain the security system."

"Then why did he send his girlfriend to poison me?"

Geraldine looked at him closely. The face was freshly shaven. She caught a whiff of the now familiar talcum powder.

"You sure it was her?"

"Positive." He slid his glass against the edge of the bar and caught the yellow sweater's attention.

"Just how close did you get to her?"

Owen looked at Geraldine and smiled. He couldn't help it. The smile was totally involuntary.

She stormed out of the bar and walked back to the motel where she lay awake till almost dawn. When she awoke at noon, he still hadn't returned.

CHAPTER FIFTY-NINE

That same afternoon, David Ko, wearing white slacks and a lime green shirt, looking very much like a tourist, got out of the car in the visitors' lot at Curran Field.

He walked across the paved roadway and followed the narrow cement strip to the field where a maze of small planes stood neatly nestled along the grassy incline. A cluster of palm trees a mile away at the edge of the furthest runway attested to the clear visibility.

He walked slowly among the gleaming, winged bodies, unmindful of the raindrops that now began to fall. A uniformed attendant skittered past on a golf cart and braked when Ko waved him down.

"I was supposed to meet LeRoy Thomas here," he yelled over a plane revving up for takeoff. "They all look the same," he shrugged.

"Get in," the man said, shifting into reverse and darting the cart around a tow bar. "I fueled him this morning."

He drove parallel to the main runway and came to a stop yards short of a tall chain link fence. David Ko noted a tear in the fence large enough for a person to crawl through, and the path pounded by years of foot traffic.

"There she is," the driver pointed.

Ko looked at the high-winged two-seater with *Grand Jury* scrawled in blue near the nose.

Although it was strictly against his training, Ko reached into his pocket and tipped the man five dollars. He hopped off the cart and walked toward the plane as the man scooted away.

Ko wandered to the far end of the field. He stopped near a cement embankment that served as the platform for a tall pole bearing a drooping wind sock. The ground swooped up to meet the fence at that point, leaving a small weather-dug crater. He found that there was enough room for him to sit comfortably on the grass with his back against the cement wall. He stretched his legs easily, careful to avoid the small puddle at the base.

In this position, he would go unnoticed by any motorist traveling the paved road. Even the attendant in the golf cart couldn't spot him from the field. The cement wall also hid him from the small aircraft circling overhead.

With the warm sun caressing his arms, Ko settled down to wait. The rain shower ended as quickly as it had come and the man felt tranquil.

Soon the hunt would be over.

At first Geraldine was worried that something had happened to him but the anxiety soon gave way to anger.

The only thing that had happened to him, she was certain, is that he got lucky with Miss Dial-a-Porn. She threw off the covers and checked the bathroom. The folded towel was still there from the night before.

Geraldine took a leisurely bath, which she hardly enjoyed. Her senses were tuned to the door, hoping for a sound of keys.

An hour later, unable to still her fears, she reached for the phone and called the Wagon Master.

"How ya doing, gal?" Earl asked.

"Okay," she replied. "You buy any fresh paint lately?"

She heard him catch his breath. "I thought you had some."

"I did. But I can't find it."

"When you see it last?"

"Around midnight. In a bar. I think some floozie took it home."

The old man laughed. "Well, she'll probably return it when she's done with it."

Geraldine groaned. "Wonderful. Anything interesting in the paper?"

"Nope. How's the money holding out?"

"It isn't," she answered.

"How much you need?"

Geraldine smiled. "Whatever you can spare."

"It'll be at Western Union in an hour."

"You're an angel," she told him.

"Take care of my buddy," Earl said.

They hung up and Geraldine dressed quickly. The bruises on her face were fading. A little pancake makeup did wonders.

She walked to the dresser and pulled out the top drawer, where she'd stashed the gray manila envelope with the Xeroxed clippings.

It was just as well that Owen wasn't around, she decided. He would never let her go ahead with the scheme she was planning. Yes, it was better if he didn't know.

She opened the envelope and spilled the clippings on the bed. She reached over and picked up the one with the photo of Marco and Kate.

They were posed by a billboard announcing a concert to benefit Ethiopian children.

Geraldine sat on the bed and looked closely at the picture.

It was startling. Claire was right.

Claire Shultz, the women's page editor at the *Herald*, had gasped in astonishment when Geraldine walked into her office.

Yes, Geraldine could see why the woman had been so startled. She could easily be Kate's sister.

CHAPTER SIXTY

LeRoy woke to the sound of Gladys Knight and The Pips doing "Midnight Train to Georgia."

It was one of his favorites so he didn't bother to reach over and turn off the clock radio. He lay in the wide bed, still smelling of last night's love.

He stared at the poster of Greece plastered on the wall next to similar travel scenes of Paris, Rome, Venice, and London.

Bruce Springsteen's voice roared out, causing Leroy to lunge, shutting off the radio.

He glanced at the clock and read the note taped to the face: "I have four days off next week. How does San Juan sound? Call me tomorrow night."

He smiled as he entered the shower. It just proved his theory that things always worked out for the best. He hadn't wanted to come to Miami, he hadn't wanted to get mixed up with the screwy sailor and his girlfriend, but he had, reluctantly, and here he was looking forward to Puerto Rico and quality sex. Grade A. Prime. Olympic gold medal.

Not that there was inferior sex, but some was just better. And this was major league caliber. Every part of his body ached. A small price to pay. He'd gladly put himself through the agony again, but his secretary was threatening to quit unless he showed up today.

Besides, his wife probably wouldn't buy the delay much longer. She might even ask to see the papers on the "million-dollar malpractice suit" that had whisked him from home.

Better to return today and not stretch credibility too thin. He needed time to clear the desk if he was going to spend four days in San Juan. He dressed quickly, scrawled a note, and took a cab to the airport. The sun baked his face as he hurried across the field.

He reached his plane, yanked the door open, and threw his canvas bag on the front seat. He walked around to the side, checked the oil, and gave the tires a quick glance. He untied the ground rope and hopped aboard.

The sun hit the windshield with the impact of a beach ball as he taxied toward the runway. He radioed the tower and retrieved his sunglasses from the net compartment on the door, which was clogged with maps.

The tower gave him the go-ahead as LeRoy looked at his watch. He would be home in time for a quick swim and maybe even take the kids to a movie.

The plane glided along the runway as he eased out the throttle, and sailed easily over the spindly trees. He could read the number on the roof of a truck lumbering up the highway. A red and blue police bubble pulsed below as cars crawled to a standstill on I-95. An ambulance raced in the opposite direction.

LeRoy swung the craft into an easy, gliding turn, pointing it south, away from the direct glare of the sun. The wings cast a gray shadow on the tin roof of a factory. He'd be home before the drivers got around the traffic jam.

It was moments like this that he didn't regret the bank loans.

He was still smiling when David Ko sat up in the back seat and pressed his fingers against LeRoy's jugular.

"We're going to have a little talk," the man informed him. The voice was a mere whisper above the engines.

"We can do this pleasantly, if you like. I can remove my hands. It's up to you."

LeRoy had known terror. He'd met it in Cuu Long near the Mekong River Delta. And once on the D Train to Brooklyn on a snowy night.

But that was a merely a dress rehearsal for this moment.

He couldn't breathe. The man was choking off the air and then releasing it. LeRoy grew dizzy. Despite the fear hammering in his brain, he managed to nod.

"Good," the man said, loosening his hold but not removing his hands from LeRoy's throat.

"A friend of mine is looking for a friend of yours. We know you brought him to Miami. We need to find him."

LeRoy stared straight ahead. "I think you have me confused with someone else."

He glanced at the instrument panel without moving his head. His hand trembled on the stick as he noted, for the first time, the oriental accent.

The unseen passenger slowly pressed his fingers against LeRoy's throat.

"You brought the sailor and the woman to Miami."

LeRoy stiffened. "I don't know what you're talking about." He thought of putting the plane into a spin but the altitude was too low. If he could just climb . . .

"Where is he?"

If he could just keep him talking till he reached a safer elevation . . . If the plane spun out he'd have to release his hold—a normal reaction. The survival glands would kick in. Especially if he looked out the window and saw the ground rushing up at him.

He eyed the altimeter and noted the steady rise. A voice came over the headset and warned him he was creeping into a restricted space.

Ko clenched his fingers and LeRoy felt a sudden blackness embrace him. He regained his senses when the plane swooped into a dive.

"Stupid fuck! You trying to get us killed?"

The man released the pressure slightly.

LeRoy thought of banking the plane sharply and throwing him off balance, but it was too risky. For one, his hands were shaking too much and he wasn't sure that once in motion he could correct the spin. He needed to get himself together first.

He knew enough to know he wasn't thinking clearly. The thoughts were jumbled. If he wasn't in control of himself how could he hope to control the aircraft? He needed time. A few minutes. Maybe seconds. He needed . . .

"Many have died. One more won't matter," the man told him calmly.

That, more than the fingers at his throat, terrified him.

Were these the hands that planted the bomb that killed Gabe?

He had dealt with psychos before. In the infantry. He'd learned it wasn't wise to lie to them. They seemed to have a built in detector.

So LeRoy Thomas, who'd been awarded three battlefield commendations, quickly revamped his strategy.

"Okay. I brought them to Miami. Had no choice. They forced me. I left them at the airport and never saw them again. That was two days ago. They were heading for New York."

The passenger leaned closer. "Did he mention a friend of mine? He disappeared two days ago."

"No. They didn't tell me shit."

The man sighed, "Why don't I believe you?"

CHAPTER SIXTY-ONE

The money was waiting at Western Union when Geraldine arrived in a cab. Earl had wired eight hundred and the words: "Call me when the paint dries."

She bought a newspaper and walked across the street to a Denny's restaurant where she sat at the counter searching the clothing ads. Unfamiliar with Miami, she had no idea of the smart dress shops. But it was soon apparent from the highly embellished prose of the advertisements that Mona's in Coconut Grove was the type of establishment that Kate would have patronized.

One blouse in the ad was listed, in tiny eye-straining print, at $149. A suggested skirt went for $225.

Clothes had never been a priority for Geraldine. She left it to Hal and friends to replenish her wardrobe at Christmas. Her money was better spent on airfare to Vegas. Clothing was less than an afterthought.

Yet, she had known women like Kate. Had interviewed them and encountered them, usually on the arm of a politician. What she called the Jackie O Campfire Girls. A society to be viewed from behind velvet ropes.

It was early afternoon when the cab dropped her off in the Grove. Tanned tourists and natives walked along the cobbled streets. Couples sat under umbrellas at white tables along the sidewalk sipping drinks festooned with fruit.

Where was that son of a bitch of a sailor? Dead? Drunk? Drowned? Wounded? In jail? Hospital? Bar? Sleazy motel?

She spotted the gold-edged orange canopy of Mona's and entered through the glittering revolving door. Mona was not only helpful but extremely tactful. She pretended not to notice Geraldine's uncoordinated Macy's/Caldor's/Shoetown ensemble and enthusiastically helped her select a plain beige silk shirtdress with tiny pearl buttons on the sleeves.

"It travels like a dream," Mona cooed. She accessorized the outfit with a small clasp leather purse and muted pearl earrings.

She also recommended a nearby shoe store, and a hair salon from which Geraldine emerged $140 poorer, with her gleaming red hair plastered severely against her skull and caught in a muffin-sized bun behind the ears. A wisp of white baby's breath flowers circled the knot.

Her nails gleamed with silver polish, and she carried the chic shopping bag that contained a pale pink lipstick and gray eye shadow.

It was almost four when she returned to the hotel and found a note propped up against the TV.

"Went to check on Gigi. Be back soon."

At least the son of a bitch was alive.

She went into the bathroom, scrubbed off her makeup, careful not to muss the hairdo that made her look like a spinster aunt, and quickly threw on the new clothes.

Glancing from the mirror, which showed pale pink lips and dull untouched lashes, to the news photo, Geraldine knew it wasn't perfect—but close.

The tiny purse wouldn't hold her usual two packs of cigarettes so she discarded them, realizing that Kate, a dancer, would never smoke.

She left Owen a note: "You free for dinner?" and hurried out of the room.

In the cab driving to the travel agency she told herself this was merely another investigative story like many she had worked on through the years.

No worse, no better, no different.

Like the time she posed as a patient to expose a hospital that refused emergency care to indigent persons.

Or the time she worked as a waitress in Donald Trump's hotel.

Or when she tried to adopt a baby through a black market ring.

This was just another story.

But why was her hand clammy and her pulse racing in her neck?

Why was she suddenly thinking of Hal?

"Ger! Are you crazy? You can't do this. You can't walk in there. Run! Go back! It's too dangerous. Stop!"

But, she reminded herself, when did she ever listen to him? Never. No point starting now that he was dead.

It was now dark and the lights in the travel agency were on. She could see a young woman sitting at a desk near the window.

She had the driver drop her off at the corner. She stood on the sidewalk as he pulled away and took a moment to smooth down the dress and pat the braided bun.

She clasped the purse at her side, waited for the traffic to break, and crossed the street quickly.

"You're a fruitcake!" Hal shouted.

Geraldine pushed the glass door open and walked into the travel agency.

The office was softly carpeted beneath wide mahogany desks. Ceiling-high wall racks stuffed with travel folders covered three walls. A huge pair of Mickey Mouse ears outlined in bright red neon flashed from a corner, advertising a Disney cruise.

"Can I help you?" A young Hispanic girl smiled from behind the desk-top computer.

Geraldine slid slowly into the thick chair.

"I'd like to visit the islands." She glanced discreetly at a glass-enclosed cubicle to her left.

A man in a gray suit stood with his back to her, talking on the phone, leaning against a wooden file cabinet.

"That's easy enough," the girl smiled. "When do you—" The phone rang, cutting off her words. "Excuse me."

Geraldine had a clear view of the man. A chunky nugget bracelet flashed on his wrist beneath the thin white sliver of a shirt cuff. The dark hair was curled tightly, with traces of white. The body was lean beneath the heavy shoulder pads. He turned slightly and she caught a glimpse of the honey-colored profile.

The secretary held up a finger as she tried to explain to the customer on the phone, apparently not for the first time, that the price of the excursion did not include meals.

Geraldine ached for a cigarette and reminded herself she was Kate. She returned her gaze to the glass partition.

It was important that she see his immediate reaction when he spotted her. She didn't want him to have time to shield his feelings. She silently willed him to look her way. She often practiced that when bored on subways and buses. It didn't always work.

The man hung up the phone and walked to his desk.

Geraldine stiffened. Any moment now he would turn her way.

If his reaction was fearful . . . if she saw even a glimmer of hostility . . . she was prepared to bolt.

The secretary said something to Geraldine but the redhead didn't respond.

"Come on. Turn around," she ordered silently.

As if instantly reacting to the unspoken command, Marco glanced her way. His face froze with disbelief. The mouth slacked open as he held onto the desk for support.

Their eyes locked for a moment and she quickly turned away, satisfied he'd never seen her before . . . except as a mirror of his dead wife.

"Sorry about that," the girl said, gesturing toward the phone. "Islands, huh?"

Geraldine heard the door open behind her and the man suddenly appeared at her side.

"Can I help you?"

She noted the slight accent.

Also the face. Gorgeous. Ricardo Montalban and then some. She could smell the flowery cologne. His hand rested inches away on the stack of telephone directories on the desk.

"It's okay," the secretary told him.

Geraldine found it impossible to believe that this fabulous creature had poisoned the country with an army of Japanese killers. The only thing he could be guilty of was breaking hearts.

But then a voice, maybe Hal's, maybe Owen's, maybe her own, whispered, "What about Ted Bundy?"

"Why don't you let me take care of it?" he said, not taking his eyes from Geraldine. "We'll be more comfortable in here," Marco said, gesturing toward his office.

Geraldine favored him with a small smile and followed.

"Please," Marco said, indicating the couch against the wall. He made no move to join her. He remained standing, much like an art patron in a museum staring adoringly at a beloved portrait.

"Tell me, where would you like to go?"

Geraldine was confident he didn't know who she was. His manner was genial and the voice relaxed. Yet the small voice buzzed. It could be a clever charade. He could at this moment be formulating a plan to follow her when she left. Or one of his men could walk in, maybe even the one who had rifled her hotel room.

She knew he wouldn't be stupid enough to try anything in the office, not with traffic whizzing by the window and people strolling past.

She edged closer to the coffee table, resting her elbow near a crystal paperweight in the form of a pyramid. It would suffice as a weapon.

"Maybe Aruba. St. Martin. I'm very flexible."

Marco leaned against the desk. His demeanor was not unlike that of a child gazing in wonder at the Christmas tree that had magically appeared in all its glowing splendor.

"You remind me of someone."

Geraldine lowered her eyes.

"I don't mean to embarrass you. Forgive me, but it's an amazing resemblance. You could be her sister."

The phone rang and he ignored it. Two rings later it was picked up by the secretary.

Geraldine replied, "I don't have any family. I lost my parents four years ago." Her voice broke. "I . . . guess I'm not quite over it yet. That's one of the reasons I want to get away for awhile. With Easter a week away . . . it's harder during the holidays." She stared at the wall behind his head.

She noted the window high in the ceiling covered by an air-conditioning unit. A door at the right partially revealed a bathroom. She couldn't tell if it had any windows.

Marco looked away as if humbled by her confession. "I also lost someone."

"I've heard it gets easier," Geraldine said. "Is that true?"

Marco replied, "I suppose so. But forget? Never."

"I appreciate your honesty."

She noted the one picture on his desk. An older woman, very

elegant, with Hispanic features. The chin and the eyes were like his.

Geraldine counted the filing cabinets, four of them, tall, legal-sized, and with a single, protruding cylinder lock at the top of each. A briefcase, also bearing a thick clasp, rested on a small table. The appointment calendar/blotter lying flat across the desk bore no notations. The gray metal Rolodex file was closed. The bulletin board near the water cooler held a single thumbtack speared into a menu for an Italian restaurant with WE DELIVER in block letters, probably put there by the secretary.

There were no personal momentoes. No baseball mug. No ashtray from a special vacation spot. No pictures on the walls, not even a travel poster. No plants. No books. Nor a scrawled reminder of a doctor's appointment. A man who keeps secrets.

"Can I be even more honest?"

She mumbled, "Of course."

"I'd like to continue our conversation over dinner. Would you give me the honor?" He smiled and just as quickly withdrew it. "I've made you angry."

"No," she answered quickly. "You just . . . took me by surprise."

She wasn't lying. Her mind raced to Owen. What if he decided to do something equally foolhardy—like watching the travel agency?

Another fear surfaced. What if the invitation was merely a ploy, and he intended to kidnap her?

"Sometimes I am accused of being impulsive," he said, "especially by my mother," he glanced at the photograph.

Geraldine smiled. "I'm the opposite. I tend to think things through. I've been planning this trip for months and I just worked up the courage today to do something about it."

"Women *should* be cautious. It's a dangerous world."

Especially if you get a headache and open a bottle of Tylenol, she wanted to say.

"I'm used to it. I'm from New York."

"Really? So was my wife. She danced there for many years. She came to Miami after she retired."

"Was?" she asked.

Marco stared at the light hitting the crystal pyramid. "She died. Many years ago. When I said it gets easier, I lied. It doesn't."

He walked out of the room to the outer office and returned with a handful of brochures.

"Okay. Where would you like to go?"

Geraldine looked up slowly. "To dinner."

"You honor me," he beamed. "I feel foolish. We haven't even been introduced. My name is Marco DelCampo."

She said, "Karen."

Earl was sitting on the porch stringing up a new net when a car whizzed up the road, its headlights bumping from ground to trees.

The old man turned to look. Probably one of the local teenagers filled with hooch and needing to pee in the creek.

The vehicle barely missed a neighbor's cat. The animal wailed and leapt to the safety of a fence.

The old man shielded his eyes from the overhead glare of the yellow bulb. He held the knitting prong in mid-air as the car came to a halt a few yards away on the grass. He watched as a large form got out of the car, not bothering to turn off the headlights or close the door.

The figure crossed swiftly toward the porch, the headlights catching the sheen of the cowhide boots.

The old man slowly reached for the open beer bottle near his foot.

The dark figure mounted the porch steps. The car radio crackled in the night. Voices mingled with the sound of a fish belly-whopping in the creek.

"Evening, Earl."

"Howdy, Ford. Get you a beer?"

He reached over to the ice chest by his leg and flipped open the Styrofoam lid.

"This isn't a social call," the man said, resting his leg on the top step.

"That so?"

"We got worries, Earl."

"What kind of worries?"

So he'd found the body after all, the old man thought. And it ain't been in the papers 'cause he wanted to tell me first, seeing as how the bastard got killed in my house.

Ford stared down the road.

I'll just out-and-out deny. What else can I do? I'll tell 'im, "Yeah, I rented her the place. She had nowhere to stay. That a goddamn crime these days?"

The chief leaned his weight forward on his knee, causing the holster to shift slightly, resting the gun squarely on his thigh.

"LeRoy Thomas is dead."

The old man stared at the uniform. He found himself gazing at the straight crease splitting the leg and wondered if Leona still ironed his clothes.

"LeRoy?"

"Murdered."

The old man's hand shook as he slowly lowered the bottle to the floor. His heart tumbled, momentarily scaring him. He waited for it to right itself.

"Just left the body. He's sitting in his airplane. Dead. Strangled, looks like."

The old man stared across the vacant lot that was a graveyard for abandoned cars. Rusted metal skeletons lay still in the moonlight, shrouded by thick weeds.

"Who did it?" he asked.

"Don't know. He flew in a couple of hours ago. Parked his plane. Then a worker making his rounds sees the door wide open. Goes over to check—"

Earl's hand closed tightly over the porch railing and he waited for his heart to stop jumping.

"He was a good man, LeRoy. Knew his daddy. We worked together on the old highway. His mama used to come by, 'fore she quit driving, every Friday. Always kept a fresh trout for her. Does she know?"

"Not yet. My men are going over to tell the wife. I came straight here," he said. "I think he took your friends to Miami and got killed for his trouble."

"You don't know that to be a fact."

"Don't fucking tell me what I don't know!" the chief yelled. He quickly glanced toward the house, hoping Molly hadn't heard. He didn't see any sign of her.

"You also oughta know that one of the mechanics said a Japanese guy was around the other day asking for LeRoy." He glared at the old man. "Earl, what the hell is going on?"

"I don't know, Ford."

"Bullshit! I got a dead cop and now LeRoy. And your fucking sailor buddy is responsible for both of them."

"You're wrong there."

He wanted to shout, "It was me. I'm the one! I found the damn note and showed it to him. I told him to call the writer."

But he didn't.

"Why are you protecting the bastard?"

Earl continued staring at the vehicular graveyard. He thought of his conversation with Geraldine. Maybe he hadn't run off with some woman. Maybe they'd killed him and were hunting her now. He had to warn her!

"Where is he, Earl?"

The old man shook his head. "I can't help you."

The chief's chest seemed to inflate with rage. His body suddenly dwarfed the porch. "Don't make me do something I don't wanna do. I came here asking for your help. I ain't the enemy."

"Neither is Owen."

"Who the fuck is he? Your illegitimate son? Why are you covering for him? I swear to God, Earl, on my daddy's grave, you tell me where the son of a bitch is right now or you're spending the night in jail. You hid that woman in your house. I was there. I saw her. I don't need no more than that to haul your ass."

Earl faced him squarely. "You go ahead and do what you have to do."

A car engine thundered in the distance. They both turned to the approaching headlights. Ford instinctively placed his hand over his gun.

They stood watching as the checkered taxi swooped under the porch light and deposited Molly and two suitcases on the lawn.

Chief Ford Baker drove to LeRoy's house and turned back when he saw the cars circling the front yard. The relatives had heard. And he wouldn't intrude on their grief.

The image of Gabe's wife screaming in her child's arms was still too vivid.

He drove home instead and was glad his mother was there. He needed someone to talk to. Someone to soothe the hurt. Someone to share his anger.

"And that son of a bitch," he said sitting at the kitchen table, his fist circling a glass of beer, "stood there and lied to my face! Swear to God I'd have run him in if Molly hadn't showed."

"Maybe he was telling the truth. Maybe he doesn't know where Owen is," the old woman told her son.

"He knows. Shifty-eyed cracker can't fool me for a second. He damn sure knows."

The woman got up from the table. "I'm going over to LeRoy's. I'll be back soon," she told him.

He protested quickly, "Ma, you know I don't like you driving at night. Let it wait till tomorrow."

She walked to the hall closet, got her purse and a lavender sweater, and held her hand out for the car keys.

But Leona, like her son, never made it to the house. She spotted Earl's truck down the block near LeRoy's place, behind a string of cars, and quickly retreated, driving as fast as her eyesight and pumping veins allowed—straight to Sweet Water Creek.

She parked in front of the old man's house and climbed quickly up the dark porch. Only a single light burned in the kitchen as she knocked on the door with the jangled car keys in her hand. She knew no one was home. Molly wouldn't let Earl pay a sympathy call alone.

She also knew the front door would open at a slight push, which it did, and she quickly entered, heading straight for the kitchen, past the living room and Earl's den, which smelled of seaweed.

It took her less than a minute to find it. There, pressed to the refrigerator under a magnetic clip in the shape of a green Coke bottle, was a penciled notation: "Owen" with a phone number.

Old habits died hard. Many a time she'd had coffee in their kitchen and commented on the stubs of papers cluttering the refrigerator.

Leona searched quickly through her purse and came up with a pencil. She copied the number onto the back of her dry cleaners' receipt and hurried away.

* * *

Geraldine ordered the fillet of sole and Marco selected the prime rib. She declined the wine, believing a dancer would not indulge, and requested mineral water.

They had driven to the small oceanside restaurant in North Miami in Marco's car. There had been one unsettling moment, when he had locked both doors from his side, but she had countered by opening her window all the way—in case she needed to scream for help.

He offered to turn on the air-conditioning, but she claimed it often gave her headaches.

They drove in near silence, listening to a Tito Rodriguez tape.

Once in the restaurant, where everyone from the valet kid to the waiters called Marco by name, she began to relax. It would be foolish of him to murder her after they had been publicly seen together.

The only other anxious moment came when Marco was called away to the phone at the bar. He gave no explanation when he returned other than, "Business."

She wondered if the caller had a Japanese accent and was now at this moment preparing to confront them when they left the restaurant. She forced the thought from her mind but it nervously kept intruding as they spoke.

"It's amazing how much you look like Kate. You don't sound anything like her. She was schooled in London so she had no New York accent," he smiled. "But, otherwise, you could be sisters."

Geraldine wondered if she would draw suspicion by going to the phone. She could say she'd had a previous appointment and in her haste had forgotten about it. She could call Owen and have him wait by the restaurant and follow them.

She could see the pay phone next to the hatcheck counter, but it was too close to the podium where the maître d' stood scrawling something on his clipboard. He would hear the conversation. Maybe there was a phone in the ladies' room.

"Do you like to sail?"

"Don't know. Never have," she answered. "There's not much opportunity in Manhattan."

"We'll have to do something about that."

She learned that he had businesses and real estate throughout

Florida, loved the theater, ballet, and boating, and adored his mother.

He learned that she was single, a childrens' book author who had come to Miami to address the English department at the university.

"Perhaps you'll autograph one of your books for me."

And perhaps you're not who we think you are and all this is just a nightmare. Perhaps you'd even laugh and enjoy the absurdity of it if I told you the truth.

Perhaps not.

CHAPTER SIXTY-TWO

YOU WHAT?" Owen raged as they sat in the motel. "You're fuckin' certifiable! You're a goddamned lunatic! I could be down at the morgue right now identifying your body 'cept I wouldn't have recognized you with that dopey hairdo."

He was naked except for white boxer shorts and the gold anchor chain. He'd been asleep and had jumped up at the sound of the key in the door.

The minute Geraldine entered the room she lit a cigarette and told him the events of the night.

She was desperate to unpin her hair and release the tension in her skull, but she was afraid that once she removed it she'd never duplicate it again—and there was no more money to spare for fancy Coconut Grove hairdressers.

Marco had dropped her off at the Concordia Hotel, a magnificent palm-shrouded palace she'd spotted earlier, and she breezed into the lobby with a cheery wave.

Once inside she'd quickly registered under the name Karen Reynolds and then took a cab immediately to the motel.

"Swear to God, I shoulda listened to Hal. He told me you were nuts. Jesus! How the hell could you do a thing like that? What if he recognized you? What if one of his Japs had walked into the restaurant and said, 'Hey, buddy, you know who that is sitting with you?' I can't believe you did that!"

Geraldine couldn't help it. She smiled. The son of a bitch really likes me, she told herself.

"You find this funny?" he thundered.

He stood leaning against the dresser, arms crossed in front of his chest, much like an exasperated parent confronting an idiot child.

She totally blotted out the tirade, wondering instead who he had spent the evening with.

"The man is a killer. A maniac. He makes Son of Sam look like a choirboy and you WENT TO DINNER WITH HIM!"

Geraldine sat on the edge of the bed, careful not to wrinkle the beige silk. "I've got another bulletin for you," she said. "He's taking me sailing tomorrow."

His face tensed and he glared at her disgustedly.

"Well, I've got one for you. LeRoy Thomas is dead and your boyfriend had it done."

It was shortly after 9:30 P.M. when Leona returned home and handed her son the slip of paper with the Miami number scribbled in pencil.

"That number there next to the other one is probably his room number," she pointed out.

He didn't stop to ask how she got it. The chief dialed the kitchen phone and heard the clerk answer, "Howard Johnson's."

He asked the address and hung up quickly. He raced to his den, where he removed a loose-leaf notebook from the bottom drawer. His mother followed, making herself comfortable in the stuffed chair, thrice upholstered, that had belonged to her great aunt Ruth and, according to family lore, had survived the Johnstown flood.

Chief Baker rifled through the notebook stained with coffee splats and cigar ashes. He found Carl Crowder's number and dialed the Miami police headquarters and asked for the deputy chief.

The call was routed through three departments before an aide informed him that the man had gone home.

"Call him and tell him Ford Baker from Key West needs to talk to him right away," the chief ordered. He gave his number and made the man repeat it.

"Is that skinny Carl?" Leona inquired.

"Yep."

She knew the man from his visits to the Tennessee cabin. He ate like a logger, but weighed all of 135 pounds.

"What's going on?" she asked. It wasn't like her son to seek favors. Nor to make calls at night from home. Especially long distance.

He didn't answer. He got up from the chair and walked to the bookcase. Leona knew better than to intrude. Whenever he was upset or disturbed he instinctively reached for his copy of Emily Dickinson poems. It had been his present from her when he graduated from high school. The worn volume lay gently in his hands as the thick fingers probed the pages. They were silent, he reading, she almost dozing, when the phone rang a half hour later.

"Carl. I need your help. I'll fill you in when I get there but I could use the best man you have and whatever other ones you can spare. I can be up there in three hours."

"We'll be ready," his friend told him.

The chief hung up and confronted a reproachful look from his mother.

"Have no choice," he said, gathering up a handful of cigars from the wooden box on the desk. He left the room and took a small suitcase from the top shelf of the hall closet.

His mother scurried to the bathroom and emerged with his toothbrush, shaving cream, toothpaste, razor, and ulcer pills.

"Go to sleep. I'll call you sometime tomorrow. If you need to get hold of me, call the office. They'll know where to reach me."

He stuffed the clothes in the suitcase, jammed the shaving gear in the side pocket, checked his wallet for money, and scooped up the car keys from the kitchen table.

"You be careful," Leona said. Her eyes flew to the gun on his waistband. She wondered if he even knew how to use it.

"If anyone asks, I've gone up to the cabin." He leaned over and kissed the top of her head.

As he drove out of town two police cars raced east in the direction of the abandoned skating rink near the railroad tracks.

From the red and blue lights flashing through the distant trees, he knew they'd found the body.

He wished now he'd taken the time to hide it better.

He stopped at the police station and stayed long enough to speak to the teenager who'd found the body.

He turned him over to the detectives to take his statement and instructed his deputy chief to maintain a news blackout till his return.

"What do I tell the mayor? He's been calling every five minutes."

"Tell him to fuck off," the chief said.

Officer Powanda rapped softly on the door and stuck his head in the office.

"Mayor's on the phone. Hot as a bitch. Threatening to come down here."

The chief reached for the phone as his deputy averted his eyes.

"What in the hell is going on here?" the mayor demanded. "What's this about a dead body in the skating rink! Another goddamn Jap—for crissakes! These people have to come here all the way from Tokyo to drop dead in my town?"

The chief opened his desk and gathered up a pack of stomach mints, two rounds of bullets, a handful of change, a small notebook, and three pens.

"I don't want anymore goddamn Japs coming in! Have cops posted at the airport and turn them back. Enough of this shit. They wanna kill themselves, let 'em go to New York. You talk to the press?"

"When I get back from Miami."

"Miami! When the hell are you going to Miami?"

"As soon as you get off this goddamn phone and let me get back to work. I don't tell you how to run the town, don't fucking tell me how to run the police department. You think you can do it better, get your fat ass over here and start right now!"

The chief slammed the phone down and told his man, "Give him ten minutes to cool off and then call and tell him about LeRoy. If he hears it on TV first, he'll be all over your ass."

He scribbled on a paper. "That's my number in Miami, but don't give it to the fat fuck. I'll check in with you from time to time. As far as anyone else, I'm up at the cabin."

"How long you gonna be gone?" It came out like a moan.

"However long it takes."

"What do I tell the reporters? The LeRoy business, and now the Jap, this place is gonna be jumping. You know I'm not good at talking to them to begin with. Last time, with the holdup, they pointed that camera and I said shit right on the six o'clock news."

"Just do the best you can."

The deputy didn't look happy.

"Charley, you've been after my job for twenty years. Well, now you got it!"

The man sputtered, "Yeah . . . but . . . the dead Jap. I mean, LeRoy and all—"

The chief headed for the door and paused. "Have a man keep an eye on Earl's place. And it would be terrific if he could do it without being seen. In other words, don't send Powanda."

The man bristled at the mention of his nephew.

"He tries, chief. He's always been slow . . . but he means well."

Ford faced the deputy. "I had a dog who was slow. Couldn't catch a raindrop in the rain forest. But he wasn't dumb. Don't confuse the two."

David Ko hadn't meant to kill LeRoy. He was just trying to scare him. But the man refused to cooperate, leaving him no option.

He was in a hotel in Key West, a room service tray lying untouched next to the bed. He could no longer postpone making the call to Marco.

He didn't know which the man would react most violently to—LeRoy or the discovery of Yan-San's body.

For more than a few moments, Ko even considered disappearing and going into hiding. It was time to get on with his own life, what was left of it. But it would mean looking over his shoulder the rest of his days. Never returning to his beloved homeland. Never seeing his family again.

He was tired of the chase. Besides, he'd hired on to slip in and out of stores with the tainted Tylenol. Not to stalk people.

The other was fun and exciting, a grotesque game played out in a time warp. When the first victim died, he was two thousand miles away. Removed, yet not entirely. He'd read every newspaper, even clipped some of the stories, and delighted in the bogus announcement that an extortion note had been received by the police.

But now the remoteness was removed, and with it, the romance of adventure.

He was reaching for the phone when a local mortuary appeared on the TV screen, its spokesman seated at a carved desk, his manner appropriately somber.

"Please remember that in your time of need," Shirley said, "we're here. And we care."

Ko no longer cared.

For himself.

For his future.

For Marco.

He wanted out. He wanted it finished. He wanted it all behind him.

The only obstacles were the woman and the sailor.

Their deaths would mean he could begin to live again.

He reached for the phone, filled with a new resolve, an exciting urgency. He was eager to convey it to Marco.

CHAPTER SIXTY-THREE

It was almost midnight when Chief Ford Baker pulled into the parking lot of the downtown Miami precinct and walked to the oval-shaped, modernistic brick building that could easily be mistaken for a university.

It annoyed him. Police stations, he felt, should look worn, beaten, and angry, just like the society that required their protection.

A young Hispanic woman officer manned the information booth and pointed him down the hall to a suite of offices, saying, "They're expecting you."

No "wanted" posters, no human debris, no stench of cigarettes and bitter coffee assaulted his senses. The only poster prominently displayed was a child's crayon drawing with the words Just Say No.

Rows of offices lined both sides of the wide corridor with signs reading: Community Affairs, Civilian Patrol Force, Lost and Found. A wide bulletin board carried notices of a flea market and a CYO car wash.

Potted plants, some five feet high, stood erect in brass buckets. Fancy floor ashtrays filled with sand guarded the elevator doors.

It depressed the hell out of him.

The chief found the door and wondered if he should wipe his feet before entering the carpeted office. A ceiling fan circled overhead, tossing a click-click sound through the otherwise silent room. A glass-enclosed ticker machine sat quietly next to a bank of computers.

A man in his early thirties, short, slightly balding, wearing glasses, bolted from a chair and crossed the room quickly with his hand extended.

"Chief Baker? Detective Carmine Ruffini," the man said. "Welcome to Miami."

Ford looked about, glanced at the closed door with the brass plate: Deputy Chief.

The detective told him, "The hour's a little late for the chief. Said he'll catch up with you in the morning."

Ford nodded. "Got any coffee?"

"In here," Carmine said, leading him to an adjacent room. "Consider it yours. It's got seven phone lines, Xerox machine, shredder, fax, microwave oven, kitchen, VCR, a couch, and full bath." The man smiled.

Ford had to admit it was impressive as hell. It's probably what they meant whenever he heard a big city department talk about a command post. He'd never seen one before.

Carmine poured the hot coffee into a ceramic mug, not the Styrofoam cup the chief was used to.

"I've got eight men on my squad on alert. One is a sharpshooter, we got a Spanish translator, a forensic expert, an ex-FBI agent, a SWAT-team leader, and a little gal, Lorraine, who's the meanest damn cop I ever saw."

Ford wondered how such a young man had made detective. He was either exceptional or well connected. It would help to know which.

Carmine opened the refrigerator and called out: "Chinese, Italian, or Cuban."

The chief had no idea what he was talking about, but not wanting to offend him, said: "Italian."

The detective removed two plates, which he quickly popped into the microwave, and Ford sat down to a dish of lasagna while the other got the tastier roast pork and black beans.

The meal was polished off with a dark foamy beer and the chief's brand of cigars.

"You did your homework," he said.

"Chief Crowder said to make you feel welcome."

Ford told him the story that had brought him in the middle of the night from Key West. He left out the part about finding and dumping the body.

When he had finished talking, Carmine snapped off the tape recorder and carried it to another office, where a secretary would have the tape transcribed and on the chief's desk by morning, along with a copy of the arrest warrant for Owen Ryder that Ford produced.

"I read about your lieutenant. Nasty way to go."

"There weren't enough pieces to put a suit over. And that son of a bitch Owen is gonna pay. What the woman reporter is doing in all this, I don't know."

The detective took two more beers from the refrigerator and poured them into tall pilsner glasses.

"Maybe she's in it for the story," Carmine said. "You sure she's here in Miami with him?"

"Can't say." He took the slip of paper from his pocket and dropped it on the desk. "That's where he is. How soon can you get your hotshots over here?"

"Only two are on duty. Rest are home sleeping." Carmine grinned. "We gonna hit 'em tonight?"

"I got nothing better to do," the chief answered.

At the motel, Geraldine was packing her clothes and emptying the bathroom of her makeup as Owen stood barefoot, dressed in his dungarees and white undershirt.

"I don't like this," he said.

She swept past him. "I have to be there in case he calls."

"We don't know what we're dealing with."

"Which is exactly what I'm trying to find out," she said, enunciating every word slowly as if speaking to a rowdy child.

She was tired and edgy. His attitude wasn't helping. Instead of "Great work!" all she'd heard the past hours was how dumb and reckless she was. "We have to get into his house. That's our only shot."

Owen heard a sound outside and glanced out at the parking lot. Two cars pulled in and he watched a man and woman emerge from one. He slid the drapes closed.

"Geraldine, I'm not gonna let you do this. I don't care if you—"

The phone rang, cutting off his threat. He stared at it for a moment and knew Earl wouldn't be calling at this hour.

"Aren't you going to—"

Owen clamped his hand over her mouth. He swept her purse off the dresser, grabbed his wallet, and pushed her out the door.

He pushed her up a flight of stairs and shoved her in the small enclosure near the top of the steps that housed a soda machine and ice maker.

He forced his body into the tight crevice, plastering her against the wall and the cold, gray surface of the soda machine. She was facing him, a look of sheer terror contorting her features.

Had Marco discovered her identity? Had he sent his men to kill her?

She was pressed so tightly to the sailor that the buttons on her dress made slight impressions on his white T-shirt.

The only sound was the chunks of ice dropping like rocks into the coffin-sized bin.

Geraldine started to whisper "What is it?" when someone shouted, "Wait for backup."

Walkie-talkies rattled with static as people raced through the corridor below.

A voice yelled, "They're gone!"

Geraldine cowered closer to the wall, her back stinging from the coldness of the metal refrigerator. She reached for Owen's hand and gripped it tightly. The chunky ring with the naval insignia cut into the side of his finger, but he didn't pull away.

Doors opened and new voices mingled as hotel guests woke to the commotion.

"Police. Everybody back inside," a man ordered. "Close your doors!"

Two cops ran up the stairs. A woman's voice could be heard shouting into a walkie-talkie: "All clear here."

"Check the roof!" a voice commanded.

A man emerged from his room and headed for the soda machine just as a cop hit the landing and ordered him away.

"But I want a soda," the man protested, extending his palm bearing three quarters.

"Move it!" he was told.

Geraldine squeezed her body deeper behind the machine and tugged Owen's sleeve to follow. Her hair snagged on the circular metal coils, which yanked out a clump of strands. Her dress was damp with sweat and she could feel the pulse beating in her neck. She didn't have enough room to raise a hand to soothe the pounding.

They stood welded together, barely breathing, for over an hour.

The corridors had been silent for the last thirty minutes or so. The only activity was confined to the floor below, where people could be heard entering and leaving the room. Just when she thought she'd be there the rest of her life, Owen nodded his head and pulled her out slowly.

He edged gingerly toward the corridor and looked down the long hallway. The canvas fire extinguisher hose had come unfastened in the turmoil and lay in a clump on the floor with the long brass nozzle pointing down the stairs.

He quietly opened the door marked Exit and listened for a moment. Behind him, Geraldine clutched his arm. A man's voice rang out from the floor below, "Who's in charge here?"

They didn't wait for the answer. Owen pulled Geraldine down the back staircase to the parking lot.

Three uniformed cops and a man in a brown suit were leaning against a car talking. Two police cars blocked the driveway to the motel.

Geraldine looked for the car she'd borrowed from Buzzy, but it was nowhere to be seen. She gazed up at Owen, who edged her quickly along the building, around the garbage bins, and toward the beach.

Detective Ruffini dismissed all but two of his men as he and the chief continued to inspect the motel room.

Ford Baker plucked a menthol cigarette from the ashtray. The same brand he had bought her in the Key West diner. A whiskey bottle and glass were removed for fingerprints, along with the telephone receiver.

The chief took the discarded dress box from the wastebasket in the bathroom and the plastic tote bearing the name of a local shoe store.

He held them up to Carmine. "You familiar with these stores?"

The detective laughed. "You're asking the wrong guy. I'm a bachelor."

"Check it out in the morning."

Carmine opened the dresser drawers and came up with the newspaper clippings. "What do you make of this?"

The older man put on his bifocals and stared at the picture of Marco and Kate.

"Must be fifty of 'em," Carmine said rifling through the newspaper photostats.

The chief spread the clippings out on the rumpled bed as Carmine peered over his shoulder.

"Who's the man?" Ford asked, staring at the well-dressed figure in the grainy photo.

"A local hood. Rich one. Has a restaurant in town. We think he's dirty but we've never been able to nail him."

"And the woman?"

"His wife. She's dead. Car accident or something. Couple years ago. Even the governor came down for the funeral. I know, 'cause I worked it."

"We'll take the clippings and pictures with us back to the office," the chief said. "I want a list of everything in the room. I'll start in the bathroom. I don't care if you find a used tissue. You write it down. Color, size, what it's made of, weight. Everything. Got that?"

Carmine nodded. He pulled a small notebook from his pocket and went to work.

It took them almost an hour, working silently and independently, to complete the inventory.

Satisfied that every inch had been covered, they left the room and sought out the manager, who paced nervously in the lobby.

"You got that phone list for us?" the chief asked.

"Right here, sir." The man handed him a computer printout. "This is the first time we've ever had any trouble here. We get families mostly. And businessmen. Even spring break, when the kids come down," the man wiped his lip nervously, "we've never had any trouble."

"What are your rates here?"

The man stuttered. "Rates?"

"How much?" Ford demanded.

"Depends. On the season. Number of people in the room. Ages . . . we give a discount to—"

"How much?"

"Sixty-five for a single. Eighty for a double."

The chief nodded. "Okay. I'll take it."

The manager looked at him, his face mirroring confusion.

"I need a room. I want a clean one, no higher than the second floor, near the fire exit, if possible."

"Certainly," the man smiled.

"Whoa," Carmine cut in. "You're staying at my place. It's all taken care of."

"Thanks," Ford told him, "but this'll be fine."

Carmine persisted. "The chief'll have my ass!"

"I snore," Ford said in a voice that ended all debate. He signed the registration card and handed it back to the manager. "See that I get enough towels."

They drove back to the police station and the chief got in his car. The black sky had begun to submit to the coming daylight.

"See you back here at nine. Work on the phone list," he told Carmine. He took a manila envelope from the glove compartment and slid out a sheet of paper.

"Send a guy over to the dress shop in the morning and have him show them Geraldine's picture. It's not great. Took it off her press card. He can mention she looks like that movie star."

Carmine waited.

The chief turned on the car ignition.

"Which movie star?" Carmine leaned into the car window.

The chief grunted, "The pretty one. The redhead."

"Kathleen Turner?"

The older man squinted. "Who? Who the hell is that?"

"She's a movie star."

"Never heard of her. The redhead," he repeated.

"Susan Sarandon?"

"Who?"

Carmine could see that at this rate they'd still be there when the sun came up.

"She was in those old movies. Black and white. Before television even."

Carmine said happily, "Oh, right. Katharine Hepburn!"

Ford shot him a disgusted look. "I said *pretty*."

The detective sighed and leaned against the car. He tapped his fingers on the roof, wondering why he always drew these assignments. He'd been on duty since 8:00 A.M. the day before and now this guy wanted him back in a couple of hours. By the time he got home and walked the dog and fed it, it'd be time to turn around and come back.

"How pretty?"

"Jesus! Long hair. Red. She was a big star for crissakes! In the forties. Fifties. Don't you watch television?"

"Yeah, football."

The old man snarled, "Everybody knows her."

Carmine grinned. "Maureen O'Hara?"

"Shit!" the chief grumbled.

Carmine looked at his watch. There was no point even trying to make it home. He'd have to call his neighbor and ask her to walk the dog. He didn't know why he didn't just give her the animal. She saw more of it than he did.

"Lucille Ball?"

The chief backed up and drove away.

The doorman at the Concordia Hotel eyed the couple walking briskly up the circular driveway. He braced himself for trouble. Drunks, obviously.

Both barefoot, no less.

He was used to worse. Sixteen years on the job and you got to see just about everything.

He couldn't refuse them entrance, as he'd done once early in his tenure. A half-naked woman carrying a bottle of vodka and a mangy cat had attempted to enter the hotel and he stopped her, threatening to call the police, only to learn she was the daughter of an IBM executive who kept a suite year-round.

So when the couple approached, the man in the braided uniform merely opened the door and closed it behind them.

Let the security people deal with them, he told himself. He wasn't paid enough to confront drunks.

He resumed his post at the curb, half listening for the security alert code from the lobby, and when it didn't come he wondered who the hotshots were.

Probably rock stars.

Geraldine and Owen crossed the lobby quickly and swept past the security guard lingering by the open elevator.

The man regarded them with a look of professional sternness, which Geraldine quickly deflected by opening her purse and producing the gold embossed room key with the signature palm tree.

When they entered the room, the red light on the phone was blinking.

Geraldine nudged Owen and said, "Marco."

He took in the antique furnishings, the canopy bed, the silver green wrapped chocolates on the pillow, and the pink robe and slippers on the foot rest.

"What the hell did this cost?" he asked.

She had the phone in hand. "This is Karen Reynolds in Room eight-ten. You have a message for me?"

He flinched. He went into the bathroom and filled a glass with cold tap water. Besides a new hairdo she'd acquired a new name, one dangerously close to that of the dead woman's. He looked into the mirror, below the string of pink-tinted light bulbs, and stared at his haggard face. He was tired of running. Tired of being scared. Tired of being tired. He thought of Lily and how uncomplicated, in retrospect, their affair had been. He thought of his kids and wondered if he had really led such a normal life. Supermarket shopping, washing the car on Saturdays. Was that Owen Ryder or someone he'd heard of?

But none of the agony came close to the realization that Earl had turned him in to the cops.

Why?

Did they threaten him? Throw him in jail?

It was as if the ground beneath his feet had suddenly opened and swallowed all his energy, all his strength. Earl, whom he felt closer to than his own father, had betrayed him. The pain in his gut was real.

He was still staring in the mirror when Geraldine appeared in the doorway. "He's picking me up for lunch tomorrow. I'm supposed to call him."

Owen didn't budge. He stood leaning on the pink fake marble counter, his palms spread open, his body listing forward, gazing in the mirror.

"You all right?" she asked. He was making her very nervous, just standing there, hunched over, staring at his reflection. Was he cracking up? Was he sick? Was he scared? He seemed smaller, somehow. Not as powerful. Something was different. "You want me to call down for drinks?"

That was probably it, she reasoned. A quick scotch and he'd be his old self.

He was still Owen, she told herself. Just tired. Sober. In need of sleep. But why was he staring at the mirror?

"Owen?"

He dropped his chin to his chest. His fingers gripped the edge of the counter till his knuckles drained the blood from the bones.

She turned quickly and left the room. A fear gripped her that was stronger even than the first night when he pulled her across the Vegas street.

She was losing him.

Chief Ford Baker overslept and didn't get to the police station till almost eleven.

Carmine had fresh coffee brewed and toasted bagels with whipped cream cheese waiting for him.

"I may never go home," the chief told him.

"There's a method to my madness," Carmine admitted. "Crowder told me about your cabin in the mountains. I got a beautiful hunting rifle still in the box."

Ford knew the feeling. "You get me through this, son, and that gun'll be worn out." He carried the coffee and bagel to a desk near the window. "Is he in?"

"Was for a few minutes. I briefed him as much as I could. He had to go to some political luncheon. Said he'll catch up with you later."

Ford looked at the young man hunched over the Xerox machine. "You get any sleep?"

"Enough," he lied.

"What do you have for me?"

"We checked the phone numbers. She called her apartment in New York twice. I called, got an answering machine. One of them, probably her, called the Miami *Herald*."

"Who she talk to?"

"Don't know yet," Carmine said, reaching over the side of the machine to gather up the duplicated copies. He carried them over to a desk and began collating. "She called the main number. They have some forty departments in the building. I figured we'd take a ride over."

"Anything else?"

"Called a guy in Key West by the name of Earl Smithers. That's it."

The chief nodded. "Figures."

The young detective sorted through a stack of color-coded file folders and carried one over to the chief, setting it next to his cup of coffee.

"My man went to the dress shop an hour ago. They remembered *Susan Hayward,*" Carmine smiled. "Bought a dress. Very expensive. Light brown. Asked about a hairdresser and the owner sent her over to—" Carmine opened the orange folder. "A Mr. G over on South Beach. We're checking that out now. My man also went to the shoe store. She bought a pair of tan shoes. Paid cash for everything."

The chief crossed to Carmine's desk and saw the folders labeled Hotel Room, Telephone List, News Clippings.

"You're very thorough," he observed.

"Chief demands it."

Baker sighed. "So do I, but I never get it."

He picked up the room file and carried it to a chair near the window. He stared at a building under construction. The empty shell was taller than anything he'd ever seen in person. Men in yellow hats darted about on wooden planks like cats in heat.

"Why would a woman who's running from the police and some maniac who beat her up take the time to go out and buy a dress and have her hair done?"

Carmine shrugged. "Got me."

"Why does a woman who has three pair of shoes go out and buy another pair?"

"Well, I can only speak for my sister. She must have, easy, a hundred pair of shoes. We call her Imelda," he laughed.

"But she's got clothes. Our gal only had a couple of things in the room. And she had a pair of white shoes. So she buys a light brown dress. Can't you wear white shoes with it? White goes with everything, isn't that what they say?"

Carmine said, "I guess."

The chief shook his head. "It doesn't add up."

A young officer came in and Carmine quickly introduced him to the chief.

"What'd you get?"

"She had her hair done. Talked to the guy who did it. Real flaming queen. He didn't agree with what she wanted and tried to talk her out of it. But she insisted. And it had to be exactly a certain way. He did it, but felt she was making a mistake."

The chief looked at Carmine. "What she get? Purple streaks?"

"No color," the cop answered. "She just wanted it combed back, very tight, into a little thing in the back of her head. Guy said it made her look like an old maid."

Carmine looked up from his paper sorting. "Maybe sailorboy is the old-fashioned type. Likes women to look like his mother."

The chief lit a cigar. "I doubt he even has one."

"Anything else?" Carmine asked the cop.

"Nope."

"Type it up and bring it back."

The cop was almost out the door when the chief hollered, "Wait. Hold on!" He left the window and grabbed the other file on Carmine's desk. With both officers hovering by, the chief thumbed through the clippings and produced a picture of Kate at a hospital dedication ceremony. It was a good, tight photo, taken at half angle, showing the side of her face.

"Go back to the beauty shop and show him this," he instructed the officer, handing him the picture. "Ask him if the hairdo was anything like that."

"Okay."

Carmine waited till the man left and said, "I should have spotted it. Really fucking dumb."

The chief brushed his protest aside. "No, you were thinking it was something between her and the sailor. Anybody would have gone that way."

Carmine observed, "You didn't."

Ford offered a half-smile. "Sometimes you get lucky."

"What next?" Carmine asked.

"Let's take a ride over to the paper."

* * *

In New York, Cardinal Thomas Ryan McHugh instructed his housekeeper to pack his suitcases sparingly.

Besides Paris, he had managed to wangle an invitation from a provincial monastery known for its cheeses and wines. He intended to bring back samples.

He also had her pack the usual tacky collection of New York souvenirs: metallic replicas of the Statue of Liberty, Big Apple key chains, plastic paperweights with photos of the UN, a pencil sharpener shaped like a subway car, notepads with pictures of King Kong dangling off the Empire State Building.

He reminded her to include three bottles of mineral water and two rolls of toilet paper. He was not going to suffer as he had in Poland.

Father Murphy entered the library–sitting parlor. It was a splendid room with magnificent artwork and a priceless collection of first editions dating back to the invention of the printing press.

It was a room that never failed to astound visitors, no matter how mighty their station.

The Arabian tapestry, with its shimmering silk threads depicting the Last Supper, covered an entire wall from floor to ceiling. The hidden, recessed lighting brought out the fine details of the master craftsmen. It was rumored that Winston Churchill, upon viewing it, had offered a king's ransom to possess it.

"Your Eminence, you're needed at the altar."

The cardinal looked up from his crossword puzzle.

"What for?"

"The television technicians want to do a light check. They'll only need you for a few minutes."

The cardinal sighed and threw his pencil down. "Every year it's the same thing. If we didn't need the money, I wouldn't do it. Five minutes—that's it!"

The aide followed him quickly.

It was all an act. He knew the cardinal enjoyed being televised at the Easter mass. He even wrote his sermon on small index cards so he wouldn't flub in front of the camera.

Father Murphy was looking forward to the Easter service in two days. For him it meant more than the Resurrection. It signified peace and contentment . . . minus the cardinal.

CHAPTER SIXTY-FOUR

Geraldine slept only three hours. The room was dark as she pulled the telephone into the bathroom and called Buzzy at home.

His wife answered and Geraldine passed herself off as a secretary from the office.

When he came on the phone, sounding annoyed, she identified herself quickly. "I'm in big trouble and I need your help."

"What is it?" The tone was irritated. She wondered if it was meant to distract his wife or if he was truly angry.

"I need money. Much as you can raise. A pair of women's shoes size seven and men's shoes size ten. Also a man's shirt. Large. Right away. Can you do it?"

"Give me at least an hour."

Geraldine relaxed. "You're a champ. I'll meet you, in exactly an hour, at the entrance to the Concordia Hotel. You know where it is?"

"Yeah."

She hung up and called Marco, leaving a message with his answering machine that she'd be available for lunch at one-thirty and would meet him in the hotel lobby.

She turned off the bathroom light and carried the phone back into the dark bedroom. She placed it on the floor and muffled it with a pillow in case it rang. There was no need to wake Owen just yet. Maybe if he got enough sleep . . .

She sat in the darkness on the half-moon upholstered chair near the dressing table and stared at the sleeping form. He was cocooned tightly in the blanket, with only one bare arm visible.

"It's going to be okay," she told him silently.

An hour later, she crept out of the room and jumped into Buzzy's station wagon, which actually belonged to his wife.

"Are you going to tell me what's going on?" he asked.

"I can't," she said, grabbing up the envelope on the seat between them and the shoe boxes.

"Hope they're okay," he said.

"Perfect."

She leaned over and kissed him on the cheek. "I'll pay you back. Promise."

"Am I going to get shot or arrested?" he asked.

She laughed and dashed back into the hotel.

Geraldine hurried upstairs to find Owen awake and frantic.

"Where the hell did you go?"

"Had to take care of something," she said, tossing the shoe boxes on the bed. "If they don't fit," she fished in the envelope, pulling out two fifties, "get another pair. Shirt's not exactly you," she said holding up the cellophane package, "but it'll do."

Owen dressed quickly and didn't ask where the clothes came from. He suspected one of various ex-husbands.

"I'm going to get the car," he told her. "I stashed it by the drugstore a couple of blocks from the motel."

"Be careful," she cautioned.

The sailor glared at her. "I don't have to be careful. I'm not going to lunch with a killer."

She tried to defuse his anger by asking, "Did you call Earl? There must have been something in the paper by now."

Owen made a strange sound that caused her to look up with alarm.

"No."

"I'll try him now," she said, reaching for the phone.

"Don't!" he yelled.

Her hand froze mid-air.

He saw the wounded expression on her face and said, "He turned us in, Ger."

The old man stood in his kitchen dialing the phone.

It was answered in two rings by a man's voice he didn't recognize. Figuring he had dialed wrong, he hung up and tried again. The same man answered.

Earl hung up. He glanced at Molly, who was soaking clothes in the sink and punching them with fists of soap.

A sudden coldness swept his body. He reached for the chair and sat down quickly till it passed.

The officer in the room made a note of the two calls and plopped back on the bed to watch the daytime quiz show.

Owen found the car where he'd left it and headed toward Key Biscayne.

The sun's heat filled the car. His clothes smelled sour. The dungarees felt like cardboard across his legs. The new shoes felt awkward on his bare feet.

He had no idea where he was driving. He mostly needed time to sort his thoughts.

The old man must have had his reasons. He would have to accept it. Maybe he was even in jail as an accomplice.

He soon found himself crossing the toll bridge to Marco's island retreat.

"You look lovely," Marco said, as Geraldine met him in the lobby.

She smiled nervously, hoping her dress was buttoned. She was barely back from the dress shop in the hotel when he rang to say he was waiting downstairs.

The simple blue polka-dotted dress with the white lace collar did nothing for her figure. But then neither did the flat blue shoes. She felt ill at ease, certainly not herself, but then, wasn't that the point?

"Thank you," she smiled.

"I invited my mother to join us," he said. "We're having a family crisis," he smiled apologetically. But with the Spanish accent, crisis came out "creases" and it took her a moment to decipher it.

A woman strolling from the elevator gave Marco more than a casual glance and Geraldine felt her envy.

She had to admit he was even more spectacular in the daylight. The white even teeth against the dark smooth skin gave his face a perpetual smile. He was wearing a gray linen suit accented only by a baby blue tie and pocket handkerchief. The gray snakeskin shoes had similar flecks of blue.

"I thought you might enjoy lunch at my place," he said, leading her to the limo parked outside.

"Then maybe we can go sailing just before sunset, if you'd like."

"I'd like," she smiled.

The driver jumped out and opened the door as they approached.

The older woman turned in the back seat at the sight of the redhead walking next to her son. She let out a gasp as they neared. "Dios mio!" she moaned, quickly making the sign of the cross on her forehead.

Marco followed Geraldine into the rear seat and told his mother, "This is Karen."

The woman tried to find her voice and instead settled for a nervous smile.

"So that's how someone looks when they've seen a ghost," Geraldine mused silently.

Carmine showed Geraldine's picture to the day city editor of the Miami *Herald*, who remembered her. He led them to the feature department and introduced them to the editor Claire Shultz, who had spent time with her.

"That beautiful lady is wanted by the police? And here I thought she was related to the late Mrs. DelCampo."

Carmine gently posed questions, almost in an offhand manner, not bothering to take notes for fear of intimidating the editor. He didn't want her to clam up.

They returned to headquarters to find memos from Key West.

Ford's mother called to say the new owners had stopped by with the kids. The deputy reported the press was hounding him and the mayor was causing a commotion. There was a second message from Leona about LeRoy's funeral. Would he be back in time?

There was also a note from Chief Crowder apologizing for missing him again.

Ford Baker tossed them aside and told Carmine, "She's up to something, dressing like his dead wife. I want to get into his house. Today."

Carmine shrugged, "I have no basis for a warrant."

"Who the fuck said anything about a warrant?"

"We can't just bust in," the detective responded.

The chief stared at Carmine. It was a wonder anybody ever solved a crime these days.

Carmine noted the man's disappointment and said softly, "I'm sorry, we just can't."

Baker lit a cigar and walked to the window. The guys in the yellow helmets were still cat-dancing. A young teacher led a group of students up the walkway into the police station, each child carrying a paper lunchbag. He wondered what they expected to learn. That people were bad? That even the most honest citizen, given the opportunity, would sway to temptation? That justice very rarely prevailed?

He wondered how many of the children would enter a police station later in life in handcuffs. He shook off the thoughts.

"You got a PBA association in this town?"

"Sure."

"You sell tickets to the policemen's ball?"

Carmine grinned, "We charter a boat and have a dinner dance at sea. Chief even wears a tux."

"You got any tickets lying around?"

Carmine bristled at the man's gruff tone. "We hold it in October. Tickets aren't even printed yet."

Ford always kept undated tickets in his desk for just such situations, but it was too late in the game to teach police work.

"This Marco have any animals?"

Carmine shrugged, "I don't know."

"Can you call the board of health and find out?"

The detective reached for the phone. He was having second thoughts about his new partner. The old bastard didn't have to talk to him like he was a retard.

They sat not speaking, waiting for the phone to ring. When it did, Carmine jumped. He spoke to the clerk and hung up.

"Nothing on record. If he has any, they're not registered. My guess is he doesn't."

Ford blew a smoke ring overhead. "I say he does. Probably attack dogs. Never met a dope dealer who didn't. Pit bulls, they seem to like. Call 'em back and get me an ID without a picture. I'll wait in the car."

* * *

Marco's cook had prepared an elaborate lunch of seafood, saffron rice, and endive salad, which was served on the second-floor patio overlooking the ocean.

The "Grand March" from *Aida* played softly from concealed speakers in the hanging plants circling the terrace.

"You have a magnificent home," Geraldine told him.

She was sitting at a glass-topped table across from Marco's mother, who had said very little throughout the meal. The woman pretended to be interested in the conversation while her eyes took in every detail of Geraldine's person.

At one point her attention centered on Geraldine's hands. She followed the woman's gaze and noted to her horror the nicotine smudges beneath the chipped nail polish.

She berated herself for being so careless.

For his part, Marco seemed oblivious to the tension as he talked animatedly on a variety of subjects from his horses in Ocala to his days as a TV producer.

The mother finished eating and slipped a cigarette case from her purse.

"Would you like one?" she asked Geraldine.

Geraldine glanced quickly at Marco and then regained her composure, smiling. "No. Thank you. I quit six months ago."

"Really?" The woman returned the smile. But the eyes remained cold under the shadow of the overhead canopy.

"What do you do in New York, Karen?" the mother asked, purposely placing the cigarette pack near Geraldine's coffee cup.

"I write. Childrens' books, mostly. Also plays."

Marco beamed. "Have you had any on Broadway?"

"No, I'm afraid I haven't been all that successful."

"Have you ever been married?"

"Mama! Por favor," Marco protested.

"It's all right," Geraldine said pleasantly, addressing the woman. "My husband was killed in Viet Nam."

"I'm sorry," Marco said. "I had no idea."

"Children?" the woman persisted.

"I'm afraid not. It's my greatest regret."

The woman looked away. A sunflower yellow butterfly flitted to the terrace railing. Geraldine thought she hadn't noticed it, but the white-haired woman said, to no one in particular, "La mariposa dice que lagrimas estan en la brisa."

Marco quickly explained: "Mama says the butterfly brings news that tears are coming." He looked at Geraldine and shrugged.

"Yes," she told Geraldine, "children can be a blessing. They can also break your heart."

Marco mumbled something in Spanish but the woman was not to be consoled.

"How many godchildren do you have? One! How many times is that child going to be engaged? Once! And you won't be there!"

"Mama—"

Marco reached across the table for the woman's hand but she quickly pulled it away.

"I don't care about business. People lose a business every day. But you lose your family, you lose everything!"

Marco's response was cut off by the housekeeper, who informed him a man waited to see him.

"Who?"

"He's from the board of health."

The mother laughed. "See! They're going to close your restaurant. Business is nothing. Family is everything!"

Marco excused himself and followed the housekeeper from the terrace with his mother in tow.

Alone for a moment, Geraldine got up quickly and walked into the house. She tried a door and found herself in what appeared to be the master bedroom. An oil painting of Kate graced the wall above the fireplace. She was wearing a lilac gown and reclining on a wicker settee. The face was pale beneath the auburn strands pulled tight behind the ears. The eyes, almost pensive, stared back with an almost pleading expression. The legs, slightly outlined beneath the sheer dress, were definitely those of a ballerina. The artist had not attempted to minimize the strong calf. It was almost as if you expected her to spring into a ballet position at any moment.

Geraldine heard voices on the lawn and crossed the room quickly to the cathedral windows overlooking the main entrance. A small compact car, definitely civil servant issue, stood near the guard shack. It appeared there was someone behind the wheel but she couldn't be certain.

The voices rose. First Marco's. Then his mother's. Geraldine crept closer to the window and looked down. She glanced at the figure on the lawn talking to Marco.

Her hand flew to her throat. She jumped back quickly, wedging herself against the thick drapes, but not before the man's eyes had met hers.

"Of course he saw me! He had to!" Geraldine shouted at Owen as she paced the hotel room. "It happened so fast. Maybe he didn't recognize me. I don't know."

She lit a cigarette even though she had two burning in the ashtray. "What the hell is the police chief of Key West doing in Miami? At Marco's house? Pretending to be from the board of health? God, Earl must have told him everything!"

"Looks that way." He slid a new shirt out of the bag and brought it to his mouth, biting off the plastic tag.

She yanked the pins out of her hair and flung them on the bed. She tossed her head from side to side, allowing the hair to tumble loose. The pain in her skull vanished.

"We're so close!" she said, collapsing on the bed. "You should have seen him with his mother. He's terrified of her. Whatever's in Chicago, it's big! His only godchild is getting engaged Sunday, his mother is giving the party, and he's not going to be there."

Owen filled a duffel bag with new clothes and toiletries he'd bought at a discount house on the highway. "Did he say what time he's leaving?"

"No. Just that he'll call me tomorrow night when he gets there."

Owen glanced out the window. The rain that had threatened an hour ago had arrived in full force. The wind pushed waves of water across the concrete driveway circling the hotel. The uniformed doorman raced to a taxi holding an open umbrella that fought to fly from his grip.

"You stay here and wait for his call. I'll go to Chicago," he said.

Geraldine sat up in the bed, hunched on her knees. "Are you crazy? What if he's going to meet one of his little Japs? It's too dangerous. I won't let you go."

Owen combed his hair in the mirror. He glanced at her reflection behind him, the blue polka-dotted dress high above her knees. Barefoot. Cigarette in hand. Hair tousled, half hiding the face. The eyes firm with resolve. The soft body. Maybe, he thought, Hal got off easy.

Ford Baker knew she was on the premises. He knew it as soon as he spotted the car hidden by the mango bushes. He didn't see the sailor, but he was willing to wager his retirement pay that he was nearby.

Carmine wanted to grab him right there, but the chief prevailed.

"Let's play it out," he told his partner. "When we take him, I want all the bad guys."

Carmine remained in the car while the chief, dressed in green polyester pants and a white golf shirt borrowed from a cop's locker, informed Marco that the dogs roaming the estate required licensing and proof of rabies shots.

Marco assured him he would personally attend to it Monday morning.

His mother promised to see that he complied.

"We didn't come to America to break the law," she told him.

Baker handed them the registration papers, pointing out the additional fee for unspayed animals, and wished them a good day.

When Ford and Carmine left the estate and crossed the toll bridge, they happily noted the presence of the rest of the squad.

Officer Lorraine Laly, looking very much like the suburban housewife she was, drove up in a four-door Jeep cluttered with stuffed animals, two baby seats, and bags of groceries.

Two hours later when Geraldine and Marco drove across the bridge in the limo, a fisherman on the bridge cast his line and reached into an empty bait bucket to radio Carmine.

When Owen's car, with the Miami *Herald* stickers on the bumper, came into view a minute later, Officer Laly steered her Jeep easily into the traffic pattern.

She didn't know anything about the out of town cop who was running the show today other than that he was a close buddy of Chief Crowder.

If she screwed up, Carmine had insinuated, oh so politely, she could find herself back behind the computer updating stolen vehicles.

She gunned the Jeep forward. The creep in the brown car was not going to thwart her plan of being the first female police chief of a major Florida city.

Give or take ten years.

CHAPTER SIXTY-FIVE

In Key West, the morning sun struggled to penetrate the clump of gray clouds.

A group of tourists lined up for the Conch train to Hemingway's house looked at the threatening sky and decided to postpone the outing.

At the tip of the island, the black-suited divers sat forlornly ashore waiting for the tour bus to arrive. They'd be lucky to make cigarette money today.

Across town, the funeral procession of over thirty cars slowed as it passed LeRoy Thomas's house en route to St. Albert's Cemetery. Earl and Molly followed in her Dodge van.

"Wonder why Ford didn't come to the church. Leona was there," Molly said. "Not like him not to pay his respects."

Earl only half heard. His mind was on Owen and the stranger's voice in the Miami hotel. Something was wrong. He could feel it. Wasn't like Owen not to call.

The hearse drove between the black gates of the cemetery and circled past the gray mausoleum with its bronze nameplates on the wall. A child's silvery balloon was taped to one of the drawers and the sight caused Earl to look away.

He parked on a slope along the dirt road and they walked behind the procession to the white tent in the distance. Up ahead, Leona strolled with three elderly ladies. The mayor walked behind LeRoy's widow and her daughters as uniformed police officers stood in attention along the dirt path.

The minister waited by the covered grave for the immediate family to take their seats near the casket. A purple silk tassle caught in the pages of his Bible waved in the wind as a rain-heavy breeze suddenly chilled the air.

"Give us strength, Almighty God, to bear this burden which has fallen upon us today. Hear our plea for mercy and serenity so that we may know Your comforting touch and glory in the knowledge that this, too, shall pass."

A red kitten skittered after a windblown plastic bag.

"As you have lifted our son, friend, father, and husband, LeRoy Thomas, to sit among your cherished angels, so lift our spirits and guide us to the closeness of Your embrace so that we, too, may know the everlasting peace that is now his."

LeRoy's mother clutched her heart and moaned. Two people quickly drew to her side.

Earl found it difficult to watch. His eyes kept straying to the young daughters whose faces were turned from the coffin. The wife stared at her hands, deep angry lines in her face pulled the chin down.

Earl walked to the far end of the tent, slipping easily through the crowd. He shouldn't have come. He never was any good at these things.

He longed for his pipe but felt it would appear disrespectful. He stood off to the side, barely able to hear the minister's words, hoping it would end soon.

The sky darkened overhead. Three silver fingers of lightning curved toward the ground. He turned his head to wait for the sound and it was then that he saw the Japanese man standing in the fold of a drooping tree.

One of the same men who'd rented his boat and left the note. He was positive.

Earl looked about quickly to see if the man was alone. He saw no one else in the vicinity.

Earl edged his way through the crowd, careful not to call attention to himself, and crouched down behind Molly, who sat on a folding chair.

"Get a ride home with Leona. Have to go," he whispered. He rushed off before she could protest and darted up the dirt road past the black limos and parked cars.

He glanced back once. The Japanese man had not moved.

Afraid of being spotted, Earl climbed into the van, disengaged the gears, and using his foot as a rudder, steered it quietly off the slope and across the grass. When he could no longer see the road behind him, he turned on the ignition and drove out of the cemetery. He parked in a mini-mall across the highway that gave him a clear view of the exit.

Less then twenty minutes later, a white car emerged, driven by the Asian. Earl followed it to the Sea Crest Motel and watched him enter the lobby.

The old man smiled. Maybe there was a God after all. He gave the man time to get inside and then left the van. He walked to a large litter basket at the far end of the lot and rummaged through newspapers and Taco Bell wrappers till he found what he wanted. A beer bottle.

A young couple strolled to their car nearby and he pretended to be busy scavenging. As soon as they drove off he slammed the bottle hard against the rim of the basket, smashing it. He gathered up the amber pieces of glass and hurried to the white car. He crouched down beside it and let the air out of the two left tires. Earl quickly sprinkled the broken glass near the vehicle and walked into the hotel lobby, where he found the manager behind the desk.

"Sam," he told him, "I need a favor."

"What?"

Earl wedged himself closer between the registration desk and the wire rack of tourist pamphlets.

"One of your guests is gonna need a tow truck. I want you to call Bumper over at Harry's station."

The manager pursed his lips tightly. "Can't. I give my business to Halsey."

"Don't worry, I'll square it with him."

The manager protested. "Can't. Just can't. We have a contract. If he found out—"

"He ain't gonna find out. I'll take care of it. Sam, this is important. I wouldn't ask you if it wasn't."

The manager sighed. "All right."

Earl used the manager's phone to alert Bumper not to leave the gas station.

"I go to lunch in an hour," Bumper yelled over a pneumatic drill in the background.

"Not today you don't! You're gonna stay there till you get a call from Sam to come out and fix a tire. I'll tell you what to do after that."

Bumper didn't like it one bit. "What if Harry sends me out on a call?"

"You don't go!" the old man yelled and slammed down the phone.

He returned to the van and drove it out of the lot, across the road to a supermarket where he sat and waited. Four hours later, thirsty and hurting to take a pee, the old man saw his quarry leave the motel and head for the car. The man spotted the flat tires and turned abruptly back to the motel.

"Please, God, don't let him call a cab," Earl prayed aloud. "If not for me, do it for LeRoy and his young'uns." He also wanted to add "and don't let me pee in my pants" but thought it wasn't fitting for God's ear.

Almost ten minutes later, the tow truck rattled into view with Bumper behind the wheel. The Japanese man hurried from the hotel to meet him.

Bumper jumped from the truck, inspected the car, and told him, "I'll have to hook her up and take her in. We should have it for you in a couple of hours."

The man insisted the flats be fixed on the spot.

"No way! I can't keep the truck off the road that long. We're too busy. Look, buddy, either I take it or you fix it."

The man gave him the keys.

Wagon Master was waiting at the garage when Bumper pulled up. He watched as Bumper unhooked the car and pushed it into the bay of the garage. They lowered the overhead doors and began inspecting the car.

"What the hell are we looking for?" the mechanic asked.

"I don't know," Earl told him, "but that son of a bitch killed LeRoy."

"What?" Bumper shot from under the car as if his ass had been prodded with a hot wire. "What the hell is going on here, Earl?"

"Just keep looking," the old man said, rifling through the glove compartment.

"Bullshit!" Bumper said. "I ain't getting involved in this. Call the chief! Let him—"

"I did," Earl yelled. "He's in Miami trying to arrest Owen. We have to do this ourselves."

"I don't like it," the mechanic told him.

"Just do it," Earl ordered, attacking the back seat.

It took them almost an hour to practically strip the car. They even removed the hubcaps.

"Nothing," Bumper said.

A customer pulled up for gas and Bumper hurried to the pump.

It gave Earl just enough time to remove his wallet, watch, and wedding ring and stuff them deep in the glove compartment.

"Now the engine," the old man ordered.

Bumper pulled a cigarette from behind his ear and lit it. "Let the cops handle it. I don't want any part of it."

"I'm gonna go home and tell Geraldine what a chickenshit piece of garbage you are!" Earl roared.

The mechanic bristled. His fists automatically balled up.

"You got no business talking to me like that!"

The old man glared back, toe to toe. "He probably killed Gabe, too. I thought he was your friend. Fucking friend like you—he's better off dead."

Bumper's body lurched forward and his belly sent the old man tumbling back. He landed hard against a metal battery box on wheels that was hooked to a car.

Bumper was sorry the minute he did it and rushed over to help the old man off the ground. "Jesus, Earl! You shouldn't be—"

"Can we check the engine now?" He refused the outstretched hand and got up by holding onto the car fender.

The mechanic stormed over to the car and threw up the hood. "There are fucking laws in this state, okay? Tampering with a vehicle is one of 'em. I ain't going to jail just to—" Bumper leaned closer over the engine and called out, "Lookie here!"

The old man hobbled over. His kidney ached from where it had hit the battery cable. "What?"

"He jump-started the car. See the wires? He put 'em back but he didn't connect them all the way. See that piece there?" His greasy thumb held up a stray copper strand. "That's a homemade job."

Earl peered in. "But I saw him give you the car keys."

"Don't mean shit. Lots of people keep an extra set taped to the underbelly. He probably found 'em after."

Earl asked, "You positive?"

"I've seen it before."

The old man nodded, "Okay. Fix the flats. I don't want him walking in here and getting wind of anything."

"What do we do then?" Bumper asked.

"We wait for him to call," Earl said.

They were playing their second hand of gin rummy when the phone rang.

"It's ready," Bumper told him.

When he hung up, Earl went to the phone and called the cops. "Guy just held me up with a gun and the son of a bitch is sitting in Harry's station gassing up to leave town. Better send someone right away," he told the officer who answered.

Bumper looked at his friend. "You nuts?"

"It'll bring 'em," Earl replied.

Within minutes a taxi deposited the Jap at the garage. Earl stayed hidden in the office while Bumper stalled him, pretending to have mislaid the keys.

Earl glanced anxiously out the dirt-smudged window, hoping to sight a police car. "If I'd said stolen car we'd be here till summer," he grumbled.

Outside, the Asian got into the car, leaving the door open. His leg was poised on the pavement. He could bolt at any moment, Earl agonized.

Even Bumper was frightened. He went through an elaborate charade of checking all the keys hanging on the wall racks. As bad luck would have it, no one came in for gas, which would have helped the delay.

He stuck his head in the office as the man got out of the car and walked toward the bay doors.

"What do I do?" he whispered.

Before Earl could answer, two police cars converged and Officer Powanda scrambled out with gun in hand. The man turned quickly and stood rigid.

"Hold it," Powanda ordered. He raced forward and tripped over the cement island by the gas pumps, falling to the pavement. The gun fired, sending a bullet through his own elbow.

His partner rushed to him while Earl bolted from the office and tackled the Jap. The man kicked high with his leg, sending his shoe heel into the old man's stomach. Earl grabbed the leg and sank his teeth into the flesh below the dark suit pants.

Bumper ran to the phone to call an ambulance, yelling over his shoulder, "You really did it now!"

The second cop grabbed a handful of blue paper towels used to clean windshields and held them to Powanda's arm to soak up the blood.

"You fucking did it now, Earl!" another cop screamed as he held his foot inches from the Jap's face on the ground.

Two more police cars and an ambulance arrived within minutes. Officer Powanda was lifted onto a stretcher and the ambulance sirened away as Earl and Bumper and the Asian were shoved into police cars.

"Shut up! Everyone shut up!" the deputy chief roared in Ford's office. He ordered the sergeant to place the Japanese in the holding cell.

"The hospital's on three!" the desk officer yelled.

The deputy grabbed up the phone. "How's my nephew?"

Earl and Bumper exchanged quick glances. The old man looked away. It wouldn't do to laugh.

"Ethel's on two!" a voice called out.

"Thank you, doctor," the chief said, hanging up.

"Ethel's hysterical," the officer reported.

"Tell her to drop dead." The deputy chief walked to the door and slammed it shut.

"How is he?" Earl asked.

"Okay. Could've been a lot worse."

Bumper exploded, "You're damn right. He could've hit the gas pump and blown us all to hell! He has no fucking business being a cop!"

The deputy confronted the mechanic. "What the hell are you doing here?"

"I'm a witness. And I may sue!"

The deputy straddled the desk and faced the old man. "Okay, Earl. What's all this about?"

The old man dug into his pocket for his pipe. "Guy robbed me."

The deputy sighed. "Oh? We searched him. He's clean. Says he never saw you before."

"Then check the car. Just make out a complaint that he robbed me and I'll sign it."

"Where and when exactly did this happen?"

Earl struck the pipe against the palm of his hand and dislodged a hunk of old tobacco. "Do that horseshit later. Send someone to check the car."

The deputy glared at the skinny old man in the black suit and paint-spattered work shoes.

"We can't just search a person's car without a warrant. The Supreme Court—"

"Fuck the Supreme Court. The guy stole the car!" Bumper yelled.

The chief regarded him with unconcealed disgust. "You see him do it? He told you he did it? I thought he robbed your friend here."

Earl looked at the brown uniform and sat up straight to his tallest height. "Charley, you're wasting time here. Write up the complaint. If we lose this guy—"

"Don't tell me what to do! I got my sister's kid lying in the hospital with a bullet in his arm, 'cause you called here saying you got robbed, and I ain't heard one detail from you!"

"If Ford Baker finds out you had the killer locked up and let him go—"

"Killer? Now he's a killer! You still drinking that moonshine? Shit's gone to your brain, Earl."

The old man stood up, knocking the chair to the floor. "I'm done talking to you. You get on that phone and call Ford in Miami. Right this minute!"

"No sir. He told me not to bother him unless the place was on fire. Those were his words."

"That right?" the old man's face hardened. He took a lighter from his pocket and held it to the papers sticking out of the wastebasket next to the deputy's leg.

Within seconds the flames leapt over the metal brim.

"You son of a bitch!" The cop flung his coffee on the fire. "You're a lunatic!"

Earl swooped forward and grabbed the man's gun out of his holster.

"Jesus, Earl!" Bumper shouted.

The old man pointed the gun at the deputy. "I'd call him if I were you."

Chief Ford Baker was sitting in the back of a florist's van two blocks from the causeway.

The lumpy mattress didn't help. At most, he'd gotten an hour's sleep.

They'd spent the night staked out by the Concordia Hotel and followed the sailor when he drove across the bridge leading to Marco's estate early that morning.

Other police reported that he was still parked by Marco's house and Geraldine had not left the fancy hotel.

If this was a potential kidnaping or a drug deal, it was the strangest one Ford had ever encountered.

The chief wrestled with the pillow and tried to tame it into a comfortable wedge. He settled back on the mattress and picked up the copy of *Arizona Highways.* He reached over and adjusted the bamboo shade to block the sun.

His foot grazed the pizza carton that had been lunch. And breakfast.

"Chief," Carmine said from the front seat. "Your office is calling."

Ford groaned. He got up on his knees and felt his leg muscles cramp. He half crawled to the front of the van and took the phone. His mouth felt like a cat had crawled in it and died.

"The fucking place better be on fire," he told Carmine.

The deputy's voice sounded strained. Ford had to ask him to talk louder.

"Earl's holding a gun on me. Says he has to talk to you," the deputy muttered.

Ford Baker moved quickly into a sitting position. "Well, put him on."

Bumper gave him a thumbs up sign as the old man took the phone.

"Chief, we got big problems here."

Ford Baker enunciated the words carefully. "You really holding a gun on Charley?"

"Had to, chief. Can't reason with him."

Baker smiled. "Okay. Talk to me."

Fifteen minutes later he told Earl to hand the phone and the gun back to Charley.

"You're fucking going to jail for twenty years!" the deputy roared. "Attempted murder of a police chief—you might even get the chair!"

The old man pointed to the phone. "He's waiting on you."

Charley put the receiver to his ear and heard Baker shout, "You're not the chief yet! And if I have any say in it, you never will be. Now you get your ass over to that gas station and check that car! Take Earl with you. Then you write up that complaint and lock that Jap up till I get there. Got that?"

"Yes, sir. But . . . what about him . . . taking my gun? I mean, we just can't—"

"He didn't take your gun, Charley. You handed it to him 'cause you were so upset over your idiot nephew almost blowing up the town and half the citizens."

Chief Baker handed the phone back just as the walkie-talkie next to Carmine's leg rattled: "Marco's moving!"

Carmine switched on the ignition and yelled through the car radio. "Everyone in place!"

A cop dressed as a telephone worker jumped from his utility truck.

Officer Lorraine Laly started the Jeep and waited near the toll bridge. She glanced in the back seat where the birthday cake lay in the white carton with the see-through cover. She had picked it up at the bakery before coming on duty. She hoped the icing didn't melt before she could get it home for the party.

Carmine and the chief stared silently as the white limo pulled into view. They allowed it to pass and watched as an officer in a taxi slid in behind it.

A moment later Owen's brown car appeared, followed by Officer Laly.

"Don't lose 'em," the chief barked as Carmine edged the van into traffic.

"I used to deliver pizzas," the detective answered. "Not to worry."

The caravan traveled easily through the city streets. At appointed times, one of the vehicles would drop from the pack to be replaced by another member of the team.

The limo turned on I-95 and picked up speed. It made a quick exit on a ramp four miles south.

"They're going to the airport!" Carmine shouted.

"Shit!" Ford Baker punched the dashboard.

"We take 'em?"

"No," he answered. "Play it out."

The detective said, "Okay. I hope it's Hawaii."

The limo headed swiftly toward Departures and parked in front of the Continental terminal. Marco jumped out carrying a small suitcase and strode into the building.

"Laly! Stick with the sailor," Carmine said into the radio.

She watched as Owen ditched the car at the curb and hurried away carrying a duffel bag. She quickly jumped from her Jeep, leaving the engine running, and raced up to the florist's van.

"What do I do now?" she asked Carmine frantically.

"Stay with him," he ordered.

"But what if he's getting on a plane?"

"You go!"

The policewoman hurried away, casting an anxious eye behind to the birthday cake. She pushed her way into the terminal and her worst fears materialized.

The sailor was in line at the ticket counter a few feet behind Marco.

She took her place, hoping Carmine would show up momentarily to replace her. She felt in her purse for her gun and readied her ID in case she had to go through the metal detector.

The chief and Carmine jumped out of the van and the detective told an officer to remove Lorraine's vehicle. "I can't go on the plane," Baker told Carmine. "Either of 'em would spot me in a minute."

Carmine told him, "Meet me in the coffee shop," and hurried into the terminal.

Officer Laly was still in line when she noticed Carmine approach the counter, apologizing profusely to those waiting, and stand next to Marco as the Cuban spoke to the ticket agent.

Moments later Carmine left the counter, walked briskly into the line of waiting passengers, and stumbled against Officer Laly. He shoved some money in her hand and whispered, "See you in New York," before he hurried off.

Less than an hour later, while Marco relaxed in the first class cabin, Laly sat in the rear of the plane, two rows behind Owen. She buckled her seat belt and looked about frantically for Carmine. He hadn't made it aboard.

She moaned to herself, "What the hell do I do when I get there?"

A new worry surfaced when the pilot informed the passengers the temperature in New York was eighteen. She looked down at her calico print dress and leather sandals. Super.

Officer Laly was expecting thirty guests that evening for a surprise party for her husband. She wondered if the shaky marriage would survive the fiasco. Things hadn't been right between them for a long time. The party was designed to patch the rift.

She gazed out the window. Maybe he was right. Maybe her job was more important.

Here she was cruising at 33,000 feet above the Atlantic while her living room sat decorated with orange balloons in the shape of footballs. Maybe Tony had a point. Maybe she did love it too much.

Chief Ford Baker was in the airport coffee shop eating a hot turkey sandwich when Carmine hurried over.

"Got us on TWA. Leaves in an hour."

"Good."

"Poor Lorraine. I'll have to call someone in authority in New York and hope—"

"Done." Ford said, sliding a cup of coffee to the detective. "I know a sergeant at the South Street precinct. Comes to the Keys every winter. He'll send someone to meet the plane."

Neither said it, but they knew if they lost her, they lost everything. Ford would never be able to explain letting Owen board the plane.

Two hours and twenty minutes later, Officer Laly hurried out of JFK terminal, trying to keep pace with Owen a few yards ahead. She had no idea where Marco was. The first class cabin was empty when she passed it. She wasn't unduly concerned. The sailor was her assignment and right now he was striding ahead, the blue denim jacket barely visible in the crush of people.

For a split second she thought she heard her name being paged, but dismissed it as highly unlikely.

She needed desperately to call a neighbor and have her alert everyone the party was off, but she couldn't risk losing the suspect.

She walked through the terminal, finding it hard to believe she was actually in New York. She stopped dead in her tracks upon seeing a famous TV star heading straight for her. No one approached him for his autograph. Maybe New Yorkers were used to that kind of thing. In Miami, he would've been tackled. It took her a moment to realize that the denim jacket had vanished.

Officer Laly broke into a sprint and caught up with Owen as he rode down the escalator.

The TV star had been well worth the momentary panic.

She followed the sailor past the baggage claim area and out onto the sidewalk.

The city welcomed her with a blast of arctic air that curled her bare toes. She stood at the curb in her sleeveless cotton dress enviously watching the parade of fur coats and tent-sized down jackets.

"What the hell do I do now?" she agonized.

It was dark and the wind whipped around her bare legs like a frozen rope. She kept a few feet behind Owen who followed Marco to the taxi stand. The overhead street lights, almost pink in color, cast a strange glow over the faces exhaling steam clouds.

Owen slagged down a cab.

She darted behind him, almost banging his leg with her shoulder bag, and ran toward a cab that was slowly approaching. She dashed for the yellow door only to be beaten out by a beautiful lanky brunette in a full-length black fur coat.

She watched, paralyzed, as Owen's driver slowly pointed the wheels into the traffic.

The beauty's leg and upper body were half into the cab as Laly reached into her purse and brought out a badge.

"Police. I need this taxi," she informed her.

The woman in the thick fur hat glanced at the badge and said, "So do I. Sorry."

The woman tossed her overnight case on the floor just as Officer

Laly yanked a fistful of fur and sent the woman spinning backward to land against a mailbox. The brunette looked up to see her suitcase fly out the cab door.

Officer Laly settled into the taxi with a grin a mile wide and told the driver, "Follow that cab!"

"You lost her," Chief Baker berated the young officer who met their plane.

"She got by us somehow."

"Jesus goddamn Christ! Amateurs—no matter where the hell I go I'm surrounded by fucking amateurs. You got eight million people in your city? How do you suggest we find her?"

Detective Carmine felt almost sorry for the ashen-faced cop, but not really. New York's finest, my ass.

The cop led them to an unmarked car. "We gave her description to all the taxi dispatchers." He neglected to mention that if she had taken a gypsy cab, it would be impossible to trace her. Instead he said, "We'll find her."

The chief got into the back seat with Carmine, muttering, "If luck was a piss ant, I couldn't get bit!"

It was almost 8:00 P.M. when Geraldine woke, fully dressed, in the dark hotel room. She hadn't meant to sleep, but the effects of three Bloody Marys postponed the anxiety of not knowing what was happening in Chicago.

Why didn't Owen call? Had Marco spotted him? Or worse, one of his men? She had a strong urge to call Earl, but resisted.

She reached across the bed and turned on the lamp. She yanked the phone cord across her stomach and dialed her New York apartment.

She bolted up fully awake at the sound of Buzzy's voice. "Ger, hope you get this message. Didn't want to call the hotel. Couple of cops came over to the paper this afternoon asking about my car. Told them I lent it to a friend. Asked me a lot of questions about you. I don't know what the hell you got me into, but I am not amused. Do me a favor. Don't call me. Send me a note where I can pick up the car."

The casino manager at the Showboat in Atlantic City alerted her to a blackjack tournament. Her landlord wanted to know when he could expect the rent.

She tried Buzzy at the paper but was told he had left for the night.

How the hell had the cops traced the car? Only one way. They followed Owen.

Which explained why he hadn't called. He was in jail.

Officer Laly was mesmerized by the sights and sounds of the city as the cab headed for the midtown tunnel to Manhattan.

It had been her lifelong dream to visit the city. Ever since she was nine years old and had seen *Miracle on 34th Street.*

The fantasy did not include racing along a highway in pursuit, on Easter weekend, with six dollars in her purse. By now her guests with presents had arrived at a dark house and Tony would soon leave the office to find his wife and car missing. She wasn't worried about the kids because they were spending their Easter vacation at her mother's house.

The taxi came out of the tunnel and turned north. It came to a halt when Owen jumped out of his cab on Madison Avenue. She scrunched down by the window and gazed up at the glitzy lights but couldn't find the name. She saw him race after Marco's gray suit and disappear into the lobby.

"What hotel is this?" she asked the Iranian driver.

"The Helmsley Palace," he said, flicking off the meter. "That'll be thirty-three seventy-five."

A doorman wearing more gold braid than Patton approached the cab and she waved him away. Officer Laly leaned across the front seat and told the driver, "I have a slight problem. No money."

The man hit a lever locking all the doors and screeched away from the curb with her screaming.

He drove to the nearest police station and yanked her out of the cab, cursing foreign obscenities.

Officer Lorraine Laly waited till they got inside the building—in front of the duty sergeant—and swung a punch, knocking the Iranian cabbie to his knees. When he crumpled over in pain she grabbed a hunk of his hair and sent him crashing into a bench.

The sergeant jumped over the desk just as she flashed her badge.

"I want that man arrested for kidnaping," she demanded.

The driver tried to crawl away but she was faster, and caught him in a choke hold with the strap of her purse.

"What the hell is going on here?" the precinct captain shouted. The rotund officer, dressed in a white shirt with military bars, eyed the petite woman in the strange clothes and the bedraggled man who stood hissing curses at her.

"Officer Lorraine Laly, Miami police," she said, holding out her hand just as the cabbie lunged for her. She kicked him into the water cooler.

"Get him out of here," the captain ordered the sergeant.

"I want to press charges. Assault and battery! I know my rights. I want that bitch arrested!"

She followed the captain to his office and threw her ID on the desk. "I need a telephone, hot coffee, and a jacket and socks would be terrific." She sank into the wooden chair and added, "Food would also help."

At this point she didn't care about the party, her husband, the sailor, the Cuban drug dealer, Detective Carmine Ruffini, the city of Miami, or her pension. Fuck 'em all!

The captain gave her his jacket from the coat rack and left the room for a few minutes. He returned with a cup of coffee. "I sent out for food."

Once the hot liquid hit her cold insides she was fine. "So I follow this guy all the way from Miami and we get to the hotel and I tell the driver I don't have any money. The son of a bitch locks the doors and brings me here."

The captain listened with amusement, especially to the part about the surprise party. Himself recently divorced, he could appreciate it more than most.

"I don't know what happened to my backup. They never made it to the plane. I had no instructions, no money—just follow the guy. So, here I am."

The sergeant knocked on the door and entered carrying a woman's black coat, scarf, and hat. "You'll have to sign for it and return it when you're done," he said. "We use it for decoy work."

"So what's your plan now?" the captain asked.

"I guess I have to get a room at the hotel and call my squad in Miami."

"What hotel?"

"I wrote it down," she said, fishing in her purse. "The Helmsley Palace."

The captain laughed. "I don't know what kind of expenses they give in Miami, but a room there has to go three a night."

"Hundred?" she gasped.

"Welcome to New York," he shrugged.

A cop arrived with the food. She grabbed a sandwich and after two quick bites called her squad in Miami.

A detective answered in Carmine's office. "Lorraine! They're going crazy looking for you. Where the hell are you?"

"Hold on," she said, cupping the phone. "Where am I?"

"Forty-third precinct, Manhattan. Fifty-first and Ninth Avenue."

She repeated it between slurps of the chocolate egg cream. The Miami officer told her to wait while he called Carmine on the other phone.

"Food's great," she told the captain as she waved the sandwich. "What is it?"

"Pastrami."

"No kidding. Never had it." She was dwarfed by the large blue wool jacket with the copper buttons.

The Miami cop got back on the line. "Carmine's on his way now to get you."

"He's in New York?" she asked.

"Yep. Just sit tight."

"No problem," Lorraine told him. "I'm on overtime."

Marco settled into his suite and called for food. After a dinner of broiled trout and lemon sherbet, he rang the florist and arranged for flowers to be sent the next day to his godchild. Western Union was told to deliver her a money order for $2,000.

That done, he opened his briefcase and removed the letter addressed to the city editor of the *New York Times*. He would carry it with him tomorrow. If God chose to call him home, it would be found on his body.

If all went well, it would be sent from a random mailbox in Queens. It read:

Your cardinal has been sacrificed. God ordained his death as a warning that the time has come to address the needs of the legion of poor and neglected souls who cry out for justice and compassion throughout the nation, from the welfare mother in Dallas to the migrant worker in Arizona.

Jesus told His disciples to feed the poor, clothe the naked, house the homeless, and heal the infirm. In His name I ask you to do God's bidding.

Jesus placed His caring hands on the lepers. He heard their cries and walked among them. This nation can no longer ignore the anguished voices. Too many innocents have perished for want of food and shelter. Now it is time for the mighty and powerful to lie beside them in endless sleep.

It was signed, "His willing apostle."

CHAPTER SIXTY-SIX

Geraldine picked up the phone on the first ring.
"I'm in New York," Owen told her.
"What?"
"That's where he is. The Chicago story was bullshit."
Geraldine didn't like the sudden change. She was unprepared for it.
"I've got a hell of a problem," he shouted above the street noise. "The hotel's got four exits. He's gonna slip by me."
She looked at the clock. It was almost ten at night. She could hear traffic in the background.
"Where are you?" she asked.
"In the goddamn street on a pay phone. I tried to get a room. They want four twenty-five a night!"
"Where the hell is he staying, the Helmsley Palace?" she asked sarcastically.
"You got it."
It annoyed her that he didn't seem glad to hear her voice.
"To top it off, I'm freezing my ass. It's goddamn winter up here."
"You can't stay in the street. Go to my apartment and get the key from my super."
"Forget it. You don't think the cops are watching your place? Or his buddies?" He shoved his hand into his pocket. The pea jacket, which was similar to the one he'd worn in the North Atlantic, did not protect him from the howling gust of wind sweeping around the corner. He wondered why it had worked in the Arctic and not in Manhattan.
"How do I get hold of you if I need you?"
"You can't. I'll keep checking in with you. Has he called?"

"No."

Owen looked toward the hotel entrance across the street. The doorman, with his thick white gloves and high leather boots below a knee-length cape, was huddled shivering near a brass-potted tree.

A cop on horseback clacked along the street unmindful of the traffic and coughing buses. Steam rose from a manhole cover and obscured the horse's legs.

"Maybe I should fly up—"

"No!" His feet were starting to numb. He kicked them awake against the sidewalk. "I'm going back in the hotel where it's warm. There's a bar near the elevators. I can watch from there."

"And when it closes?" she asked.

"I'll worry about it then."

She wanted to say, "I miss you," but settled for, "Be careful."

He started to say something and then blurted, "Shit! He just came out!"

She heard the receiver fall.

Carmine finished talking with his partner in Miami and told Chief Baker, "Call your office. Some kind of emergency." They were sitting in the conference room of the South Street precinct overlooking the East River. "Your deputy's been calling every hour."

First thing that came to mind was his mother. She'd been taken ill. Or had a car accident. The second thought was guilt for not having called since he left home. It wasn't like him to cause her any worry.

Ford took the phone and dialed.

"Chief here. Put Charley on."

The conversation was brief. Ford said very little. He ended it with, "I'll be back tomorrow." When he hung up he glanced out the window at the string of lights adorning the Brooklyn Bridge and told Carmine, his back to the man, "The Jap is dead. Hanged himself in the cell."

Owen hurried from the pay phone, sidestepping a panhandler who asked him for a subway token. He kept an even pace with Marco, who strolled ahead, unmindful of the cruel temperatures.

It had to be ten below. Maybe fifteen. He couldn't remember ever being this cold, not even above deck in the Alaskan peninsula.

Owen crossed the street and looked up to read the green marker that told him he was on Madison Avenue. Not that it meant anything. The one time he'd been in New York, as a young recruit, he was confined to Governor's Island, and shore leave was spent gawking at the sights of Times Square.

Marco paused by a shop window that displayed electronic gadgetry. Owen ducked quickly into the doorway of a fancy supermarket. It stank of urine. Cigarette packs and beer cans littered the subway grating where a man lay huddled under a cardboard box. The huge carton had once housed a refrigerator. Now it was home to an old man in torn pants and a pink blanket laced with soot.

The sidewalk was practically free of pedestrians. Two teenage girls with purple/orange/green hair and motorcycle jackets lounged against a parked car. A woman in a silvery evening gown and white fur exited a cab, then entered a dimly lighted restaurant.

Marco resumed walking, turned the corner on Fiftieth Street, and headed directly for St. Patrick's Cathedral.

Owen recognized it from long-ago postcards. It seemed smaller, somehow, in the frigid night. The golden spires gleamed under the spotlights. Soot-coated clumps of snow clung to the frozen bushes alongside the church.

He raced up the steps and was momentarily halted by a German family, two adults and three kids, who asked him how to get to Chinatown.

He tried circling around them, but the man produced a camera with a flash attachment. He extended it for him to take a picture of the family.

Owen shook his head and darted into the church. The pews were empty except for small pockets of people sprinkled throughout the cavernous cathedral.

Two Spanish women with infants stood quietly at the rear of the church by the bank of flickering gold candles.

Owen stood near them. He took some change from his pocket and deposited it in the metal grating, as they did, and reached for the thin, wooden stick to light a candle.

He had a clear view of the gray topcoat as Marco paused along the far aisle to admire the marble saints lining the long wall beneath the stained glass windows.

Owen glanced up at the wooden scaffolding high over the altar. Thick cables curled down from the platform like rubber snakes. A technician sat on the wooden plank, his legs dangling, reading a newspaper. Three TV cameras stood mounted and covered with plastic sheets.

Marco crossed to the altar, which was bedecked with shimmering brass vases filled with white lilies. Behind it, a huge gold crucifix glistened against the marble wall.

Marco knelt at the altar as Owen slowly took a seat in one of the last rows off to the side, giving him a full view of most of the exits should the man suddenly bolt.

Marco remained with head bowed in prayer. He praised God for the chance to serve Him. He was prepared to give his life . . . a better one awaited at the side of his father, Kate, and Yan-San. His only request was that He give his mother the serenity to live out her days in peace, should he fail in his mission.

Geraldine couldn't take it any longer. The not knowing. Unable to sleep, she booked a flight and arrived at LaGuardia shortly after 8:15 A.M.

She was prepared for Owen's argument, but it was a small price to pay for knowing.

He had called after midnight to report that Marco was back in his room. She hadn't heard from him by the time she left for the airport at 5 A.M.

She took a cab to the Helmsley and got off a block away. It felt good being back in New York. It felt right. Key West and Japanese assassins seemed another lifetime ago. Today the sun was bright and the street was clogged with people. The city even smelled new. Alive.

She headed toward the hotel, walking past a French restaurant she'd gone to often with Hal.

She forced the memories away and crossed the street to the hotel. She scanned the area. No sign of her sailor. She walked past the side of the building, the freight delivery area. Nothing.

Geraldine headed back to Madison, turned the corner, and stopped dead in her tracks.

Marco came out of the hotel and walked briskly up the block. Geraldine looked around for Owen. Surely he'd show now. But he didn't. She couldn't risk waiting and took off after Marco.

Geraldine darted across the street and followed when he headed west toward Fifth Avenue.

She wasn't scared as much as confused. Where was Owen? Had something happened to him? And if he was hidden, mingling with the pedestrians that clogged the sidewalk, wouldn't he have spotted her by now and hurried over?

She found herself suddenly having to jockey around large groups of people, and Marco was getting too far ahead.

She broke into a sprint, dashing between the waves of pedestrians that had swollen to an army. Where had they all suddenly come from? The crowds spilled over the sidewalk into the street.

Any minute now he would vanish from sight. Geraldine ran in the gutter and pushed herself into the mob, scooting around backs and shoulders, trying to keep him in view.

The madness suddenly became clear when a family decked out in flowery hats stopped to be photographed.

"It's the damn Easter parade!" she moaned.

Madison was choked with traffic that had been diverted from Fifth Avenue.

Geraldine panicked as she realized he was leading her straight to Fifth Avenue and the crush of bodies that looked like sea gulls in a feeding frenzy.

If she didn't catch up with him soon she'd lose him for sure.

A woman's flowery hat, complete with gilded birdcage and a canary on a perch, totally obscured her view.

CHAPTER SIXTY-SEVEN

Chief Ford Baker stood in the small office at the precinct leaning against the window. Behind him a garbage-filled scow moved gracefully under the bridge with a tugboat clamped to its side.

A subway train rattled below the bridge casings while cars and trucks rumbled a few feet above.

Owen sat in a chair with his hands cuffed to the wooden arm rests. Carmine read the Sunday comics in the *Daily News* while munching on a knish. Officer Laly was at that moment atop the Empire State Building listening to a tour guide point out the five boroughs. She was in no hurry to go home. Tony wasn't speaking to her.

"You can talk here or back home in the cell. Doesn't matter to me," Ford told his prisoner.

"I told you everything."

Ford snarled, "Your girlfriend help you come up with that bullshit about the Tylenol?"

"Ask her yourself."

"Intend to do just that. As soon as we locate her."

"What do you mean?"

"She flew the coop."

Owen yelled, "Then find her, goddamn it! Before something happens to her!"

The chief swung his elbow and caught Owen in the neck. He fell back into the chair, knocking it over.

Carmine walked over and picked him and the chair up, never losing his reading place.

"I'm telling you, she's in danger!"

"You don't tell me shit."

Owen lowered his voice to a menacing growl. It was more animal than human. "If anything happens to her . . .

The chief's fist crashed into Owen's nose, splattering the air with blood.

Geraldine pushed and stalled and swayed and elbowed and squeezed through the thousands of people filling the avenue. She was no longer concerned that he would spot her. Only that she would lose him.

She was only inches behind when he made his way through the doors of St. Patrick's Cathedral. All the pews were jammed and latecomers were forced to stand at the rear and against the side walls.

An elderly man, pushing his wife in a wheelchair, pleaded with the standees to give her a view of the cardinal.

A choir of young voices led by a soprano filled the cathedral from a hidden perch. The sun streaming through the stained glass windows cast purple and blue rays across the altar.

Cardinal Thomas Ryan McHugh, in his white vestments of celebration, moved about the shrine while an army of black-robed altar boys clustered in the background.

The cardinal held a gold goblet over his head and blessed the body of Christ. He took a thin wafer, placed it in his mouth, and thumped his chest three times, praising the glory of God.

Father Murphy sat behind the altar in a high-backed carved chair along the far wall between two other priests. Facing them, from the distant raised platform, sat three other priests in white vestments.

Above in the scaffolding, now concealed by a shimmering white cloak, a technician checked the sound meter and adjusted his equipment.

Marco made his way slowly down the far aisle and stood a few feet from the altar. Geraldine kept him in view as she wedged herself behind one of the marble pillars.

None of this made sense to her. He could've gone to Easter Mass in Miami. And why the charade about Chicago? Was he meeting someone here, knowing it would go unnoticed? She looked about uneasily for any Asian men in his vicinity, but saw none.

The cardinal gestured to the heavens as the priests moved to the altar with heads bowed in prayer, led by Father Murphy.

The choir sang joyfully when the cardinal, flanked by two altar boys, took his position at the golden rail.

Spectators rose silently and walked, heads bowed, hands held in prayer, toward the altar.

Geraldine was amazed to see Marco join the procession. He took his place in line and waited for those ahead to receive Communion before kneeling at the altar. After receiving the wafer, the people would rise, bless themselves, and return to their seats.

The cardinal's magnificent robes swept the air as he hastened along the bowed heads, closely followed by the altar boy carrying the gold goblet. As His Emminence approached the kneeling figure of Marco, Geraldine tried to anticipate which route he would take after receiving Communion. He could walk up the center aisle, which made her vulnerable to detection. She was pondering her next move when a noise rang out.

It sounded like the dull thud when you hit a highway reflector at high speed.

She heard it again, followed by a woman's scream.

Father Murphy bolted forward toward the sound. People rushed from the altar in panic, shoving and trampling those who had run forward.

The choir stopped singing when a youngster's voice in its midst screamed, "He's been shot!"

Geraldine pushed ahead as the worshipers fled from the altar. She saw the cardinal clutch his chest. His white silk vestments glistened with a red blotch as the holy man slumped to his knees and then the floor. His head lay cradled in Father Murphy's lap. The priest, weeping loudly, tried to keep the cardinal's stiff-tiered hat from toppling to the ground. He did not want him to be seen bareheaded on the altar.

"Get help! Get a doctor!" he yelled at the escaping legs.

Marco swept by Geraldine, attempting to navigate through the stampede.

"Lock the doors!" someone yelled.

His face placid and unconcerned, Marco moved slowly through the crowd.

Geraldine flung herself through the mob and felt strands of hair rip from her head as they caught on a woman's bracelet.

The gray topcoat was suddenly inches away. Her hand flew out like a snake's tongue and grabbed the sleeve.

Her foot crashed against the foot of a pew as she fought to hold on.

Marco felt himself being pulled back. He looked around quickly, but all he saw was the purple flowers of a straw hat worn by a woman who wept openly. Geraldine circled the woman and lunged forward, tightening her grip on the coat.

The woman in the hat with the purple flowers was swept away by the swollen crowd, and Marco's eyes came to rest on Geraldine's face.

The initial flash of surprise gave way to anger. He made no attempt to escape. He turned and faced her.

Geraldine focused on the lips that now parted in a smile.

A wide band of sunlight invaded the church as an army of cops stormed through the doors.

Geraldine felt herself falling slowly. . . . She tried to hold onto the coat but couldn't.

Someone screamed and it sounded like her own voice.

She tried to get up but the pain increased sharply. She lay on the floor staring at the shoes . . . so many shoes . . . so many colors.

She woke up days later to find Owen grinning at her. "Hi, babe," he said.

She drifted back to sleep wondering what he was so happy about. Probably found a new bartender.

The next time she opened her eyes, later that same night, she saw a pair of boots propped against the white sheets. She followed the pointed toes up to the legs and the reclining form of Chief Ford Baker.

"Shit," moaned Geraldine.

She thought she heard laughter, but couldn't be sure as she sank deeply into a pleasant dream. She was sitting on a park swing talking to a lady dressed as the queen of hearts. The woman carried a silvery balloon dotted with crimson hearts, black spades, and shimmering diamonds.

Geraldine started to ask her a question but the swing suddenly rose high in the air. She turned quickly to see who was pushing her and spied a young man dressed as the ace of clubs.

He carried two ice cream cones and handed her one. Vanilla. But the cone was made out of a new hundred dollar bill and she started to cry when the ice cream dripped onto the green currency.

"It's okay," a voice told her.

Upon being released from the hospital, Geraldine went home to find a letter from Ida, postmarked a month earlier.

In it Ida told of going out to dinner with her husband on their anniversary.

"Harry," she wrote on pink lined paper, "wore one of the cardigan sweaters that used to belong to Hal, and when he went for change to tip the boy who parked our car, he found a tape in the pocket.

"We played it when we got home. It must be a book Hal was writing. About a man who put poison in Tylenol. Crazy stuff like that. Very strange stuff. I was going to throw it out but Harry said maybe you wanted it, seeing as how you're a writer. Do you?"

Accompanied by an FBI agent from Atlanta and Chief Baker, Geraldine traveled to Alabama to pick up the tape.

"I kinda thought it might be important," Harry said, producing it from the foot locker in the bedroom.

Ida dispensed coffee and pecan pie while the solemn visitors listened to the recording. She was asked to sign a statement releasing the tape to their custody, explaining how it came into her possession.

"Would you like it back when we're done with it?" Geraldine whispered when they were momentarily alone.

The woman thought about it for a few seconds. "No. That's what killed him, isn't it?"

Geraldine left the question unanswered.

The trio flew back to Atlanta, where a task force had been hurriedly assembled to track Marco. The popular theory had him hiding in Costa Rica. Others, high in the Washington bureau, placed him in the Far East.

By early June the cardinal had recovered from his wounds and was greeted in Paris by cheering throngs who waited hours along the parade route for a glimpse of the holy man many said was next in line to become pope.

Father Murphy accompanied him in the motorcade, whispering basic French phrases which the cardinal still managed to mangle.

Officer Laly was promoted to detective, mainly on Ruffini's strong endorsement, and wasn't unduly surprised when her husband moved out of the house. She used her "comp" time for a five-day visit to New York, spending it with the precinct captain who'd introduced her to pastrami.

Geraldine recovered from the gunshot wound and sold the story rights to Ted Turner's production company for a movie of the week. She held little hope that his wife, Jane Fonda, would play the female lead.

Ford Baker and Leona followed the moving van to Fox Creek and discovered someone had broken into the cabin, helping himself to all the food supplies, some blankets, and the chief's fishing equipment. No valuables were taken.

Powanda and Ethel were quietly married in a small ceremony attended by the new chief of police who was so intimidated by the mayor that he took to stopping by city hall each day for a chat. The officers quickly tagged him Charlene, and some even spoke fondly of Baker.

Earl sold the house in Little Cuba and used the money to hire a contractor to add a dining room. He socked the rest of it in the bank for his old age.

Patrick Shirley introduced "Drive By" viewing, patterned after a funeral home in Los Angeles, and was subjected to death threats by an outraged community.

Marco's mother became accustomed to the familiar car parked near her home which followed her wherever she went. She knew her phone was tapped and suspected her mail was checked before it was delivered daily. She and her son communicated through a busboy at the restaurant who delivered her dinner every so often, along with a concealed letter from Marco in Salt Lake City, Utah, where he'd become friendly with an elder of the Church of Latter-day Saints.

On a hot August afternoon, Geraldine sat aboard *Nathan* enjoying the saltwater breeze on her face.

Owen was nearby brushing the dog Molly had given him, a mutt she'd found wandering dazed outside the supermarket.

The dog scratched its ear vigorously, thumping his leg against the deck. He was a drab shade of brown, with a chunk of exposed pink skin about the neck where another animal had torn it away. He had not, as yet, displayed a fondness for booze. But it was too soon to tell. The sailor had only had him two days.

"What are you going to call him?" she asked.

Owen said, "Porky."

Geraldine wailed, "That's awful."

"Hell, Molly found him at the Piggy-Wiggly."

The sailor pulled his chair closer. "I have an idea. Wanna hear it?"

"Sure."

She was wearing a blue sundress and a gold chain and crucifix, which had been a gift from the cardinal.

Owen stared out at the water, knowing it would be easier if he wasn't looking directly into her brown eyes.

"Awhile back I kinda kidnaped you, sort of, in Las Vegas. Now that you're feeling better, I'd like to take you there and maybe have dinner . . . drive to California. I have a buddy in San Diego, we can take his boat, go down to Acapulco. We can find out how we are together, without people chasing us, I mean. What do you think?"

He still bore a slight scar where the chief's PBA ring had caught him on the side of the nose, but you had to look close to notice it.

Geraldine reached down and petted the dog that sat at her feet.

She had expected something like this when he'd first called to issue the invitation to come to Key West. Sure, the thought had crossed her mind. He was an attractive man and there were even flashes of intelligence, now and then.

But a sailor with a drinking problem was not high on her wish list.

Besides, he wasn't her type. Whatever that was. He didn't care about movies or books. His idea of a gourmet meal was Swiss cheese on a burger. And for some perverse reason he rooted for the Houston Astros.

Not to mention she'd have to put up with bikini gals renting him and the boat.

Obviously, he could only make her miserable.

"What the hell," she said laughing. "Why not?"